THE ADVENTURES OF TOM SWIFT

VOLUME 3

Tom Swift and His Sky Racer

Tom Swift and His Electric Rifle

Tom Swift in the City of Gold

Tom Swift and His Air Glider

THE ADVENTURES OF TOM SWIFT

VOLUME 3

VICTOR APPLETON

BROWNSTONE BOOKS

THE ADVENTURES OF TOM SWIFT, VOL. 3

Published by Brownstone Books,
a division of Wildside Press LLC.
www.wildsidebooks.com

CONTENTS

TOM SWIFT AND HIS SKY RACER

Or, The QUICKEST FLIGHT ON RECORD

CHAPTER I

THE PRIZE OFFER

"Is this Tom Swift, the inventor of several airships?"

The man who had rung the bell glanced at the youth who answered his summons.

"Yes, I'm Tom Swift," was the reply. "Did you wish to see me?"

"I do. I'm Mr. James Gunmore, secretary of the Eagle Park Aviation Association. I had some correspondence with you about a prize contest we are going to hold. I believe—"

"Oh, yes, I remember now," and the young inventor smiled pleasantly as he opened wider the door of his home. "Won't you come in? My father will be glad to see you. He is as much interested in airships as I am." And Tom led the way to the library, where the secretary of the aviation society was soon seated in a big, comfortable leather chair.

"I thought we could do better, and perhaps come to some decision more quickly, if I came to see you, than if we corresponded," went on Mr. Gunmore. "I hope I haven't disturbed you at any of your inventions," and the secretary smiled at the youth.

"No. I'm through for today," replied Tom. "I'm glad to see you. I thought at first it was my chum, Ned Newton. He generally runs over in the evening."

"Our society, as I wrote you, Mr. Swift, is planning to hold a very large and important aviation meet at Eagle Park, which is a suburb of Westville, New York State. We expect to have all the prominent 'bird-men' there, to compete for prizes, and your name was mentioned. I wrote to you, as you doubtless recall, asking if you did not care to enter."

"And I think I wrote you that my big aeroplane-dirigible, the Red Cloud, was destroyed in Alaska, during a recent trip we made to the caves of ice there, after gold," replied Tom.

"Yes, you did," admitted Mr. Gunmore, "and while our committee was very sorry to hear that, we hoped you might have some other air craft that you could enter at our meet. We want to make it as complete as possible, and we all feel that it would not be so unless we had a Swift aeroplane there."

"It's very kind of you to say so," remarked Tom, "but since my big craft was destroyed I really have nothing I could enter."

"Haven't you an aeroplane of any kind? I made this trip especially to get you to enter. Haven't you anything in which you could compete for the prizes? There are several to be offered, some for distance flights, some for altitude, and the largest, ten thousand dollars, for the speediest craft. Ten thousand dollars is the grand prize, to be awarded for the quickest flight on record."

"I surely would like to try for that," said Tom, "but the only craft I have is a small monoplane, the Butterfly, I call it, and while it is very speedy, there have been such advances made in aeroplane construction since I made mine that I fear I would be distanced if I raced in her. And I wouldn't like that."

"No," agreed Mr. Gunmore. "I suppose not. Still, I do wish we could induce you to enter. I don't mind telling you that we consider you a drawing-card. Can't we induce you, some way?"

"I'm afraid not. I haven't any machine which—"

"Look here!" exclaimed the secretary eagerly. "Why can't you build a special aeroplane to enter in the next meet? You'll have plenty of time, as it doesn't come off for three months yet. We are only making the preliminary arrangements. It is now June, and the meet is scheduled for early in September. Couldn't you build a new and speedy aeroplane in that time?"

Eagerly Mr. Gunmore waited for the answer. Tom Swift seemed to be considering it. There was an increased brightness to his eyes, and one could tell that he was thinking deeply. The secretary sought to clinch his argument.

"I believe, from what I have heard of your work in the past, that you could build an aeroplane which would win the ten-thousand-dollar prize," he went on. "I would be very glad if you did win it, and, so I think, would be the gentlemen associated with me in this enterprise. It would be fine to have a New York State youth win the grand prize. Come, Tom Swift, build a special craft, and enter the contest!"

As he paused for an answer footsteps were heard coming along the hall, and a moment later an aged gentleman opened the door of the library.

"Oh! Excuse me, Tom," he said, "I didn't know you had company." And he was about to withdraw.

"Don't go, father," said Tom. "You will be as much interested in this as I am. This is Mr. Gunmore, of the Eagle Park Aviation Association. This is my father, Mr. Gunmore."

"I've heard of you," spoke the secretary as he shook hands with the aged inventor. "You and your son have made, in aeronautics, a name to be proud of."

"And he wants us to go still farther, dad," broke in the youth. "He wants me to build a specially speedy aeroplane, and race for ten thousand dollars."

"Hum!" mused Mr. Swift. "Well, are you going to do it, Tom? Seems to me you ought to take a rest. You haven't been back from your gold-hunting trip to Alaska long enough to more than catch your breath, and now—"

"Oh, he doesn't have to go in this right away," eagerly explained Mr. Gunmore. "There is plenty of time to make a new craft."

"Well, Tom can do as he likes about it," said his father. "Do you think you could build anything speedier than your Butterfly, son?"

"I think so, father. That is, if you'd help me. I have a plan partly thought out, but it will take some time to finish it. Still, I might get it done in time."

"I hope you'll try!" exclaimed the secretary. "May I ask whether it would be a monoplane or a biplane?"

"A monoplane, I think," answered Tom. "They are much more speedy than the double-deckers, and if I'm going to try for the ten thousand dollars I need the fastest machine I can build."

"We have the promise of one or two very fast monoplanes for the meet," went on Mr. Gunmore. "Would yours be of a new type?"

"I think it would," was the reply of the young inventor. "In fact, I am thinking of making a smaller monoplane than any that have yet been constructed, and yet one that will carry two persons. The hardest work will be to make the engine light enough and still have it sufficiently powerful to make over a hundred miles an hour, if necessary.

"A hundred miles an hour in a small monoplane! It isn't possible!" cried the secretary.

"I'll make better time than that," said Tom quietly, and with not a trace of boasting in his tones.

"Then you'll enter the meet?" asked Mr. Gunmore eagerly.

"Well, I'll think about it," promised Tom. "I'll let you know in a few days. Meanwhile, I'll be thinking out the details for my new craft. I have been going to build one ever since I got back, after having seen my Red Cloud crushed in the ice cave. Now I think I had better begin active work."

"I hope you will soon let me know," resumed the secretary. "I'm going to put you down as a possible contestant for the ten-thousand-dollar prize. That can do no harm, and I hope you win it. I trust—"

He paused suddenly, and listened. So did Tom Swift and his father, for they all distinctly heard stealthy footsteps under the open windows of the library.

"Some one is out there, listening," said Tom in low tones.

"Perhaps it's Eradicate Sampson," suggested Mr. Swift, referring to the eccentric colored man who was employed by the inventor and his son to help around the place. "Very likely it was Eradicate, Tom."

"I don't think so," was the lad's answer. "He went to the village a while ago, and said he wouldn't be back until late tonight. He had to get some medicine for his mule, Boomerang, who is sick. No, it wasn't Eradicate; but some one was under that window, trying to hear what we said."

As he spoke in guarded tones, Tom went softly to the casement and looked out. He could observe nothing, as the night was dark, and the new moon, which had been shining, was now dimmed by clouds.

"See anything?" asked Mr. Gunmore as he advanced to Tom's side.

"No," was the low answer. "I can't hear anything now, either."

"I'll go speak to Mrs. Baggert, the housekeeper," volunteered Mr. Swift. "Perhaps it was she, or she may know something about it."

He started from the room, and as he went Tom noticed, with something of a start, that his father appeared older that night than he had ever looked before. There was a trace of pain on the face of the aged inventor, and his step was lagging.

"I guess dad needs a rest and doctoring up," thought the young inventor as he turned the electric chandelier off by a button on the wall, in order to darken the room, so that he might peer out to better advantage. "I think he's been working too hard on his wireless motor. I must get Dr. Gladby to come over and see dad. But now I want to find out who that was under this window."

Once more Tom looked out. The moon had emerged from behind a thin bank of clouds, and gave a little light.

"See anything?" asked Mr. Gunmore cautiously.

"No," whispered the youth, for it being a warm might, the windows were open top and bottom, a screen on the outside keeping out mosquitoes and other insects. "I can't see a thing," went on Tom, "but I'm sure—"

He paused suddenly. As he spoke there sounded a rustling in the shrubbery a little distance from the window.

"There's something!" exclaimed Mr. Gunmore.

"I see!" answered the young inventor.

Without another word he softly opened the screen, and then, stooping down to get under the lower sash (for the windows in the library ran all the way to the floor), Tom dropped out of the casement upon the thick grass.

As he did so he was aware of a further movement in the bushes. They were violently agitated, and a second later a dark object sprang from them and sprinted along the path.

"Here! Who are you? Hold on!" cried the young inventor.

But the figure never halted. Tom sprang forward, determined to see who it was, and, if possible, capture him.

"Hold on!" he cried again. There was no answer.

Tom was a good runner, and in a few seconds he had gained on the fugitive, who could just be seen in the dim light from the crescent moon.

"I've got you!" cried Tom.

But he was mistaken, for at that instant his foot caught on the out-cropping root of a tree, and the young inventor went flat on his face.

"Just my luck!" he cried.

He was quickly on his feet again, and took after the fugitive. The latter glanced back, and, as it happened, Tom had a good look at his face. He almost came to a stop, so startled was he.

"Andy Foger!" he exclaimed as he recognized the bully who had always proved himself such an enemy of our hero. "Andy Foger sneaking under my windows to hear what I had to say about my new aeroplane! I wonder what his game can be? I'll soon find out!"

Tom was about to resume the chase, when he lost sight of the figure. A moment later he heard the puffing of an automobile, as some one cranked it up.

"It's too late!" exclaimed Tom. "There he goes in his car!" And knowing it would be useless to keep up the chase, the youth turned back toward his house.

CHAPTER TWO

Mr. Swift is Ill

"Who was it?" asked Mr. Gunmore as Tom again entered the library. "A friend of yours?"

"Hardly a friend," replied Tom grimly. "It was a young fellow who has made lots of trouble for me in the past, and who, lately, with his father, tried to get ahead of me and some friends of mine in locating a gold claim in Alaska. I don't know what he's up to now, but certainly it wasn't any good. He's got nerve, sneaking up under our windows!"

"What do you think was his object?"

"It would be hard to say."

"Can't you find him tomorrow, and ask him?"

"There's not much satisfaction in that. The less I have to do with Andy Foger the better I'm satisfied. Well, perhaps it's just as well I fell, and couldn't catch him. There would have been a fight, and I don't want to worry dad any more than I can help. He hasn't been very well of late."

"No, he doesn't look very strong," agreed the secretary. "But I hope he doesn't get sick, and I hope no bad consequences result from the eavesdropping of this Foger fellow."

Tom started for the hall, to get a brush with which to remove some of the dust gathered in his chase after Andy. As he opened the library door to go out Mr. Swift came in again.

"I saw Mrs. Baggert, Tom," he said. "She wasn't out under the window, and, as you said, Eradicate isn't about. His mule is in the barn, so it couldn't have been the animal straying around."

"No, dad. It was Andy Foger."

"Andy Foger!"

"Yes. I couldn't catch him. But you'd better go lie down, father. It's getting late, and you look tired."

"I am tired, Tom, and I think I'll go to bed. Have you finished your arrangements with Mr. Gunmore?"

"Well, I guess we've gone as far as we can until I invent the new aeroplane," replied Tom, with a smile.

"Then you'll really enter the meet?" asked the secretary eagerly.

"I think I will," decided Tom. "The prize of ten thousand dollars is worth trying for, and besides that, I'll be glad to get to work again on a speedy craft. Yes, I'll enter the meet."

"Good!" exclaimed Mr. Gunmore, shaking hands with the young inventor. "I didn't have my trip for nothing, then. I'll go back in the morning and report to the committee that I've been successful. I am greatly obliged to you."

He left the Swift home, after refusing Tom's invitation to remain all night, and went to his hotel. Tom then insisted that his father retire.

As for the young inventor, he was not satisfied with the result of his attempt to catch Andy Foger. He had no idea why the bully was hiding under the library window, but Tom surmised that some mischief might be afoot.

"Sam Snedecker or Pete Bailey, the two cronies of Andy, may still be around here, trying to play some trick on me," mused Tom. "I think I'll take a look outside." And taking a stout cane from the umbrella rack, the youth sallied forth into the yard and extensive grounds surrounding his house.

While he is thus looking for possible intruders we will tell you a little more about him than has been possible since the call of the aviation secretary.

Tom Swift lived with his father, Barton Swift, in the town of Shopton, New York State. The young man had followed in the footsteps of his parent, and was already an inventor of note.

Their home was presided over by Mrs. Baggert, as housekeeper, since Mrs. Swift had been dead several years. In addition, there was Garret Jackson, an engineer, who aided Tom and his father, and Eradicate Sampson, an odd colored man, who, with his mule, Boomerang, worked about the place.

In the first volume of this series, entitled "Tom Swift and his Motor-Cycle," here was related how he came to possess that machine. A certain Mr. Wakefield Damon, an eccentric gentleman, who was always blessing himself, or something about him, owned the cycle, but he came to grief on it, and sold it to Tom very cheaply.

Tom had a number of adventures on the wheel, and, after having used the motor to save a valuable patent model from a gang of unscrupulous men, the lad acquired possession of a power boat, in which he made several trips, and took part in many exciting happenings.

Some time later, in company with John Sharp, an aeronaut, whom Tom had rescued from Lake Carlopa, after the airman had nearly lost his life in a burning balloon, the young inventor made a big airship, called the Red Cloud. With Mr. Damon, Tom made several trips in this craft, as set forth in the book, "Tom Swift and His Airship."

It was after this that Tom and his father built a submarine boat, and went under the ocean for sunken treasure, and, following that trip Tom built a speedy electric runabout, and by a remarkable run in that, with Mr. Damon, saved a bank from ruin, bringing gold in time to stave off a panic.

"Tom Swift and His Wireless Message" told of the young inventor's plan to save the castaways of Earthquake Island, and how he accomplished it by constructing a wireless plant from the remains of the wrecked airship Whizzer. After Tom got back from Earthquake Island he went with Mr. Barcoe Jenks, whom he met on the ill-fated bit of land, to discover the secret of the diamond makers. They found the mysterious men, but the trip was not entirely successful, for the mountain containing the cave where the diamonds were made was destroyed by a lightning shock, just as Mr. Parker, a celebrated scientist, who accompanied the party, said it would be.

But his adventure in seeking to discover the secret of making precious stones did not satisfy Tom Swift, and when he and his friends got back from the mountains they prepared to go to Alaska to search for gold in the caves of ice. They were almost defeated in their purpose by the actions of Andy Foger and his father, who in an under-hand manner, got possession of a valuable map, showing the location of the gold, and made a copy of the drawing.

Then, when Tom and his friends set off in the Red Cloud, as related in "Tom Swift in the Caves of Ice," the Fogers, in another airship, did likewise. But Tom and his party were first on the scene, and accomplished their purpose, though they had to fight the savage Indians. The airship was wrecked in a cave of ice, that collapsed on it, and the survivors had desperate work getting away from the frozen North.

Tom had been home all the following winter and spring, and he had done little more than work on some small inventions, when a new turn was given his thoughts and energies by a visit from Mr. Gunmore, as narrated in the first chapter of the present volume.

"Well, I guess no one is here," remarked the young inventor as he completed the circuit of the grounds and walked slowly back toward the house. "I think I scared Andy so that he won't come back right away. He had the laugh on me, though, when I stumbled and fell."

As Tom proceeded he heard some one approaching, around the path at the side of the house.

"Who's there?" he called quickly, taking a firmer grasp of his stick.

"It's me, Massa Swift," was the response. "I jest come back from town. I got some peppermint fo' mah mule, Boomerang, dat's what I got."

"Oh! It's you, is it, Rad?" asked the youth in easier tones.

"Dat's who it am. Did yo' t'ink it were some un else?"

"I did," replied Tom. "Andy Foger has been sneaking around. Keep your eyes open the rest of the night, Rad."

"I will, Massa Tom."

The youth went into the house, having left word with the engineer, Mr. Jackson, to be on the alert for anything suspicious.

"And now I guess I'll go to bed, and make an early start tomorrow morning, planning my new aeroplane," mused Tom. "I'm going to make the speediest craft of the air ever seen!"

As he started toward his room Tom Swift heard the voice of the housekeeper calling to him:

"Tom! Oh, Tom! Come here, quickly!"

"What's the matter?" he asked, in vague alarm.

"Something has happened to your father!" was the startling reply. "He's fallen down, and is unconscious! Come quickly! Send for the doctor!"

Tom fairly ran toward his father's room.

CHAPTER THREE

THE PLANS DISAPPEAR

Mr. Swift was lying on the floor, where he had fallen, in front of his bed, as he was preparing to retire. There was no mark of injury upon him, and at first, as he knelt down at his father's side, Tom was at a loss to account for what had taken place.

"How did it happen? When was it?" he asked of Mrs. Baggert, as he held up his father's head, and noted that the aged man was breathing slightly.

"I don't know what happened, Tom," answered the housekeeper, "but I heard him fall, and ran upstairs, only to find him lying there, just like that. Then I called you. Hadn't you better have a doctor?"

"Yes; we'll need one at once. Send Eradicate. Tell him to run—not to wait for his mule—Boomerang is too slow. Oh, no! The telephone, of course! Why didn't I think of that at first? Please telephone for Dr. Gladby, Mrs. Baggert. Ask him to come as soon as possible, and then tell Garret Jackson to step here. I'll have him help me get father into bed."

The housekeeper hastened to the instrument, and was soon in communication with the physician, who promised to call at once. The engineer was summoned from another part of the house, and then Eradicate was aroused.

Mrs. Baggert had the colored man help her get some kettles of hot water in readiness for possible use by the doctor. Mr. Jackson aided Tom to lift Mr. Swift up on the bed, and they got off some of his clothes.

"I'll try to see if I can revive him with a little aromatic spirits of ammonia," decided Tom, as he noticed that his father was still unconscious. He hastened to prepare the strong spirits, while he was conscious of a feeling of fear and alarm, mingled with sadness.

Suppose his father should die? Tom could not bear to think of that. He would be left all alone, and how much he would miss the companionship and comradeship of his father none but himself knew.

"Oh! but I mustn't think he's going to die!" exclaimed the youth, as he mixed the medicine.

Mr. Swift feebly opened his eyes after Tom and Mr. Jackson had succeeded in forcing some of the ammonia between his lips.

"Where am I? What happened?" asked the aged inventor faintly.

"We don't know, exactly," spoke Tom softly. "You are ill, father. I've sent for the doctor. He'll fix you up. He'll be here soon."

"Yes, I'm—I'm ill," murmured the aged man. "Something hurts me—here," and he put his hand over his heart.

Tom felt a nameless sense of fear. He wished now that he had insisted on his parent consulting a physician some time before, when Mr. Swift first complained of a minor ailment. Perhaps now it was too late.

"Oh! when will that doctor come?" murmured Tom impatiently.

Mrs. Baggert, who was nervously going in and out of the room, again went to the telephone.

"He's on his way," the housekeeper reported. "His wife said he just started out in his auto."

Dr. Gladby hurried into the room a little later, and cast a quick look at Mr. Swift, who had again lapsed into unconsciousness.

"Do you think he—think he's going to die?" faltered Tom. He was no longer the self-reliant young inventor. He could meet danger bravely when it threatened himself alone, but when his father was stricken he seemed to lose all courage.

"Die? Nonsense!" exclaimed the doctor heartily. "He's not dead yet, at all events, and while there's life there's hope. I'll soon have him out of this spell."

It was some little time, however, before Mr. Swift again opened his eyes, but he seemed to gain strength from the remedies which Dr. Gladby administered, and in about an hour the inventor could sit up.

"But you must be careful," cautioned the physician. "Don't overdo yourself. I'll be in again in the morning, and now I'll leave you some medicine, to be taken every two hours."

"Oh, I feel much better," said Mr. Swift, and his voice certainly seemed stronger. "I can't imagine what happened. I came upstairs, after Tom had received a visit from the minister, and that's all I remember."

"The minister, father!" exclaimed Tom, in great amazement. "The minister wasn't here this evening! That was Mr. Gunmore, the aviation secretary. Don't you remember?"

"I don't remember any gentleman like that calling here tonight," Mr. Swift said blankly. "It was the minister, I'm sure, Tom."

"The minister was here last night, Mr. Swift," said the housekeeper.

"Was he? Why, it seems like tonight. And I came upstairs after talking to him, and then it all got black, and—and—"

"There, now; don't try to think," advised the doctor. "You'll be all right in the morning."

"But I can't remember anything about that aviation man," protested Mr. Swift. "I never used to be that way—forgetting things. I don't like it!"

"Oh, it's just because you're tired," declared the physician. "It will all come back to you in the morning. I'll stop in and see you then. Now try to go to sleep." And he left the room.

Tom followed him, Mrs. Baggert and Mr. Jackson remaining with the sick man.

"What is the matter with my father, Dr. Gladby?" asked Tom earnestly, as the doctor prepared to take his departure. "Is it anything serious?"

"Well," began the medical man, "I would not be doing my duty, Tom, if I did not tell you what it is. That is, it is comparatively serious, but it is curable, and I think we can bring him around. He has an affection of the heart, that, while it is common enough, is sometimes fatal.

"But I do not think it will be so in your father's case. He has a fine constitution, and this would never have happened had he not been run down from overwork. That is the principal trouble. What he needs is rest; and then, with the proper remedies, he will be as well as before."

"But that strange lapse of memory, doctor?"

"Oh, that is nothing. It is due to the fact that he has been using his brain too much. The brain protests, and refuses to work until rested. Your father has been working rather hard of late hasn't he?"

"Yes; on a new wireless motor."

"I thought so. Well, a good rest is what he needs, and then his mind and body will be in tune again. I'll be around in the morning."

Tom was somewhat relieved by the doctor's words, but not very much so, and he spent an anxious night, getting up every two hours to administer the medicine. Toward morning Mr. Swift fell into a heavy sleep, and did not awaken for some time.

"Oh, you're much better!" declared Dr. Gladby when he saw his patient that day.

"Yes, I feel better," admitted Mr. Swift.

"And can't you remember about Mr. Gunmore calling?" asked Tom.

The aged inventor shook his head, with a puzzled air.

"I can't remember it at all," he said. "The minister is the last person I remember calling here."

Tom looked worried, but the physician said it was a common feature of the disease from which Mr. Swift suffered, and would doubtless pass away.

"And you don't remember how we talked about me building a speedy aeroplane and trying for the ten-thousand-dollar prize?" asked Tom.

"I can't remember a thing about it," said the inventor, with a puzzled shake of his head, "and I'm not going to try, at least not right away. But, Tom, if you're going to build a new aeroplane, I want to help you. I'll give you the benefit of my advice. I think my new form of motor can be used in it."

"Now! now! No inventions—at least not just yet!" objected the physician. "You must have a good rest first, Mr. Swift, and get strong. Then you and Tom can build as many airships as you like."

Mr. Swift felt so much better about three days later that he wanted to get right to work planning the airship that was to win the big prize, but the doctor would not hear of it. Tom, however, began to make rough sketches of what he had in mind changing them from time to time. He also worked on a type of motor, very light, and modeled after one his father had recently patented.

Then a new idea came to Tom in regard to the shape of his aeroplane, and he worked several days drawing the plans for it. It was a new idea in construction, and he believed it would give him the great speed he desired.

"But I'd like dad to see it," he said. "As soon as he's well enough I'll go over it with him."

That time came a week later, and with a complete set of the plans, embodying his latest ideas, Tom went into the library where his father was seated in an easy-chair. Dr. Gladby had said it would not now harm the aged inventor to do a little work. Tom spread the drawings out in front of his father, and began to explain them in detail.

"I really think you have something great there, Tom!" exclaimed Mr. Swift, at length. "It is a very small monoplane, to be sure, but I think with the new principle you have introduced it will work; but, if I were you, I'd shape those wing tips a little differently."

"No, they're better that way," said Tom pleasantly, for he did not often disagree with his father. "I'll show you from a little model I have made. I'll get it right away."

Anxious to demonstrate that he was right in his theory, Tom hurried from the library to get the model of which he had spoken. He left the roll of plans lying on a small table near where his father was seated.

"There, you see, dad," said the young inventor as he re-entered the library a few minutes later, "when you warp the wing tips in making a spiral ascent it throws your tail wings out of plumb, and so—"

Tom paused in some amazement, for Mr. Swift was lying back in his chair, with his eyes closed. The lad started in alarm, laid aside his model, and sprang to his father's side.

"He's had another of those heart attacks!" gasped Tom. He was just going to call Mrs. Baggert, when Mr. Swift opened his eyes. He looked at Tom, and the lad could see that they were bright, and did not show any signs of illness.

"Well, I declare!" exclaimed the inventor. "I must have dozed off, Tom, while you were gone. That's what I did. I fell asleep!"

"Oh!" said Tom, much relieved. "I was afraid you were ill again. Now, in this model, as you will see by the plans, it is necessary—"

He paused, and looked over at the table where he had left the drawings. They were not there!

"The plans, father!" Tom exclaimed. "The plans I left on the table! Where are they?"

"I haven't touched them," was the answer. "They were on that table, where you put them, when I closed my eyes for a little nap. I forgot all about them. Are you sure they're missing?"

"They're not here!" And Tom gazed wildly about the room. "Where can they have gone?"

"I wasn't out of my chair," said Mr. Swift, "I ought not to have gone to sleep, but—"

Tom fairly jumped toward the long library window, the same one from which he had leaped to pursue Andy Foger. The casement was open, and Tom noted that the screen was also unhooked. It had been closed when he went to get the model, he was sure of that.

"Look, dad! See!" he exclaimed, as he picked up from the floor a small piece of paper.

"What is it, Tom?"

"A sheet on which I did some figuring. It is no good, but it was in with the plans. It must have dropped out."

"Do you mean that some one has been in here and taken the plans of your new aeroplane, Tom?" gasped his father.

"That's just what I mean! They sneaked in here while you were dozing, took the plans, and jumped out of the window with them. On the way this paper fell out. It's the only clue we have. Stay here, dad. I'm going to have a look." And Tom jumped from the library window and ran down the path after the unknown thief.

CHAPTER FOUR

ANXIOUS DAYS

Peering on all sides as he dashed along the gravel walk, hoping to catch a glimpse of the unknown intruder in the garden or shrubbery, Tom sprinted on at top speed. Now and then he paused to listen, but no sound came to him to tell of some one in retreat before him. There was only Silence.

"Mighty queer," mused the youth. "Whoever it was, he couldn't have had more than a minute start of me—no, not even half a minute—and yet they've disappeared as completely as though the ground had opened and let them down; and the worst of it is, that they've taken my plans with them!"

He turned about and retraced his steps, making a careful search. He saw no one, until, turning a corner, a little later, he met Eradicate Sampson.

"You haven't seen any strangers around here just now, have you, Rad?" asked Tom anxiously.

"No, indeedy, I hasn't, Massa Tom. What fo' kind ob a stranger was him?"

"That's just what I don't know. Rad. But some one sneaked into the library just now and took some of my plans while my father dozed off. I jumped out after him as soon as I could, but he has disappeared."

"Maybe it were th' man who done stowed hisself away on yo' airship, de time yo' all went after de diamonds," suggested the colored man.

"No, it couldn't have been him. If it was anybody, it was Andy Foger, or some of his crowd. You didn't see Andy, did you, Rad?"

"No, indeedy; but if I do, I suah will turn mah mule, Boomerang, loose on him, an' he won't take any mo' plans—not right off, Massa Tom."

"No, I guess not. Well, I must get back to dad, or he'll worry. Keep your eyes open, Rad, and if you see Andy Foger, or any one else, around here, let me know. Just sing out for all you're worth."

"Shall I call out, Massa Tom, ef I sees dat blessin' man?"

"You mean Mr. Damon?"

"Dat's de one. De gen'man what's allers a-blessin' ob hisself or his shoelaces, or suffin laik dat. Shall I sing out ef I sees him?"

"Well, no; not exactly, Rad. Just show Mr. Damon up to the house. I'd be glad to see him again, though I don't fancy he'll call. He's off on a little trip, and won't be back for a week. But watch out, Rad." And with that Tom turned toward the house, shaking his head over the puzzle of the missing plans.

"Did you find any one?" asked his father eagerly as the young inventor entered the library.

"No," was the gloomy answer. "There wasn't a sign of any one."

Tom went over to the window and looked about for clues. There was none that he could see, and a further examination of the ground under the window disclosed nothing. There was gravel beneath the casement, and this was not the best medium for retaining footprints. Nor were the gravel walks any better.

"Not a sign of any one," murmured Tom. "Are you sure you didn't hear any noise, dad, when you dozed off?"

"Not a sound, Tom. In fact, it's rather unusual for me to go to sleep like that, but I suppose it's because of my illness. But I couldn't have been asleep long—not more than two minutes."

"That's what I think. Yet in that time someone, who must have been on the watch, managed to get in here and take my plans for the new sky racer. I don't see how they got the wire screen open from the outside, though. It fastens with a strong hook."

"And was the screen open?" asked Mr. Swift

"Yes, it was unhooked. Either they pushed a wire in through the mesh, caught it under the hook, and pulled it up from the outside, or else the screen was opened from the inside."

"I don't believe they could get inside to open the screen without some of us seeing them," spoke the older inventor. "More likely, Tom, it wasn't hooked, and they found it an easy matter to simply pull it open."

"That's possible. I'll ask Mrs. Baggert if the screen was unhooked."

But the housekeeper could not be certain on that point, and so that part of the investigation amounted to nothing.

"It's too bad!" exclaimed Mr. Swift. "It's my fault, for dozing off that way."

"No, indeed, it isn't!" declared Tom stoutly.

"Is the loss a serious one?" asked his father. "Have you no copy of the plans?"

"Yes, I have a rough draft from which I made the completed drawings, and I can easily make another set. But that isn't what worries me—the mere loss of the plans."

"What is it, then, Tom?"

"The fact that whoever took them must know that they are the plans for a sky racer that is to take part in the big meet. I have worked it out on a new principle, and it is not yet patented. Whoever stole my plans can make the same kind of a sky racer that I intended to construct, and so stand as good a chance to win the prize of ten thousand dollars as I will."

"That certainly is too bad, Tom. I never thought of that. Do you suspect any one?"

"No one, unless it's Andy Foger. He's mean enough to do a thing like that, but I didn't think he'd have the nerve. However, I'll see if I can learn anything about him. He may have been sneaking around, and if he has my plans he'd ask nothing better than to make a sky racer and beat me."

"Oh, Tom, I'm so sorry!" exclaimed Mr. Swift "I—I feel very bad about it!"

"There, never mind!" spoke the lad, seeing that his father was looking ill again. "Don't think any more about it, dad. I'll get back those plans. Come, now. It's time for your medicine, and then you must lie down." For the aged inventor was looking tired and weak.

Wearily he let Tom lead him to his room, and after seeing that the invalid was comfortable Tom called up Dr. Gladby, to have him come and see Mr. Swift. The doctor said his patient had been overdoing himself a little, and must rest more if he was to completely recover.

Learning that his father was no worse, Tom set off to find Andy Foger.

"I can't rest until I know whether or not he has my plans," he said to himself. "I don't want to make a speedy aeroplane, and find out at the last minute that Andy, or some of his cronies, have duplicated it."

But Tom got little satisfaction from Andy Foger. When that bully was accused of having been around Tom's house he denied it, and though the young inventor did not actually accuse him of taking the plans, he hinted at it. Andy muttered many indignant negatives, and called on some of his cronies to witness that at the time the plans were taken he and they were some distance from the Swift home.

So Tom was baffled; and though he did not believe the red-haired lad's denial, there was no way in which he could prove to the contrary.

"If he didn't take the plans, who did?" mused Tom.

As the young inventor turned away after cross-questioning Andy, the bully called out:

"You'll never win that ten thousand dollars!"

"What do you know about that?" demanded Tom quickly.

"Oh, I know," sneered Andy. "There'll be bigger and better aeroplanes in that meet than you can make, and you'll never win the prize."

"I suppose you heard about the affair by sneaking around under our windows, and listening," said Tom.

"Never mind how I know it, but I do," retorted the bully.

"Well, I'll tell you one thing," said Tom calmly. "If you come around again it won't be healthy for you. Look out for live wires, if you try to do the listening act any more, Andy!" And with that ominous warning Tom turned away.

"What do you suppose he means, Andy?" asked Pete Bailey, one of Andy's cronies.

"It means he's got electrical wires strung around his place," declared Sam Snedecker, "and that we'll be shocked if we go up there. I'm not going!"

"Me, either," added Pete, and Andy laughed uneasily.

Tom heard what they said, and in the next few days he made himself busy by putting some heavy wires in and about the grounds where they would show best. But the wires carried no current, and were only displayed to impress a sense of fear on Andy and his cronies, which purpose they served well.

But it was like locking the stable door after the horse had been stolen, for with all the precautions he could take Tom could not get back his plans, and he spent many anxious days seeking them. They seemed to have completely disappeared, however, and the young inventor decided there was nothing else to do but to draw new ones.

He set to work on them, and in the meanwhile tried to learn whether or not Andy had the missing plans. He sought this information by stealth, and was aided by his chum, Ned Newton. But all to no purpose. Not the slightest trace or clue was discovered.

CHAPTER FIVE

BUILDING THE SKY RACER

"What will you do, if, after you have your little monoplane all constructed, and get ready to race, you find that some one else has one exactly like it at the meet?" asked Ned Newton one day, when he and Tom were out in the big workshop, talking things over. "What will you do, Tom?"

"I don't see that there is anything I can do. I'll go on to the meet, of course, and trust to some improvements I have since brought out, and to what I know about aeroplanes, to help me win the race. I'll know, too, who stole my plans."

"But it will be too late, then."

"Yes, too late, perhaps, to stop them from using the drawings, but not too late to punish them for the theft. It's a great mystery, and I'll be on the anxious seat all the while. But it can't be helped."

"When are you going to start work on the sky racer?"

"Pretty soon, now. I've got another set of plans made, and I've fixed them so that if they are stolen it won't do any one any good."

"How's that?"

"I've put in a whole lot of wrong figures and measurements, and scores of lines and curves that mean nothing. I have marked the right figures and lines by a secret mark, and when I work on them I'll use only the proper ones. But any one else wouldn't know this. Oh, I'll fool 'em this time!"

"I hope you do. Well, when you get the machine done I'd like to ride in it. Will it carry two, as your Butterfly does?"

"Yes, only it will be much different; and, of course, it will go much faster. I'll give you a ride, all right, Ned. Well, now I must get busy and see what material I need for what I hope will prove to be the speediest aeroplane in the world."

"That's going some! I must be leaving now. Don't forget your promise. I saw Mary Nestor on my way over here. She was asking for you. She said you must be very busy, for she hadn't seen you in some time."

"Um!" was all Tom answered, but by the blush that mounted to his face it was evident that he was more interested in Mary Nestor than his mere exclamation indicated.

When Ned had gone Tom got out pencil and paper, and was busily engaged in making some intricate calculations. He drew odd little sketches on the margin of the sheet, and then wrote out a list of the things he would need to construct the new aeroplane.

This finished, he went to Mr. Jackson, the engineer, and asked him to get the various things together, and to have them put in the special shop where Tom did most of his work.

"I want to get the machine together as soon as I can," he remarked to the engineer, "for it will need to be given a good tryout before I enter in the race, and I may find that I'll have to make several changes in it."

Mr. Jackson promised to attend to the matter right away, and then Tom went in to talk to his father about the motor that was to whirl the propeller of the new air craft.

Mr. Swift had improved very much in the past few days, and though Dr. Gladby said he was far from being well, the physician declared there was no reason why he should not do some inventive work.

He and Tom were deep in an argument of gasoline motors, discussing the best manner of attaching the fins to the cylinders to make them air-cooled, when a voice sounded outside, the voice of Eradicate:

"Heah! Whar yo' goin'?" demanded the colored man. "Whar yo' goin'?"

"Somebody's out in the garden!" exclaimed Tom, jumping up suddenly.

"Perhaps it's the same person who took the plans!" suggested Mr. Swift.

"Hold on, dere!" yelled Eradicate again.

Then a voice replied:

"Bless my insurance policy! What's the matter? Have there been burglars around? Why all these precautions? Bless my steam heater! Don't you know me?"

"Mr. Damon!" cried Tom, a look of pleasure coming over his face. "Mr. Damon is coming!"

"So I should judge," responded Mr. Swift, with a smile. "I wonder why Eradicate didn't recognize him?"

They learned why a moment later, for on looking from the library window, Tom saw the colored man coming up the walk behind a well-dressed gentleman.

"Why, mah goodness! It's Mr. Damon!" exclaimed Eradicate. "I didn't know yo', sah, wif dem whiskers on! I didn't, fo' a fac'!"

"Bless my razor! I suppose it does make a difference," said the eccentric man. "Yes, my wife thought I'd look better, and more sedate, with a beard, so I grew one to please her. But I don't like it. A beard is too warm this kind of weather; eh, Tom?" And Mr. Damon waved his hand to the young inventor and his father, who stood in the low windows of the library. "Entirely too warm, bless my finger-nails, yes!"

"I agree with you!" exclaimed Tom. "Come in! We're glad to see you!"

"I called to see if you aren't going on another trip to the North Pole, or somewhere in the Arctic regions," went on Mr. Damon.

"Why?" inquired Tom.

"Why, then this heavy beard of mine would come in handy. It would keep my throat and chin warm." And Mr. Damon ran his hands through his luxuriant whiskers.

"No more northern trips right away," said Tom. "I'm about to build a speedy monoplane, to take part in the big meet at Eagle Park."

"Oh, yes, I heard about the meet," said Mr. Damon. "I'd like to be in that."

"Well, I'm building a machine that will carry two," went on Tom, "and if you think you can stand a speed of a hundred miles an hour, or better, I'll let you come with me. There are some races where a passenger is allowed."

"Have you got a razor?" asked Mr. Damon suddenly.

"What for?" inquired Mr. Swift, wondering what the eccentric man was going to do.

"Why, bless my shaving soap! I'm going to cut off my beard. If I go in a monoplane at a hundred miles an hour I don't want to make any more resistance to the wind than possible, and my whiskers would certainly hold back Tom's machine. Where's a razor? I'm going to shave at once. My wife won't mind when I tell her what it's for. Lend me a razor, please, Tom."

"Oh, there's plenty of time," explained the lad, with a laugh. "The race doesn't take place for over two months. But when it does, I think you would be better off without a beard."

"I know it," said Mr. Damon simply. "I'll shave before we enter the contest, Tom. But now tell me all about it."

Tom did so, relating the story of the theft of the plans. Mr. Damon was for having Andy arrested at once, but Mr. Swift and his son pointed out that they had no evidence against him.

"All we can do," said the young inventor, "is to keep watch on him, and see if he is building another aeroplane. He has all the facilities, and he may attempt to get ahead of me. If he enters a sky craft at the meet I'll be pretty sure that he has made it from my stolen plans."

"Bless my wing tips!" cried Mr. Damon. "But can't we do anything to stop him?"

"I'm afraid not," answered Tom; and then he showed Mr. Damon his re-drawn plans, and told in detail of how he intended to construct the new aeroplane.

The eccentric man remained as the guest of the Swift family that night, departing for his home the next day, and promising to be on hand as soon as Tom was ready to test his new craft, which would be in about a month.

As the days passed, Tom, with the help of his father, whose health was slightly better, and with the aid of Mr. Jackson, began work on the speedy little sky racer.

As you boys are all more or less familiar with aeroplanes, we will not devote much space to the description of the new one Tom Swift made.

We can describe it in general terms, but there were some features of it which Tom kept a secret from all save his father.

Suffice it to say that Tom had decided to build a small air craft of the single-wing type, known as the monoplane. It was to be a cross between the Bleriot and the Antoinette, with the general features of both, but with many changes or improvements.

The wings were shaped somewhat like those of a humming-bird, which, as is well known, can, at times, vibrate its wings with such velocity that the most rapid camera lens cannot quite catch.

And when it is known that a bullet in flight has been successfully photographed, the speed of the wings of the humming-bird can be better appreciated.

The writer has seen a friend, with a very rapid camera, which was used to snap automobiles in flight, attempt to take a picture of a humming-bird. He got the picture, all right, but the plate was blurred, showing that the wings had moved faster than the lens could throw them on the sensitive plate.

Not that Tom intended the wings of his monoplane to vibrate, but he adopted that style as being the best adapted to allow of rapid flight through the air; and the young inventor had determined that he would clip many minutes from the best record yet made.

The body of his craft, between the forward wings and the rear ones, where the rudders were located, was shaped like a cigar, with side wings somewhat like the fin keels of the ocean liner to prevent a rolling motion. In addition, Tom had an ingenious device to automatically adapt his monoplane to sudden currents of air that might overturn it, and this device was one of the points which he kept secret.

The motor, which was air-cooled, was located forward, and was just above the heads of the operator and the passenger who sat beside him. The single propeller, which was ten feet in diameter, gave a minimum thrust of one thousand pounds at two thousand revolutions per minute.

This was one feature wherein Tom's craft differed from others. The usual aeroplane propeller is eight feet in diameter, and gives from four to five hundred pounds thrust at about one thousand revolutions per minute, so it can be readily seen wherein Tom had an advantage.

"But I'm building this for speed," he said to Mr. Jackson, "and I'm going to get it! We'll make a hundred miles an hour without trouble."

"I believe you," replied the engineer. "The motor you and your father have made is a wonder for lightness and power."

In fact, the whole monoplane was so light and frail as to give one the idea of a rather large model, instead of a real craft, intended for service. But a careful inspection showed the great strength it had, for it was braced and guyed in a new way, and was as rigid as a steel-trussed bridge.

"What are you going to call her?" asked Mr. Jackson, about two weeks after they had started work on the craft, and when it had begun to assume shape and form.

"I'm going to name her the Humming-Bird," replied Tom. "She's little, but oh, my!"

"And I guess she'll bring home the prize," added the engineer.

And as the days went by, and Tom, his father and Mr. Jackson continued to work on the speedy craft, this hope grew in the heart of the young inventor. But he could not rid himself of worry as to the fate of the plans that had disappeared. Who had them? Was some one making a machine like his own from them? Tom wished he knew.

CHAPTER SIX

ANDY FOGER WILL CONTEST

One afternoon, as Tom was working away in the shop on his sky racer, adjusting one of the rear rudders, and pausing now and then to admire the trim little craft, he heard some one approaching. Looking out through a small observation peephole made for this purpose, he saw Mrs. Baggert hurrying toward the building.

"I wonder what's the matter?" he said aloud, for there was a look of worriment on the lady's face. Tom threw open the door. "What is it, Mrs. Baggert?" he called. "Some one up at the house who wants to see me?"

"No, it's your father!" panted the housekeeper, for she was quite stout. "He is very ill again, and I can't seem to get Dr. Gladby on the telephone. Central says he doesn't answer."

"My father worse!" cried Tom in alarm, dropping his tools and hurrying from the shop. "Where's Eradicate? Send him for the doctor. Perhaps the wires are broken. If he can't locate Dr. Gladby, get Dr. Kurtz. We must have some one. Here, Rad! Where are you?" he called, raising his voice.

"Heah I be!" answered the colored man, coming from the direction of the garden, which he had been weeding.

"Get out your mule, and go for Dr. Gladby. If he isn't home, get Dr. Kurtz. Hurry, Rad!"

"I's mighty sorry, Massa Tom," answered the colored man, "but I cain't hurry, nohow."

"Why not?"

"Because Boomerang done gone lame, an' he won't run. I'll go mahse'f, but I cain't take dat air mule."

"Never mind. I'll go in the Butterfly," decided Tom quickly. "I'll run up to the house and see how dad is, and while I'm gone, Rad, you get out the Butterfly. I can make the trip in that. If Dr. Kurtz had a 'phone I could get him, but he lives over on the back road, where there isn't a line. Hurry, Rad!"

"Yes, sah, Massa Tom, I'll hurry!"

The colored man knew how to get the monoplane in shape for a flight, as he had often done it.

Tom found his father in no immediate danger, but Mr. Swift had had a slight recurrence of his heart trouble, and it was thought best to have a doctor. So Tom started off in his air craft, rising swiftly above the house-top, and sailed off toward the old-fashioned residence of Dr. Kurtz, a sturdy, elderly German physician, who sometimes attended Mr. Swift. Tom decided that as long as Dr. Gladby did not answer his 'phone, he could not be at home, and this, he learned later, was the case, the physician being in a distant town on a consultation.

"My, this Butterfly seems big and clumsy beside my Humming-Bird," mused Tom as he slid along through the air, now flying high and now low, merely for practice. "This machine can go, but wait until I have my new one in the air! Then I'll show 'em what speed is!"

He was soon at the physician's house, and found him in.

"Won't you ride back with me in the monoplane?" asked Tom. "I'm anxious to have you see dad as soon as you can.

"Vot! Me drust mineself in one ob dem airships? I dinks not!" exclaimed Dr. Kurtz ponderously. "Vy, I vould not efen ride in an outer-mobile, yet, so vy should I go in von contrivance vot is efen more dangerous? No, I gomes to your fader in der carriage, mit mine old Dobbin horse. Dot vill not drop me to der ground, or run me up a tree, yet! Vot?"

"Very well," said Tom, "only hurry, please."

The young inventor, in his airship, reached home some time before the slow-going doctor got there in his carriage. Mr. Swift was no worse, Tom was glad to find, though he was evidently quite ill.

"So, ve must take goot care of him," said the doctor, when he had examined the patient. "Dr. Gladby he has done much for him, und I can do little more. You must dake care of yourself, Herr Swift, or you vill—but den, vot is der use of being gloomy-minded? I am sure you vill go more easy, und not vork so much."

"I haven't worked much," replied the aged inventor. "I have only been helping my son on a new airship."

"Den dot must stop," insisted the doctor. "You must haf gomplete rest—dot's it—gomplete rest."

"We'll do just as you say, doctor," said Tom. "We'll give up the aeroplane matters, dad, and go away, you and I, where we can't see a blueprint or a pattern, or hear the sound of machinery. We'll cut it all out."

"Dot vould he goot," said Dr. Kurtz ponderously.

"No, I couldn't think of it," answered Mr. Swift. "I want you to go in that race, Tom—and win!"

"But I'll not do it, dad, if you're going to be ill."

"He is ill now," interrupted the doctor. "Very ill, Dom Swift."

"That settles it. I don't go in the race. You and I'll go away, dad—to California, or up in Canada. We'll travel for your health."

"No! no!" insisted the old inventor gently. "I will be all right. Most of the work on the monoplane is done now, isn't it, Tom?"

"Yes, dad."

"Then you go on, and finish it. You and Mr. Jackson can do it without me now. I'll take a rest, doctor, but I want my son to enter that race, and, what's more, I want him to win!"

"Vell, if you don't vork, dot is all I ask. I must forbid you to do any more. Mit Dom, dot is different. He is young und strong, und he can vork. But you—not, Herr Swift, or I doctor you no more." And the physician shook his big head.

"Very well. I'll agree to that if Tom will promise to enter the race," said the inventor.

"I will," said Tom.

The physician took his leave shortly after that, the medicine he gave to Mr. Swift somewhat relieving him. Then the young inventor, who felt in a little better spirits, went back to his workshop.

"Poor dad," he mused. "He thinks more of me and this aeroplane than he does of himself. Well, I will go in the race, and I'll—yes, I'll win!" And Tom looked very determined.

He was about to resume work on his craft when something about the way one of the forward planes was tilted attracted his attention.

"I never left it that way," mused Tom. "Some one has been in here. I wonder if it was Mr. Jackson?"

Tom stepped to the door and called for Eradicate. The colored man came from the direction of the garden, which he was still weeding.

"Has Mr. Jackson been around, Rad?" asked the lad.

"No, sah. I ain't seed him."

"Have you been in here, looking at the Humming-Bird?"

"No, Massa Tom. I nebber goes in dere, lessen as how yo' is dere. Dem's yo' orders."

"That's so, Rad. I might have known you wouldn't go in. But did you see any one enter the shop?"

"Not a pusson, sab."

"Have you been here all the while?"

"All but jes' a few minutes, when I went to de barn to put some liniment on Boomerang's so' foot."

"H'm! Some one might have slipped in here while I was away," mused Tom. "I ought to have locked the doors, but I was in a hurry. This thing is getting on my nerves. I wonder if it's Andy Foger, or some one else, who is after my secret?"

He made a hasty examination of the shop, but could discover nothing more wrong, except that one of the planes of the Humming-Bird had been shifted.

"It looks as if they were trying to see how it was fastened on, and how it worked," mused Tom. "But my plans haven't been touched, and no damage has been done. Only I don't like to think that people have been in here. They may have stolen some of my ideas. I must keep this place locked night and day after this."

Tom spent a busy week in making improvements on his craft. Mr. Swift was doing well, and after a consultation by Dr. Kurtz and Dr. Gladby it was decided to adopt a new style of treatment. In the meanwhile, Mr. Swift kept his promise, and did no work. He sat in his easy-chair, out in the garden, and dozed away, while Tom visited him frequently to see if he needed anything.

"Poor old dad!" mused the young inventor. "I hope he is well enough to come and see me try for the ten-thousand-dollar prize—and win it! I hope I do; but if some one builds, from my stolen plans, a machine on this model, I'll have my work cut out for me." And he gazed with pride on the Humming-Bird.

For the past two weeks Tom had seen nothing of Andy Foger. The red-haired bully seemed to have dropped out of sight, and even his cronies, Sam Snedecker and Pete Bailey, did not know where he had gone.

"I hope he has gone for good," said Ned Newton, who lived near Andy. "He's an infernal nuisance. I wish he'd never come back to Shopton."

But Andy was destined to come back.

One day, when Tom was busy installing a wireless apparatus on his new aeroplane, he heard Eradicate hurrying up the path that led to the shop.

"I wonder if dad is worse?" thought Tom, that always being his first idea when he knew a summons was coming for him. Quickly be opened the door.

"Some one's comin' out to see you, Massa Tom," said the colored man.

"Who is it?" asked the lad, taking the precaution to put his precious plans out of sight.

"I dunno, sah; but yo' father knows him, an' he said fo' me to come out heah, ahead ob de gen'man, an' tell yo' he were comin'. He'll be right heah."

"Oh, well, if dad knows him, it's all right. Let him come, Rad."

"Yes, sah. Heah he comes." And the colored man pointed to a figure advancing down the gravel path. Tom watched the stranger curiously. There was something familiar about him, and Tom was sure he had met him before, yet he could not seem to place him.

"How are you, Tom Swift?" greeted the newcomer pleasantly. "I guess you've forgotten me, haven't you?" He held out his hand, which Tom took. "Don't know me, do you?" he went on.

"Well, I'm afraid I've forgotten your name," admitted the lad, just a bit embarrassed. "But your face is familiar, somehow, and yet it isn't."

"I've shaved off my mustache," went on the other. "That makes a difference. But you haven't forgotten John Sharp, the balloonist, whom you rescued from Lake Carlopa, and who helped you build the Red Cloud? You haven't forgotten John Sharp, have you, Tom?"

"Well, I should say not!" cried the lad heartily. "I'm real glad to see you. What are you doing around here? Come in. I've got something to show you," and he motioned to the shop where the Humming-Bird was housed.

"Oh, I know what it is," said the veteran balloonist.

"You do?"

"Yes. It's your new aeroplane. In fact, I came to see you about it."

"To see me about it?"

"Yes. I'm one of the committee of arrangements for the meet to be held at Eagle Park, where I understand you are going to contest. I came to see how near you were ready, and to get you to make a formal entry of your machine. Mr. Gunmore sent me."

"Oh, so you're in with them now, eh?" asked Tom. "Well, I'm glad to know I've got a friend on the committee. Yes, my machine is getting along very well. I'll soon be ready for a trial flight. Come in and look at it. I think it's a bird—a regular Humming-Bird!" And Tom laughed.

"It certainly is something new," admitted Mr. Sharp as his eyes took in the details of the trim little craft. "By the way, Shopton is going to be well represented at the meet."

"How is that? I thought I was the only one around here to enter an aeroplane."

"No. We have just received an entry from Andy Foger."

"From Andy Foger!" gasped Tom. "Is he going to try to win some of the prizes?"

"He's entered for the big one, the ten-thousand-dollar prize," replied the balloonist. "He has made formal application to be allowed to compete, and we have to accept any one who applies. Why, do you object to him, Tom?"

"Object to him? Mr. Sharp, let me tell you something. Some time ago a set of plans of my machine here were stolen from my house. I suspected Andy Foger of taking them, but I could get no proof. Now you say he is building a machine to compete for the big prize. Do you happen to know what style it is?"

"It's a small monoplane, something like the Antoinette, his application states, though he may change it later."

"Then he's stolen my ideas, and is making a craft like this!" exclaimed Tom, as he sank upon a bench, and gazed from the balloonist to the Humming-Bird, and back to Mr. Sharp again. "Andy Foger is trying to beat me with my own machine!"

CHAPTER SEVEN

SEEKING A CLUE

John Sharp was more than surprised at the effect his piece of information had on Tom Swift. Though the young inventor had all along suspected Andy of having the missing plans, yet there had been no positive evidence on this point. That, coupled with the fact that the red-haired bully had not been seen in the vicinity of Shopton lately, had, in a measure, lulled Tom's suspicions to rest, but now his hope had been rudely shattered.

"Do you really think that's his game?" asked Mr. Sharp.

"I'm sure of it," replied the youth. "Though where he is building his aeroplane I can't imagine, for I haven't seen him in town. He's away."

"Are you sure of that?"

"Well, not absolutely sure," replied Tom. "It's the general rumor that he's out of town."

"Well, old General Rumor is sometimes a person not to be relied upon," remarked the balloonist grimly. "Now this is the way I size it up: Of course, all I know officially is that Andy Foger has sent in an entry for the big race for the ten-thousand-dollar prize which is offered by the Eagle Park Aviation Association. I'm a member of the arrangements committee, and so I know. I also know that you and several others are going to try for the prize. That's all I am absolutely sure of.

"Now, when you tell me about the missing plans, and you conclude that Andy is doing some underhanded work, I agree with you. But I go a step farther. I don't believe he's out of town at all."

"Why not?" exclaimed Tom.

"Because when he has an airship shed right in his own backyard, where, you tell me, he once made a craft in which he tried to beat you out in the trip to Alaska, when you think of that, doesn't it seem reasonable that he'd use that same building in which to make his new craft?"

"Yes, it does," admitted Tom slowly, "but then everybody says he's out of town."

"Well, what everybody says is generally not So. I think you'll find that Andy is keeping himself in seclusion, and that he's working secretly in his shop, building a machine with which to beat you."

"Do you, really?"

"I certainly do. Have you been around his place lately?"

"No. I've been too busy; and then I never have much to do with him."

"Then take my advice, and see if you can't get a look inside that shop. You may see something that will surprise you. If you find that Andy is infringing on your patented ideas, you can stop him by an injunction. You've got this model patented, I take it?"

"Oh, yes. I didn't have at the time the plans were stolen, but I've patented it since. I could get at him that way."

"Then take my advice, and do it. Get a look inside that shed, and you'll find Andy working secretly there, no matter if his cronies do think he's out of town."

"I believe I will," agreed Tom, and somehow he felt better now that he had decided on a plan of action. He and the balloonist talked over at some length just the best way to go about it, for the young inventor recalled the time when he and Ned Newton had endeavored to look into Andy's shed, with somewhat disastrous results to themselves; but Tom knew that the matter at stake justified a risk, and he was willing to take it.

"Well, now that's settled," said Mr. Sharp, "tell me more about yourself and your aeroplane. My! To think that the Red Cloud was destroyed! That was a fine craft."

"Indeed she was," agreed Tom. "I'm going to make another on similar lines, some day, but now all my time is occupied with the Humming Bird."

"She is a hummer, too," complimented Mr. Sharp. "But I almost forgot the real object of my trip here. There is no doubt about you going in the race, is there?"

"I fully expect to," replied Tom. "The only thing that will prevent me will be—"

"Don't say you're worried on account of what Andy Foger may do," interrupted Mr. Sharp.

"I'm not. I'll attend to Andy, all right. I was going to say that my father's illness might interfere. He's not well at all. I'm quite worried about him."

"Oh, I sincerely hope he'll be all right," remarked the balloonist. "We want you in this race. In fact, we're going to feature you, as they say about the actors and story-writers. The committee is planning to do considerable advertising on the strength of Tom Swift, the well-known young inventor, being a contestant for the ten-thousand-dollar prize."

"That's very nice, I'm sure," replied Tom, "and I'm going to do my best. Perhaps dad will take a turn for the better. He wants me to win as much as I want to myself. Well, we'll not worry about it, anyhow, until the time comes. I want to show you some new features of my latest aeroplane."

"And I want to see them, Tom. Don't you think you're making a mistake, though, in equipping it with a wireless outfit?"

"Why so?"

"Well, because it will add to the weight, and you want such a small machine to be as light as possible."

"Yes, but you see I have a very light engine. That part my father helped me with. In fact, it is the lightest air-cooled motor made, for the amount of horsepower it develops, so I can afford to put on the extra weight of the wireless outfit. I may need to signal when I am flying along at a hundred miles an hour."

"That's so. Well, show me some of the other good points. You've certainly got a wonderful craft here."

Tom and Mr. Sharp spent some time going over the Humming-Bird and in talking over old times. The balloonist paid another visit to Mr. Swift, who was feeling pretty good, and who expressed his pleasure in seeing his old friend again.

"Can't you stay for a few days?" asked Tom, when Mr. Sharp was about to leave. "If you wait long enough you may be able to help me work up the clues against Andy Foger, and also witness a trial flight of the Humming-Bird."

"I'd like to stay, but I can't," was the answer. "The committee will be anxious for me to get back with my report. Good luck to you. I'll see you at the time of the race, if not before."

Tom resolved to get right to work seeking clues against his old enemy, Andy, but the next day Mr. Swift was not so well, and Tom had to remain in the house. Then followed several days, during which time it was necessary to do some important work on his craft, and so a week passed without any information having been obtained.

In the meanwhile Tom had made some cautious inquiries, but had learned nothing about Andy. He had no chance to interview Pete or Sam, the two cronies, and he did not think it wise to make a bald request for information at the Foger home.

Ned Newton could not be of any aid to his friend, as he was kept busy in the bank night and day, working over a new set of books.

"I wonder how I can find out what I want to know?" mused Tom one afternoon, when he had done considerable work on the Humming-Bird. "I certainly ought to do it soon, so as to be able to stop Andy if he's infringing on my patents. Yet, I don't see how—"

His thoughts were interrupted by hearing a voice outside the shop, exclaiming:

"Bless my toothpick! I know the way, Eradicate, my good fellow. It isn't necessary for you to come. As long as Tom Swift is out there, I'll find him. Bless my horizontal rudder! I'm anxious to see what progress he's made. I'll find him, if he's about!"

"Yes, sah, he's right in dere," spoke the colored man. "He's workin' on dat Dragon Fly of his." Eradicate did not always get his names right.

"Mr. Damon!" exclaimed Tom in delight, at the sound of his friend's voice. "I believe he can help me get evidence against Andy Foger. I wonder I didn't think of it before! The very thing! I'll do it!"

CHAPTER EIGHT

THE EMPTY SHED

"Bless my dark-lantern! Where are you, Tom?" called Mr. Damon as he entered the dim shed where the somewhat frail-appearing aeroplane loomed up in the semi-darkness, for it was afternoon, and rather cloudy. "Where are you?"

"Here!" called the young inventor. "I'm glad to see you! Come in!"

"Ah! there it is, eh?" exclaimed the odd man, as he looked at the aeroplane, for there had been much work done on it since he had last seen it. "Bless my parachute, Tom! But it looks as though you could blow it over."

"It's stronger than it seems," replied the lad. "But, Mr. Damon, I've got something very important to talk to you about."

Thereupon Tom told all about Mr. Sharp's visit, of Andy's entry in the big race, and of the suspicions of himself and the balloonist.

"And what is it you wish me to do?" asked Mr. Damon.

"Work up some clues against Andy Foger."

"Good! I'll do it! I'd like to get ahead of that bully and his father, who once tried to wreck the bank I'm interested in. I'll help you, Tom! I'll play detective! Let me see—what disguise shall I assume? I think I'll take the part of a tramp. Bless my ham sandwich! That will be the very thing. I'll get some ragged clothes, let my beard grow again—you see I shaved it off since my last visit—and I'll go around to the Foger place and ask for work. Then I can get inside the shed and look around. How's that for a plan?"

"It might be all right," agreed Tom, "only I don't believe you're cut out for the part of a tramp, Mr. Damon."

"Bless my fingernails! Why not?"

"Oh, well, it isn't very pleasant to go around in ragged clothes."

"Don't mind about me. I'll do it." And the odd gentleman seemed quite delighted at the idea. He and Tom talked it over at some length, and then adjourned to the house, where Mr. Swift, who had seemed to improve in the last few days, was told of the plan.

"Couldn't you go around after evidence just as you are?" asked the aged inventor. "I don't much care for this disguising business."

"Oh, it's very necessary," insisted Mr. Damon earnestly. "Bless my gizzard! but it's very necessary. Why, if I went around the Foger place as I am now, they'd know me in a minute, and I couldn't find out what I want to know."

"Well, if you keep on blessing yourself," said Tom, with a laugh, "they'll know you, no matter what disguise you put on, Mr. Damon."

"That's so," admitted the eccentric gentleman. "I must break myself of that habit. I will. Bless my topknot! I'll never do it any more. Bless my trousers buttons!"

"I'm afraid you'll never do it!" exclaimed Tom.

"It is rather hard," said Mr. Damon ruefully, as he realized what he had said. "But I'll do it. Bless—"

He paused a moment, looked at Tom and his father, and then burst into a laugh. The habit was more firmly fastened on him than he was aware.

For several hours Tom, his father and Mr. Damon discussed various methods of proceeding, and it was finally agreed that Mr. Damon should first try to learn what Andy was doing, if anything, without resorting to a disguise.

"Then, if that doesn't work, I'll become a tramp," was the decision of the odd character. "I'll wear the raggedest clothes I can find Bless—" But he stopped in time.

Mr. Damon took up his residence in the Swift household, as he had often done before, and for the next week he went and came as he pleased, sometimes being away all night.

"It's no use, though," declared Mr. Damon at the end of the week. "I can't get anywhere near that shed, nor even get a glimpse inside of it. I haven't been able to learn anything, either. There are two gardeners on guard all the while, and several times when I've tried to go in the side gate, they've stopped me."

"Isn't there any news of Andy about town?" asked Tom. "I should think Sam or Pete would know where he is."

"Well, I didn't ask them, for they'd know right away why I was inquiring," said Mr. Damon, "but it seems to me as if there was something queer going on. If Andy Foger is working in that shed of his, he's keeping mighty quiet about it. Bless my—"

And once more he stopped in time. He was conquering the habit in a measure.

"Well, what do you propose to do next?" asked Tom.

"Disguise myself like a tramp, and go there looking for work," was the firm answer. "There are plenty of odd jobs on a big place such as the Foger family have. I'll find out what I want to know, you see."

It seemed useless to further combat this resolution, and, in a few days Mr. Damon presented a very different appearance. He had on a most ragged suit, there was a scrubby beard on his face, and he walked with a curious shuffle, caused by a pair of big, heavy shoes which he had donned, first having taken the precaution to make holes in them and get them muddy.

"Now I'm all ready," he said to Tom one day, when his disguise was complete. "I'm going over and try my luck."

He left the house by a side door, so that no one would see him, and started down the walk. As he did so a voice shouted:

"Hi, there! Git right out oh heah! Mistah Swift doan't allow no tramps heah, an' we ain't got no wuk fo' yo', an' there ain't no cold victuals. I does all de wuk, me an' mah mule Boomerang, an' we takes all de cold victuals, too! Git right along, now!"

"It's Eradicate. He doesn't know you," said Tom, with a chuckle.

"So much the better," whispered Mr. Damon. But the disguise proved almost too much of a success, for seeing the supposed tramp lingering near the house, Eradicate caught up a stout stick and rushed forward. He was about to strike the ragged man, when Tom called out:

"That's Mr. Damon, Rad!"

"Wh—what!" gasped the colored man; and when the situation had been explained to him, and the necessity for silence impressed upon him, he turned away, too surprised to utter a word. He sought consolation in the stable with his mule.

Just what methods Mr. Damon used he never disclosed, but one thing is certain: That night there came a cautious knock on the door of the Swift home, and Tom, answering it, beheld his odd friend.

"Well," he asked eagerly, "what luck?"

"Put on a suit of old clothes, and come with me," said Mr. Damon. "We'll look like two tramps, and then, if we're discovered, they won't know it was you."

"Have you found out anything?" asked Tom eagerly.

"Not yet; but I've got a key to one of the side doors of the shed, and we can get in as soon as it's late enough so that everybody there will be in bed."

"A key? How did you get it?" inquired the youth.

"Never mind," was the answer, with a chuckle. "That was because of my disguise; and I haven't blessed anything today. I'm going to, soon, though. I can feel it coming on. But hurry, Tom, or we may be too late."

"And you haven't had a look inside the shed?" asked the young inventor. "You don't know what's there?"

"No; but we soon will."

Eagerly Tom put on some of the oldest and most ragged garments he could find, and then he and the odd gentleman set off toward the Foger home. They waited some time after getting in sight of it, because they saw a light in one of the windows. Then, when the house was dark, they stole cautiously forward toward the big, gloomy shed.

"On this side," directed Mr. Damon in a whisper. "The key I have opens this door."

"But we can't see when we get inside," objected Tom. "I should have brought a dark lantern."

"I have one of those pocket electric flashlights," said Mr. Damon. "Bless my candlestick! but I thought of that." And he chuckled gleefully.

Cautiously they advanced in the darkness. Mr. Damon fumbled at the lock of the door. The key grated as he turned it. The portal swung back, and Tom and his friend found themselves inside the shed which, of late, had been such an object of worry and conjecture to the young inventor. What would he find there?

"Flash the light," he called to Mr. Damon in a hoarse whisper.

The eccentric man drew it from his packet. He pressed the spring switch, and in an instant a brilliant shaft of radiance shot out, cutting the intense blackness like a knife. Mr. Damon flashed it on all sides.

But to the amazement of Tom and his companion, it did not illuminate the broad white wings and stretches of canvas of an aeroplane. It only shone on the bare walls of the shed, and on some piles of rubbish in the corners. Up and down, to right and left, shot the pencil of light.

"There's—there's nothing here!" gasped Tom.

"I—I guess you're right!" agreed Mr. Damon "The shed is empty!"

"Then where is Andy Foger building his aeroplane?" asked Tom in a whisper; but Mr. Damon could not answer him.

CHAPTER NINE

A TRIAL FLIGHT

For a few moments after their exclamations of surprise Tom and Mr. Damon did not know what else to say. They stared about in amazement, hardly able to believe that the shed could be empty. They had expected to see some form of aeroplane in it, and Tom was almost sure his eyes would meet a reproduction of his Humming Bird, made from the stolen plans.

"Can it be possible there's nothing here?" went on Tom, after a long pause. He could not seem to believe it.

"Evidently not," answered Mr. Damon, as he advanced toward the center of the big building and flashed the light on all sides. "You can see for yourself."

"Or, rather, you can't see," spoke the youth. "It isn't here, that's sure. You can't stick an aeroplane, even as small a one as my Humming Bird, in a corner. No; it isn't here."

"Well, we'll have to look further," went on Mr. Damon. "I think—"

But a sudden noise near the big main doors of the shed interrupted him.

"Come on!" exclaimed Tom in a whisper. "Some one's coming! They may see us! Let's get out!"

Mr. Damon released the pressure on the spring switch, and the light went out. After waiting a moment to let their eyes become accustomed to the darkness, he and Tom stole to the door by which they had entered. As they swung it cautiously open they again heard the noise near the main portals by which Andy had formerly taken in and out the Anthony, as he had named the aeroplane in which he and his father went to Alaska, where, like Tom's craft, it was wrecked.

"Some one is coming in!" whispered Tom.

Hardly had he spoken when a light shone in the direction of the sound. The illumination came from a big lantern of the ordinary kind, carried by some one who had just entered the shed.

"Can you see who it is?" whispered Mr. Damon, peering eagerly forward; too eagerly, for his foot struck against the wooden side wall with a loud bang.

"Who's there?" suddenly demanded the person carrying the lantern.

He raised it high above his head, in order to cast the gleams into all the distant corners. As he did so a ray of light fell upon his face. "Andy Foger!" gasped Tom in a hoarse whisper.

Andy must have heard, for he ran forward just as Tom and Mr. Damon slipped out.

"Hold on! Who are you?" came in the unmistakable tones of the red-haired bully.

"I don't think we're going to tell," chuckled Tom softly, as he and his friend sped off into the darkness. They were not followed, and as they looked back they could see a light bobbing about in the shed.

"He's looking for us!" exclaimed Mr. Damon with an inward laugh. "Bless my watch chain! But it's a good thing we got in ahead of him. Are you sure it was Andy himself?"

"Sure! I'd know his face anywhere. But I can't understand it. Where has he been? What is he doing? Where is he building his aeroplane? I thought he was out of town."

"He may have come back tonight," said Mr. Damon. "That's the only one of your questions I can answer. We'll have to wait about the rest, I'm sure he wasn't around the house today, though, for I was working at weeding the flower beds, in my disguise as a tramp, and if he was home I'd have seen him. He must have just come back, and he went out to his shed to get something. Well, we did the best we could."

"Indeed we did," agreed Tom, "and I'm ever so much obliged to you, Mr. Damon."

"And we'll try again, when we get more clues. Bless my shoelaces! but it's a relief to be able to talk as you like."

And forthwith the eccentric man began to call down so many blessings on himself and on his belongings, no less than on his friends, that Tom laughingly warned him that he had better save some for another time.

The two reached home safely, removed their "disguises," and told Mr. Swift of the result of their trip. He agreed with them that there was a mystery about Andy's aeroplane which was yet to be solved.

But Tom was glad to find that, at any rate, the craft was not being made in Shopton, and during the next two weeks he devoted all his time to finishing his own machine. Mr. Jackson was a valuable assistant, and Mr. Damon gave what aid he could.

"Well, I think I'll be ready for a trial flight in another week," said Tom one day, as he stepped back to get a view of the almost completed Humming-Bird.

"Shall you want a passenger?" asked Mr. Damon.

"Yes, I wish you would take a chance with me. I could use a bag of sand, not that I mean you are to be compared to that," added Tom quickly, "but I'd rather have a real person, in order to test the balancing apparatus. Yes, we'll make a trial trip together."

In the following few days Tom went carefully over the aeroplane, making some slight changes, strengthening it here and there, and testing the motor thoroughly. It seemed to work perfectly.

At length the day of the trial came, and the Humming-Bird was wheeled out of the shed. In spite of the fact that it was practically finished, there yet remained much to do on it. It was not painted or decorated, and looked rather crude. But what Tom wanted to know was how it would fly, what control he had over it, what speed it could make, and how it balanced. For it was, at best, very frail, and the least change in equilibrium might be fatal.

Before taking his place in the operator's seat Tom started the motor, and by means of a spring balance tested the thrust of the propellers. It was satisfactory, though he knew that when the engine had been run for some time, and had warmed up, it would do much better.

"All ready, I guess, Mr. Damon!" he called, and the odd gentleman took his place. Tom got up into his own seat, in front of several wheels and levers by which he operated the craft.

"Start the propeller!" he requested of Mr. Jackson, and soon the motor was spitting fire, while the big, fan-like blades were whirring around like wings of light. The engineer and Eradicate were holding back the Humming-Bird.

"Let her go!" cried Tom as he turned on more gasoline and further advanced the spark of the motor. The roar increased, the propeller looked like a solid circle of wood, and the trim little monoplane moved slowly across the rising ground, increasing its speed every second, until, like some graceful bird, it suddenly rose in the air as Tom tilted the wing tips, and soared splendidly aloft!

CHAPTER TEN

A MIDNIGHT INTRUDER

Tom Swift sent his wonderful little craft upward on a gentle slant. Higher and higher it rose above the ground. Now it topped the trees; now it was well over them.

On the earth below stood Mr. Swift, Mr. Jackson, Eradicate and Mrs. Baggert. They were the only witnesses of the trial flight, and as the aged inventor saw his son's latest design in aeroplanes circling in the air he gave a cheer of delight. It was too feeble for Tom to hear, but the lad, glancing down, saw his father waving his hand to him.

"Dear old dad!" thought Tom, waving in return. "I hope he's well enough to see me win the big prize."

Tom and Mr. Damon went skimming easily through the air, at no great speed, to be sure, for the young inventor did not want to put too sudden a strain on his motor.

"This is glorious!" cried the odd gentleman. "I never shall have enough of aeroplaning, Tom!"

"Nor I, either," added his companion. "But how do you like it? Don't you think it's an improvement on my Butterfly, Mr. Damon?"

"It certainly is. You're a wonder, Tom! Look out! What are you up to?" for the machine had suddenly swerved in a startling manner.

"Oh, that's just a new kind of spiral dip I was trying," answered Tom. "I couldn't do that with my other machine, for I couldn't turn sharp enough."

"Well, don't do it right away again," begged Mr. Damon, who had turned a little white, and whose breath was coming in gasps, even though he was used to hair-raising stunts in the frail craft of the air.

Tom did not take his machine far away, for he did not want to exhibit it to the public yet, and he preferred to remain in the vicinity of his home, in case of any accident. So he circled around, did figures of eight, went up and down on long slants, took sharp turns, and gave the craft a good tryout.

"Does it satisfy you?" asked Mr. Damon, when Tom had once more made the spiral dip, but not at high speed.

"In a way, yes," was the answer. "I see a chance for several changes and improvements. Of course, I know nothing about the speed yet, and that's something that I'm anxious about, for I built this with the idea of breaking all records, and nothing else. I know, now, that I can construct a craft that will successfully navigate the air; in fact, there are any number of people who can do that; but to construct a monoplane that will beat anything ever before made is a different thing. I don't yet know that I have done it."

"When will you?"

"Oh, when I make some changes, get the motor tuned up better, and let her out for all she's worth. I want to do a hundred miles an hour, at least. I'll arrange for a speedy flight in about two weeks more."

"Then I think I will stay home," said Mr. Damon.

"No; I'll need you," insisted Tom, laughing. "Now watch. I'm going to let her out just a little."

He did, with the result that they skimmed through the air so fast that Mr. Damon's breath became a mere series of gasps.

"We'll have to wear goggles and mouth protectors when we really go fast!" yelled Tom above the noise of the motor, as he slowed down and turned about for home.

"Go fast! Wasn't that fast?" asked Mr. Damon.

Tom shook his head.

"You wait, and you'll see," he announced.

They made a good landing, and Mr. Swift hastened up to congratulate his son.

"I knew you could do it, Tom!" he cried.

"I couldn't, though, if it hadn't been for that wonderful engine of yours, dad! How do you feel?"

"Pretty good. Oh! but that's a fine machine, Tom!"

"It certainly is," agreed Mr. Jackson.

"It will be when I have it in better trim," admitted the young inventor modestly.

"By golly!" cried Eradicate, who was grinning almost from ear to ear, "I's proud oh yo', Massa Tom, an' so will mah mule Boomerang be, when I tells him. Yes, sah, dat's what he will be—proud ob yo', Massa Tom!"

"Thanks, Rad."

"Well, some folks is satisfied with mighty little under 'em, when they go up in the air, that's my opinion," said Mrs. Baggert.

"Why, wouldn't you ride in this?" asked Tom of the buxom house-keeper.

"Not if you was to give me ten thousand dollars!" she cried firmly. "Oh, dear! I think the potatoes are burning!" And she rushed back into the house.

The next day Tom started to work overhauling the Humming-Bird, and making some changes. He altered the wing tips slightly, and adjusted the motor, until in a thrust test it developed nearly half again as much power as formerly.

"And I'll need it all," declared Tom as he thought of the number of contestants that had entered the great race.

For the Eagle Park meet was to be a large and important one, and the principal "bird-men" of the world were to have a part in it. Tom knew that he must do his very best, and he spared no efforts to make his mono-plane come up to his ideal, which was a very exacting one.

"We'll have a real speed test tomorrow," Tom announced to Mr. Damon one night. "I'll see what the Humming-Bird can really do. You'll come, won't you?"

"Oh, I suppose so. Bless my insurance policy! I might as well take the same chance you do. But if you're going to have such a nerve-racking thing as that on the program, you'd better get to bed early and have plenty of sleep."

"Oh, I'm not tired. I think I'll go out this evening."

"Where?"

"Oh, just around town, to see some of the fellows." But if Tom was only going around town merely to see his male friends, why did he dress so carefully, put on a new necktie, and take several looks in the glass before he went out? We think you can guess, and also the girl's name.

The young inventor got in rather late, and after a visit to the aeroplane shed, to see that all was right there, he went to bed, first connecting up the burglar-alarm wires that guarded the doors and windows of the aerodrome.

How long he had been asleep Tom did not know, but he was suddenly awakened by hearing the buzzing of the alarm at the head of his bed. At first he took it for the droning and humming of the aeroplane motor, as he had a hazy notion, and a sort of dream, that he was in his craft.

Then, with a start, he realized what it was—the burglar alarm.

"Some one's in the shed!" he gasped.

Out of bed he leaped, drawing on his trousers and coat, and putting on a pair of slippers, with speed worthy of a fireman. He grabbed up a revolver and rushed from his room, pounding on the door of Mr. Jackson's apartment in passing.

"Some one in the shed, after the Humming-Bird!" shouted Tom. "Get a gun, and come down!"

CHAPTER ELEVEN

TOM IS HURT

As Tom passed down the hall on his way to the side door, from which he could more quickly reach the aeroplane shed, he saw his father coming from his room.

"What's the matter? What is it?" asked Mr. Swift, and alarm showed on his pale face.

"It's nothing much, dad," said the youth, as quietly as he could, for he realized that to excite his father might have a bad effect on the invalid.

"Then why are you in such a hurry? Why have you that revolver? I know there is something wrong, Tom. I am going to help you!"

In his father's present weakened state Tom desired this least of all, so he said:

"Now, never mind, dad. I thought I heard a noise out in the yard, and I'm not going to take any chances. So I roused Mr. Jackson, and I'm going down to see what it is. Perhaps it may only be Eradicate's mule, Boomerang, kicking around, or it may be Rad himself, or some one after his chickens. Don't worry. Mr. Jackson and I can attend to it. You go back to bed, father."

Tom spoke with such assurance that Mr. Swift believed him, and retired to his room, just as the engineer, partly dressed, came hurrying out in response to Tom's summons. He had his rifle, and, had the invalid inventor seen that, he surely would have worried more.

"Come on!" whispered Tom. "Don't make any noise. I don't want to excite my father."

"What was it?" asked the engineer.

"I don't know. Burglar alarm went off, that's all I can say until we get to the shed."

Together the two left the house softly, and soon were hurrying toward the aeroplane shed.

"Look!" exclaimed Mr. Jackson. "Didn't you see a light just then, Tom?"

"Where?"

"By the side window of the shed?"

"No, I didn't notice it! Oh, yes! There it is! Some one is in there! If it's Andy Foger, I'll have him arrested, sure!"

"Maybe we can't catch him."

"That's so. Andy is a pretty slippery customer. Say, Mr. Jackson, you go around and get Eradicate, and have him bring a club. We can't trust him with a gun. Tell him to get at the back door, and I'll wait for you to join me, and we'll go in the front door. Then we'll have 'em between two fires. They can't get away."

"How about the windows?"

"They're high up, and hard to open since I put the new catches on them. Whoever got in must have forced the lock of the door. There goes the light again!"

As Tom spoke there was seen the faint glimmer of a light. It moved slowly about the interior of the shed, and with a peculiar bobbing motion, which indicated that some one was carrying it.

"Go for Eradicate, and don't make any more noise than you can help in waking him up," whispered Tom, for they were now close to the shed, and might be heard.

Mr. Jackson slipped off in the darkness, and Tom drew nearer to the building that housed his Humming-Bird. There was one window lower than the others, and near it was a box, that Tom remembered having seen that afternoon. He planned to get up on that and look in, before making a raid to capture the intruder.

Tom raised himself up to the window. The light had been visible a moment before he placed the box in position, but an instant later it seemed to go out, and the place was in darkness.

"I wonder if they've gone away?" thought Tom. "I can't hear any noise."

He listened intently. It was dark and silent in the shop. Suddenly the light flashed up brighter than before, and the young inventor caught sight of a man walking around the new aeroplane, examining it carefully. He carried, as Tom could see, a large-sized electric flash-lamp, with a brilliant tungsten filament, which gave a powerful light.

As the youth watched, he saw the intruder place the light on a bench, in such a position that the rays fell full upon the Humming-Bird. Then, adjusting the spring switch so that the light would continue to glow, the man stepped back and drew something from an inner pocket.

"I wonder what he's up to?" mused Tom. "I wish Eradicate and Mr. Jackson would hurry back. Who can that fellow be, I wonder? I've never seen him before, as far as I know. I thought sure it was going to turn out to be Andy Foger!"

Tom turned around to look into the dark yard surrounding the shed. He was anxious to hear the approach of his two allies, but there was no sound of their footsteps.

As he turned back to watch the man he could not repress a cry of alarm, for what the intruder had drawn from his pocket was a small hatchet, and he was advancing with it toward the Humming-Bird!

"He's going to destroy my aeroplane!" gasped Tom, and he raised his revolver to fire.

He did not intend to shoot at the man, but only to fire to scare him, and thus hasten the coming of Mr. Jackson and the colored man. But there was no need of this, for an instant later the two came running up silently, Eradicate with a big club.

"Whar am he?" he asked in a hoarse whisper. "Let me git at him, Massa Tom!"

"Hush!" exclaimed the young inventor. "We have no time to lose! He's in there, getting ready to chop my aeroplane to bits! Go to the back door, Rad, and if he tries to come out don't let him get away."

"I won't!" declared the colored man emphatically, and he shook his club suggestively.

"Come on! We'll go in the front door," whispered Tom to the engineer. "I have the key. We'll catch him red-handed, and hand him over to the police."

Waiting a few seconds, to enable Eradicate to get to his place, Tom and the engineer stole softly toward the big double doors. Every moment the youth expected to hear the crash of the hatchet on his prize machine. He shivered in anticipation, but the blows did not fall.

Tom pushed open the door and stepped inside, followed by Mr. Jackson. As they did so they saw the man standing in front of the Humming-Bird. He again raised the little hatchet, which was like an Indian tomahawk, and poised it for an instant over the delicate framework and planes of the air craft. Then his arm began to descend.

"Stop!" yelled Tom, and at the same time he fired in the air.

The man turned as suddenly as though a bullet had struck him, and for a moment Tom was afraid lest he had hit him by accident; but an instant later the intruder grabbed up his flashlight, and holding it before him, so that its rays shone full on Tom and Mr. Jackson, while it left him in the shadow, sprang toward them, the hatchet still in his hand.

"Look out, Tom!" cried Mr. Jackson.

"Out of my way!" shouted the man.

Bravely Tom stood his ground. He wished now that he had a club instead of his revolver. The would-be vandal was almost upon him. Mr. Jackson clubbed his rifle and swung it at the fellow. The latter dodged, and came straight at Tom.

"Look out!" yelled the engineer again, but it was too late. There was the sound of a blow, and Tom went down like a log. Then the place was in darkness, and the sound of footsteps in rapid flight could be heard outside the shed.

The intruder, after wounding the young inventor, had made his escape.

CHAPTER TWELVE

MISS NESTOR CALLS

"What's de mattah? Shall I come in? Am anybody hurted?" yelled Eradicate Sampson as he pounded on the rear door of the aeroplane shed. "Let me in, Massa Tom!"

"All right! Wait a minute! I'm coming!" called Mr. Jackson. He tried to peer through the darkness, to where a huddled heap indicated the presence of Tom. Then he thought of the electric lights, which were run by a storage battery when the dynamo was shut down, and a moment later the engineer had switched on the incandescents, filling the big shed with radiance.

"Tom, are you badly hurt?" gasped Mr. Jackson.

There was no answer, for Tom was unconscious.

"Let me in! Let me git at dat robber wif mah club!" cried the colored man eagerly.

Knowing that he would need help in carrying Tom to the house, Mr. Jackson hurried to the back door. He had a key to it, and it was quicker to open it than to send Eradicate away around the shed to the front portals.

"Whar am he?" gasped the faithful darky, as he took a firmer grasp of his club and looked around the place. "Let me git mah hands on him! I'll feed him t' Boomerang, when I gits froo wif him!"

"He's gone," said the engineer. "Help me look after Tom. I'm afraid he's badly hurt."

They hastened to the unconscious lad. On one side of his head was a bad cut, which was bleeding freely.

"Oh! he's daid! I know he's daid!" wailed Eradicate.

"Not a bit of it. He isn't dead, but he may die, if we don't get him into the house, and have a doctor here soon," said Mr. Jackson sternly. "Catch hold of him, Rad, and, mind, don't carry on, and get excited, and scare Mr. Swift. Just pretend it isn't very bad, or we'll have two patients on our hands instead of only Tom."

They managed to get the youth into the house, and, contrary to their fears, Mr. Swift was not nearly so nervous as they had expected. Calmly he took charge of matters, and even telephoned for Dr. Gladby himself, while Mr. Jackson and Eradicate undressed Tom and got him to bed. Mrs. Baggert busied herself heating water and getting things in readiness for the doctor, who had promised to come at once.

Tom was just regaining consciousness when the physician came in, having driven over at top speed.

"What—what happened? Did the Humming Bird fall?" asked Tom in a whisper, putting his hand to his head.

"No, something fell on you, I guess," said the doctor, who had been hurriedly told of the circumstances. "But don't worry, Tom. You'll be all right in a few days. You got a bad cut on the head, but the skull isn't fractured, I'm glad to say. Here, now, just drink this," and he gave Tom some medicine he had mixed in a glass.

The cut was soon dressed, and Tom felt much better, though weak and a trifle dizzy.

"Did he hit me with the hatchet?" he asked Mr. Jackson.

"I couldn't tell," was the engineer's reply, "it all happened so quickly. In another instant I'd have bowled him over, instead of him landing on you, but I just missed him. He either used the hatchet, or some blunt instrument."

"Well, don't talk about it now," urged the doctor. "I want Tom to get quiet and go to sleep. We'll be much better in the morning, but I must forbid any aeroplane flights." And he shook his finger at Tom in warning. "You'll have to lie quiet for several days," he added.

"All right," agreed the young inventor weakly, and then he dozed off, for the physician had given him a quieting medicine.

"Haven't you any idea who it was?" asked Dr. Gladby of Mr. Jackson, as he prepared to leave.

"Not the slightest. It was no one Tom or I had ever seen before. But whoever it was, he intended to destroy the Humming-Bird, that was evident!"

"The scoundrel! I'm glad you foiled him in time; but it's too bad about Tom. However, we'll soon have him all right again."

"I knows who done it!" broke in Eradicate, who was a sort of privileged character about the Swift home.

"Who?" asked Mr. Jackson.

"It were dat Andy Foger. Leastways, he send dat man heah t' make mincemeat oh de Hummin'-Bird. I's positib 'bout dat, so I am!" And Eradicate grinned triumphantly.

"Well, perhaps Andy did have a hand in it," admitted Mr. Swift, "but we have no proof of it, I can't see what his object would be in wanting to destroy Tom's new craft."

"Pure meanness. Afraid that Tom will beat him in the race," suggested Mr. Jackson.

"It's too big a risk to take," went on the aged inventor. "I'm inclined to think it might be one of the gang of men who made the diamonds in the cave in the mountains. They might have sent a spy on East, and he might try to damage the aeroplane to be revenged for what Tom and Mr. Jenks did to them."

"It's possible," agreed the engineer. "Well, we'll wait until Tom can talk, and we'll go over it with him."

"Not until he is stronger, though," stipulated the physician as he went away. "Don't excite Tom for a few days."

The young inventor was much better the following day, and when Dr. Gladby called he said Tom could sit up for a little while. Two days later Tom was well enough to be talked to, and his father and Mr. Jackson went over all the details of the matter. Mr. Damon, who had returned home, came to see his friend as soon as he heard of his plight, and was also a member of the consulting party.

"Bless my dictionary!" exclaimed the eccentric man. "I wish I had been here to take a hand in it. But, Tom, do you believe it was one of the diamond-making gang?"

"I hardly think so," was the reply. "They would take some other means of revenge than by destroying my new aeroplane. I'm inclined to think it was some one who is in with Andy Foger."

"Then we'll hire detectives, and locate him and them," declared Mr. Damon, blessing several things in succession.

Tom, however, did not like that plan, and it was decided to do nothing right away. In another few days Tom was able to be up, though he was still a semi-invalid, not venturing out of the house.

It was one afternoon, when, rather tired of his confinement, he was wishing he could resume work on his air craft, that Mrs. Baggert came in, and said:

"Some one to see you, Tom."

"Is it Mr. Damon?"

"No, it's a lady. She—"

"Oh, Tom! How are you?" cried a girlish voice, and Mary Nestor walked into the room, holding out both hands to the young inventor. Tom, with a blush, arose hastily.

"No! no! Sit still!" commanded the girl. "Oh! I'm so sorry to hear about your accident! In fact, I only heard this morning. We've been away, mamma and I, and we just got back. Tell me all about it, that is, if you feel able. But don't exert yourself. Oh! I wish I had hold of that man!"

And Miss Nestor clenched her two pretty little hands and set her white, even teeth grimly together, as though she would do most desperate things indeed.

"I wish you did, too!" exclaimed Tom. "That is, so you could hold him until I had a chance at him. But I'm all right now. It was very good of you to call. How are you, and how are your folks?"

"Very well. But I came to hear about you. Tell me," and she looked anxiously at Tom, while Mrs. Baggert discreetly withdrew to the adjoining room, and made a great noise, rattling papers and moving chairs about.

Thereupon Tom told what had happened, while Mary Nestor listened interestedly and with expressions of fear at times.

"But if Andy had anything to do with it," concluded Tom, "I can't understand what his object is. Andy is acting very strangely lately. We can't locate him, nor find out where he is building his airship. That's what I want to know; but Mr. Damon and I, after a lot of trouble, only found his aeroplane shed empty."

"And you want to find out where Andy Foger is building his aeroplane which he has entered in the big race?" asked Miss Nestor.

"That's what I'd like to know," declared Tom earnestly. "Only we can't seem to do it. No one knows."

"Why don't you write to Mr. Sharp, or some one of the aviation meet committee?" asked the girl simply. "They would know, for you say Andy made his formal entry with them, and the rules require him to tell from what city and State he will enter his craft. Write to the committee, Tom."

For a moment the young inventor stared at her. Then he banged his fist down on the arm of his chair.

"By Jove, Mary! That's the very thing!" he cried. "I wonder why I never thought of that, instead of fiddling around in disguises, and things like that? I wonder why I never thought of that plan?"

"Perhaps because it was so simple," she answered, with a pretty blush.

"I guess that's it," agreed Tom. "It takes a woman to jump across a bridge to a conclusion every time. I'll write to Mr. Sharp at once."

CHAPTER THIRTEEN

A CLASH WITH ANDY

Tom lost no time in writing to Mr. Sharp. He wondered more and more at his own neglect in not before having asked the balloonist, when the latter was in Shopton, where Andy was building his aeroplane. But, as it developed later, Mr. Sharp did not know at that time.

While waiting for a reply to his letter, Tom busied himself about his own craft, making several changes he had decided on. He also began to paint and decorate it, for he wanted to have the Humming-Bird present a neat appearance when she was officially entered in the great race.

Miss Nestor called on Tom again, and Mr. Damon was a frequent visitor. He agreed to accompany Tom to the aviation park when it was time for the race, and also to be a passenger in the ten-thousand-dollar contest.

"It must be perfectly wonderful to fly through the air," said Miss Nestor one day, when Tom and Mr. Damon had the Humming-Bird out on the testing ground, trying the engine, which had been keyed up to a higher pitch of speed. "I consider it perfectly marvelous, and I can't imagine how it must seem to skim along that way."

"Come and try it," urged Tom suddenly. "There's not a bit of danger. Really there isn't."

"Oh! I'd never dare do it!" replied the girl, with a gasp. "That machine is too swift by name and swift by nature for me."

"Why don't you take Miss Nestor on a grass-cutting flight, Tom?" suggested Mr. Damon. "Bless my lawn mower! but she wouldn't be frightened at that."

"Grass cutting?" repeated the girl. "What in the world does that mean?"

"It means skimming along a few feet up in the air," answered the young inventor, who had now fully recovered from the effects of the blow given him by the midnight intruder. In spite of many inquiries, no clues to his identity had been obtained.

"How high do you go when you 'cut grass,' as you call it?" asked Miss Nestor, and Tom thought he detected a note of eager curiosity in her voice.

"Not high at all," he said. "In fact, sometimes I do cut off the tops of tall daisies. Come, Mary! Won't you try that? I know you'll like it, and when you've been over the lawn a few times you'll be ready for a high flight. Come! there's no danger."

"I—I almost believe I will," she said hesitatingly. "Will you take me down when I want to come?"

"Of course," said Tom. "Get in, and we'll start."

The Humming-Bird was all ready for a trial flight, and Tom was glad of the chance to test it, especially with such a pretty passenger as was Miss Nestor.

"Bless my shoelaces!" cried Mr. Damon. "I can see where I am going to be cut out, Tom Swift. I'll not get many more rides with you now that Miss Nestor is taking to aeroplaning, you young rascal!" And he playfully shook his finger at Tom.

"Oh, I don't expect to get enthusiastic over it," said Miss Nestor, who, now that she had taken her place in one of the small seats under the engine, appeared as if she would be glad of the chance to change her mind. But she did not.

"Now, if you take me more than five feet up in the air, I'll never speak to you again, Tom Swift!" she exclaimed.

"Five feet it shall be, unless you yourself ask to go higher," was the youth's reply, as he winked at Mr. Damon. Well he knew the fascination of aeroplaning, and he was almost sure of what would happen. "You can take a tape measure along, and see for yourself," he added to his fair passenger. "The barograph will hardly register such a little height."

"Well, it's as high as I want to go," said the girl. "Oh!" with a scream, as Tom started the propeller. "Are we going?"

"In a moment," was his reply. He took his seat beside the girl. The motor was speeded up until it sounded like the roar of the ocean surf in a storm.

"Let her go!" cried Tom to Mr. Damon and Mr. Jackson, who were holding back the Humming-Bird. They gave her a slight shove to overcome the inertia, and the trim little craft darted across the ground at every increasing speed.

Miss Nestor caught her breath with a gasp, glanced at Tom, and noted how cool he was, and then her frantic grip of the uprights slightly relaxed.

"We'll go up a little way in a minute!" shouted Tom in her ear as they were speeding over the level ground.

He pulled a lever slightly, and the Humming-Bird rose a little in the air, but only for a short distance, not more than five feet, and Tom held her there, though he had to run the engine at a greater speed than would have been the case had he been in the sustaining upper currents. It was as if the Humming-Bird resented being held so closely to the earth.

Around in a big circle, back and forth went the craft, at no time being more than seven feet from the ground. Tom glanced at Miss Nestor. Her cheeks were unusually red, and there was a bright sparkle in her eyes.

"It's glorious!" she cried. "Do you—do you think there's any danger in going higher? I believe I'd like to go up a bit."

"I knew it!" cried Tom. "Up we go!" And he pulled the wind-bending plane lever toward him. Upward shot the craft, as if alive.

"Oh!" gasped Mary.

"Sit still! It's all right!" commanded Tom.

"It's glorious; glorious!" she cried. "I'm not a bit afraid now!"

"I knew you wouldn't be," declared the young inventor, who had calculated on the fascination which the motion through the air, untrammeled and free, always produces. "Shall we go higher?"

"Yes!" cried Miss Nestor, and she gazed fearlessly down at the earth, which was falling away from beneath their feet. She was in the grip of the air, and it was a new and wonderful sensation.

Tom went up to a considerable distance, for, once a person loses his first fright, one hundred feet or one thousand feet elevation makes little difference to him. It was this way with Miss Nestor.

Now, indeed, could Tom demonstrate to her some of the fine points of navigation in the upper currents, and though he did no risky "stunts," he showed the girl what it means to do an ascending spiral, how to cut corners, how to twist around in the figure eight, and do other things. Tom did not try for the great speed of which he knew his craft was capable, for he knew there was some risk with Miss Nestor aboard. But he did nearly everything else, and when he sent the Humming-Bird down he had made another convert and devotee to the royal sport of aeroplaning.

"Oh! I never would have dared believe I could do it!" exclaimed the girl, as with flushed cheeks and dancing eyes she dismounted from the seat. "Mamma and papa will never believe I did it!"

"Bring them over, and I'll take them for a flight," said Tom, with a laugh, as Mary departed.

Tom received an answer to his letter to Mr. Sharp that night.

"Andy Foger's entry blank states," wrote the balloonist, "that he is constructing his aeroplane in the village of Hampton, which is about fifty miles from your place. If there is anything further I can do for you, Tom, let me know. I will see you at the meet. Hope you win the prize."

"In Hampton, eh?" mused Tom. "So that's where Andy has been keeping himself all this while. His uncle lives there, and that's the reason for it. He wanted to keep it a secret from me, so he could use my stolen plans for his craft. But he shan't do it! I'll go to Hampton!"

"And I'll go with you!" declared Mr. Damon, who was with Tom when he got the note from the balloonist. "We'll get to the bottom of this mystery after a while, Tom."

Delaying a few days, to make the final changes in his aeroplane, Tom and Mr. Damon departed for Hampton one morning. They thought first of going in the Butterfly, but as they wanted to keep their mission as secret as possible, they decided to go by train, and arrive in the town quietly and unostentatiously. They got to Hampton late that afternoon.

"What's the first thing to be done?" asked Mr. Damon as they walked up from the station, where they were almost the only persons who alighted from the train.

"Go to the hotel," decided Tom. "There's only one, I was told, so there's not much choice."

Hampton was a quiet little country town of about five thousand inhabitants, and Tom soon learned the address of Mr. Bentley, Andy's uncle, from the hotel clerk.

"What business is Mr. Bentley in?" asked Tom, for he wanted to learn all he could without inquiring of persons who might question his motives.

"Oh, he's retired," said the clerk. "He lives on the interest of his money. But of late he's been erecting some sort of a building on his back lot, like a big shed, and folks are sort of wondering what he's doing in it. Keeps mighty secret about it. He's got a young fellow helping him."

"Has he got red hair?" asked Tom, while his heart beat strangely fast.

"Who? Mr. Bentley? No. His hair's black."

"I mean the young fellow."

"Oh! his? Yes, his is red. He's a nephew, or some relation to Mr. Bentley. I did hear his name, but I've forgotten it. Sandy, or Andy, or some such name as that."

This was near enough for Tom and Mr. Damon, and they did not want to risk asking any more questions. They turned away to go to their rooms, as the clerk was busy answering inquiries from some other guests. A little later, supper was served, and Tom, having finished, whispered to Mr. Damon to join him upstairs as soon as he was through.

"What are you going to do?" asked the eccentric man.

"We're going out and have a look at this new shed by moonlight," decided Tom. "I want to see what it's like, and, if possible, I want to get a peep inside. I'll soon be able to tell whether or not Andy is using my stolen plans."

"All right. I'm with you. Bless my bill of fare! But we seem to be doing a lot of mysterious work of late."

"Yes," agreed Tom. "But if you have to bless anything tonight, Mr. Damon, please whisper it. Andy, or some of his friends, may be about the shed, and as soon as they hear one of your blessings they'll know who's coming."

"Oh, I'll be careful," promised Mr. Damon.

"Andy will find out, sooner or later, that we are in town," went on Tom, "but we may be able to learn tonight what we want to know, and then we can tell how to act."

A little later, as if they were merely strolling about, Mr. Damon and Tom headed for Mr. Bentley's place, which was on the outskirts of the town. There was a full moon, and the night was just right for the kind of observation Tom wanted to make. There were few persons abroad, and the young inventor thought he would have no one spying on him.

They located the big house of Andy's uncle without trouble. Going down a side street, they had a glimpse of a shed, built of new boards, standing in the middle of a large lot. About the structure was a new, high wooden fence, but as Tom and his friend passed along it they saw that a gate in it was open.

"I'm going in!" whispered Tom.

"Will it be safe?" asked Mr. Damon.

"I don't care whether it will be or not. I've got to know what Andy is doing. Come on! We'll take a chance!"

Cautiously they entered the enclosure. The big shed was dark, and stood out conspicuously in the moonlight.

"There doesn't seem to be any one here," whispered Tom. "I wonder if we could get a look in the window?"

"It's worth trying, anyhow," agreed Mr. Damon. "I'm with you, Tom."

They drew nearer to the shed. Suddenly Tom stepped on a stick, which broke with a sharp report.

"Bless my spectacles!" cried Mr. Damon, half aloud.

There was silence for a moment, and then a voice cried out:

"Who's there? Hold on! Don't come any farther! It's dangerous!"

Tom and Mr. Damon stood still, and from behind the shed stepped Andy Foger and a man.

"Oh! it's you, is it, Tom Swift?" exclaimed the red-haired bully. "I thought you'd come sneaking around. Come on, Jake! We'll make them wish they'd stayed home!" And Andy made a rush for Tom.

CHAPTER FOURTEEN

THE GREAT TEST

"Bless my gizzard!" exclaimed Mr. Damon, who hardly knew what to do. "We'd better be getting out of here, Tom!"

"Not much!" exclaimed the young inventor. "I never ran from Andy Foger yet, and I'm not going to begin now."

He assumed an attitude of defense, and stood calmly awaiting the onslaught of the bully; but Andy knew better than to come to a personal argument with Tom, and so the red-haired lad halted some paces off. The man, who had followed young Foger, also stopped.

"What do you want around here, Tom Swift?" demanded Andy.

"You know very well what I want," said the young inventor, calmly. "I want to know what you did with the aeroplane plans you took from my house."

"I never took any!" declared Andy vigorously

"Well, there's no use discussing that," went on Tom. "What I came here to find out, and I don't mind telling you, is whether or not you are building a monoplane to compete against me, and building it on a model invented by me; and what's more, Andy Foger, I intend to find this out, too!"

Tom started toward the big shed, which loomed up in the moonlight.

"Stand back!" cried Andy, getting in Tom's way. "I can build any kind of an aeroplane I like, and you can't stop me!"

"We'll see about that," declared the young inventor, as he kept on. "I'm not going to allow my plans to be stolen, and a monoplane made after them, and do nothing about it."

"You keep away!" snarled Andy, and he grabbed Tom by the shoulder and struck him a blow in the chest. He must have been very much excited, or otherwise he never would have come to hostilities this way with Tom, whom he well knew could easily beat him.

The blow, together with the many things he had suffered at Andy's hands, was too much for our hero. He drew back his fist, and a moment later Andy Foger was stretched out on the grass. He lay there for a moment, and then rose up slowly to his knees, his face distorted with rage.

"You—you hit me!" he snarled.

"Not until you hit first," said Tom calmly.

"Bless my punching bag! That's so!" exclaimed Mr. Damon.

"You'll suffer for this!" whined Andy, getting to his feet, but taking care to retreat from Tom, who stood ready for him. "I'll get square with you for this! Jake, come on, and we'll get our guns!"

Andy turned and hurried back toward the shed, followed by the evil-looking man, who had apparently been undecided whether to attack Mr. Damon or Tom. Now the bully and his companion were in full retreat.

"We'll get our guns, and then we'll see whether they'll want to stay where they're not wanted!" went on Andy, threateningly.

"Bless my powderhorn! What had we better do?" asked Mr. Damon.

"I guess we'd better go back," said Tom calmly. "Not that I'm afraid of Andy. His talk about guns is all bluff; but I don't want to get into any more of a row, and he is just ugly and reckless enough to make trouble. I'm afraid we can't learn what we came to find out, though I'm more convinced than ever that Andy is using my plans to make his aeroplane."

"But what can you do?"

"I'll see Mr. Sharp, and send a protest to the aviation committee. I'll refuse to enter if Andy flies in a model of my Humming-Bird, and I'll try to prevent him from using it after he gets it on the ground. That is all I can do, it seems, lacking positive information. Come on, Mr. Damon. Let's get back to our hotel, and we'll start for home in the morning."

"I have a plan," whispered the odd man.

"What is it?" asked Tom, narrowly watching for the reappearance of Andy and the man.

"I'll stay here until they come, then I'll pretend to run away. They'll chase after me, and get all excited, and you can go up and look in the shed windows. Then you can join me later. How's that?"

"Too risky. They might fire at you by mistake. No. We'll both go. I've found out more than enough to confirm my suspicions."

They turned out of the lot which contained the shed, and walked toward the road, just as Andy and his crony came back.

"Huh! You'd better go!" taunted the bully.

Tom had a bitter feeling in his heart. It seemed as if he was defeated, and he did not like to retreat before Andy.

"You'd better not come back here again, either," went on Andy.

Tom and Mr. Damon did not reply, but kept on in silence. They returned to Shopton the next day.

"Well," remarked Tom, when he had gone out to look at his Humming-Bird, "I know one thing. Andy Foger may build a machine something like this, but I don't believe he can put in all the improvements I have, and certainly he can't equal that engine; eh, dad?"

"I hope not, Tom," replied his father, who seemed to be much improved in health.

"When are you going to try for speed?" asked Mr. Damon.

"Tomorrow, if I can get it tuned up enough," replied Tom, "and I think I can. Yes, we'll have the great test tomorrow, and then I'll know whether I really have a chance for that ten thousand dollars."

Never before had Tom been so exacting in his requirements of his air craft as when, the next day, the Humming-Bird was wheeled out to the flight ground, and gotten ready for the test. The young inventor went over every bolt, brace, stay, guy wire and upright. He examined every square inch of the wings, the tips, planes and rudders. The levers, the steering wheel, the automatic equilibrium attachments and the balancing weights were looked at again and again.

As for the engine, had it been a delicate watch, Tom could not have scrutinized each valve, wheel, cam and spur gear more carefully. Then the gasoline tank was filled, the magneto was looked after, the oil reservoirs were cleaned out and freshly filled, and finally the lad remarked:

"Well, I guess I'm ready. Come along, Mr. Damon."

"Am I going with you in the test?"

"Surely. I've been counting on you. If you're to be with me in the race, you want to get a sample of what we can do. Take your place. Mr. Jackson, are you ready to time us?"

"All ready, Tom."

"And, dad, do you feel well enough to check back Mr. Jackson's results? I don't want any errors."

"Oh, yes, Tom. I can do it."

"Very well, then. Now this is my plan. I'm going to mount upward on an easy slant, and put her through a few stunts first, to warm up, and see that everything is all right. Then, when I give the signal, by dropping this small white ball, that means I'm ready for you to start to time me. Then I'll begin to try for the record. I'll go about the course in a big ellipse, and—well, we'll see what happens."

While Mr. Damon was in his seat the young inventor started the propeller, and noted the thrust developed. It was satisfactory, as measured on the scale, and then Tom took his place.

"Let her go!" he cried to Mr. Jackson and Eradicate, after he had listened to the song of the motor for a moment. The Humming-Bird flew across the course, and a moment later mounted into the air.

Tom quickly took her up to about two thousand feet, and there, finding the conditions to his liking, he began a few evolutions designed to severely test the craft's stability, and to learn whether the engine was working properly.

"How about it?" asked Mr. Damon anxiously.

"All right!" shouted Tom in his ear, for the motor was making a great racket. "I guess we'll make the trial next time we come around. Get ready to drop the signal ball."

Tom slowly brought the aeroplane around in a graceful curve. He sighted down, and saw the first tall white pole that marked the beginning of the course.

"Drop!" he called to Mr. Damon.

The white rubber ball went to the earth like a shot. Mr. Jackson and Mr. Swift saw it, and started their timing-watches. Tom opened the throttle and advanced the spark. The great test was on!

The Humming-Bird trembled and throbbed with the awful speed of the motor, like a thing alive. She seemed to rush forward as an eagle dropping down from a dizzy height upon some hapless prey.

"Faster yet!" murmured Tom. "We must go faster yet!"

The motor was warming up. Streaks of fire came from it. The exhaust of the explosions was a continuous roar. Faster and faster flew the frail craft.

Around and around the air course she circled. The wind appeared to be rushing beneath the planes and rudders with the velocity of a hurricane. Had it not been for the face protectors they wore, Tom and Mr. Damon could not have breathed. For ten minutes this fearful speed was kept up. Then Tom, knowing he had run the motor to the limit, slowed it down. Next he shut it off completely, and prepared to volplane back to earth. The silence after the terrific racket was almost startling. For a moment neither of the aviators spoke. Then Mr. Damon said:

"Do you think you did it, Tom?"

"I don't know. We'll soon find out. They'll have the record." And he motioned toward the earth, which they were rapidly nearing.

CHAPTER FIFTEEN

A NOISE IN THE NIGHT

"Well, did I make it? Make any kind of a record?" asked Tom eagerly, as he brought the trim little craft to a stop, after it had rolled along the ground on the bicycle wheels.

"What do you think you did?" asked Mr. Jackson, who had been busy figuring on a slip of paper.

"Did I get her up to ninety miles an hour?" inquired Tom eagerly. "If I did, I know when the motor wears down a bit smoother that I can make her hit a hundred in the race, easily. Did I touch ninety, Mr. Jackson?"

"Better than that, Tom! Better than that!" cried his father.

"Yes," joined in Mr. Jackson. "Allowing for the difference in our watches, Tom, your father and I figure that you did the course at the rate of one hundred and twelve miles an hour!"

"One hundred and twelve!" gasped the young inventor, hardly able to believe it.

"I made it a hundred and fifteen," said Mr. Swift, who was almost as pleased as was his son, "and Mr. Jackson made it one hundred and eleven; so we split the difference, so to speak. You certainly have a sky racer, Tom, my boy!"

"And I'll need it, too, dad, if I'm to compete with Andy Foger, who may have a machine almost like mine."

"But I thought you were going to object to him if he has," said Mr. Damon, who had hardly recovered from the speedy flight through space.

"Well, I was just providing for a contingency, in case my protest was overruled," remarked Tom. "But I'm glad the Humming-Bird did so well on her first trial. I know she'll do better the more I run her. Now we'll get her back in her 'nest,' and I'll look her over, when she cools down, and see if anything has worked loose."

But the trim little craft needed only slight adjustments after her try-out, for Tom had built her to stand up under a terrific strain.

"We'll soon be in shape for the big race," he announced, "and when I bring home that ten thousand dollars I'm going to abandon this sky-scraping business, except for occasional trips."

"What will you do to occupy your mind?" asked Mr. Damon.

"Oh, I'm going to travel," announced Tom. "Then there's my new electric rifle, which I have not perfected yet. I'll work on that after I win the big race."

For several days after the first real trial of his sky racer Tom was busy going over the Humming-Bird, making slight changes here and there. He was the sort of a lad who was satisfied with nothing short of the best, and though neither his father nor Mr. Jackson could see where there was room for improvement, Tom was so exacting that he sat up for several nights to perfect such little details as a better grip for the steering-lever, a quicker way of making the automatic equilibriumizer take its position, or an improved transmitter for the wireless apparatus.

That was a part of his monoplane of which Tom was justly proud, for though many aeroplanes today are equipped with the sending device, few can receive wireless messages in mid-air. But Tom had seen the advantage of this while making a trip in the ill-fated Red Cloud to the cave of the diamond makers, and he determined to have his new craft thus provided against emergencies. The wireless outfit of the Humming-Bird was a marvel of compactness.

Thus the days passed, with Tom very busy; so busy, in fact, that he hardly had time to call on Miss Nestor. As for Andy Foger, he heard no more from him, and the bully was not seen around Shopton. Tom concluded that he was at his uncle's place, working on his racing craft.

The young inventor sent a formal protest to the aviation committee, to be used in the event of Andy entering a craft which infringed on the Humming-Bird, and received word from Mr. Sharp that the interests of the young inventor would be protected. This satisfied Tom.

Still, at times, he could not help wondering how the first plans had so mysteriously disappeared, and he would have given a good deal to know just how Andy got possession of them, and how he knew enough to use them.

"He, or some one whom he hired, must have gotten into our house mighty quickly that day," mused Tom, "and then skipped out while dad fell into a little doze. It was a mighty queer thing, but it's lucky it was no worse."

The time was approaching for the big aviation meet. Tom's craft was in readiness, and had been given several other trials, developing more speed each time. Additional locks were put on the doors of the shed, and more burglar-alarm wires were strung, so that it was almost a physical impossibility to get into the Humming-Bird's "nest" without arousing some one in the Swift household.

"And if they do, I guess we'll be ready for them," said Tom grimly. He had been unable to find out who it was that had attempted once before to damage the monoplane, but he suspected it was the ill-favored man who was working with Andy.

As for Mr. Swift, at times he seemed quite well, and again he required the services of a physician.

"You will have to be very careful of your father, Tom," said Dr. Gladby. "Any sudden shock or excitement may aggravate his malady, and in that case a serious operation will be necessary."

"Oh, we'll take good care of him," said the lad; but he could not help worrying, though he tried not to let his father see the strain which he was under.

It was some days after this, and lacking about a week until the meet was to open, when a peculiar thing happened. Tom had given his Humming-Bird a tryout one day, and had then begun to make arrangements for taking it apart and shipping it to Eagle Park. For he would not fly to the meet in it, for fear of some accident. So big cases had been provided.

"I'll take it apart in the morning," decided Tom, as he went to his room, after seeing to the burglar alarm, "and ship her off. Then Mr. Damon and I will go there, set her up, and get ready to win the race."

Tom had opened all the windows in his room, for it was very warm. In fact it was so warm that sleep was almost out of the question, and he got up to sit near the windows in the hope of feeling a breeze.

There it was more comfortable, and he was just dozing off, and beginning to think of getting back into bed, when he was aware of a peculiar sound in the air overhead.

"I wonder if that's a heavy wind starting up?" he mused. "Good luck, if it is! We need it." The noise increased, sounding more and more like wind, but Tom, looking out into the night, saw the leaves of the trees barely moving.

"If that's a breeze, it's taking its own time getting here," he went on.

The sound came nearer, and then Tom knew that it was not the noise of the wind in the trees. It was more like a roaring and rumbling.

"Can it be distant thunder?" Tom asked himself. "There is no sign of a storm." Once more he looked from the window. The night was calm and clear—the trees as still as if they were painted.

The sound was even more plain now, and Tom, who had sharp ears, at once decided that it was just over the house—directly overhead. An instant later he knew what it was.

"The motor of an aeroplane, or a dirigible balloon!" he exclaimed. "Some one is flying overhead!"

For an instant he feared lest the shed had been broken into, and his Humming-Bird taken, but a glance toward the place seemed to show that it was all right.

Then Tom hastily made his way to where a flight of stairs led to a little enclosed observatory on the roof.

"I'm going to see what sort of a craft it is making that noise," he said.

As he opened the trap door, and stepped out into the little observatory the sound was so plain as to startle him. He looked up quickly, and, directly overhead he saw a curious sight.

For, flying so low as to almost brush the lightning rod on the chimney of the Swift home, was a small aeroplane, and, as Tom looked up, he saw in a light that gleamed from it, two figures looking down on him.

CHAPTER SIXTEEN

A MYSTERIOUS FIRE

For a few moments Tom did not know what to think. Not that the sight of aeroplanes in flight were any novelty to him, but to see one flying over his house in the dead of night was a little out of the ordinary. Then, as he realized that night-flights were becoming more common, Tom tried to make out the details of the craft.

"I wish I had brought the night glasses with me," he said aloud.

"Here they are," spoke a voice at his side, and so suddenly that Tom was startled. He looked down, and saw Mr. Jackson standing beside him.

"Did you hear the noise, too?" the lad asked the engineer.

"Yes. It woke me up. Then I heard you moving around, and I heard you come up here. I thought maybe it was a flight of meteors you'd come to see, and I knew the glasses would be handy, so I stopped for them. Take a look, Tom. It's an aeroplane; isn't it?"

"Yes, and not moving very fast, either. They seem to be circling around here."

The young inventor was peering through the binoculars, and, as soon as he had the mysterious craft in focus, he cried:

"Look, Mr. Jackson, it's a new kind of monoplane. I never saw one like it before. I wonder who could have invented that? It's something like a Santos-Dumont and a Bleriot, with some features of Cornu's Helicopter. That's a queer machine."

"It certainly is," agreed the engineer, who was now sighting through the glasses. In spite of the darkness the binoculars brought out the peculiarities of the aeroplane with considerable distinctness.

"Can you make out who are in it?" asked Tom.

"No," answered Mr. Jackson. "You try."

But Tom had no better luck. There were two persons in the odd machine, which was slowly flying along, moving in a great circle, with the Swift house for its center.

"I wonder why they're hanging around here?" asked Tom, suspiciously.

"Perhaps they want to talk to you," suggested Mr. Jackson. "They may be fellow inventors—perhaps one of them is that Philadelphia man who had the Whizzer."

"No," replied the lad. "He would have sent me word if he intended calling on me. Those are strangers, I think. There they are, coming back again."

The mysterious aeroplane was once more circling toward the watchers on the roof. There was a movement on the steps, near which Tom was standing, and his father came up.

"Is anything the matter?" he asked anxiously.

"Only a queer craft circling around up here," was the reply. "Come and see, dad."

Mr. Swift ascended to the roof. The aeroplane was higher now, and those in her could not so easily be made out. Tom felt a vague sense of fear, as though he was being watched by the evil eyes of his enemies. More than once he looked over to the shed where his craft was housed, as though some danger might threaten it. But the shed of the Humming-Bird showed no signs of invaders.

Suddenly the mysterious aeroplane increased its speed. It circled about more quickly, and shot upward, as though to show the watchers of what it was capable. Then, with a quick swoop it darted downward, straight for the building where Tom's newest invention was housed.

"Look out! They'll hit something!" cried the young inventor, as though those in the aeroplane could hear him.

Then, just as though they had heeded his warning, the pilots of the mysterious craft shot her upward, after she had hovered for an instant over the big shed.

"That was a queer move," said Tom. "It looked as if they lost control of her for a moment."

"And they dropped something!" cried Mr. Jackson. "Look! something fell from the aeroplane on the roof of the shed."

"Some tool, likely," spoke Tom. "I'll get it in the morning, and see what sort of instruments they carry. I'd like to examine that machine, though."

The queer aeroplane was now shooting off in the darkness and Tom followed it with the glasses, wondering what its construction could be like. He was to have another sight of it sooner than he expected.

"Well, we may as well get back to bed," said Mr. Jackson. "I'm tired, and we've got lots to do tomorrow."

"Yes," agreed Tom. "It's cooler now. Come on, dad."

Tom fell into a light doze. He thought afterward he could not have slept more than half an hour when he heard a commotion out in the yard.

For an instant he could not tell what it was, and then, as he grew wider awake he knew that it was the shouting of Eradicate Sampson, and the braying of Boomerang.

But what was Eradicate shouting?

"Fire! Fire! Fire!"

Tom leaped to his window.

"Wake up, Massa Tom! Wake up! De areoplane shed am on fire, an' de Humming-Bird will burn up! Hurry! Hurry!"

Tom looked out. Flames were shooting up from the roof of the shed where his precious craft was kept.

CHAPTER SEVENTEEN

MR. SWIFT IS WORSE

Almost before the echoes of Eradicate's direful warning cry had died away, Tom was on his way out of the house, pausing only long enough to slip on a pair of shoes and his trousers. There was but one thought in his mind. If he could get the Humming-Bird safely out he would not care if the shed did burn, even though it contained many valuable tools and appliances.

"We must save my new aeroplane!" thought Tom, desperately. "I've got to save her!"

As he raced through the hall he caught up a portable chemical fire-extinguisher. Tom saw his father's door open, and Mr. Swift looked out.

"What is it?" he called anxiously.

"Fire!" answered the young inventor, almost before he thought of the doctor's warning that Mr. Swift must not be excited. Tom wished he could recall the word, but it was too late. Besides Eradicate, down in the yard was shouting at the top of his voice:

"Fire! Fire! Fire!"

"Where, Tom?" gasped Mr. Swift, and his son thought the aged inventor grew suddenly paler.

"Aeroplane shed," answered the lad. "But don't worry dad. It's only a small blaze. We'll get it out. You stay here. We'll attend to it—Mr. Jackson and Eradicate and I."

"No—I'm going to help!" exclaimed Mr. Swift, sturdily. "I'll be with you, Tom. Go on!"

The lad rushed down to the yard, closely followed by the engineer, who had caught up another extinguisher. Eradicate was rushing about, not knowing what to do, but still keeping up his shouting.

"It's on de roof! De roof am all blazin'!" he yelled.

"Quit your noise, and get to work!" cried Tom. "Get out a ladder, Rad, and raise it to the side of the shed. Then play this extinguisher on the blaze. Mr. Jackson, you help me run the Humming-Bird out. After she's safe we'll tackle the fire."

Tom cast a hurried look at the burning shed. The flames were shooting high up from the roof, now, and eating their way down. As he rushed toward the big doors, which he intended to open to enable him to run out his sky racer, he was wondering how the fire came to start so high up as the roof. He wondered if a meteor could have fallen and caused it.

As the doors, which were quickly unlocked by Tom, swung back, and as he and the engineer started to go in, they were met by choking fumes as if of some gas. They recoiled for the moment.

"What—what's that?" gasped Tom, coughing and sneezing.

"Some chemical—I—I don't know what kind," spluttered Mr. Jackson. "Have you any carboys of acid in there Tom, that might have exploded by the heat?"

"No; not a thing. Let's try again."

Once more they tried to go in, but were again driven back by the distressing fumes. The fire was eating down, now. There was a hole burned in the roof, and by the leaping tongues of flame Tom could see his aeroplane. It was almost in the path of the blaze.

"We must get her out!" he shouted. "I'm going in!"

But it was impossible, and the daring young inventor nearly succumbed to the choking odors. Mr. Jackson dragged him back.

"We can't go in!" he cried. "There has been some mysterious work here! Those fumes were put here to keep us from saving the machine. This fire has been set by some enemy! We can't go in!"

"But I am going!" declared Tom. "We'll try the back door."

They rushed to that, but again were driven out by the gases and vapors, which were mingled with the smoke. Disheartened, yet with a wild desire to do something to save his precious craft, Tom Swift drew back for a moment.

As he did so he heard a hiss, as Eradicate turned the chemical stream on the blaze. Tom looked up. The faithful colored man was on a ladder near the burning roof, acting well his part as a fireman.

"That's the stuff!" cried Tom. "Come on, Mr. Jackson. Maybe if we use the chemical extinguishers we can drive out those fumes!"

The engineer understood. He took up the extinguisher he had brought, and Tom got a second one from a nearby shed. Then Mr. Swift came out bearing another.

"You shouldn't have come, dad! We can attend to it!" cried Tom, fearing for the effect of the excitement on his invalid parent.

"Oh, I couldn't stay there and see the shed burn. Are you getting it under control? Why don't you run out the Humming-Bird?"

Tom did not mention the choking fumes. He passed up a full extinguisher to Eradicate, who had used all the chemical in his. Then Tom got another ladder, and soon three streams were being directed on the flames. They had eaten, a pretty big hole in the roof, but the chemicals were slowly telling on them.

As soon as he saw that Eradicate and Mr. Jackson could control the blaze, Tom descended to the ground, and ran once more to the big doors. He was determined to make another try to wheel out the aeroplane, for he saw from above that the flames were now on the side wall, and might reach the craft any minute. And it would not take much to inflict serious damage on the sky racer.

"I'll get her, fumes or no fumes!" murmured Tom, grimly. And, whether it was the effect of the chemical streams, or whether the choking odors were dissipated through the hole in the roof was not manifested, but, at any rate, Tom found that he could go in, though he coughed and gasped for breath.

He wheeled the aeroplane outside, for the Humming-Bird was almost as light as her namesake. A hurried glance by the gleam of the dying fire assured Tom that his craft was not damaged beyond a slight scorching of one of the wing tips.

"That was a narrow escape!" he murmured, as he wheeled the sky racer far away, out of any danger from sparks. Then he went back to help fight the fire, which was extinguished in about ten minutes more.

"It was a mighty queer blaze," said Mr. Jackson, "starting at the top that way. I wonder what caused it?"

"We'll investigate in the morning," decided Tom. "Now, dad, you must get back to your room." He turned to help his father in, but at that moment Mr. Swift, who was trying to say something, fell over in a dead faint.

"Quick! Help me carry him into the house!" cried Tom. "Then telephone for Dr. Gladby, Mr. Jackson."

The physician looked grave when, half an hour later, he examined his patient.

"Mr. Swift is very much worse," he said in a low voice. "The excitement of the fire has aggravated his ailment. I would like another doctor to see him, Tom."

"Another doctor?" Tom's voice showed his alarm.

"Yes, we must have a consultation. I think Dr. Kurtz will be a good one to call in. I should like his opinion before I decide what course to take."

"I'll send Eradicate for him at once," said the young inventor, and he went to give the colored man his instructions, while his heart was filled with a great fear for his father.

CHAPTER EIGHTEEN

THE BROKEN BRIDGE

Dr. Kurtz looked as grave as did Dr. Gladby when he had made an examination of the patient. Mr. Swift was still in a semi-conscious condition, hardly breathing as he rested on the bed where they had placed him after the fire.

"Vell," said the German physician, after a long silence, "vot is your obinion, my dear Gladby?"

"I think an operation is necessary."

"Yes, dot is so; but you know vot kind of an operation alone vill safe him; eh, my dear Gladby?"

Dr. Gladby nodded.

"It will be a rare and delicate one," he said. "There is but one surgeon I know of who can do it."

"You mean Herr Hendrix?" asked Dr. Kurtz.

"Yes, Dr. Edward Hendrix, of Kirkville. If he can be induced to come I think there is a chance of saving Mr. Swift's life. I'll speak to Tom about it."

The two physicians, who had been consulting together, summoned the youth from another room, where, with Mrs. Baggert and Mr. Jackson he had been anxiously awaiting the verdict.

"What is it?" the young inventor asked Dr. Gladby.

The medical man told him to what conclusion he and his colleague had arrived, adding:

"We advise that Dr. Hendrix be sent for at once. But I need hardly tell you, Tom, that he is a noted specialist, and his services are in great demand. He is hard to get."

"I'll pay him any sum he asks!" burst out the youth. "I'll spend all my fortune—and I have made considerable money of late—I'll spend every cent to get my father well! Money need not stand in the way, Dr. Gladby."

"I knew that, Tom. Still Dr. Hendrix is a very busy man, and it is hard to induce him to come a long distance. It is over a hundred miles to Kirkville, and it is an out-of-the-way place. I never could understand why Dr. Hendrix settled there. But there he is, and if we want him he will have to come from there. The worst of it is that there are few trains, and only a single railroad line from there to Shopton."

"Then I'll telegraph," decided Tom. "I'll offer him his own price, and ask him to rush here as soon as he can."

"You had better let Dr. Kurtz and me attend to that part of it," suggested the physician. "Dr. Hendrix would hardly come on the request of some one whom he did not know. I'll prepare a telegram, briefly explaining the case. It is the sort of an operation Dr. Hendrix is much interested in, and I think he will come on that account, if for no other reason. I'll write out the message, and you can have Eradicate take it to the telegraph office."

"I'll take it myself!" exclaimed Tom, as he got ready to go out into the night with the urgent request. "Is there any immediate danger for my father?" he asked.

"No; not any immediate danger," replied Dr. Gladby. "But the operation is imperative if he is to live. It is his one and only chance."

Tom thought only of his father as he hurried on through the night. Even the prospect of the great race, so soon to take place, had no part in his mind.

"I'll not race until I'm sure dad is going to get better," he decided. With the message to the noted specialist Tom also sent one to Mr. Damon, telling him the news, and asking him to come to Shopton. Tom felt that the presence of the odd gentleman would help him, and Mr. Damon, who first intended to stay on at the Swift home until he and Tom departed for Eagle Park, had gone back to his own residence to attend to some business Tom knew he would come in the morning, and Mr. Damon did arrive on the first train.

"Bless my soul!" he exclaimed with ready sympathy, as he extended his hand to Tom. "What's all this?" The young inventor told him, beginning with the fire that had been the cause of the excitement which produced the change in Mr. Swift.

"But I have great hopes that the specialist will be able to cure him," said Tom, for, with the coming of daylight, his courage had returned to him. "Dr. Gladby and Dr. Kurtz depend a great deal on Dr. Hendrix," he said.

"Yes, he certainly is a wonderful man. I have heard a great deal about him. I have no doubt but what he will cure your father. But about the fire? How did it start?"

"I don't know, but now that I have a few hours to spare before the doctor can get here, I'm going to make an examination."

"Bless my penwiper, but I'll help you."

Tom went into the house, to inquire of Mrs. Baggert, for probably the tenth time that morning, how his father was doing. Mr. Swift was still in a semi-conscious condition, but he recognized Tom, when the youth stood at his bedside.

"Don't worry about me, son," said the brave old inventor, as he took Tom's hand. "I'll be all right. Go ahead and get ready for the race. I want you to win!"

Tears came into Tom's eyes. Would his father be well enough to allow him to take part in the big event? He feared not.

By daylight it was seen that quite a hole had been burned in the aeroplane shed. Tom and Mr. Damon, accompanied by Mr. Jackson, walked through the place.

"And you say the fire broke out right after you had seen the mysterious airship hovering over the house?" asked the eccentric man.

"Well, not exactly after," answered Tom, "but within an hour or so. Why do you ask?"

But Mr. Damon did not answer. Something on the floor of the shed, amid a pile of blackened and charred pieces of wood, attracted his attention. He stooped over and picked it up.

"Is this yours?" he asked Tom.

"No. What is it?"

The object looked like a small iron ball, with a tube about half an inch in diameter projecting slightly from it. Tom took it'.

"Why, it looks like an infernal machine or a dynamite bomb," he said. "I wonder where it came from? Guess I'd better drop it in a pail of water. Maybe Eradicate found it and brought it here. I never saw it before. Mr. Jackson, please hand me that pail of water. We'll soak this bomb."

"There is no need," said Mr. Damon, quietly. "It is harmless now. It has done its work. It was that which set fire to your shed, and which caused the stifling fumes."

"That?" cried Tom.

"Yes. This ball is hollow, and was filled with a chemical. It was dropped on the roof, and, after a certain time, the plug in the tube was eaten through, the chemicals ran out, set the roof ablaze, and, dripping down inside spread the choking odors that nearly prevented you from getting out your aeroplane."

"Are you sure of this?" asked the young inventor.

"Positive. I read about these bombs recently. A German invented them to be used in attacking a besieged city in case of war."

"But how did this one get on my shed roof?" asked Tom.

"It was dropped there by the mysterious airship!" exclaimed the odd man. "That was why the aeroplane moved about over your place. Those in it hoped that the fire would not break out until you were all asleep, and that the shed and the Humming-Bird would be destroyed before you came to the rescue. Some of your enemies are still after you, Tom."

"And it was Andy Foger, I'll wager!" he cried. "He was in that aircraft! Oh, I'll have a long score to settle with him!"

"Of course you can't be sure it was he," said Mr. Damon, "but I wouldn't be a bit surprised but what it was. Andy is capable of such a thing. He wanted to prevent you from taking part in the race."

"Well, he sha'n't!" cried Tom, and then he thought of his invalid father. They made a further examination of the shed, and discovered another empty bomb. Then Tom recalled having seen something drop from the mysterious aeroplane as it passed over the shed.

"It was these bombs," he said. "We certainly had a narrow escape! Oh, wait until I settle my score with Andy Foger!"

As there would be but little use for the aeroplane shed now, if Tom sent his craft off to the meet, it was decided to repair it temporarily only, until he returned.

Accordingly, a big tarpaulin was fastened over the hole in the roof. Then Tom put a new wing tip on in place of the one that had been scorched. He looked all over his sky racer, and decided that it was in fit condition for the coming meet.

"I'll begin to take it apart for shipment, as soon as I hear from the specialist that dad is well enough for me to go," he said.

It was a few hours after the discovery of the empty bomb that Tom saw Dr. Gladby coming along. The physician was urging his horse to top speed. Tom felt a vague fear in his heart.

"I've got a message from Dr. Hendrix, Tom," he said, as he stopped his carriage, and approached the lad.

"When can he come?" asked the young inventor, eagerly.

"He can't get here, Tom."

"Can't get here! Why not?"

"Because the railroad bridge has collapsed, and there is no way to come. He can't make any other connections to get here in time—in time to do your father any good, Tom. He has just sent me a telegram to that effect. Dr. Hendrix can't get here, and..." Dr. Gladby paused.

"Do you mean that my father may die if the operation is not performed?" asked Tom, in a low voice.

"Yes," was the answer.

"But can't Dr. Hendrix drive here in an auto?" asked the lad. "Surely there must be some way of getting over the river, even if the railroad bridge is down. Can't he cross in a boat and drive here?"

"He wouldn't be in time, Tom. Don't you understand, Dr. Hendrix must be here within four hours, if he is to save your father's life. He never could do it by driving or by coming on some other road, or in an auto. He can't make the proper connections. There is no way."

"Yes, there is!" cried Tom, suddenly. "I know a way!"

"How?" asked Dr. Gladby, thrilled by Tom's ringing tones. "How can you do it, Tom?"

"I'll go for Dr. Hendrix in my Humming-Bird."

"Going for him would do no good. He must be brought here."

"And so he shall be!" cried Tom. "I'll bring him here in my sky racer—if he has the nerve to stand the journey, and I think he has! I'll bring Dr. Hendrix here!" and Tom hurried away to prepare for the thrilling trip.

CHAPTER NINETEEN

A NERVY SPECIALIST

There was little time to lose. Every moment of delay meant so much less chance for the recovery of Mr. Swift. Even now the periods of consciousness were becoming shorter and farther apart. He seemed to be sinking.

Tom resolutely refused to think of the possibility of death, as he went in to bid his parent good-by before starting off on his trip through the air. Mr. Swift barely knew his son, and, with tears in his eyes, though he bravely tried to keep them back, the young inventor went out into the yard.

There stood the Humming-Bird, with Mr. Jackson, Mr. Damon and Eradicate working over her, to get her in perfect trim for the race before her—a race with death.

Fortunately there was little to be done to get the speedy craft ready. Tom had accomplished most of what was necessary, while waiting for word from Dr. Hendrix. Now about all that needed to be done was to see that there was plenty of gasoline and oil in the reservoirs.

"I'll give you a note to Dr. Hendrix," said Mr. Gladby, as Tom was fastening on his faceguard. "I—I trust you won't be disappointed, Tom. I hope he will consent to return with you."

"He's got to come," said the young inventor, simply, as if that was all there was to it.

"Do you think you can make the trip in time?" asked Mr. Damon. "It is a little less than a hundred miles in an airline, but you have to go and go back. Can the aeroplane do it?"

"I'd be ashamed of her if she couldn't," said Tom, with a grim tightening of his lips. "She's just got to do it; that's all! But I know she will," and he patted the big propeller and the motor's shining cylinders as though the machine was a thing alive, like a horse or a dog, who could understand him.

He climbed to his seat, the other one holding a bag of sand to maintain a good balance.

"Start her," ordered Tom, and Mr. Jackson twisted the propeller. The motor caught at once, and the air throbbed with the noise of the explosions. Tom listened to the tune of the machinery. It sang true.

"Two thousand pounds thrust!" called the engineer, as he looked at the scale.

"Let her go!" cried Tom, whose voice was hardly heard above the roar. The trim little aeroplane scudded over the ground, gathering speed at every revolution of the wheels. Then with a spring like that of some great bird launching itself in flight, she left the earth, and took to the air. Tom was off on his trip.

Those left behind sent up a cautious cheer, for they did not want to disturb Mr. Swift. They waved their hands to the young inventor, and he waved his in reply. Then he settled down for one of the swiftest flights he had ever undertaken.

Tom ascended until he struck a favorable current of air. There was a little wind blowing in the direction he wished to take, and that aided him. But even against a powerful head-wind the Humming-Bird could make progress.

The young inventor saw the ground slipping backward beneath him. Carefully he watched the various indicators, and listened intently to the sound of the cylinders' explosions. They came rapidly and regularly. The motor was working well.

Tom glanced at the barograph. It registered two thousand feet, and he decided to keep at about that height, as it gave him a good view, and he could see to steer, for a route had been hastily mapped out for him by his friends.

Over cities, towns, villages, scattered farmhouses; across stretches of forest; over rivers, above big stretches of open country he flew. Often he could see eager crowds below, gazing up at him. But he paid no heed. He was looking for a sight of a certain broad river, which was near Kirkville. Then he knew he would be close to his goal.

He had speeded up the motor to the limit, and there was nothing to do now, save to manage the planes, wing tips and rudders, and to see that the gasoline and oil were properly fed to the machine.

Faster and faster went the Humming-Bird, but Tom's thoughts were even faster. He was thinking of many things—of his father—of what he would do if Mr. Swift died—of the mysterious airship—of the stolen plans—of the fire in the shed—of the great race—and of Andy Foger.

He took little note of time, and when, in less than an hour he sighted the river that told him he was near to Kirkville, he was rather startled.

"You certainly did come right along, Humming-Bird!" he murmured proudly.

He descended several hundred feet, and, as he passed over the town, the people of which grew wildly excited, he looked about for the house of the noted specialist. He knew how to pick it out, for Dr. Gladby had described it to him, and Tom was glad to see, as he came within view of the residence, that it was surrounded by a large yard.

"I can land almost at his door," he said, and he did, volplaning to earth with an ease born of long practice.

To say that Dr. Hendrix was astonished when Tom dropped in on him in this manner, would not be exactly true. The specialist was not in the habit of receiving calls from youths in aeroplanes, but the fact was, that Dr. Hendrix was so absorbed in his work, and thought so constantly about it, that it took a great deal to startle him out of his usual calm.

"And so you came for me in your aeroplane?" he asked of Tom, as he gazed at the trim little craft. It is doubtful if he really saw it, however, as Dr. Hendrix was just then thinking of an operation he had performed a few hours before. "I'm sorry you had your trip for nothing," he went on. "I'd like very much to come to your father, but didn't you get my telegram, telling about the broken bridge? There is no way for me to get to Shopton in time."

"Yes, there is!" cried Tom, eagerly.

"How?"

"The same way I came—in the aeroplane! Dr. Hendrix you must go back with me! It's the only way to save my father's life. Come with me in the Humming-Bird. It's perfectly safe. I can make the trip in less than an hour. I can carry you and your instruments. Will you come? Won't you come to save my father's life?" Tom was fairly pleading now.

"A trip in an aeroplane," mused Dr. Hendrix "I've never taken such a thing. I—"

"Don't be afraid, there's really no danger," said Tom.

The physician seemed to reach a sudden conclusion. His eyes brightened. He walked over and looked at the little Humming-Bird. For the time being he forgot about his operations.

"I'll go with you!" he suddenly cried. "I'll go with you, Tom Swift! If you've got the nerve, so have I! and if my science and skill can save your father's life, he'll live to be an old man! Wait until I get my bag and I'll be with you!"

TOM'S HEART GAVE A BOUND OF HOPE. CHAPTER TWENTY

JUST IN TIME

While Dr. Hendrix was in his office, getting ready to make the thrilling trip through the air with Tom, the young inventor spent a few minutes going over his monoplane. The wonderful little craft had made her first big flight in excellent time, though Tom knew she could do better the farther she was flown. Not a stay had started, not a guy wire was loose. The motor had not overheated, and every bearing was as cool as though it had not taken part in thousands of revolutions.

"Oh, I can depend on you!" murmured Tom, as he looked to see that the propeller was tight on the shaft. He gave the bearing a slight adjustment to make sure of it.

He was at this when the specialist reappeared. Dr. Hendrix, after his first show of excitement, when he had made his decision to accompany Tom, had resumed his usual calm demeanor. Once again he was the grave surgeon, with his mind on the case before him.

"Well, is my auto ready?" he asked absentmindedly. Then, as he saw the little aeroplane, and Tom standing waiting beside it, he added: "Oh, I forgot for the moment that I was to make a trip through the air, instead of in my car. Well, Mr. Swift, are we all ready?"

"All ready," replied the young inventor. "We're going to make fast time, Dr. Hendrix. You'd better put this on," and Tom extended a face protector.

"What's it for?" The physician looked curiously at it.

"To keep the air from cutting your cheeks and lips. We are going to travel a hundred miles an hour this trip."

"A hundred miles an hour!" Dr. Hendrix spoke as though he would like to back out.

"Maybe more, if I can manage it," went on Tom, calmly, as he proceeded to remove the bag of sand from the place where the surgeon was to sit. Then he looked to the various equilibrium arrangements and the control levers. He was so cool about it, taking it all for granted, as if rising and flying through the air at a speed rivaling that of the fastest birds, was a matter of no moment, that Dr. Hendrix was impressed by the calm demeanor of the young inventor.

"Very well," said the surgeon with a shrug of his shoulders, "I guess I'm game, Tom Swift."

The doctor took the seat Tom pointed out to him, with his bag of instruments on his knees. He put on the face protector, and had, at the suggestion of our hero, donned a heavy coat.

"For it's cold in the upper regions," said Tom.

Several servants in the physician's household had gathered to see him depart in this novel fashion, and the chauffeur of the auto, in which the specialist usually made his calls, was also there.

"I'll give you a hand," said the chauffeur to the young inventor. "I was at an aviation meet once, and I know how it's done."

"Good," exclaimed Tom. "Then you can hold the machine, and shove when I give the word."

Tom started the propeller himself, and quickly jumped into his seat. The chauffeur held back the Humming-Bird until the young aviator had speeded up the motor.

"Let go!" cried the youthful inventor, and the man gave the little craft a shove. Across the rather uneven ground of the doctor's yard it ran, straight for a big iron barrier.

"Look out! We'll be into the fence!" shouted the surgeon. "We'll be killed!" He seemed about to leap off.

"Sit still!" cried Tom, and at that instant he tilted the elevation planes, and the craft shot upward, going over the fence like a circus horse taking a seven-barred gate.

"Oh!" exclaimed the physician in a curious voice. They were off on their trip to save the life of Mr. Swift.

What the sensations of the celebrated specialist were, Tom never learned. If he was afraid, his fright quickly gave place to wonder, and the wonder soon changed to delight as the machine rose higher and higher, acquired more speed, and soared in the air over the country that spread out in all directions from Kirkville.

"Magnificent! Magnificent!" murmured the doctor, and then Tom knew that the surgeon was in the grip of the air, and was one of the "bird-men."

Every moment the Humming-Bird increased her speed. They passed over the river near where men were working on the broken bridge. It was now no barrier to them. Tom, noting the barograph, and seeing that they were twenty-two hundred feet high, decided to keep at about that distance from the earth.

"How fast are we going?" cried Dr. Hendrix, into the ear of the young inventor.

"Just a little short of a hundred an hour!" Tom shouted back. "We'll hit a hundred and five before long."

His prediction proved true, and when about forty miles from Shopton that terrific speed had been attained. It seemed as if they were going to have a trip devoid of incident, and Tom was congratulating himself on the quick time made, when he ran into a contrary strata of air. Almost before he knew it the Humming-Bird gave a dangerous and sickening dive, and tilted at a terrifying angle.

"Are we going to turn turtle?" cried the doctor.

"I—I hope not!" gasped Tom. He could not understand why the equilibrium weights did not work, but he had no time then to investigate. Quickly he warped the wing tips and brought the craft up on an even keel.

He gave a sigh of relief as the aeroplane was once more shooting forward, and he was not mistaken when he thought he heard Dr. Hendrix murmur a prayer of thankfulness. Their escape had been a narrow one. Tom's nerve, and the coolness of the physician, had alone saved them from a fall to death.

But now, as if ashamed of her prank, the Humming-Bird went along even better than before. Tom was peering through the slight haze that hung over the earth, for a sight of Shopton. At length the spires of the churches came into view.

"There it is," he called, pointing downward. "We'll land in two minutes more."

"No time to spare," murmured the doctor, who knew the serious nature of the aged inventor's illness. "How long did it take us?"

"Fifty-one minutes," replied Tom, glancing at a small clock in front of him. Then he shut off the motor and volplaned to earth, to the no small astonishment of the surgeon. He made a perfect landing in the yard before the shed, leaped from his seat, and called:

"Come, Dr. Hendrix!"

The surgeon followed him. Dr. Gladby and Dr. Kurtz came to the door of the house. On their faces were grave looks. They greeted the celebrated surgeon eagerly.

"Well?" he asked quickly, and they knew what he meant.

"You are only just in time," said Dr. Gladby, softly, and Tom, following the doctors into the house, wondered if his trip with the specialist had been in vain.

CHAPTER TWENTY-ONE

"WILL HE LIVE?"

Soon there were busy scenes in the Swift home, as preparations were made for a serious operation on the aged inventor. Tom's father had sunk into deep unconsciousness, and was stretched out on the bed as though there was no more life in him. In fact, Tom, for the moment, feared that it was all over. But good old Dr. Kurtz, noting the look on the lad's face, said:

"Ach, Dom, doan't vorry! Maybe it vill yet all be vell, und der vater vill hear of der great race. Bluck up your courage, und doan't gif up. Der greatest surgeon in der vorld is here now, und if anybody gan safe your vater, Herr Hendriz gan. Dot vos a great drip you made—a great drip!"

Tom felt a little comforted and, after a sight of his father, and a silent prayer that God would spare his life for years to come, the young inventor went out in the yard. He wanted to be busy about something, for he knew, with the doctors, and a trained nurse who had been hastily summoned, there was no immediate need for him. He wanted to get his mind off the operation that would soon take place, and so he decided to look over his aeroplane.

Mr. Damon came out when Tom was going over the guy wires and braces, to see how they had stood the strain.

"Well, Tom, my lad," said the eccentric man, sadly, as he grasped our hero's hand, "it's too bad. But hope for the best. I'm sure your father will pull through. We will have to begin taking the Humming-Bird apart soon; won't we, if we're going to ship it to Eagle Park?" He wanted to take Tom's mind off his troubles.

"I don't know whether we will or not," was the answer, and Tom tried to speak unbrokenly, but there was a troublesome lump in his throat, and a mist of tears in his eyes that prevented him from seeing well. The Humming-Bird, to him, looked as if she was in a fog.

"Nonsense! Of course we will!" cried Mr. Damon. "Why, bless my wishbone! Tom, you don't mean to say you're going to let that little shrimp Andy Foger walk away with that ten-thousand-dollar prize without giving him a fight for it; are you?"

This was just what Tom needed, and it seemed good to have Mr. Damon bless something again, even if it was only a wishbone.

"No!" exclaimed Tom, in ringing tones. "Andy Foger isn't going to beat me, and if I find out he is going to race with a machine made after my stolen plans, I'll make him wish he'd never taken them."

"But if the machine he had flying over here when he dropped that bomb on the shed roof, and set fire to it, is the one he's going to race with, it isn't like yours," suggested Mr. Damon, who was glad he had turned the conversation into a more cheerful channel.

"That's so," agreed the young inventor. "Well, we'll have to wait and see." He was busy now, going over every detail of the Humming-Bird. Mr. Damon helped him, and they discovered the defect in the equilibrium weights, and remedied it.

"We can't afford to have an accident in the race," said Tom. He glanced toward the house, and wondered if the operation had begun yet. He could see the trained nurse hurrying here and there, Mrs. Baggert helping her.

Eradicate Sampson shuffled out from the stable where he kept his mule Boomerang. On the face of the honest colored man there was a dejected look.

"Am Massa Swift any better, Massa Tom?" he asked.

"We can't tell yet," was the answer.

"Well, if he doan' git well, den I'm goin' t' sell mah mule," went on the dirt-chaser, from which line of activity Eradicate had derived his name.

"Sell Boomerang! Bless my curry comb! what for?" asked Mr. Damon.

"'Case as how he wouldn't neber be any good fo' wuk any mo'," explained Eradicate. "He's got so attached t' dis place, an' all de folkes on it, dat he'd feel so sorry ef—ef—well, ef any ob 'em went away, dat I couldn't git no mo' wuk out ob him, no how. So ef Massa Swift doan' git well, den I an' Boomerang parts!"

"Well, we hope it won't happen," said Tom, greatly touched by the simple grief of Eradicate. The young inventor was silent a moment, and then he softly added: "I—I wonder when—when we'll know?"

"Soon now, I think," answered Mr. Damon, in a low voice.

Silently they waited about the aeroplane. Tom tried to busy himself, but he could not. He kept his eyes fastened on the house.

It seemed like several hours, but it was not more than one, ere the white-capped nurse came to the door and waved her hand to Tom. He sprang to his feet and rushed forward. What would be the message he was to receive?

He stood before the nurse, his heart madly beating. She looked gently at him.

"Will he—will he live?" Tom asked, pantingly.

"I think so," she answered gently. "The operation is over. It was a success, so far. Time alone will tell, now. Dr. Hendrix says you can see your father for just a moment."

CHAPTER TWENTY-TWO

OFF TO THE MEET

Softly Tom tiptoed into the room where his father lay. At the bedside were the three doctors, and the nurse followed the young inventor in. Mrs. Baggert stood in the hall, and near her was Garret Jackson. The aged housekeeper had been weeping, but she smiled at Tom through her tears.

"I think he's going to get well," she whispered. She always looked on the bright side of things. Tom's heart felt better.

"You must only speak a few words to him," cautioned the specialist, who had performed such a rare and delicate operation, near the heart of the invalid. "He is very weak, Tom."

Mr. Swift opened his eyes as his son approached. He looked around feebly.

"Tom—are you there?" he asked in a whisper.

"Yes, dad," was the eager answer

"They tell me you—you made a great trip to get Dr. Hendrix—broken bridge—came through the air with him. Is that right?"

"Yes, dad. But don't tire yourself. You must get well and strong."

"I will, Tom. But tell me; did you go in—in the Humming-Bird?"

"Yes, dad."

"How did she work?"

"Fine. Over a hundred, and the motor wasn't at its best."

"That's good. Then you can go in the big race, and win."

"No, I don't believe I'll go, dad."

"Why not?" Mr. Swift spoke more strongly.

"I—because—well, I don't want to."

"Nonsense, Tom! I know; it's on my account. I know it is. But listen to me. I want you to go in! I want you to win that race! Never mind about me. I'm going to get well, and I'll recover all the more quickly if you win that race. Now promise me you'll go in it and—and—win!"

The invalid's strength was fast leaving him.

"I—I—," began Tom.

"Promise!" insisted the aged inventor, trying to rise. Dr. Hendrix made a hasty move toward the bed.

"Promise!" whispered the surgeon to Tom.

"I—I promise!" exclaimed Tom, and the aged inventor sank back with a smile of satisfaction on his pale face.

"Now you must go," said Dr. Gladby to Tom. "He has talked long enough. He must sleep now, and get up his strength."

"Will he get better?" asked Tom, anxiously.

"We can't say for sure," was the answer. "We have great hopes."

"I don't want to enter the race unless I know he is going to live," went on Tom, as Dr. Gladby followed him out of the room.

"No one can say for a certainty that he will recover," spoke the physician. "You will have to hope for the best, that is all, Tom. If I were you I'd go in the race. It will occupy your mind, and if you could send good news to your father it might help him in the fight for life he is making."

"But suppose—suppose something happens while I am away?" suggested the young inventor.

The doctor thought for a moment. Then he exclaimed:

"You have a wireless outfit on your craft; haven't you?"

"Yes."

"Then you can receive messages from here every hour if you wish. Garret Jackson, your engineer, can send them, and you can pick them up in mid-air if need be."

"So I can!" cried Tom. "I will go to the meet. I'll take the Humming-Bird apart at once, and ship it to Eagle Park. Unless Dr. Hendrix wants to go back in it," he added as an after thought.

"No," spoke Dr. Gladby, "Dr. Hendrix is going to remain here for a few days, in case of an emergency. By that time the bridge will have been repaired, and he can go back by train. I gather, from what he said, that though he liked the air trip, he will not care for another one."

"Very well," assented Tom, and Mr. Damon and he were kept busy, packing the Humming-Bird for shipment. Mr. Jackson helped them, and Eradicate and his mule Boomerang were called on occasionally when boxes or crates were to be taken to the railroad station.

In the meanwhile, Mr. Swift, if he did not improve any, at least held his own. This the doctors said was a sign of hope, and, though Tom was filled with anxiety, he tried to think that fate would be kind to him, and that his father would recover. Dr. Hendrix left, saying there was nothing more he could do, and that the rest depended on the local physicians, and on the nurse.

"Und ve vill do our duty!" ponderously exclaimed Dr. Kurtz. "You go off to dot bird race, Dom, und doan't vorry. Ve vill send der with-out-vire messages to you venever dere is anyt'ing to report. Go mit a light heart!"

How Tom wished he could, but it was out of the question. The last of the parts of the Humming-Bird had been sent away, and our hero forwarded a telegram to Mr. Sharp, of the arrangement committee, stating that he and Mr. Damon would soon follow. Then, having bidden his father a fond farewell, and after arranging with Mr. Jackson to send frequent wireless messages, Tom and the eccentric man left for the meet.

There was a wireless station at Eagle Park, and Tom had planned to receive the messages from home there until he could set up his own plant. He would have two outfits. One in the big tent where the Humming-Bird was to be put together, and another on the machine itself, so that when in the air, practicing, or even in the great race itself, there would be no break in the news that was to be flashed through space.

Tom and Mr. Damon arrived at Eagle Park on time, and Tom's first inquiry was for a message from home. There was one, stating that Mr. Swift was fairly comfortable, and seemed to be doing well. With happiness in his heart, the young inventor then set about getting the parts of his craft from the station to the park, where he and Mr. Damon, with a trusty machinist whom Mr. Sharp had recommended, would assemble it. Tom arranged that in his absence the wireless operator on the grounds would take any message that came for him.

The Humming-Bird, in the big cases and boxes, had safely arrived, and these were soon in the tent which had been assigned to Tom. It was still several days until the opening of the meet, and the grounds presented a scene of confusion.

Workmen were putting up grand stands, tents and sheds were being erected, exhibitors were getting their machines in shape, and excited contestants of many nationalities were hurrying to and fro, inquiring about parts delayed in shipment, or worrying lest some of their pet ideas be stolen.

Tom and Mr. Damon, with Frank Forker, the young machinist, were soon busy in their big tent, which was a combined workshop and living quarters, for Tom had determined to stay right on the ground until the big race was over.

"I don't see anything of Andy Foger," remarked Mr. Damon, on the second day of their residence in the park. "There are lots of new entries arriving, but he doesn't seem to be on hand."

"There's time enough," replied Tom. "I am afraid he's hanging back until the last minute, and will spring his machine so late that I won't have time to lodge a protest. It would be just like him."

"Well, I'll be on the lookout for him. Have you heard from home today, Tom?"

"No. I'm expecting a message any minute." The young inventor glanced toward the wireless apparatus which had been set up in the tent. At that moment there came the peculiar sound which indicated a message coming through space, and down the receiving wires. "There's something now!" exclaimed Tom, as he hurried over and clamped the telephone receiver to his ear. He listened a moment.

"Good news!" he exclaimed. "Dad sat up a little today! I guess he's going to get well!" and he clicked back congratulations to his father and the others in Shopton.

Another day saw the Humming-Bird almost in shape again, and Tom was preparing for a tryout of the engine.

Mr. Damon had gone over to the committee headquarters to consult with Mr. Sharp about the steps necessary for Tom to take in case Andy did attempt to enter a craft that infringed on the ideas of the young inventor, and on his way back he saw a newly-erected tent. There was a young man standing in the entrance, at the sight of whom the eccentric man murmured:

"Bless my skate-strap! His face looks very familiar!"

The youth disappeared inside the tent suddenly, and, as Mr. Damon came opposite the canvas shelter, he started in surprise.

For, on a strip of muslin which was across the tent, painted in gay colors, were the words:

THE FOGER AEROPLANE

"Bless my elevation rudder!" cried Mr. Damon. "Andy's here at last! I must tell Tom!"

CHAPTER TWENTY-THREE

THE GREAT RACE

"Well," remarked Mr. Sharp, when Tom and Mr. Damon had called on him, to state that Andy Foger's machine was now on the grounds, and demanding to be allowed to view it, to see if it was an infringement on the one entered by the young inventor, "I'll do the best I can for you. I'll lay the case before the committee. It will meet at once, and I'll let you know what they say."

"Understand," said Tom, "I don't want to interfere unless I am convinced that Andy is trying an underhand trick. My plans are missing, and I think he took them. If his machine is made after those plans, it is, obviously, a steal, and I want him ruled out of the meet."

"And so he shall be!" exclaimed Mr. Sharp. "Get the evidence against him, and we'll act quickly enough."

The committee met in about an hour, and considered the case. Meanwhile, Tom and Mr. Damon strolled past the tent with its flaring sign. There was a man on guard, but Andy was not in sight.

Then Tom was sent for, and Mr. Sharp told him what conclusion had been arrived at. It was this:

"Under the rules of the meet," said the balloonist, "we had to guarantee privacy to all the contestants until such time as they choose to exhibit their machines. That is, they need not bring them out until just before the races," he added. "This is not a handicap affair, and the speediest machine, or the one that goes to the greatest height, according to which class it enters, will win. In consequence we cannot force any contestant to declare what kind of a machine he will use until he gets ready.

"Some are going to use the familiar type of biplanes and, as you can see, there is no secret about them. They are trying them out now." This was so, for several machines of this type were either in the air, circling about, or were being run over the ground.

"But others," continued Mr. Sharp, "will not even take the committee into their confidence until just before the race. They want to keep their craft a secret. We can't compel them to do otherwise. I'm sorry, Tom, but the only thing I see for you to do is to wait until the last minute. Then, if you find Andy has infringed on your machine, lodge a protest—that is unless you can get evidence against him before that time."

Tom well knew the uselessness of the latter plan. He and Mr. Damon had tried several times to get a glimpse of the craft Andy had made, but without success. As to the other alternative—that of waiting until the last moment—Tom feared that, too, would be futile.

"For," he reasoned, "just before the race there will be a lot of confusion, officials will be here and there, scattered over the ground, they will be hard to find, and it will be almost useless to protest then. Andy will enter the race, and there is a possibility that he may win. Almost any one could with a machine like the Humming-Bird. It's the machine almost as much as the operator, in a case like this."

"But you can protest after the race," suggested Mr. Damon.

"That would be little good, in case Andy beat me. The public would say I was a sorehead, and jealous. No, I've either got to stop Andy before the race, or not at all. I will try to think of a plan."

Tom did think of several, but abandoned them one after the other. He tried to get a glimpse inside the tent where the Foger aeroplane was housed, but it was too closely guarded. Andy himself was not much in evidence, and Tom only had fleeting glimpses of the bully.

Meanwhile he and Mr. Damon, together with their machinist, were kept busy. As Tom's craft was fully protected by patents now, he had no hesitation in taking it out, and it was given several severe tests around the aerial course. It did even better than Tom expected of it, and he had great hopes.

Always, though, there were two things that worried him. One was his father's illness, and the other the uneasiness he felt as to what Andy Foger might do. As to the former, the wireless reports indicated that Mr. Swift was doing as well as could be expected, but his improvement was not rapid. Regarding the latter worry, Tom saw no way of getting rid of it.

"I've just got to wait, that's all," he thought.

The day before the opening of the meet, Tom and Mr. Damon had given the Humming-Bird a grueling tryout. They had taken her high up—so high that no prying eyes could time them, and there Tom had opened the motor for all the power in it. They had flashed through space at the rate of one hundred and twenty miles an hour.

"If we can only do that in the race, the ten thousand dollars is mine!" exulted Tom, as he slanted the nose of the aeroplane toward the earth.

The day of the race dawned clear and beautiful. Tom was up early, for there remained many little things to do to get his craft in final trim for the contest. Then, too, he wanted to be ready to act promptly as soon as

Andy's machine was wheeled out, and he also wanted to get a message from home.

The wireless arrived soon after breakfast, and did not contain very cheering news.

"Your father not so well," Mr. Jackson sent. "Poor night, but doctor thinks day will show improvement. Don't worry."

"Don't worry! I wonder who could help it," mused poor Tom. "Well, I'll hope for the best," and he wired back to tell the engineer in Shopton to keep in touch with him, and to flash the messages to the Humming-Bird in the air, after the big race started.

"Now I'll go out and see if I can catch a glimpse of what that sneak Andy has to pit against me," said Tom.

The Foger tent was tightly closed, and Tom turned back to his own place, having arranged with a messenger to come and let him know as soon as Andy's craft was wheeled out.

All about was a scene of great activity. The grand stands were filled, and a big crowd stood about the field anxiously waiting for the first sight of the "bird-men" in their wonderful machines. Now and then the band blared out, and cheers arose as one after another the frail craft were wheeled to the starting place.

Men in queer leather costumes darted here and there—they were the aviators who were soon to risk life and limb for glory and gold. Most of them were nervously smoking cigarettes. The air was filled with guttural German or nasal French, while now and then the staccato Russian was heard, and occasionally the liquid tones of a Japanese. For men of many nations were competing for the prizes.

The majority of the machines were monoplanes and biplanes though one triplane was entered, and there were several "freaks" as the biplane and monoplane men called them—craft of the helicopter, or the wheel type. There was also one Witzig Liore Dutilleul biplane, with three planes behind.

Tom was familiar with most of these types, but occasionally he saw a new one that excited his curiosity. However, he was more interested in what Andy Foger would turn out. Andy's machine had not been tried, and Tom wondered how he dared risk flying in it, without at least a preliminary tryout. But Andy, and those with him, were evidently full of confidence.

News of the suspicions of Tom, and what he intended to do in case these suspicions proved true, had gotten around, and there was quite a crowd about his own tent, and another throng around that of Andy.

Tom and Mr. Damon had wheeled the Humming-Bird out of her canvas "nest.". There was a cheer as the crowd caught sight of the trim little craft. The young inventor, the eccentric man, and the machinist were busy going over every part.

Meanwhile the meet had been officially opened, and it was announced that the preliminary event would be some air evolutions at no great height, and for no particular prize. Several biplanes and monoplanes took part in this. It was very interesting, but the big ten-thousand-dollar race, over a distance of a hundred miles was the principal feature of the meet, and all waited anxiously for this.

The opening stunts passed off successfully, save that a German operator in a Bleriot came to grief, crashing down to the ground, wrecking his machine, and breaking an arm. But he only laughed at that, and coolly demanded another cigarette, as he crawled out of the tangle of wires, planes and the motor.

After this there was an exhibition flight by a French aviator in a Curtis biplane, who raced against one in a Baby Wright. It was a dead heat, according to the judges. Then came a flight for height; and while no records were broken, the crowd was well satisfied.

"Get ready for the hundred-mile ten-thousand-dollar-prize race!" shouted the announcer, through his megaphone.

Tom's heart gave a bound. There were seven entrants in this contest besides Tom and Andy Foger, and as announced by the starter they were as follows:

CONTESTANT / MACHINE
Von Bergen… Wright Biplane
Alameda… Antoinette Monoplane
Perique…Bleriot Monoplane
Loi Tong…Santos-Dumont Monoplane
Wendell…Curtis Biplane
De Tromp…Farman Biplane
Lascalle…Demoiselle Monoplane
Andy Foger…——
Tom Swift…Humming-Bird Monoplane

"What is the style of the Foger machine?" yelled some one in the crowd, as the announcer lowered his megaphone.

"It has not been announced," was the reply. "It will at once be wheeled out though, in accordance with the conditions of the race."

There was a craning of necks, and an uneasy movement in the crowd, for Tom's story was now generally known.

"Get ready to make your protest," advised Mr. Damon to the young inventor. "I'll stay by the machine here until you come back. Bless my radiator! I hope you beat him!"

"I will, if it's possible!" murmured Tom, with a grim tightening of his lips.

There was a movement about Andy's tent, whence, for the last half hour had come spasmodic noises that indicated the trying-out of the motor. The flaps were pulled back and a curious machine was wheeled into view. Tom rushed over toward it, intent on getting the first view. Would it prove to be a copy of his speedy Humming-Bird?

Eagerly he looked, but a curious sight met his eyes. The machine was totally unlike any he had expected to see. It was large, and to his mind rather clumsy, but it looked powerful. Then, as he took in the details, he knew that it was the same one that had flown over his house that night— it was the one from which the fire bomb had been dropped.

He pushed his way through the crowd. He saw Andy standing near the curious biplane, which type of air craft it nearest resembled, though it had some monoplane features. On the side was painted the name:

SLUGGER

Andy caught sight of Tom Swift.

"I'm going to beat you!" the bully boasted, "and I haven't a machine like yours, after all. You were wrong."

"So I see," stammered Tom, hardly knowing what to think. "What did you do with my plans then?"

"I never had them!"

Andy turned away, and began to assist the men he had hired to help him. Like all the others, his machine had two seats, for in this race each operator must carry a passenger.

Tom turned away, both glad and sorry,—glad that his rival was not to race him in a duplicate of the Humming-Bird, but sorry that he had as yet no track of the strangely missing plans.

"I wonder where they can be?" mused the young inventor.

Then came the firing of the preliminary gun. Tom rushed back to where Mr. Damon stood waiting for him.

There was a last look at the Humming-Bird. She was fit to race any machine on the ground. Mr. Damon took his place. Tom started the propeller. The other contestants were in their seats with their passengers. Their assistants stood ready to shove them off. The explosions of so many motors in action were deafening.

"How much thrust?" cried Tom to his machinist.

"Twenty-two hundred pounds!"

"Good!"

The report of the starting-gun could not be heard. But the smoke of it leaped into the air. It was the signal to go.

Tom's voice would not have carried five feet. He waved his hands as a signal. His helper thrust the Humming-Bird forward. Over the smooth ground it rushed. Tom looked eagerly ahead. On a line with him were the other machines, including Andy Foger's Slugger.

Tom pulled a lever. He felt his craft soar upward. The other machines also pointed their noses into the air.

The big race for the ten-thousand-dollar prize was under way!

CHAPTER TWENTY-FOUR

WON BY A LENGTH

Rising upward, on a steep slant, for he wanted to get into the upper currents as soon as possible, Tom looked down and off to his left and saw one machine going over the ground in curious leaps and bounds. It was the tiny Demoiselle—the smallest craft in the race, and its peculiar style of starting was always thus manifested.

"I don't believe he's going to make it," thought Tom.

He was right. In another moment the tiny craft, after rising a short distance, dove downward, and was wrecked. The young inventor saw the two men crawling out from the tangled planes and wings, apparently uninjured.

"One contestant less," thought Tom, grimly, though with pity in his heart for the unfortunates.

However, he must think of himself and his own craft now. He glanced at Mr. Damon sitting beside him. That odd gentleman, with never a thought of blessing anything now, unless he did it silently, was watching the lubricating system. This was a vital part of the craft, for if anything went wrong with it, and the bearings overheated, the race would have to be abandoned. So Tom was not trusting to any automatic arrangement, but had instituted, almost at the last moment, a duplicate hand-worked system, so that if one failed him he would have the other.

"A good start!" shouted Mr. Damon in his ear.

Tom nodded, and glanced behind him. On a line with the Humming-Bird, and at about the same elevation, were the Bleriot monoplane and a Wright biplane. Below were the Santos-Dumont and the Antoinette.

"Where's the Slugger?" called Tom to his friend.

Mr. Damon motioned upward. There, in the air above Tom's machine, and slightly in advance, was Andy Foger's craft. He had gotten away in better shape than had the Humming-Bird.

For a moment Tom's heart misgave him. Then he turned on more power, and had the satisfaction of mounting upward and shooting on-ward until he was on even terms with Andy.

The bully gave one glance over toward his rival, and pulled a lever. The Slugger increased her speed, but Tom was not a second behind him.

There was a roaring noise in the rear, and up shot De Tromp in the Farman, and Loi Tong, the little Japanese, in the Santos-Dumont. Truly the race was going to be a hotly contested one. But the end was far off yet.

After the first jockeying for a start and position, the race settled down into what might be termed a "grind." The course was a large one, but so favorable was the atmosphere that day, and such was the location of Eagle Park in a great valley, that even on the far side of the great ellipse the contestants could be seen, dimly with the naked eye, but very plainly with glasses, with which many of the spectators were provided.

Around and around they went, at no very great height, for it was necessary to make out the signals set up by the race officials, so that the contestants would know when they were near the finish, that they might use the last atom of speed. So at varying heights the wonderful machines circled about the course.

The Humming-Bird was working well, and Tom felt a sense of pride as he saw the ground slipping away below him. He felt sure that he would win, even when Alameda, the Spaniard, in the Antoinette, came creeping up on him, and even when Andy Foger, with a burst of speed, placed himself and his passenger in the lead.

"I'll catch him!" muttered Tom, and he opened the throttle a trifle wider, and went after Andy, passing him with ease.

They had covered about thirty miles of the course, when the hum-ming and crackling of the wireless apparatus told Tom that a message was coming. He snapped the receiver to his ear, adjusting the outer cov-ering to shut out the racket of the motor, and listened.

"Well?" asked Mr. Damon, as Tom took off the receiver.

"Dad isn't quite so well," answered the lad. "Mr. Jackson says they have sent for Dr. Hendrix again. But dad is game. He sends me word to go on and win, and I'll do it, too, only—"

Tom paused, and choked back a sob. Then he prepared to get more speed out of his motor.

"Of course you will!" cried Mr. Damon. "Bless my—!"

But they encountered an adverse current of wind at that moment, and it required the attention of both of the aviators to manage the machine. It was soon on an even keel again, and once more was shooting forward around the course.

At times Tom would be in advance, and again he would have to give place to the Curtis, the Farman, or the Santos-Dumont, as these speedy machines, favored by a spurt from their motors, or by some current of air, shot ahead. But, in general, Tom maintained the lead, and among the spectators there began a series of guesses as to how much he would win by.

Tom glanced at the barograph. It registered a little over twelve hundred feet. He looked at the speed gage. He was doing a trifle better than a hundred miles an hour. He looked down at the signals. There was twenty miles yet to go. It was almost time for the spurt for which he had been holding back. Yet he would wait until five miles from the end, and then he felt that he could gain and maintain a lead.

"Andy seems to be doing well," said Mr. Damon.

"Yes, he has a good machine," conceded Tom.

Five miles more were reeled off. Then another five. Another round of that distance and Tom would key his motor up to the highest pitch, and then the Humming-Bird would show what she could do. Eagerly Tom waited for the right signal.

Suddenly the wireless began buzzing again. Quickly the young inventor clamped the receiver to his ear. Mr. Damon saw him turn pale.

"Dr. Gladby says dad has a turn for the worse. There is little hope," translated Tom.

"Will you—are you going to quit?" asked Mr. Damon.

Tom shook his head.

"No!" he cried. "My father has become unconscious, so Mr. Jackson says, but his last words were to me: 'Tell Tom to win the race!' And I'm going to do it!"

Tom suddenly changed his plans. There was to be no waiting for the signal now. He would begin his final spurt, and if possible finish the hundred miles at his utmost speed, win the race and then hasten to his father's side.

With a menacing roar the motor of the Humming-Bird took up the additional power that Tom sent into her. She shot ahead like an eagle darting after his prey. Tom opened up a big gap between his machine and the one nearest him, which, at that moment, was the Antoinette, with the Spaniard driving her.

"Now to win!" cried Tom, grimly.

Surely no race was ever flown as was that one! Tom flashed through the air so quickly that his speed was almost incredible. The gage registered one hundred and thirty miles an hour!

Down below in the grand stands, and on the aviation field, there were yells of approval—of wonder—of fear. But Tom and Mr. Damon could not hear them. They only heard the powerful song of the motor.

Faster and faster flew the Humming-Bird. Tom looked down, and saw the signal put up which meant that there were but three miles more to go. He felt that he could do it. He was half a lap ahead of them all now. But he saw Andy Foger's machine pulling away from the bunch.

"He's going to try to catch me!" exulted Tom.

Then something happened. The motor of the Humming-Bird suddenly slackened its speed, it missed explosions, and the trim little craft began to drop behind.

"What's the matter?" cried Mr. Damon.

"Three of the cylinders are out of business!" yelled Tom. "We're done for, I guess."

On came the other machines, Andy in the lead, then the Santos-Dumont, then the Farman, and lastly the Wright. They saw the plight of the Humming-Bird and determined to beat her. Tom cast a despairing look up at the motor. There was nothing to be done. He could not reach it in mid-air. He could only keep on, crippled as he was, and trust to luck.

Andy passed by his rival with an evil smile on his ugly face. Then the Antoinette flashed by. In turn all the others left Tom in the rear. His heart was like lead. Mr. Damon gazed blankly forward. They were beaten. It did not seem possible.

There was but a single chance. If Tom shut off all power, coasted for a moment, and then, ere the propeller had ceased revolving, if he could start the motor on the spark, the silent cylinders might pick up, with the others, and begin again. He would try it. They could be no worse off than they were.

"A mile behind!" gasped Tom. "It's a long chance, but I'll take it."

He shut off the power. The motor was silent, the Humming-Bird began to fall. But ere she had gone down ten feet Tom suddenly switched on the batteries. There was a moment of silence, and then came the welcome roar that told of the rekindled motor. And such a roar as it was! Every cylinder was exploding as though none of them had ever stopped!

"We did it!" yelled Tom. Opening up at full speed, he sent the sky racer on the course to overtake and pass his rivals.

Slowly he crept on them. They looked back and saw him coming. They tried to put on more speed, but it was impossible. Andy Foger was in the lead. He was being slowly overhauled by the Santos-Dumont, with the queer tail-rudders.

"I'll get him!" muttered Tom. "I'll pass 'em all!"

And he did. With a wonderful burst of speed the little Humming-Bird overtook one after another of her larger rivals, and passed them. Then she crept up on Andy's Slugger.

In an instant more it was done, and, a good length in advance of the Foger craft, Tom shot over the finish line a winner, richer by ten thousand dollars, and, not only that, but he had picked up a mile that had been lost, and had snatched victory from almost certain defeat.

There was a succession of thundering cheers as he shut off the motor, and volplaned to earth, but he paid little attention to them. He brought his craft to a stop just as the wireless on it buzzed again.

He listened with a look of pain on his face.

"My father is dying," he said simply. "I must go to him. Mr. Damon, will you fill the tanks with oil and gasoline, while I send off a message?"

"Oil and gasoline," murmured the odd man, while hundreds pressed up to congratulate Tom Swift "What are you going to do?"

"I'm going to my father in the Humming-Bird," said Tom. "It's the only way I can see him alive," and he began to click off a message to Mr. Jackson, stating that he had won the race and was going to fly to Shopton, while Mr. Damon and several others replenished the fuel and oil of the aeroplane.

Tom Swift had won one race. Could he win the other?

CHAPTER TWENTY-FIVE

HOME AGAIN—CONCLUSION

Mr. Sharp pushed his way through the crowd.

"The committee has the certified check ready for you, Tom," called the balloonist. "Will you come and get it?"

"Send it to me, please," answered the young inventor. "I must go to my father."

"Huh! I'd have beaten him in another round," boasted Andy Foger. No one paid any attention to him.

"Monsieur ezz plucky!" said the Frenchman, Perique. "I am honaired to shake his hand! He has broken all ze records!"

"Dot's der best machine I effer saw," spoke the Dutchman, De Tromp, ponderously. "Shake hands!"

"Ver' fine, ver' good!" came from the little Japanese, and all the contestants congratulated Tom warmly. Never before had a hundred miles been covered so speedily.

A man elbowed his way through the press of people.

"Is your machine fully protected by patents?" he inquired earnestly.

"It is," said Tom.

"Then, as a representative of the United States Government, I would like an option to purchase the exclusive right to use them," said the man. "Can you guarantee that no one else has any plans of them? It will mean a fortune to you."

Tom hesitated. He thought of the stolen plans. If he could only get possession of them! He glanced at Andy Foger, who was wheeling his machine back into the tent. But there was no time now to have it out with the bully.

"I will see you again," said Tom to the government agent. "I must go to my father, who is dying. I can't answer you now."

The tanks were filled. Tom gave a hasty look to his machine, and, bidding his new friends farewell, he and Mr. Damon took their places aboard the Humming-Bird. The little craft rose in the air, and soon they had left Eagle Park far behind. Eagerly Tom strained his eyes for a sight of his home town, though he knew it would be several hours ere he could hover over it.

Would he be in time? Would he be in time? That question came to him again and again.

For a time the Humming-Bird skimmed along as though she delighted in the rapid motion, in slipping through the air and sliding along on the billows of wind. Tom, with critical ears, listened to the hum of the motor, the puffing of the exhaust, the grinding of the gear wheels, and the clicking of the trips, as valve after valve opened or closed to admit the mixture of air and gasoline, or closed to give the compression necessary for the proper explosion.

"Is she working all right?" asked Mr. Damon, anxiously, and, such was the strain on him that he did not think to bless anything. "Is she all right, Tom, my lad?"

"I think so. I'm speeding her to the limit. Faster than I ever did before, but I guess she'll do. She was built to stand a strain, and she's got to do it now!"

Then there was silence again, as they slid along through the air like a coaster gliding down a steep descent.

"It was a great race, wasn't it?" asked Mr. Damon, as he shifted to an easier position in his seat. "A great race, Tom. I didn't think you'd do it, one spell there."

"Neither did I," came the answer, as the young inventor changed the spark lever. "But I made up my mind I wouldn't be beaten by Andy Foger, if I could help it. Though it was taking a risk to shut off the current the way I did."

"A risk?"

"Yes; it might not have started again," and Tom looked down at the earth below them, as if measuring the distance he would have fallen had not his sky racer kept on at the critical moment.

"And—and if the current hadn't come on again; eh, Tom? Would we—?"

Mr. Damon did not finish, but Tom knew what he meant.

"It would have been all up with us," he said simply. "I might have volplaned back to earth, but at the speed we were going, and at the height, around a curve, we might have turned turtle."

"Bless my—!" began Mr. Damon, and then he stopped. The thought of Tom's trouble came to him, and he realized that his words might grate on the feelings of his companion.

On they rushed through the air with the Humming-Bird speeded up faster and faster as she warmed to her task. The machinery seemed to be working perfectly, and as Tom listened to the hum a look of pleasure replaced the look of anxiety on his face.

"Don't you think we'll make it?" asked Mr. Damon, after another pause, during which they passed over a large city, the inhabitants exhibiting much excitement as they sighted the airship over their heads.

"We've got to make it!" declared Tom between his clenched teeth.

He turned on a little more gasoline, and there was a spurt in their speed which made Mr. Damon grasp the upright braces near him with firm hands, and his face became a little paler.

"It's all right," spoke Tom, reassuringly. "There's no danger."

But Tom almost reckoned without his host, for a few moments later, as he was trying to get more revolutions out of the propellers, he ran into an adverse current of air.

In an instant the Humming-Bird was tilted up almost on her "beams' ends," so to speak, and had it not been that the young inventor quickly warped the wing tips, to counteract the pressure on one side, there might have been a different end to this story.

"Bless my——!" began Mr. Damon, but he got no further, for he had to bend his body as Tom did, to equalize the pressure of the wind current.

"A little farther over!" yelled the lad. "A little farther over this way, Mr. Damon!"

"But if I come any more toward you I'll be out of my seat!" objected the eccentric man.

"If you don't you'll be out of the aeroplane!" cried Tom grimly, and his companion leaned over as far as he could until the young pilot had brought the craft to an even keel again.

Then Tom speeded up the motor, which he had partly shut down as they passed through the danger zone, and again they were racing through space.

They were nearing Shopton now, as the lad and Mr. Damon could tell by the familiar landmarks which loomed up in sight. Tom strained his eyes for the first view of his home.

Suddenly, as they were skimming along, there came a cessation of the hum and roar that told of the perfectly-working motor. It was an ominous silence.

"What's—what's wrong?" gasped Mr. Damon.

"Something's given way," answered Tom quickly. "I'm afraid the magneto isn't sparking as it ought to."

"Well, can't we volplane back to earth?" asked the odd man, for he had become familiar with this feat when anything happened to the motor.

"We could," answered Tom, "but I'm not going to."

"Why not?"

"Because we're too far from Shopton—and dad! I'm going to keep on. I've got to—if I want to be there in time!"

"But if the motor doesn't work?"

"I'll make her work!"

Tom was desperately manipulating the various levers and handles connected with the electrical ignition system. He tried in vain to get the magneto to resume the giving out of sparks, and, failing in that, he switched on the batteries. But, to his horror, the dry cells had given out. There was no way of getting a spark unless the little electrical machine would work.

The propellers were still whirring around by their own momentum, and if Tom could switch in the magneto in time all might yet be well.

They had started to fall, but, by quickly bringing up the head plane tips, Tom sent his craft soaring upward again on a bank of air.

"Here!" he cried to Mr. Damon. "Take the steering-wheel and kept her on this level as long as you can."

"What are you going to do?"

"I've got to fix that magneto!"

"But if she dips down?"

"Throw up the head planes as I did. It's our only chance! I can't go down now, so far from Shopton!"

Mr. Damon reached over and took the wheel from Tom's hands. Then the young inventor, leaning forward, for the magneto was within easy reach, looked to see what the trouble was. He found it quickly. A wire had vibrated loose from a binding-post. In a second Tom had it in place again; and, ere the propellers had ceased revolving, he had turned the switch. The magneto took up the work in a flash. Once more the spark exploded the gasoline mixture, and the propellers sent the Humming-Bird swiftly ahead.

"We'll make it now!" declared Tom grimly.

"We're almost there," added Mr. Damon, as he relinquished the wheel to the young pilot. The craft had gone down some, but Tom sent her up again.

Nearer and nearer home they came, until at last the spires of the Shopton churches loomed into view. Then he was over the village. Now he was within sight of his own house.

Tom coasted down a bank of air, and brought the Humming-Bird up with a jerk of the ground brakes. Before the wheels had ceased turning he had leaped out.

"It's Massa Tom!" cried Eradicate, as he saw Tom alight.

The young inventor hurried into the house. He was met by the nurse, who held up a warning finger. Tom's heart almost stopped beating. He was aware that Dr. Gladby came from the room where Mr. Swift lay.

"Is he—is he—am I too late?" gulped Tom.

"Hush!" cautioned the nurse.

Tom reeled, and would have fallen had not the doctor caught him, for the lad was weak and worn out.

"He is going to get well!" were the joyful words he heard, as if in a dream, and then his strength suddenly came back to him. "The crisis is just passed, Tom," went on Dr. Gladby, "and your father will recover, and be stronger than ever. Your good news of winning was like a tonic to him. Now let me congratulate you on the race." Tom had flashed by wireless a brief message of his success.

"Dad's news is better than all the congratulations in the world," he said softly, as he grasped the doctor's hand.

* * * * *

It was a week later. Mr. Swift improved rapidly once the course of the disease was permanently checked, and he was soon able to sit up. Tom was with him in the room, talking of the great race, and how he had won. He fingered the certified check for ten thousand dollars that had just come to him by mail.

"You certainly did wonderfully well," said the aged inventor, softly. "Wonderfully well, Tom. I'm proud of you."

"You may well be," added Mr. Damon. "Bless my shoelaces, but I thought Andy Foger had us there one spell; didn't you, Tom?"

"Indeed I did. But you helped me win, Mr. Damon."

"Nonsense!" exclaimed the odd man.

"Yes, you did. You helped me a lot."

"Well, are you going to keep after more air-prizes, Tom, or are you going to try for something else?" asked his father.

"I don't believe I'll go in any more aeroplane races right away," answered the young inventor. "For some time I've been wanting to complete and perfect my electric rifle. I think I'll begin work on that soon."

"And go hunting?" asked Mr. Damon.

"I think so," answered Tom, dreamily. "I don't know just where, though."

Where he went, and what he shot, will be told in the next volume of this series, to be called: "Tom Swift and His Electric Rifle; or, Daring Adventures in Elephant Land."

For a few moments after Tom's announcement no one spoke, then the young inventor said:

"It's too bad that first set of plans were stolen. If I had them I could make a good deal with the Government about my little aeroplane. But they don't want to take up with it as long as there is a chance of some foreign nation getting information about the secret parts, and my patents won't hold abroad. I wonder if there is any way of getting those plans away from Andy Foger? I don't understand why he hasn't used them before this. I thought sure he would make a craft like the Humming-Bird to race against me."

"What plans are those?" asked Mr. Swift.

"Why, don't you remember?" asked Tom. "The ones I showed you one day, in the library, when you fell asleep, and some one slipped in and stole them."

A curious look came over Mr. Swift's face. He passed his hand across his brow.

"I am beginning to remember something I have been trying to recall ever since I became ill," he said slowly. "It is coming back to me. Those plans—in the library—I fell asleep, but before I did so I hid those plans, Tom!"

"You hid those plans!" Tom fairly shouted the words.

"Yes, I remember feeling a drowsy feeling coming on, and I feared lest some one might see the drawings. I got up and put them under the window, in a little, hollow place in the foundation wall. Then I came back in through the window again, and went to sleep. Then, on account of my illness, just as I once before forgot something, and thought the minister had called, I lost all recollection of them. I hid those plans."

Tom leaped to his feet. He rushed to the place named by his father. Soon his triumphant shout told of his success. He came hurrying back into the house with a roll of papers in his hands.

And there were the long-missing plans! damp and stained by the weather, but all there. No enemy had them, and Tom's secret was safe.

"Now I can accept the Government offer!" he cried. And a few weeks later he made a most advantageous deal with the United States officials for his patents.

Dr. Gladby explained that Mr. Swift's queer action was due to his illness. He became liable to lapses of memory, and one happened just after he hid away the plans. Even the hiding of them was caused by the peculiar condition of his brain. He had opened the library window, slipped out with the papers, and hastened in again, to fall asleep in his chair, during the short time Tom was gone.

"And Andy Foger never took them at all," remarked Mary Nestor, when Tom was telling her about it a few days afterward.

"No. I guess I must apologize to him." Which Tom did, but Andy did not receive it very graciously, especially as Tom accused him of trying to destroy the Humming-Bird.

Andy denied this and denied having anything to do with the mysterious fire, and, as there was no way to prove him guilty, Tom could not proceed against him. So the matter was dropped.

Mr. Swift continued to improve, and was soon himself again, and able to resume his inventive work. Tom received several offers to give exhibition flights at big aero meets, but refused, as he was busy on his new rifle. Mr. Damon helped him.

Andy Foger made several successful flights in his queer aeroplane, which turned out to be the product of a German genius who was supplied with money by Mr. Foger. Andy became very proud, and boasted that he and the German were going abroad to give flights in Europe.

"I'd be glad if he would," said Tom, when he heard of the plan. "He wouldn't bother me then."

With the money received from winning the big race, and from his contracts from the Government, Tom Swift was now in a fair way to become quite wealthy. He was destined to have many more adventures; yet, come what might, never would he forget the thrilling happenings that fell to his lot while flying for the ten-thousand dollar prize in his sky racer.

TOM SWIFT AND HIS ELECTRIC RIFLE

OR, DARING ADVENTURES IN ELEPHANT LAND

CHAPTER I

TOM WANTS EXCITEMENT

"Have you anything special to do tonight, Ned?" asked Tom Swift, the well-known inventor, as he paused in front of his chum's window, in the Shopton National Bank.

"No, nothing in particular," replied the bank clerk, as he stacked up some bundles of bills. "Why do you ask?"

"I wanted you to come over to the house for a while."

"Going to have a surprise party, or something like that?"

"No, only I've got something I'd like to show you."

"A new invention?"

"Well, not exactly new. You've seen it before, but not since I've improved it. I'm speaking of my new electric rifle. I've got it ready to try, now, and I'd like to see what you think of it. There's a rifle range over at the house, and we can practice some shooting, if you haven't anything else to do."

"I haven't, and I'll be glad to come. What are you doing in the bank, anyhow; putting away more of your wealth, Tom?"

"Yes, I just made a little deposit. It's some money I got from the government for the patents on my sky racer, and I'm salting it down here until Dad and I can think of a better investment."

"Good idea. Bring us all the money you can," and the bank clerk, who held a small amount of stock in the financial institution, laughed, his chum joining in with him.

"Well, then. I'll expect you over this evening," went on the youthful inventor, as he turned to leave the bank.

"Yes, I'll be there. Say, Tom, have you heard the latest about Andy Foger?"

"No, I haven't heard much since he left town right after I beat him in the aeroplane race at Eagle Park."

"Well, he's out of town all right, and I guess for a long time this trip. He's gone to Europe."

"To Europe, eh? Well, he threatened to go there after he failed to beat me in the race, but I thought he was only bluffing."

"No, he's really gone this time."

"Well, I, for one, am glad of it. Did he take his aeroplane along?"

"Yes, that's what he went for. It seems that this Mr. Landbacher, the German who really invented it, and built it with money which Mr. Foger supplied, has an idea he can interest the German or some other European government in the machine. Andy wanted to go along with him, and as Mr. Foger financed the scheme, I guess he thought it would be a good thing to have some one represent him. So Andy's gone."

"Then he won't bother me. Well, I must get along. I'll expect you over tonight," and with a wave of his hand Tom Swift hurried from the bank.

The young inventor jumped into his electric runabout which stood outside the institution, and was about to start off when he saw a newsboy selling papers which had just come in from New York, on the morning train.

"Here, Jack, give me a TIMES," called Tom to the lad, and he tossed the newsboy a nickel. Then, after glancing at the front page, and noting the headings, Tom started off his speedy car, in which, on one occasion, he had made a great run, against time. He was soon at home.

"Well, Dad, I've got the money safely put away," he remarked to an aged gentleman who sat in the library reading a book. "Now we won't have to worry about thieves until we get some more cash in."

"Well, I'm glad it's coming in so plentifully," said Mr. Swift with a smile. "Since my illness I haven't been able to do much, Tom, and it all depends on you, now."

"Don't let that worry you, Dad. You'll soon be as busy as ever," for, following a serious operation for an ailment of the heart, Mr. Swift, who was a veteran inventor, had not been able to do much. But the devices of his son, especially a speedy monoplane, which Tom invented, and sold to the United States Government, were now bringing them in a large income. In fact with royalties from his inventions and some gold and diamonds which he had secured on two perilous trips, Tom Swift was quite wealthy.

"I'll never be as busy as I once was," went on Mr. Swift, a little regretfully, "but I don't know that I care as long as you continue to turn out new machines, Tom. By the way, how is the electric rifle coming on? I haven't heard you speak of it lately."

"It's practically finished, Dad. It worked pretty well the time I took it when we went on the trip to the caves of ice, but I've improved it very much since then. In fact I'm going to give it a severe test tonight. Ned Newton is coming over, and it may be that then we'll find out something about it that could be bettered. But I think not. It suits me as it is."

"So Ned is coming over to see it; eh? You ought to have Mr. Damon here to bless it a few times."

"Yes, I wish I did. And he may come along at any moment, as it is. You never can tell when he is going to turn up. Mrs. Baggert says you were out walking while I was at the bank, Dad. Do you feel better after it?"

"Yes, I think I do, Tom. Oh, I'm growing stronger every day, but it will take time. But now tell me something about the electric gun."

Thereupon the young inventor related to his father some facts about the improvements he had recently made to the weapon. It was dinner time when he had finished, and, after the meal Tom went out to the shed where he built his aeroplanes and his airships, and in which building he had fitted up a shooting gallery.

"I'll get ready for the trial tonight," he said "I want to see what it will do to a dummy figure. Guess I'll make a sort of scarecrow and stuff it with straw. I'll get Eradicate to help me. Rad! I say, Rad! Where are you?"

"Heah I is, Massa Tom! Heah I is," called a colored man as he came around the corner of a small stable where he kept his mule Boomerang. "Was yo'-all callin' me?"

"Yes, Rad, I want you to help make a scarecrow."

"A scarecrow, Massa Tom! Good land a' massy! What fo' yo' want ob a scarecrow? Yo'-all ain't raisin' no corn, am yo'?"

"No, but I want something to shoot at when Ned Newton comes over tonight."

"Suffin t' shoot at? Why Massa Tom! Good land a' massy! Yo'-all ain't gwine t' hab no duel, am yo'?"

"No, Rad, but I want a life-size figure on which to try my new electric gun. Here are some old clothes, and if you will stuff them with rags and straw and fix them so they'll stand up, they'll do first-rate. Have it ready by night, and set it up at the far end of the shooting gallery."

"All right, Massa Tom. I'll jest do dat, fo' yo'," and leaving the colored man to stuff the figure, after he had showed him how, Tom went back into the house to read the paper which he had purchased that morning.

He skimmed over the news, thinking perhaps he might see something of the going abroad of Andy Foger with the German aeroplane, but there was nothing.

"I almost wish I was going to Europe," sighed Tom. "I will certainly have to get busy at something, soon. I haven't had any adventure since I won the prize at the Eagle Park aviation meet in my sky racer. Jove! That was some excitement! I'd like to do that over again, only I shouldn't want to have Dad so sick," for just before the race, Tom had saved his father's life by making a quick run in the aeroplane, to bring a celebrated surgeon to the invalid's aid.

"I certainly wish I could have some new adventures," mused Tom, as he turned the pages of the paper. "I could afford to take a trip around the earth after them, too, with the way money is coming in now. Yes, I do wish I could have some excitement. Hello, what's this! A big elephant hunt in Africa. Hundreds of the huge creatures captured in a trap—driven in by tame beasts. Some are shot for their tusks. Others will be sent to museums."

He was reading the headlines of the article that had attracted his attention, and, as he read, he became more and more absorbed in it. He read the story through twice, and then, with sparkling eyes, he exclaimed:

"That's just what I want. Elephant shooting in Africa! My! With my new electric rifle, and an airship, what couldn't a fellow do over in the dark continent! I've a good notion to go there! I wonder if Ned would go with me? Mr. Damon certainly would. Elephant shooting in Africa! In an airship! I could finish my new sky craft in short order if I wanted to. I've a good notion to do it!"

CHAPTER II

TRYING THE NEW GUN

While Tom Swift is thus absorbed in thinking about a chance to hunt elephants, we will take the opportunity to tell you a little more about him, and then go on with the story.

Many of you already know the young inventor, but those who do not may be interested it hearing that he is a young American lad, full of grit and ginger, who lives with his aged father in the town of Shopton, in New York State. Our hero was first introduced to the public in the book, "Tom Swift and His Motorcycle."

In that volume it was related how Tom bought a motor-cycle from a Mr. Wakefield Damon, of Waterford. Mr. Damon was an eccentric individual, who was continually blessing himself, some one else, or something belonging to him. His motor-cycle tried to climb a tree with him, and that was why he sold it to Tom. The two thus became acquainted, and their friendship grew from year to year.

After many adventures on his motor-cycle Tom got a motor-boat, and had some exciting times in that. One of the things he and his father and his chum, Ned Newton, did, was to rescue, from a burning balloon that had fallen into Lake Carlopa, an aeronaut named John Sharp. Later Tom and Mr. Sharp built an airship called the Red Cloud, and with Mr. Damon and some others had a series of remarkable fights.

In the Red Cloud they got on the track of some bank robbers, and captured them, thus foiling the plans of Andy Foger, a town bully, and one of Tom's enemies, and putting to confusion the plot of Mr. Foger, Andy's father.

After many adventures in the air Tom and his friends, in a submarine boat, invented by Mr. Swift, went under the ocean for sunken treasure and secured a large part of it.

It was not long after this that Tom conceived the idea of a powerful electric car, which proved, to be the speediest of the road, and in it he won a great race, and saved from ruin a bank in which his father and Mr. Damon were interested.

The sixth book of the series, entitled "Tom Swift and His Wireless Message," tells how, in testing a new electric airship, which a friend of Mr. Damon's had invented, Tom, the inventor and Mr. Damon were lost on an island in the middle of the ocean. There they found some castaways, among whom were Mr. and Mrs. Nestor, parents of Mary Nestor of Shopton, a girl of whom Tom was quite fond.

Tom Swift, after his arrival home, went on an expedition among a gang of men known as the "Diamond Makers" who were hidden in the Rocky Mountains. He was accompanied by Mr. Barcoe Jenks, one of the castaways of Earthquake Island. They found the diamond makers, and had some surprising adventures, barely escaping with their lives.

This did not daunt Tom, however, and he once more started off on an expedition in his airship the Red Cloud to Alaska, amid the caves of ice. He was searching for a valley of gold, and though he and his friends found it, they came to grief. The Fogers, father and son, tried to steal the gold from them, and, failing in that, incited the Eskimos against our friends. There was a battle, but the forces of nature were even more to be dreaded than the terrible savages.

The ice cave, in which the Red Cloud was stored, collapsed, crushing the gallant craft, and burying it out of sight forever under thousand of tons of the frozen bergs.

After a desperate journey Tom and his friends reached civilization, with a large supply of gold. Tom regretted very much the destruction of the airship, but he at once set to work on another—a monoplane this time, instead of a combined aeroplane and dirigible balloon. This new craft he called the Humming-Bird and it was a "sky racer" of terrific speed. In it, as we have said, Tom brought a specialist to operate on his father, when, because of a broken railroad bridge, the physician could not otherwise have gotten to Shopton. He and Tom traveled through the air at the rate of over one hundred miles an hour. Later, Tom took part in a big race for a ten-thousand-dollar prize, and won, defeating Andy Foger, and a number of well-known "bird-men" who used biplanes and monoplanes of a more or less familiar type.

The government became interested in Tom's craft, the Humming-Bird, and, as told in the ninth book of this series, Tom Swift and His Sky Racer, they secured some rights in the invention.

And now Tom, who had done nothing for several months following the great race—that is, nothing save to work on his new rifle—Tom, we say, sighed for new adventures.

"Well, Tom, what is on your mind?" asked his father at the supper table that evening. "What is worrying you?"

"Nothing is worrying me, Dad."

"You are thinking of something. I can see that. Are you afraid your electric rifle won't work as well as you hope, when Ned comes over to try it?"

"No, it isn't that, Dad. But I may as well tell you, I guess. I've been reading in the paper about a big elephant hunt in Africa, and I—"

"That's enough, Tom! You needn't say any more," interrupted Mr. Swift. "I can see which way the wind is blowing. You want to go to Africa with your new rifle."

"Well, Dad, not exactly—that is—"

"Now, Tom, you needn't deny it," and Mr. Swift laughed. "Well, I don't blame you a bit. You have been rather idle of late."

"I would like to go, Dad," admitted the young inventor, "only I'd never think of it while you weren't well."

"Don't worry about me, Tom. Of course I will be lonesome while you are gone, but don't let that stand in the way. If you want to go to Africa, you may start tomorrow, and take your new rifle with you."

"The rifle part would be all right, Dad, but if I went I'd want to take an airship along, and it will take me some little time to finish the Black Hawk, as I have named my new craft."

"Well, there's no special hurry, is there?" asked Mr. Swift. "The elephants in Africa are likely to stay there for some time. If you want to go, why don't you get right to work on the Black Hawk and make the trip? I'd like to go myself."

"I wish you would, Dad," exclaimed Tom eagerly.

"No, son, I couldn't think of it. I want to stay here and get well. Then I am going to resume work on my wireless motor. Perhaps I'll have it finished when you come back from Africa with an airship load of elephants' tusks."

"Perhaps," admitted the young inventor. "Well, Dad, I'll think of it. But now I'm going after my rifle, and—"

Tom was interrupted by a ring of the front-door bell, and Mrs. Baggert, the housekeeper, who was almost like a mother to the youth, went to answer it.

"It's Ned Newton, I guess," murmured Tom, and, a little later, his chum entered the room.

"Oh, I guess I'm early," said Ned. "Haven't you had supper yet, Tom?"

"Yes, we're just finished. Come on out and we'll try the gun."

"And practice shooting elephants," added Mr. Swift with a laugh, as he mentioned to Ned the latest idea of Tom.

"Say! That would be great!" cried the bank clerk. "I wish I could go!"

"Come along!" invited Tom cordially. "We'll have more fun than we did in the caves of ice," for Ned had gone on the voyage to Alaska.

The two youths went out to the shed where the rifle gallery had been built. The new electric weapon was out there, and Eradicate Sampson, the colored man, who was a sort of servant and man-of-all-work about the Swift household, had set up the scarecrow figure at the end of the gallery.

"Now we'll try some shots," said Tom, as he took the gun out of the case. "Just turn on a few more lights, will you, Mr. Jackson," and the engineer, who was employed by Tom and his father to aid them in their inventive work, did as requested.

The gallery was now brilliantly illuminated, with the reflectors throwing the beams on the big stuffed figure, which, save for a face, looked very much like a human being, standing at the end of the gallery.

"I don't suppose you want to go down there and hold it, while I shoot at it; do you, Rad?" asked Tom jokingly, as he prepared the electric rifle for use.

"No indeedy, I don't!" cried Eradicate. "Yo'-all will hab t' scuse me, Massa Tom. I think I'll be goin' now."

"What's your hurry?" asked Ned, as he saw the colored man hastily preparing to leave the improvised gallery.

"I spects I'd better fro' down some mo' straw fo' a bed fo' my mule Boomerang!" exclaimed Eradicate, as he hastily slid out of the door, and shut it after him.

"Rad is nervous," remarked Tom. "He doesn't like this gun. Well, it certainly does great execution."

"How does it work'" asked Ned, as he looked at the curious gun. The electric weapon was not unlike an ordinary heavy rifle in appearance save that the barrel was a little longer, and the stock larger in every way. There were also a number of wheels, levers, gears and gages on the stock.

"It works by electricity," explained Tom.

"That is, the force comes from a powerful current of stored electricity."

"Oh, then you have storage batteries in the stock?"

"Not exactly. There are no batteries, but the current is a sort of wireless kind. It is stored in a cylinder, just as compressed air or gases are stored, and can be released as I need it."

"And when it's all gone, what do you do?"

"Make more power by means of a small dynamo."

"And does it shoot lead bullets?"

"Not at all. There are no bullets used."

"Then how does it kill?"

"By means of a concentrated charge of electricity which is shot from the barrel with great force. You can't see it, yet it is there. It's just as if you concentrated a charge of electricity of five thousand volts into a small globule the size of a bullet. That flies through space, strikes the object aimed at and—well, we'll see what it does in a minute. Mr. Jackson, just put that steel plate up in front of the scarecrow; will you?"

The engineer proceeded to put into place a section of steel armor-plate before the stuffed figure.

"You don't mean to say you're going to shoot through that, do you?" asked Ned in surprise.

"Surely. The electric bullets will pierce anything. They'll go through a brick wall as easily as the x-rays do. That's one valuable feature of my rifle. You don't have to see the object you aim at. In fact you can fire through a house, and kill something on the other side."

"I should think that would be dangerous."

"It would be, only I can calculate exactly, by means of an automatic arrangement, just how far the charge of electricity will go. It stops short just at the limit of the range, and is not effective beyond that. Otherwise, if I did not limit it and if I fired at the scarecrow, through the piece of steel, and the bullet hit the figure, it would go on, passing through whatever else was in the way, until its power was lost. I use the term 'bullet,' though as I said, it isn't properly one."

"By Jove, Tom, it certainly is a dangerous weapon!"

"Yes, the range-limit idea is a new one. That's what I've been working on lately. There are other features of the gun which I'll explain later, particularly the power it has to shoot out luminous bars of light. But now we'll see what it will do to the image."

Tom took his place at the end of the range, and began to adjust some valves and levers. In spite of the fact that the gun was larger than an ordinary rifle, it was not as heavy as the United States Army weapon.

Tom aimed at the armor-plate, and, by means of an arrangement on the rifle, he could tell exactly when he was pointing at the scarecrow, even though he could not see it.

"Here she goes!" he suddenly exclaimed.

Ned watched his chum. The young inventor pressed a small button at the side of the rifle barrel, about where the trigger should have been. There was no sound, no smoke, no flame and not the slightest jar.

Yet as Ned watched he saw the steel plate move slightly. The next instant the scarecrow figure seemed to fly all to pieces. There was a shower of straw, rags and old clothes, which fell in a shapeless heap at the end of the range.

"Say. I guess you did for that fellow, all right!" exclaimed Ned.

"It looks so," admitted Tom, with a note of pride in his voice. "Now we'll try another test."

As he laid aside his rifle in order to help Mr. Jackson shift the steel plate there was a series of yells outside the shed.

"What's that?" asked Tom, in some alarm.

"Sounds like some one calling," answered Ned.

"It is," agreed Mr. Jackson. "Perhaps Eradicate's mule has gotten loose. I guess we'd better—"

He did not finish, for the shouts increased in volume, and Tom and Ned could hear some one yelling:

"I'll have the law on you for this! I'll have you arrested, Tom Swift! What do you mean by trying to kill me? Where are you? Don't try to hide away, now. You were trying to shoot me, and I'm not going to have it!"

Some one pounded on the door of the shed.

"It's Barney Moker!" exclaimed Tom. "I wonder what can have happened?"

CHAPTER III

A DIFFICULT TEST

Tom Swift opened the door of the improvised rifle gallery and looked out. By the light of a full moon, which shone down from a cloudless sky, he saw a man standing at the portal. The man's face was distorted with rage, and he shook his fist at the young inventor.

"What do you mean by shooting at me?" he demanded. "What do you mean, I say? The idea of scaring honest folks out of their wits, and making 'em think the end of the world has come! What do you mean by it? Why don't you answer me? I say, Tom Swift, why don't you answer me?"

"Because you don't give me a chance, Mr. Moker," replied our hero.

"I want to know why you shot at me? I demand to know!" and Mr. Moker, who was a sort of miserly town character, living all alone in a small house, just beyond Tom's home, again shook his fist almost in the lad's face. "Why don't you tell me? Why don't you tell me?" he shouted.

"I will, if you give me a chance!" fairly exploded Tom. "If you can be cool for five minutes, and come inside and tell me what happened I'll be glad to answer any of your questions, Mr. Moker. I didn't shoot at you."

"Yes, you did! You tried to shoot a hole through me!"

"Tell me about it?" suggested Tom, as the excited man calmed down somewhat. "Are you hurt?"

"No, but it isn't your fault that I'm not. You tried hard enough to hurt me. Here I am, sitting at my table reading, and, all at once something goes through the side of the house, whizzes past my ear, makes my hair fairly stand up on end, and goes outside the other side of the house. What kind of bullets do you use, Tom Swift? that's what I want to know. They went through the side of my house, and never left a mark. I demand to know what kind they are."

"I'll tell you, if you'll only give me a chance," went on Tom wearily. "How do you know it was me shooting?"

"How do I know? Why, doesn't the end of this shooting gallery of yours point right at my house? Of course it does; you can't deny it!"

Tom did not attempt to, and Mr. Moker went on:

"Now what do you mean by it?"

"If any of the bullets from my electric gun went near you, it was a mistake, and I'm sorry for it," said Tom.

"Well, they did, all right," declared the excited man. "They went right past my ear."

"I don't see how they could," declared Tom. "I was trying my new electric rifle, but I had the limit set for two hundred feet, the length of the gallery. That is, the electrical discharge couldn't go beyond that distance."

"I don't know what it was, but it went through the side of my house all the same," insisted Mr. Moker. "It didn't make a hole, but it scorched the wall paper a little."

"I don't see how it could," declared Tom. "It couldn't possibly have gone over two hundred feet with the gage set for that distance." He paused suddenly, and hurried over to where he had placed his gun. Catching up the weapon he looked at the gage dial. Then he uttered an exclamation.

"I'm sorry to admit that you are right, Mr. Moker!" he said finally. "I made a mistake. The gage is set for a thousand feet instead of two hundred. I forgot to change it. The charge, after passing through the steel plate, and the scarecrow figure, destroying the latter, went on, and shot through the side of your house."

"Ha! I knew you were trying to shoot me!" exclaimed the still angry man. "I'll have the law on you for this!"

"Oh, that's all nonsense!" broke in Ned Newton "Everybody knows Tom Swift wouldn't try to shoot you, or any one else, Mr. Moker."

"Then why did he shoot at me?"

"That was a mistake," explained Tom, "and I apologize to you for it."

"Humph! A lot of good that would do me, if I'd been killed!" muttered the miser. "I'm going to sue you for this. You might have put me in my grave."

"Impossible!" exclaimed Tom.

"Why impossible?" demanded the visitor.

"Because I had so set the rifle that almost the entire force of the electrical bullet was expended in blowing apart the scarecrow figure I made for a test," explained Tom. "All that passed through your house was a small charge, and, if it HAD hit you there would have been no more than a little shock, such as you would feel in taking hold of an electric battery."

"How do I know this?" asked the man cunningly. "You say so, but for all I know you may have wanted to kill me."

"Why?" asked Tom, trying not to laugh.

"Oh, so you might get some of my money. Of course I ain't got none," the miser went on quickly, "but folks thinks I've got a lot, and I have to be on the lookout all the while, or they'd murder me for it."

"I wouldn't," declared the young inventor. "It was a mistake. Only part of the spent charge passed near you. Why, if it had been a powerful charge you would never have been able to come over here. I set the main charge to go off inside the scarecrow, and it did so, as you can see by looking at what's left of it," and he pointed to the pile of clothes and rags.

"How do I know this?" insisted the miser with a leer at the two lads.

"Because if the charge had gone off either before or after it passed through the figure, it would not have caused such havoc of the cloth and straw," explained Tom. "First the charge would have destroyed the steel plate, which it passed through without even denting it. Why, look here, I will now fire the rifle at short range, and set it to destroy the plate. See what happens."

He quickly adjusted the weapon, and aimed it at the plate, which, had again been set up on the range. This time Tom was careful to set the gage so that even a small part of the spent charge would not go outside the gallery.

The young inventor pressed the button, and instantly the heavy steel plate was bent, torn and twisted as though a small sized cannon ball had gone through it.

"That's what the rifle will do at short range," said Tom. "Don't worry, Mr. Moker, you didn't have a narrow escape. You were in no danger at all, though I apologize for the fright I caused you."

"Humph! That's an easy way to get out of it!" exclaimed the miser. "I believe I could sue you for damages, anyhow. Look at my scorched wall paper."

"Oh, I'll pay for that," said Tom quickly, for he did not wish to have trouble with the unpleasant man. "Will ten dollars be enough?" He knew that the whole room could be repapered for that, and he did not believe the wall-covering was sufficiently damaged for such work to be necessary.

"Well, if you'll make it twelve dollars, I won't say anything more about it," agreed the miser craftily, "though it's worth thirteen dollars, if it is a penny. Give me twelve dollars, Tom Swift, and I won't prosecute you."

"All right, twelve dollars it shall be," responded the young inventor, passing over the money, and glad to be rid of the unpleasant character.

"And after this, just fire that gun of yours the other way," suggested Mr. Moker as he went out, carefully folding the bills which Tom had handed him.

"Hum! that was rather queer," remarked Ned, after a pause.

"It sure was," agreed his chum. "This rifle will do more than I thought it would. I'll have to be more careful. I was sure I set the gage for two hundred feet. I'll have to invent some automatic attachment to prevent it being discharged when the gage is set wrong." Let us state here that Tom did this, and never had another accident.

"Well, does this end the test?" asked Ned.

"No, indeed. I want you to try it, while I look on," spoke Tom. "We haven't any more stuffed figures to fire at, but I'll set up some targets. Come on, try your luck at a shot."

"I'm afraid I might disturb Mr. Moker, or some of the neighbors."

"No danger. I've got it adjusted right now. Come on, see if you can shatter this steel target," and Tom set up a small one at the end of the range.

Then, having properly fixed the weapon, Tom handed it to his chum, and, taking his place in a protected part of the gallery, prepared to watch the effect of the shot.

"Let her go!" cried Tom, and Ned pressed the button.

The effect was wonderful. Though there was no noise, smoke nor flame, the steel plate seemed to crumple up, and collapse as if it had been melted in the fire. There was a jagged hole through the center, but some frail boards back of it were not even splintered.

"Good shot!" cried Tom enthusiastically. "I had the distance gage right that time."

"You sure did," agreed Ned. "The electric bullet stopped as soon as it did its work on the plate. What's next?"

"I'm going to try a difficult test," explained Tom. "You know I said the gun would shoot luminous charges?"

"Yes."

"Well, I'm going to try that, now. I wish we had another image to shoot at, but I'll take a big dry-goods box, and make believe it's an elephant. Now, this is going to be a hard test, such as we'd meet with, if we were hunting in Africa. I want you to help me."

"What am I to do?" asked Ned.

"I want you to go outside," explained Tom, "set up a dry-goods box against the side of the little hill back of the shed, and not tell me where you put it. Then I'll go out, and, by means of the luminous charge, I'll locate the box, set the distance gage, and destroy it."

"Well, you can see it anyhow, in the moonlight," objected Ned.

"No, the moon is under a cloud now," explained Tom, looking out of a window. "It's quite dark, and will give me just the test I want for my new electric rifle."

"But won't it be dangerous, firing in the dark? Suppose you misjudge the distance, and the bullet, or charge, files off and hits some one?"

"It can't. I'll set the distance gage before I shoot. But if I should happen to make a mistake the charge will go into the side of the hill, and spend itself there. There is no danger. Go ahead, and set up the box, and then come and tell me. Mr. Jackson will help you."

Ned and the engineer left the gallery. As Tom had said, it was very dark now, and if Tom could see in the night to hit a box some distance away, his weapon would be all that he claimed for it.

"This will do," said the engineer, as he pointed to a box, one of several piled up outside the shed. The two could hardly see to make their way along, carrying it to the foot of the hill, and they stumbled several times. But at last it was in position, and then Ned departed to call Tom, and have him try the difficult test—that of hitting an object in the dark.

CHAPTER IV

BIG TUSKS WANTED

"Well, are you all ready for me?" asked the young inventor, as he took up his curious weapon, and followed Ned out into the yard. It was so dark that they had fairly to stumble along.

"Yes, we're ready," answered Ned. "And you'll be a good one, Tom, if you do this stunt. Now stand here" he went on, as he indicated a place as well as he could in the dark. "The box is somewhere in that direction," and he waved his hand vaguely. "I'm not going to tell you any more, and let's see you find it."

"Oh, I will, all right—or, rather, my electric rifle will," asserted Tom.

The inventor of the curious and terrible weapon took his position. Behind him stood Ned and Mr. Jackson, and just before Tom was ready to fire, his father came stalking through the darkness, calling to them.

"Are you there, Tom?"

"Yes Dad, is anything the matter?"

"No, but I thought I'd like to see what luck you have. Rad was saying you were going to have a test in the dark."

"I'm about ready for it," replied Tom. "I'm going to blow up a box that I can't see. You know how it's done, Dad, for you helped me in perfecting the luminous charge, but it's going to be something of a novelty to the others. Here we go, now!"

Tom raised his rifle, and aimed it in the dark. Ned Newton, straining his eyes to see, was sure the young inventor was pointing the gun at least twenty feet to one side of where the box was located, but he said nothing, for from experiences in the past, he realized that Tom knew what he was doing.

There was a little clicking sound, as the youth moved some gear wheel on his gun. Then there came a faint crackling noise, like some distant wireless apparatus beginning to flash a message through space.

Suddenly a little ball of purplish light shot through the darkness and sped forward like some miniature meteor. It shed a curious illuminating glow all about, and the ground, and the objects on it were brought into relief as by a lightning flash.

An instant later the light increased in intensity, and seemed to burst like some piece of aerial fireworks. There was a bright glare, in which Ned and the others could see the various buildings about the shed. They could see each other's faces, and they looked pale and ghastly in the queer glow. They could see the box, brought into bold relief, where Ned and the engineer had placed it.

Then, before the light had died away, they witnessed a curious sight. The heavy wooden box seemed to dissolve, to collapse and to crumple up like one of paper, and ere the last rays of the illuminating bullet faded, the watchers saw the splinters of wood fall back with a clatter in a little heap on the spot where the dry-goods case had been.

A silence followed, and the darkness was all the blacker by contrast with the intense light. At length Tom spoke, and he could not keep from his voice a note of triumph.

"Well, did I do it?" he asked.

"You sure did!" exclaimed Ned heartily.

"Fine!" cried Mr. Swift.

"Golly! I wouldn't gib much fo' de hide ob any burglar what comed around heah!" muttered Eradicate Sampson. "Dat box am knocked clean into nuffiness, Massa Tom."

"That's what I wanted to do," explained the lad. "And I guess this will end the test for tonight."

"But I don't exactly understand it," spoke Ned, as they all moved toward the Swift home, Eradicate going to the stable to see how his mule was. "Do you have two kinds of bullets, Tom, one for night and one for the daytime?"

"No," answered Tom, "there is only one kind of bullet, and, as I have said, that isn't a bullet at all. That is, you can't see it, or handle it, but you can feel it. Strictly speaking, it is a concentrated discharge of wireless electricity directed against a certain object. You can't see it any more than you can see a lightning bolt, though that is sometimes visible as a ball of fire. My electric rifle bullets are similar to a discharge of lightning, except that they are invisible."

"But we saw the one just now," objected Ned.

"No, you didn't see the bullet," said Tom.

"You saw the illuminating flash which I send out just before I fire, to reveal the object I am to hit. That is another part of my rifle and is only used at night."

"You see I shoot out a ball of electrical fire which will disclose the target, or the enemy at whom I am firing. As soon as that is discharged the rifle automatically gets ready to shoot the electric charge, and I have only to press the proper button, and the 'bullet,' as I call it, follows on the heels of the ball of light. Do you see?"

"Perfectly," exclaimed Ned with a laugh. "What a gun that would be for hunting, since most all wild beasts come out only at night."

"That was one object in making this invention," said Tom. "I only hope I get a chance to use it now."

"I thought you were going to Africa after elephants," spoke Mr. Swift.

"Well, I did think of it," admitted Tom, "but I haven't made any definite plans. But come into the house, Ned, and I'll show you more in detail how my rifle works."

Thereupon the two chums spent some time going into the mysteries of the new weapon. Mr. Swift and Mr. Jackson were also much interested, for, though they had seen the gun previously and had helped Tom perfect it, they had not yet tired of discussing its merits.

Ned stayed quite late that night, and promised to come over the next day, and watch Tom do some more shooting.

"I'll show you how to use it, too," promised the young inventor, and he was as good as his word, initiating Ned into the mysteries of the electric rifle, and showing him to store the charges of death-dealing electricity in the queer-looking stock.

For a week after that Tom and Ned practiced with the terrible gun, taking care not to have any more mishaps like the one that had marked the first night. They were both good shots with ordinary weapons and it was not long before they had equaled their record with the new instrument.

It was one warm afternoon, when Tom was out in the meadow at one side of his house, practicing with his rifle on some big boxes he had set up for targets, that he saw an elderly man standing close to the fence watching him. When Tom blew to pieces a particularly large packing-case, standing a long distance away from it, the stranger called to the youth.

"I beg your pardon," he said, "but is that a dynamite gun you are using?"

"No, it's an electric rifle," was the answer.

"Would you mind telling me something about it?" went on the elderly man, and as Tom's weapon was now fully protected by patents, the young inventor cordially invited the stranger to come nearer and see how it worked.

"That's the greatest thing I ever saw!" exclaimed the man enthusiastically when Tom had blown up another box, and had told of the illumination for night firing. "The most wonderful weapon I ever heard of! What a gun it would be in my business."

"What is your trade?" asked Tom curiously, for he had noted that the man, while aged, was rugged and hearty, and his skin was tanned a leathery brown, showing that he was much in the open air.

"I'm a hunter," was the reply, "a hunter of big game, principally elephants, hippos and rhinoceroses. I've just finished a season in Africa, and I'm going back there again soon. I came on to New York to get a new elephant gun. I've got a sister living over in Waterford, and I've been visiting her. I went out for a stroll today, and I came farther than I intended. That's how I happened to be passing here."

"A sister in Waterford, eh?" mused Tom, wondering whether the elephant hunter had met Mr. Damon. "And how soon are you going back to Africa, Mr.—er—" and Tom hesitated.

"Durban is my name, Alexander Durban," said the old man. "Why, I am to start back in a few weeks. I've got an order for a pair of big elephant tusks—the largest I can get for a wealthy New York man,— and I'm anxious to fulfil the contract. The game isn't what it once was. There's more competition and the elephants are scarcer. So I've got to hustle."

"I got me a new gun. But my! it's nothing to what yours is. With that weapon I could do about as I pleased. I could do night hunting, which is hard in the African jungle. Then I wouldn't have any trouble getting the big tusks I'm after. I could get a pair of them, and live easy the rest of my life. Yes, I wouldn't ask anything better than a gun like yours. But I s'pose they cost like the mischief?" He looked a question at Tom.

"This is the only one there is," was the lad's answer. "But I am very glad to have met you, Mr. Durban. Won't you come into the house? I'm sure my father will be glad to see you, and I have something I'd like to talk to you about," and Tom, with many wild ideas in his head, led the old elephant hunter toward the house.

The dream of the young inventor might come true after all.

CHAPTER V

RUSH WORK

Mr. Swift made the African hunter warmly welcome, and listened with pride to the words of praise Mr. Durban bestowed on Tom regarding the rifle.

"Yes, my boy has certainly done wonders along the inventive line," said Mr. Swift.

"Not half as much as you have, Dad," interrupted the lad, for Tom was a modest youth.

"You should see his sky racer," went on the old inventor.

"Sky racer? What's that?" asked Mr. Durban. "Is it another kind of gun or cannon?"

"It's an aeroplane—an airship," explained Mr. Swift.

"An airship!" exclaimed the old elephant hunter. "Say, you don't mean that you make balloons, do you?"

"Well, they're not exactly balloons," replied Tom, as he briefly explained what an aeroplane was, for Mr. Durban, having been in the wilds of the jungle so much, had had very little chance to see the wonders and progress of civilization.

"They are better than balloons," went on Tom, "for they can go where you want them to."

"Say! That's the very thing!" cried the old hunter enthusiastically. "If there's one thing more than another that is needed in hunting in Africa it's an airship. The travel through the jungle is something fierce, and that, more than anything else, interferes with my work. I can't cover ground enough, and when I do get on the track of a herd of elephants, and they get away, it's sometimes a week before I can catch up to them again."

"For, in spite of their size, elephants can travel very fast, and once they get on the go, nothing can stop them. An airship would be the very thing to hunt elephants with in Africa—an airship and this electric rifle. I wonder why you haven't thought of going, Tom Swift."

"I have thought of it," answered the young inventor, "and that's why I asked you in. I want to talk about it."

"Do you mean you want to go?" demanded the old man eagerly.

"I certainly do!"

"Then I'm your man! Say, Tom Swift, I'd be proud to have you go to Africa with me. I'd be proud to have you a member of my hunting party, and, though I don't like to boast, still if you'll ask any of the big-game people they'll tell you that not every one can accompany Aleck Durban."

Tom realized that he was speaking to an authority and a most desirable companion, should he go to Africa, and he was very glad of the chance that had made him acquainted with the veteran hunter.

"Will you go with me?" asked Mr. Durban. "You and your electric gun and your airship? Will you come to Africa to hunt elephants, and help me get the big tusks I'm after?"

"I will!" exclaimed Tom.

"Then we'll start at once. There's no need of delaying here any longer."

"Oh, but I haven't an airship ready," said the young inventor. The face of the old hunter expressed his disappointment.

"Then we'll have to give up the scheme," he said ruefully.

"Not at all," Tom told him. "I have all the material on hand for building a new airship. I have had it in mind for some time, and I have done some work on it. I stopped it to perfect my electric rifle, but, now that is done, I'll tackle the Black Hawk again, and rush that to completion."-

"The Black Hawk?" repeated Mr. Durban, wonderingly.

"Yes, that's what I will name my new craft. The RED CLOUD was destroyed, and so I thought I'd change the color this time, and avoid bad luck."

"Good!" exclaimed the hunter. "When do you think you can have it finished?"

"Oh, possibly in a month—perhaps sooner, and then we will go to Africa and hunt elephants!"

"Bless my ivory paper cutter!" exclaimed a voice in the hall just outside the library. "Bless my fingernails! But who's talking about going to Africa?"

The old hunter looked at Tom and his father in surprise, but the young inventor laughing and going to the door, called out:

"Come on in, Mr. Damon. I didn't hear you ring. There is some one here from your town."

"Is it my wife?" asked the odd gentleman who was always blessing something. "She said she was going to her mother's to spend a few weeks, and so I thought I'd come over here and see if you had anything new on the program. The first thing I hear is that you are going to Africa. And so there's some one from Waterford in there, eh? Is it my wife?"

"No," answered Tom with another laugh. "Come on in Mr. Damon."

"Bless my toothpick!" exclaimed the odd gentleman, as he saw the grizzled elephant hunter sitting between Tom and Mr. Swift. "I have seen you somewhere before, my dear sir."

"Yes," admitted Mr. Durban, "if you're from Waterford you have probably seen me traveling about the streets there. I'm stopping with my sister, Mrs. Douglass, but I can't stand it to be in the house much, so I'm out of doors, wandering about a good bit of the time. I miss my jungle. But we'll soon be in Africa, Tom Swift and me."

"Is it possible, Tom?" asked Mr. Damon. "Bless my diamond mines! but what are you going to do next?"

"It's hard to say," was the answer. "But you came just in time. Mr. Damon. I'm going to rush work on the Black Hawk, my newest airship, and we'll leave for elephant land inside of a month, taking my new electric rifle along. Will you come?"

"Bless my penknife! I never thought of such a thing. I—I—guess—no, I don't know about it—yes, I'll go!" he suddenly exclaimed. "I'll go! Hurrah for the elephants!" and he jumped up and shook hands in turn with Mr. Durban, to whom he had been formally introduced, and with Tom and Mr. Swift.

"Then it's all settled but the details," declared the youth, "and now I'll call in Mr. Jackson, and we'll talk about how soon we can have the airship ready."

"My, but you folks are almost as speedy as a herd of the big elephants themselves!" exclaimed Mr. Durban, and with the advent of the engineer the talk turned to things mechanical among Tom and Mr. Jackson and Mr. Damon, while Mr. Durban told Mr. Swift hunting stories which the old inventor greatly enjoyed.

The next day Tom engaged two machinists who had worked for him building airships before, and in the next week rush work began on the new Black Hawk. Meanwhile Mr. Durban was a frequent visitor at Tom's home, where he learned to use the new rifle, declaring it was even more wonderful than he had at first supposed.

"That will get the elephants!" he exclaimed. It did, as you shall soon learn, and it also was the means of saving several lives in the wilds of the African jungle.

CHAPTER VI

NEWS FROM ANDY

Tom Swift's former airship, the Red Cloud, had been such a fine craft, and had done such good service that he thought, in building a successor, that he could do no better than to follow the design of the skyship which had been destroyed in the ice caves. But, on talking with the old elephant hunter, and learning something of the peculiarities of the African jungle the young inventor decided on certain changes.

In general the Black Hawk would be on the lines of the Red Cloud but it would be smaller and lighter and would also be capable of swifter motion.

"You want it so that it will rise and descend quickly and at sharp angles," said Mr. Durban.

"Why," inquired Tom.

"Because in Africa, at least in the part where we will go, there are wide patches of jungle and forest, with here and there big open places. If you are skimming along close to the ground, in an open place, in pursuit of a herd of elephants and they should suddenly plunge into the forest, you would want to be able to rise above the trees quickly."

"That's so," admitted Tom. "Then I'll have to use a smaller gas bag than we had on the other ship, for the air resistance to that big one made us go slowly at times."

"Will it be as safe with a small bag?" Mr. Damon wanted to know.

"Yes, for I will use a more powerful gas, so that we will be more quickly lifted," said the young inventor. "I will also retain the aeroplane feature, so that the Black Hawk will be a combined biplane and dirigible balloon. But it will have many new features. I have the plans all drawn for a new style of gas generating apparatus, and I think it can be made in time."

There were busy days about the Swift home. Mrs. Baggert, the housekeeper, was in despair. She said the good meals she got ready were wasted, because no one would come to table when they were ready. She would ring the bell, and announce that dinner would be served in five minutes.

Then Tom would shout from his workshop that he could not leave until he had inserted a certain lever in place. Mr. Jackson would positively decline to sit down until he had screwed fast some part of a machine. Even Mr. Swift, who, because of his recent illness, was not allowed to do much, would often delay his meal to test some new style of gears.

As for Mr. Damon, it was to be expected that he would be eccentric as he always was. He was not an expert mechanic, but he knew something of machinery and was of considerable help to Tom in the rush work on the airship. He would hear the dinner bell ring, and would exclaim:

"Bless my napkin ring! I can't come now. I have to fix up this electrical register first."

And so it would go. Eradicate and Boomerang, his mule, were the only ones who ate regularly, and they always insisted on stopping at exactly twelve o'clock to partake of the noonday meal.

"'Cause ef I didn't," explained the colored man, "dat contrary mule ob mine would lay down in de dust ob de road an' not move a step, lessen' he got his oats. So dat's why we has t' eat, him an' me."

"Well, I'm glad there's some one who's got sense," murmured Mrs. Baggert. Eradicate and Boomerang were of great service in the hurried work that followed, for the colored man in his cart brought from town, or from the freight depot, many things that Tom needed.

The young inventor was very enthusiastic about his proposed trip, and at night, after a hard day's work in the shop, he would read books on African hunting, or he would sit and listen to the stories told by Mr. Durban. And the latter knew how to tell hunting tales, for he had been long in his dangerous calling, and had had many narrow escapes.

"And there are other dangers than from elephants and wild beasts in Africa," he said.

"Bless my toothbrush!" exclaimed Mr. Damon. "Do you mean cannibals, Mr. Durban?"

"Some cannibals," was the reply. "But they're not the worst. I mean the red pygmies. I hope we don't get into their clutches."

"Red pygmies!" repeated Tom, wonderingly.

"Yes, they're a tribe of little creatures, about three feet high, covered with thick reddish hair, who live in the central part of Africa, near some of the best elephant-hunting ground. They are wild, savage and ferocious, and what they lack individually in strength, they make up in numbers. They're like little red apes, and woe betide the unlucky hunter who falls into their merciless hands. They treat him worse than the cannibals do."

"Then we'll look out for them," said Tom. "But I fancy my electric rifle will make them give us a wide berth."

"It's a great gun," admitted the old hunter with a shake of his head, "but those red pygmies are terrible creatures. I hope we don't get them on our trail. But tell me, Tom, how are you coming on with the airship? for I don't know much about mechanics, and to me it looks as if it would never be put together. It's like one of those queer puzzles I've seen 'em selling in the streets of London."

"Oh, it's nearer ready than it looks to be," said Tom. "We'll have it assembled, and ready for a trial in about two weeks more."

Work on the Black Hawk was rushed more than ever in the next few days, another extra machinist being engaged. Then the craft began to assume shape and form, and with the gas bag partly inflated and the big planes stretching out from either side, it began to look something like the ill-fated Red Cloud.

"It's going to be a fine ship!" cried Tom enthusiastically, one day, as he went to the far side of the ship to get a perspective view of it. "We'll make good time in this."

"Are you going to sail all the way to Africa—across the ocean—in her?" asked Mr. Durban, in somewhat apprehensive tones.

"Oh, no," replied Tom. "I believe she would be capable of taking us across the ocean, but there is no need of running any unnecessary risks. I want to get her safely to Africa, and have her do stunts in elephant land."

"Then what are your plans?" asked the hunter.

"We'll put her together here," said Tom, "give her a good try-out to see that she works well, and then pack her up for shipment to the African coast by steamer. We'll go on the same ship, and when we arrive we'll put the Black Hawk together again, and set sail for the interior."

"Good idea," commented Mr. Durban. "Now, if you've no objections, I'm going to do a little practice with the electric rifle."

"Go ahead," assented Tom. "There comes Ned Newton; he'll be glad of a chance for a few shots while I work on this new propeller motor. It just doesn't suit me."

The bank clerk, who had arranged to go to Africa with Tom, was seen advancing toward the aeroplane shed. In his hand Ned held a paper, and as he saw Tom he called out:

"Have you heard the news?"

"What news?" inquired the young inventor.

"About Andy Foger. He and his aeroplane are lost!"

"Lost!" cried Tom, for in spite of the mean way the bully had treated him our hero did not wish him any harm.

"Well, not exactly lost," went on Ned, as he held out the paper to Tom, "but he and his sky-craft have disappeared."

"Disappeared?"

"Yes. You know he and that German, Mr. Landbacher, went over to Europe to give some aviation exhibitions. Well, I see by this paper that they went to Egypt, and were doing a high-flying stunt there, when a gale sprang up, they lost control of the aeroplane and it was swept out of sight."

"In which direction; out to sea?"

"No, toward the interior of Africa."

"Toward the interior of Africa!" cried Tom. "And that's where we're going in a couple of weeks. Andy in Africa!"

"'Maybe we'll see him there," suggested Ned.

"Well, I certainly hope we do not!" exclaimed Tom, as he turned back to his work, with an undefinable sense of fear in his heart.

CHAPTER VII

THE BLACK HAWK FLIES

It was with no little surprise that the news of the plight that was said to have befallen Andy Foger was received by Tom and his associates. The newspaper had quite an account of the affair, and, even allowing the usual discount for the press dispatches, it looked as if the former bully was in rather distressing circumstances.

"He won't have to be carried very far into Africa to be in a bad country," said the old hunter. "Of course, some parts of the continent are all right, and for me, I like it all, where there's hunting to be had. But I guess your young friend Foger won't care for it."

"He's no friend of ours," declared Ned, as Tom was reading the newspaper account. "Still, I don't wish him any bad luck, and I do hope he doesn't become the captive of the red pygmies."

"So do I," echoed the old hunter fervently. There was no news of Andy in the papers the next day, though there were cable dispatches speculating on what might have happened to him and the airship. In Shopton the dispatches created no little comment, and it was said that Mr. Foger was going to start for Africa at once to rescue his son. This, however, could not be confirmed.

Meanwhile Tom and his friends were very busy over the Black Hawk. Every hour saw the craft nearer completion, for the young inventor had had much experience in this sort of work now, and knew just how to proceed.

To Mr. Damon were intrusted certain things which he could well attend to, and though he frequently stopped to bless his necktie or his shoelaces, still he got along fairly well.

There would be no necessity of purchasing supplies in this country, for they could get all they needed in the African city of Majumba, on the western coast, where they planned to land. There the airship would be put together, stocked with provisions and supplies, and they would begin their journey inland. They planned to head for Buka Meala, crossing the Congo River, and then go into the very interior of the heart of the dark continent.

As we have described in detail, in the former books of this series, the construction of Tom Swift's airship, the Red Cloud, and as the Black Hawk was made in a similar manner to that, we will devote but brief space to it now. As the story proceeds, and the need arises for a description of certain features, we will give them to you, so that you will have a clear idea of what a wonderful craft it was.

Sufficient to say that there was a gas bag, made of a light but strong material, and capable of holding enough vapor, of a new and secret composition, to lift the airship with its load. This was the dirigible-balloon feature of the craft, and with the two powerful propellers, fore and aft (in which particular the Black Hawk differed from the Red Cloud which had two forward propellers);—with these two powerful wooden screws, as we have said, the new ship could travel swiftly without depending on the wing planes.

But as there is always a possibility of the gas bag being punctured, or the vapor suddenly escaping from one cause or another, Tom did not depend on this alone to keep his craft afloat. It was a perfect aeroplane, and with the gas bag entirely empty could be sent scudding along at any height desired. To enable it to rise by means of the wings, however, it was necessary to start it in motion along the ground, and for this purpose wheels were provided.

There was a large body or car to the craft, suspended from beneath the gas bag, and in this car were the cabins, the living, sleeping and eating apartments, the storerooms and the engine compartment.

This last was a marvel of skill, for it contained besides the gas machine, and the motor for working the propellers, dynamos, gages, and instruments for telling the speed and height, motors for doing various pieces of work, levers, wheels, cogs, gears, tanks for storing the lifting gas, and other features of interest.

There were several staterooms for the use of the young captain and the passengers, an observation and steering tower, a living-room, where they could all assemble as the ship was sailing through the air, and a completely equipped kitchen.

This last was Mr. Damon's special pride, as he was a sort of cook, and he liked nothing better than to get up a meal when the craft was two or three miles high, and scudding along at seventy-five miles an hour.

In addition there were to be taken along many scientific instruments, weapons of defense and offense, in addition to the electric rifle, and various other objects which will be spoken of in due time.

"Well," remarked Tom Swift one afternoon, following a hard day's work in the shop, "I think, if all goes well, and we have good weather, I'll give the Black Hawk a trial tomorrow."

"Do you think it will fly?" asked Ned.

"There is no telling," was the answer of the young inventor. "These things are more or less guesswork, even when you make two exactly alike. As far as I can tell, we have now a better craft than the Red Cloud was, but it remains to be seen how she will behave."

They worked late that night, putting the finishing touches on the Black Hawk, and in the morning the new airship was wheeled out of the shed, and placed on the level starting ground, ready for the trial flight.

Only the bare machinery was in her, as yet, and the gas bag had not been inflated as Tom wanted to try the plane feature first. But the vapor machine was all ready to start generating the gas whenever it was needed. Nor was the Black Hawk painted and decorated as she would be when ready to be sent to Africa. On the whole, she looked rather crude as she rested there on the bicycle wheels, awaiting the starting of the big propellers. As the stores and supplies were not yet in, Tom took aboard, in addition to Mr. Damon, Ned, his father, Mr. Jackson and Mr. Durban, some bags of sand to represent the extra weight that would have to be carried.

"If she'll rise with this load she'll do," announced the young inventor, as he went carefully over the craft, looking to see that everything was in shape.

"If she does rise it will be a new experience for me," spoke the old elephant hunter. "I've never been in an airship before. It doesn't seem possible that we can get up in the air with this machine."

"Maybe we won't," spoke Tom, who was always a little diffident about a new piece of machinery.

"Well, if it doesn't do it the first time, it will the second, or the fifty-second," declared Ned Newton. "Tom Swift doesn't give up until he succeeds."

"Stop it! You'll make me blush!" cried the Black Hawk's owner as he tried the different gages and levers to see that they were all right.

After what seemed like a long time he gave the word for those who were to make the trial trip to take their places. They did so, and then, with Mr. Jackson, Tom went to the engine room. There was a little delay, due to the fact that some adjustment was necessary on the main motor. But at last it was fixed.

"Are you all ready?" called Tom.

"All ready," answered Mr. Damon. The old elephant hunter sat in a chair, nervously gripping the arms, and with a grim look on his tanned face. Mr. Swift was cool, as Ned, for they had made many trips in the air. Outside were Eradicate Sampson and Mrs. Baggert.

"Here we go!" suddenly cried Tom, and he yanked over the lever that started the main motor and propellers. The Black Hawk trembled throughout her entire length. She shivered and shook. Faster and faster whirled the great wooden screws. The motor hummed and throbbed.

Slowly the Black Hawk moved across the ground. Then she gathered speed. Now she was fairly rushing over the level space. Tom Swift tilted the elevation rudder, and with a suddenness that was startling, at least to the old elephant hunter, the new airship shot upward on a steep slant.

"The Black Hawk flies!" yelled Ned Newton. "Now for elephant land and the big tusks!"

"Yes, and perhaps for the red pygmies, too," added Tom in a low voice. Then he gave his whole attention to the management of his new machine, which was rapidly mounting upward, with a speed rivalling that of his former big craft.

CHAPTER VIII

OFF FOR AFRICA

Higher and higher went the Black Hawk, far above the earth, until the old elephant hunter, looking down, said in a voice which he tried to make calm and collected, but which trembled in spite of himself:

"Of course I'm not an expert at this game, Tom Swift, but it looks to me as if we'd never get down. Don't you think we're high enough?"

"For the time being, yes," answered the young inventor. "I didn't think she'd climb so far without the use of the gas. She's doing well."

"Bless my topknot, yes!" exclaimed Mr. Damon. "She beats the Red Cloud, Tom. Try her on a straight-away course."

Which the youth did, pointing the nose of the craft along parallel to the surface of the earth, and nearly a mile above it. Then, increasing the speed of the motor, and with the big propellers humming, they made fast time.

The old elephant hunter grew more calm as he saw that the airship did not show any inclination to fall, and he noted that Tom and the others not only knew how to manage it, but took their flight as much a matter of course as if they were in an automobile skimming along on the surface of the ground.

Tom put his craft through a number of evolutions, and when he found that she was in perfect control as an aeroplane, he started the gas machine, filled the big black bag overhead, and, when it was sufficiently buoyant, he shut off the motor, and the Black Hawk floated along like a balloon.

"That's what we'll do if our power happens to give out when we get over an African jungle, with a whole lot of wild elephants down below, and a forest full of the red pygmies waiting for us," explained Tom to Mr. Durban.

"And I guess you'll need to do it, too," answered the hunter. "I don't know which I fear worse, the bad elephants wild with rage, as they get some times, or the little red men who are as strong as gorillas, and as savage as wolves. It would be all up with us if we got into their hands. But I think this airship will be just what we need in Africa. I'd have been able to get out of many a tight place if I had had one on my last trip."

While the Black Hawk hung thus, up the air, not moving, save as the wind blew her, Tom with his father and Mr. Jackson made an inspection of the machinery to find out whether it had been strained any. They found that it had worked perfectly, and soon the craft was in motion again, her nose this time being pointed toward the earth. Tom let out some of the gas, and soon the airship was on the ground in front of the shed she had so recently left.

"She's all right," decided the young inventor after a careful inspection. "I'll give her a couple more trials, put on the finishing touches and then we'll be ready for our trip to Africa. Have you got everything arranged to go, Ned?"

"Sure. I have a leave of absence from the bank, thanks to your father and Mr. Damon, most of my clothes are packed, I've bought a gun and I've got a lot of quinine in case I get a fever."

"Good!" cried the elephant hunter. "You'll do all right, I reckon. I'm glad I met you young fellows. Well, I've lived through my first trip in the air, which is more than I expected when I started."

They discussed their plans at some length, for, now that the airship had proved all that they had hoped for, it would not be long ere they were under way. In the days that followed Tom put the finishing touches on the craft, arranged to have it packed up for shipment, and spent some time practicing with his electric rifle. He got to be an expert shot, and Mr. Durban, who was a wonder with the ordinary rifle, praised the young inventor highly.

"There won't many of the big tuskers get away from you, Tom Swift," he said. "And that reminds me, I got a letter the other day, from the firm I collect ivory for, stating that the price had risen because of a scarcity, and urging me to hurry back to Africa and get all I could. It seems that war has broken out among some of the central African tribes, and they are journeying about in the jungle, on the war path here and there, and have driven the elephants into the very deepest wilds, where the ordinary hunters can't get at them."

"Maybe we won't have any luck, either," suggested Ned.

"Oh, yes, we will," declared the hunter. "With our airship, the worst forest of the dark continent won't have any terrors for us, for we can float above it. And the fights of the natives won't have any effect. In a way, this will be a good thing, for with the price of ivory soaring, we can make more money than otherwise. There's a chance for us all to get a lot of money."

"Bless my piano keys!" exclaimed Mr. Damon, "if I can get just one elephant, and pull out his big ivory teeth, I'll be satisfied. I want a nice pair of tusks to set up on either side of my fireplace for ornaments."

"A mighty queer place for such-like ornaments," said Mr. Durban in a low voice. Then he added: "Well, the sooner we get started the better I'll like it, for I want to get that pair of big tusks for a special customer of mine."

"I'll give the Black Hawk one more trial flight, and then take her apart and ship her," decided Tom, and the final flight, a most successful one, took place the following day.

Then came another busy season when the airship was taken apart for shipment to the coast of Africa by steamer. It was put into big boxes and crates, and Eradicate and his mule took them to the station in Shopton.

"Don't you want to come to Africa with us, Rad?" asked Tom, when the last of the cases had been sent off. "You'll find a lot of your friends there."

"No, indeedy, I doan't want t' go," answered the colored man, "though I would like to see dat country."

"Then why don't you come?"

"Hu! Yo' think, Massa Tom, dat I go anywhere dat I might meet dem little red men what Massa Durban talk about? No, sah, dey might hurt mah mule Boomerang."

"Oh, I wasn't going to take the mule along," said Tom, wondering how the creature might behave in the airship.

"Not take Boomerang? Den I SUTTINLY ain't goin'," and Eradicate walked off, highly offended, to give some oats to his faithful if somewhat eccentric steed.

After the airship had been sent off there yet remained much for Tom Swift to do. He had to send along a number of special tools and appliances with which to put the ship together again, and also some with which to repair the craft in case of accident. So that this time was pretty well occupied. But at length everything was in readiness, and with his electric rifle knocked down for transportation, and with his baggage, and that of the others, all packed, they set off one morning to take the train for New York, where they would get a steamer for Africa.

Numerous good-bys had been said, and Tom had made a farewell call on Mary Nestor, promising to bring her some trophy from elephant land, though he did not quite know what it would be.

Mr. Damon, as the train started, blessed everything he could think of. Mr. Swift waved his hand and wished his son and the others good luck, feeling a little lonesome that he could not make one of the party. Ned was eager with excitement, and anticipation of what lay before him. Tom Swift was thinking of what he could accomplish with his electric rifle, and of the wonderful sights he would see, and, as for the old elephant hunter, he was very glad to be on the move again, after so many weeks of idleness, for he was a very active man.

Their journey to New York was uneventful, and they found that the parts of the airship had safely arrived, and had been taken aboard the steamer. The little party went aboard themselves, after a day spent in sight-seeing, and that afternoon the Soudalar, which was the vessel's name, steamed away from the dock at high tide.

"Off for Africa!" exclaimed Tom to Ned, as they stood at the rail, watching the usual crowd wave farewells. "Off for Africa, Ned."

As Tom spoke, a gentleman who had been standing near him and his chum, vigorously waving his hand to some one on the pier, turned quickly. He looked sharply at the young inventor for a moment, and then exclaimed:

"Well, if it isn't Tom Swift! Did I hear you say you were going to Africa?"

Tom looked at the gentleman with rather a puzzled air for a moment. The face was vaguely familiar, but Tom could not recall where he had seen it. Then it came to him in a flash.

"Mr. Floyd Anderson!" exclaimed our hero. "Mr. Anderson of—"

"Earthquake Island!" exclaimed the gentleman quickly, as he extended his hand. "I guess you remember that place, Tom Swift."

"Indeed I do. And to think of meeting you again, and on this African steamer," and Tom's mind went back to the perilous days when his wireless message had saved the castaways of Earthquake Island, among whom were Mr. Anderson and his wife.

"Did I hear you say you were going to Africa?" asked Mr. Anderson, when he had been introduced to Ned, and the others in Tom's party.

"That's where we're bound for," answered the lad. "We are going to elephant land. But where are you going, Mr. Anderson?"

"Also to Africa, but not on a trip for pleasure or profit like yourselves. I have been commissioned by a missionary society to rescue two of its workers from the heart of the dark continent."

"Rescue two missionaries?" exclaimed Tom, wonderingly.

"Yes, a gentleman and his wife, who, it is reported, have fallen into the hands of a race known as the red pygmies, who hold them captives!"

CHAPTER IX

ATTACKED BY A WHALE

Surprise at Mr. Anderson's announcement held Tom silent for a moment. That the gentleman whom he had been the means of rescuing, among others, from Earthquake Island, should be met with so unexpectedly, was quite a coincidence, but when it developed that he was bound to the same part of the African continent as were Tom and his friends, and when he said he hoped to rescue some missionaries from the very red pygmies so feared by the old elephant hunter—this was enough to startle any one.

"I see that my announcement has astonished you," said Mr. Anderson, as he noted the look of surprise on the face of the young inventor.

"It certainly has! Why, that's where we are bound for, in my new airship. Come down into our cabin, Mr. Anderson, and tell us all about it. Is your wife with you?"

"No, it is too dangerous a journey on which to take her. I have little hope of succeeding, for it is now some time since the unfortunate missionaries were captured, but I am going to do my best, and organize a relief expedition when I get to Africa."

Tom said nothing at that moment, but he made up his mind that if it was at all possible he would lend his aid, that of his airship, and also get his friends to assist Mr. Anderson. They went below to a special cabin that had been reserved for Tom's party, and there, as the ship slowly passed down New York Bay, Mr. Anderson told his story.

"I mentioned to you, when we were on Earthquake Island," he said to Tom, "that I had been in Africa, and had done some hunting. That is not my calling, as it is that of your friend, Mr. Durban, but I know the country pretty well. However, I have not been there in some time."

"My wife and I are connected with a church in New York that, several years ago, raised a fund and sent two missionaries, Mr. and Mrs. Jacob

Illingway, to the heart of Africa. They built up a little mission there, and for a time all went well, and they did good work among the natives."

"They are established in a tribe of friendly black men, of simple nature, and, while the natives did not become Christianized to any remarkable extent, yet they were kind to the missionaries. Mr. and Mrs. Illingway used frequently to write to members of our church, telling of their work. They also mentioned the fact that adjoining the country of the friendly blacks there was a tribe of fierce little red men,—red because of hair of that color all over their bodies."

"That's right," agreed Mr. Durban, shaking his head solemnly. "They're red imps, too!"

"Mr. Illingway often mentioned in his letters," went on Mr. Anderson, "that there were frequent fights between the pygmies and the race of blacks, but the latter had no great fear of their small enemies. However, it seems that they did not take proper precautions, for not long ago there was a great battle, the blacks were attacked by a large force of the red pygmies, who overwhelmed them by numbers, and finally routed them, taking possession of their country."

"What became of the missionaries?" asked Ned Newton.

"I'll tell you," said Mr. Anderson. "For a long time we heard nothing, beyond the mere news of the fight, which we read of in the papers. The church people were very anxious about the fate of Mr. and Mrs. Illingway, and were talking of sending a special messenger to inquire about them, when a cablegram came from the headquarters of the society in London."

"It seems that one of the black natives, named Tomba, who was a sort of house servant to Mr. and Mrs. Illingway, escaped the general massacre, in which all his friends were killed. He made his way through the jungle to a white settlement, and told his story, relating how the two missionaries had been carried away captive by the pygmies."

"A terrible fate," commented Mr. Durban.

"Yes, they might better be dead, from all the accounts we can hear," went on Mr. Anderson.

"Bless my Sunday hat! Don't say that!" exclaimed Mr. Damon. "Maybe we can save them, Mr. Anderson."

"That is what I am going to try to do, though it may be too late. As soon as definite news was received, our church held a meeting, raised a fund, and decided to send me off to find Mr. and Mrs. Illingway, if alive, or give them decent burial, if I could locate their bones. The reason they selected me was because I had been in Africa, and knew the country."

"I made hurried arrangements, packed up, said good-by to my wife, and here I am. But to think of meeting you, Tom Swift! And to hear that you are also going to Africa. I wish I could command an airship for the rescue. It might be more easily accomplished!"

"That's just what I was going to propose!" exclaimed Tom. "We are going to the land of the red pygmies, and while I have promised to help Mr. Durban in getting ivory, and while I want to try my electric rifle on big game, still we can do both, I think. You can depend on us, Mr. Anderson, and if the Black Hawk can be of any service to you in the rescue, count us in!"

"Gosh!" cried the former castaway of Earthquake Island. "This is the best piece of luck I could have! Now tell me all about your plans." which Tom and the others did, listening in turn, to further details about the missionaries.

Just how they would go to work to effect the rescue, or how they could locate the particular tribe of little red men who had Mr. and Mrs. Illingway, they did not know.

"We may be able to get hold of this Tomba," said Mr. Durban. "If not I guess between Mr. Anderson and myself we can get on the trail, somehow. I'm anxious to get to the coast, see the airship put together again, and start for the interior."

"So am I," declared Tom, as he got out his electric rifle, and began to put it together, for he wanted to show Mr. Anderson how it worked.

They had a pleasant and uneventful voyage for two weeks. The weather was good, and, to tell the truth, it was rather monotonous for Tom and the others, who were eager to get into activity again. Then came a storm, which, while it was not dangerous, yet gave them plenty to think and talk about for three days. Then came more calm weather, when the Soudalar plowed along over gently heaving billows.

They were about a week from their port of destination, which was Majumba, on the African coast, when, one afternoon, as Tom and the others were in their cabin, they heard a series of shouts on deck, and the sound of many feet running to and fro.

"Something has happened!" exclaimed the young inventor.

Tom raced for the companionway, and was soon on deck, followed by Mr. Durban and the others. They saw a crowd of sailors and passengers leaning over the port rail.

"What's the matter?" asked Tom, of the second mate, who was just passing.

"Fight between a killer and a whale," was the reply. "The captain has ordered the ship to lay-to so it can be watched."

Tom made his way to the rail. About a quarter of a mile away there could be observed a great commotion in the ocean. Great bodies seemed to be threshing about, beating the water to foam, and, with the foam could be seen bright blood mingled. Occasionally two jets of water, as from some small fountain, would shoot upward.

"He's blowing hard!" exclaimed one of the sailors. "I guess he's about done for!"

"Which one?" asked Tom.

"The whale," was the reply. "The killer has the best of the big fellow," and the sailor quickly explained how the smaller killer fish, by the peculiarity of its attack, and its great ferocity, often bested its larger antagonist.

The battle was now at its height, and Tom and the others were interested spectators. At times neither of the big creatures could be seen, because of the smother of foam in which they rolled and threshed about. The whale endeavored to sound, or go to the bottom, but the killer stuck to him relentlessly.

Suddenly, however, as Tom looked, the whale, by a stroke of his broad tail, momentarily stunned his antagonist. Instantly realizing that he was free the great creature, which was about ninety feet long, darted away, swimming on the surface of the water, for he needed to get all the air possible.

Quickly acquiring momentum, the whale came on like a locomotive, spouting at intervals, the vapor from the blowholes looking not unlike steam from some submarine boat.

"He looks to be heading this way," remarked Mr. Durban to Tom.

"He is," agreed the young inventor, "but I guess he'll dive before he gets here. He only wants to get away from the killer. Look, the other one is swimming this way, too!"

"Bless my harpoon, but he sure is!" called Mr. Damon. "They'll renew the fight near here."

But he was mistaken, for the killer, after coming a little distance after the whale, suddenly turned, hesitated for a moment, and then disappeared in the depths of the ocean.

The whale, however, continued to come on, speeding through the water with powerful strokes. There was an uneasy movement among some of the passengers.

"Suppose he strikes the ship," suggested one woman.

"Nonsense! He couldn't," said her husband.

"The old man had better get under way, just the same," remarked a sailor near Tom, as he looked up at the bridge where the captain was standing.

The "old man," or commander, evidently thought the same thing, for, after a glance at the oncoming leviathan, which was still headed directly for the vessel, he shoved the lever of the telegraph signal over to "full speed ahead."

Hardly had he done so than the whale sank from sight.

"Oh, I'm so glad!" exclaimed the woman who had first spoken of the possibility of the whale hitting the ship, "I am afraid of those terrible creatures."

"They're as harmless as a cow, unless they get angry," said her husband.

Slowly the great ship began to move through the water. Tom and his friends were about to go back to their cabin, for they thought the excitement over, when, as the young inventor turned from the rail, he felt a vibration throughout the whole length of the steamer, as if it had hit on a sand-bar.

Instantly there was a jangling of bells in the engine room, and the Soudalar lost headway.

"What's the matter?" asked several persons.

They were answered a moment later, for the big whale, even though grievously wounded in his fight with the killer, had risen not a hundred feet away from the ship, and was coming toward it with the speed of an express train.

"Bless my blubber!" cried Mr. Damon. "We must have hit the whale, or it hit us under the water and now it's going to attack us!"

He had no more than gotten the words out of his mouth ere the great creature of the deep came on full tilt at the vessel, struck it a terrific blow which made it tremble from stem to stern, and career violently.

There was a chorus of frightened cries, sailors rushed to and fro, the engine-room bells rang violently, and the captain and mates shouted hoarse orders.

"Here he comes again!" yelled Mr. Durban, as he hurried to the side of the ship. "The whale takes us for an enemy, I guess, and he's going to ram us again!"

"And if he does it many times, he'll start the plates and cause a leak that won't be stopped in a hurry!" cried a sailor as he rushed past Tom.

The young inventor looked at the oncoming monster for a moment, and then started on the run for his cabin.

"Here! Where are you going?" cried Mr. Damon, but Tom did not answer.

CHAPTER X

OFF IN THE AIRSHIP

As Tom Swift hurried down the companionway he again felt the ship career as the whale struck it a powerful blow, and he was almost knocked off his feet. But he kept on.

Below he found some frightened men and women, a number of whom were adjusting life preservers about them, under the impression that the ship had struck a rock and was going down. They had not been up on deck, and did not know of the battle between the killer and the whale, nor what followed.

"Oh, I know we're sinking!" cried one timid woman. "What has happened?" she appealed to Tom.

"It will be all right in a little while," he assured her.

"But what is it? I want to know. Have we had a collision."

"Yes, with a whale," replied Tom, as he grabbed up something from his stateroom, and again rushed up on deck. As he reached it the whale came on once more, and struck the ship another terrific blow. Then the monster sank and could be seen swimming back, just under the surface of the water, getting ready to renew the attack.

"He's going to ram us again!" cried Mr. Damon. "Bless my machine oil! Why doesn't the captain do something?"

At that moment the commander cried from the bridge:

"Send a man below, Mr. Laster, to see if we are making any water. Then tell half a dozen of the sailors to get out the rifles, and see if they can't kill the beast. He'll put us in Davy Jones's locker if he keeps this up! Lively now, men!"

The first mate, Mr. Laster, called out the order. A sailor went below to see if the ship was leaking much, and the captain rang for full speed ahead. But the Soudalar was slow in getting under way again, and, even at top speed she was no match for the whale, which was again rushing toward the vessel.

"Quick with those rifles!" cried the captain. "Fire a volley into the beast!"

"There's no need!" suddenly called Mr. Damon, who had caught sight of Tom Swift, and the object which the lad carried.

"No need?" demanded the commander. "Why, has the whale sunk, or made off?"

"No," answered the eccentric man, "the whale is still coming on, but Tom Swift will fix him. Get there, Tom, and let him have a good one!"

"What sort of a gun is that?" demanded the commander as the young inventor took his place at the rail, which was now almost deserted.

Tom did not answer. Bracing himself against the rolling and heaving of the vessel, which was now under about half speed, Tom aimed his electric rifle at the oncoming leviathan. He looked at the automatic gage, noted the distance and waiting a moment until the crest of a wave in front of the whale had subsided, he pressed the button.

If those watching him expected to hear a loud report, and see a flash of flame, they were disappointed. There was absolutely no sound, but what happened to the whale was most surprising.

The great animal stopped short amid a swirl of foam, and the next instant it seemed to disintegrate. It went all to pieces, just as had the dummy figure which Tom on one occasion fired at with his rifle and as had the big packing-cases. The whale appeared to dissolve, as does a lump of sugar in a cup of hot tea, and, five seconds after Tom Swift had fired his electric gun, there was not a sign of the monster save a little blood on the calm sea.

"What—what happened?" asked the captain in bewilderment. "Is—is that monster gone?"

"Completely gone!" cried Mr. Damon. "Bless my powder horn, Tom, but I knew you could do it!"

"Is that a new kind of whale gun, firing an explosive bullet?" inquired the commander, as he came down off the bridge and shook hands with Tom. "If it is, I'd like to buy one. We may be rammed again by another whale."

"This is my new, electric rifle," explained the young inventor modestly, "and it fires wireless charges of electricity instead of bullets. I'm sorry I can't let you have it, as it's the only one I have. But I guess no more whales will ram us. That one was evidently crazed by the attack of the killer, and doubtless took us for another of its enemies."

Sailors and passengers crowded around Tom, eager to shake his hand, and to hear about the gun. Many declared that he had saved the ship.

This was hardly true, for the whale could not have kept up its attacks much longer. Still he might have done serious damage, by causing a leak, and, while the Soudalar was a stanch craft, with many water-tight compartments, still no captain likes to be a week from land with a bad leak, especially if a storm comes up. Then, too, there was the danger of a panic among the passengers, had the attacks been kept up, so, though Tom wanted to make light of his feat, the others would not let him.

"You're entitled to the thanks of all on board," declared Captain Wendon, "and I'll see that the owners hear of what you did. Well, I guess we can go on, now. I'll not stop again to see a fight between a killer and a whale."

The steamer resumed her way at full speed, and the sailor, who had gone below, came up to report that there was only a slight leak, which need not cause any uneasiness.

Little was talked of for the next few days but the killing of the whale, and Tom had to give several exhibitions of his electric rifle, and explain its workings. Then, too, the story of his expedition became known, and also the object of Mr. Anderson's quest, and Tom's offer of aid to help rescue the missionaries, so that, altogether, our hero was made much of during the remainder of the voyage.

"Well, if your gun will do that to a whale, what will it do to an elephant?" asked Mr. Durban one morning, when they were within a day's steaming of their port. "I'm afraid it's almost too strong, Tom. It will leave nothing—not even the tusks to pick up."

"Oh, I can regulate the power," declared the lad. "I used full force on the whale, just to see what it would do. It was the first tine I'd tried it on anything alive. I can so regulate the charge that it will kill even an elephant, and leave scarcely a mark on the beast."

"I'd like to see it done," remarked the old hunter.

"I'll show you, if we sight any sharks," promised Tom. He was able to keep his word for that afternoon a school of the ugly fish followed the steamer for the sake of the food scraps thrown overboard. Tom took his position in the stern, and gave an exhibition of shooting with his electric gun that satisfied even Mr. Durban, exacting as he was.

For the lad, by using his heaviest charges, destroyed the largest sharks so that they seemed to instantly disappear in the water, and from that he toned down the current until he could kill some of the monsters so easily and quickly that they seemed to float motionless on the surface, yet there was no life left in them once the electric charge touched them.

"We'll use the light charges when we're killing elephants for their tusks," said Tom, "and the heavy ones when we're in danger from a rush of the beasts."

He little knew how soon he would have to put his plan into effect.

They arrived safely at Majumba, the African coast city, and for two days Tom was kept busy superintending the unloading of the parts of his airship. But it was safely taken ashore, and he and his friends hired a disused warehouse in which to work at reassembling the Black Hawk.

Tom had everything down to a system, and, in less than a week the aircraft was once more ready to be sent aloft. It was given a try-out, much to the astonishment of the natives, and worked perfectly. Then Tom and his friends busied themselves laying in a stock of provisions and stores for the trip into the interior.

They made inquiries about the chances of getting ivory and were told that they were good if they went far enough into the jungle and forests, for the big beasts had penetrated farther and farther inland.

They also tried to get some news regarding the captive missionaries, but were unsuccessful nor could they learn what had become of Tomba, who had brought the dire news to civilization.

"It's too soon to hope for anything yet," said Mr. Anderson. "Wait until we get near the country of the red pygmies."

"And then it may be too late," said Tom in a low voice.

It was two weeks after their arrival in Majumba that Tom announced that all was in readiness. The airship was in perfect working order, it was well stocked with food, arms, articles and trinkets with which to trade among the natives, spare parts for the machinery, special tools and a good supply of the chemicals needed to manufacture the lifting gas.

Of course Tom did not leave behind his electric weapon and Mr. Durban and the others took plenty of ammunition for the ordinary rifles which they carried.

One morning, after cabling to his father that they were about to start, Tom gave a last careful look to his airship, tested the motor and dynamos, took a hasty survey of the storeroom, to see that nothing had been forgotten, and gave the word to get aboard.

They took their places in the cabin. Outside a crowd of natives, and white traders of many nationalities had gathered. Tom pulled the starting lever. The Black Hawk shot across a specially prepared starting ground, and, attaining sufficient momentum, suddenly arose into the air.

There was a cheer from the watching crowd, and several superstitious blacks, who saw the airship for the first time, ran away in terror.

Up into the blue atmosphere Tom took his craft. He looked down on the city over which he was flying. Then he pointed the prow of the Black Hawk toward the heart of the dark continent.

"Off for the interior!" he murmured. "I wonder if we'll ever get out again?"

No one could answer. They had to take their chances with the dangers and terrors of elephant land, and with the red pygmies. Yet Tom Swift was not afraid.

CHAPTER XI

ANCHORED TO EARTH

With the voyage on the steamer, their arrival in Africa, the many strange sights of the city of Majumba, and the refitting of the airship, our friends had hardly had time to catch their breath since Tom Swift's determination to go elephant hunting. Now, as the Black Hawk was speeding into the interior, they felt, for the first time in many weeks, that they "could take it easy," as Ned Newton expressed it.

"Thank goodness," said the bank clerk, "I can sit down and look at something for a while," and he gazed out of the main cabin windows down at the wild country over which they were then flying.

For, so swiftly had the airship moved that it was hardly any time at all before it had left Majumba far behind, and was scudding over the wilderness.

"Bless my camera," exclaimed Mr. Damon, who had brought along one of the picture machines, "bless my camera! I don't call that much to look at," and he pointed to the almost impenetrable forest over which they then were.

"No, it isn't much of a view," said the old elephant hunter, "but wait. You'll soon see all you want to. Africa isn't all like this. There are many strange sights before us yet. But, Tom Swift, tell us how the airship is working in this climate. Do you find any difficulty managing it?"

"Not at all," answered Tom, who was in the cabin then, having set the automatic steering apparatus in the pilot house, and come back to join the others. "It works as well as it did in good old York State. Of course I can't tell what affect the continual hot and moist air will have on the gas bag, but I guess we'll make out all right."

"I certainly hope so," put in Mr. Anderson. "It would be too bad to be wrecked in the middle of Africa, with no way to get out."

"Oh, you needn't worry about that," said Ned with a laugh. "If the airship should smash, Tom would build another out of what was left, and we'd sail away as good as before."

"Hardly that," answered the young inventor.

"But we won't cross a bridge until we hear it coming, as Eradicate would say. Hello, that looks like some sort of native village."

He pointed ahead to a little clearing in the forest, where a number of mud and grass huts were scattered about. As they came nearer they could see the black savages, naked save for a loin cloth, running about in great excitement, and pointing upward.

"Yes, that's one of the numerous small native villages we'll see from now on," said Mr. Durban. "Many a night have I spent in those same grass huts after a day's hunting. Sometimes, I've been comfortable, and again not. I guess we've given those fellows a scare."

It did seem so, for by this time the whole population, including women and children, were running about like mad. Suddenly, from below there sounded a deep booming noise, which came plainly to the ears of the elephant hunters through the opened windows of the airship cabin.

"Hark! What's that?" cried Tom, raising his hand for silence.

"Bless my umbrella! it sounds like thunder," said Mr. Damon.

"No, it's one of their war drums," explained Mr. Durban. "The natives make large ones out of hollow trees, with animal skins stretched over the ends, and they beat them to sound a warning, or before going into battle. It makes a great noise."

"Do you think they want to fight us?" asked Ned, looking anxiously at Tom, and then toward where his rifle stood in a corner of the cabin.

"No, probably that drum was beaten by some of the native priests," explained the hunter. "The natives are very superstitious, and likely they took us for an evil spirit, and wanted to drive us away."

"Then we'll hustle along out of their sight," said Tom, as he went to the pilot house to increase the speed of the airship, for he had been letting it drift along slowly to enable the adventurers to view the country over which they were passing. A few minutes later, under the increased force of the machinery, the Black Hawk left the native village, and the crowd of frightened blacks, far behind.

The travelers passed over a succession of wild stretches of forest or jungle, high above big grassy plains, over low but rugged mountain ranges, and big rivers. Now and then they would cross some lake, on the calm surface of which could be made out natives, in big canoes, hollowed out from trees. In each case the blacks showed every appearance of fright at the sight of the airship throbbing along over their heads.

On passing over the lake, Ned Newton looked down and cried out excitedly:

"Look! Elephants! They're in swimming, and the natives are shooting them! Now's our chance, Tom!"

Mr. Anderson and Mr. Durban, after a quick glance, drew back laughing.

"Those are hippopotami!" exclaimed the old elephant man. "Good hunting, if you don't care what you shoot, but not much sport in it. It will be some time yet before we see any elephants, boys."

Ned was rather chagrined at his mistake, but the African travelers told him that any one, not familiar with the country, would have made it, especially in looking down from a great height.

They sailed along about half a mile above the earth, Tom gradually increasing the speed of the ship, as he found the machinery to be working well. Dinner was served as they were crossing a high grassy plateau, over which could be seen bounding a number of antelopes.

"Some of those would go good for a meal," said Mr. Durban, after a pause during which he watched the graceful creatures.

"Then we'll go down and get some for supper," decided Tom, for in that hot climate it was impossible to carry fresh meat on the airship.

Accordingly, the Black Hawk was sent down, and came to rest in a natural clearing on the edge of the jungle. After waiting until the fierce heat of noonday was over, the travelers got out their rifles and, under the leadership of Mr. Durban and Mr. Anderson, who was also an experienced hunter, they set off.

Game was plentiful, but as they could only eat a comparatively small quantity, and as it would not keep, they only shot what they needed. Tom had his electric rifle, but hesitated to use it, as Mr. Durban and Mr. Anderson had each already bowled over a fine buck.

However, a chance came most unexpectedly, for, as they were passing along the banks of a little stream, which was almost hidden from view by thick weeds and rank grass, there was a sudden commotion in the bushes, and a fierce wild buffalo sprang out at the party.

There are few animals in Africa more dreaded by hunters than the wild buffalo, for the beast, with its spreading sharp horns is a formidable foe, and will seldom give up the attack until utterly unable to move. They are fierce and relentless.

"Look out!" yelled Mr. Durban. "To cover, everybody! If that beast gets after you it's no fun! You and I will fire at him, Mr. Anderson!"

Mr. Durban raised his rifle, and pulled the trigger, but, for some reason, the weapon failed to go off. Mr. Anderson quickly raised his, but his foot slipped in a wet place and he fell. At that moment the buffalo, with a snort of rage, charged straight for the fallen man.

"Tom! your electric rifle!" yelled Ned Newton, but he need not have done so, for the young inventor was on the alert.

Taking instant aim, and adjusting his weapon for the heaviest charge, Tom fired at the advancing beast. The result was the same as in the case of the whale, the buffalo seemed to melt away. And it was stopped only just in time, too, for it was close to the prostrate Mr. Anderson, who had sprained his ankle slightly, and could not readily rise.

It was all over in a few seconds, but it was a tense time while it lasted.

"You saved my life again, Tom Swift," said Mr. Anderson, as he limped toward our hero. "Once on Earthquake Island, and again now. I shan't forget it," and he shook hands with the young inventor.

The others congratulated Tom on his quick shot, and Mr. Damon, as usual blessed everything in sight, and the electric rifle especially.

They went back to the airship, taking the fresh meat with them, but on account of the injury to Mr. Anderson's ankle could not make quick progress, so that it was almost dusk when they reached the craft.

"Well, we'll have supper, and then start off," proposed Tom, "I don't think it would be wise to remain on the ground so near the jungle."

"No' it's safer in the air," agreed Mr. Durban. The meal was much enjoyed, especially the fresh meat, and, after it was over, Tom took his place in the pilot house to start the machinery, and send the airship aloft.

The motor hummed and throbbed, and the gas hissed into the bag, for the ground was not level enough to permit of a running start by means of the planes. Lights gleamed from the Black Hawk and the big search-lantern in front cast a dazzling finger of light into the black forest.

"Well, what are you waiting for?" called Ned, who heard the machinery in motion, but who could not feel the craft rising. "Why don't you go up, Tom?"

"I'm trying to," answered the young inventor. "Something seems to be the matter." He pulled the speed lever over a few more notches, and increased the power of the gas machine. Still the Black Hawk did not rise.

"Bless my handkerchief box!" cried Mr. Damon, "what's the matter?"

"I don't know," answered Tom. "We seem to be held fast."

He further increased the speed of the propellers, and the gas machine was set to make vapor at its fullest capacity, and force it into the bag. Still the craft was held to the earth.

"Maybe the gas has no effect in this climate," called Ned.

"It can't be that," replied Tom. "The gas will operate anywhere. It worked all right today."

Suddenly she airship moved up a little way, and then seemed to be pulled down again, hitting the ground with a bump.

"Something is holding us!" cried Tom. "We're anchored to earth! I must see what it is!" and, catching up his electric rifle, he dashed out of the cabin.

CHAPTER XII

AMONG THE NATIVES

For a moment after Tom's departure the others stared blankly at one another. They could hear the throbbing and hum of the machinery, and feel the thrill of the anchored airship. But they could not understand what the trouble was.

"We must help Tom!" cried Ned Newton at length as he caught up his rifle. "Maybe we are in the midst of a herd of elephants, and they have hold of the ship in their trunks."

"It couldn't be!" declared Mr. Durban, yet they soon discovered that Ned's guess was nearer the truth then any of them had suspected at the time.

"We must help him, true enough!" declared Mr. Anderson, and he and the others followed Ned out on deck.

"Where are you Tom?" called his chum.

"Here." was the answer. "I'm on the forward deck."

"Do you see anything?"

"No, it's too dark. Turn the search-light this way."

"I will," shouted Mr. Damon, and a moment later the gleam of the powerful lantern brought Tom clearly into view, as he stood on the small forward observation platform in the bow of the Black Hawk.

An instant later the young inventor let out a startled cry.

"What is it?" demanded Mr. Durban.

"An immense snake!" shouted Tom. "It's wound around a tree, and partly twined around the ship! That's why we couldn't go up! I'm going to shoot it."

They looked to where he pointed, and there, in the glare of the light, could be seen an immense python, fully twenty-five feet long, the forward part of its fat ugly body circled around the slender prow of the airship, while the folds of the tail were about a big tree.

Tom Swift raised his electric rifle, took quick aim, and, having set it to deliver a moderate charge, pressed the button. The result was surprising, for the snake being instantly killed the folds uncoiled and the ship shot upward, only, instead of rising on an even keel, the bow pointed toward the sky, while the stern was still fast to the earth. Tilted at an angle of forty-five degrees the Black Hawk was in a most peculiar position, and those standing on the deck began to slide along it.

"There's another snake at the stern!" cried Mr. Damon as he grasped a brace to prevent falling off. "Bless my slippers! it's the mate of the one you killed! Shoot the other one, Tom!"

The young inventor needed no urging. Making his way as best he could to the stern of the airship, he killed the second python, which was even larger than the first, and in an instant the Black Hawk shot upward, this time level, and as it should be. Things on board were soon righted, and the travelers could stand upright. High above the black jungle rose the craft, moving forward under the full power of the propellers, until Tom rushed into the engine room, and reduced speed.

"Well, talk about things happening!" exclaimed Ned, when they had somewhat recovered from the excitement. "I should say they were beginning with a vengeance!"

"That's the way in Africa," declared Mr. Durban. "It's a curious country. Those pythons generally go in pairs, but it's the first time I ever knew them to tackle an airship. They probably stay around here where there is plenty of small game for them, and very likely they merely anchored to our craft while waiting for a supper to come along."

"It was a very odd thing," said Tom. "I couldn't imagine what held us. After this I'll see that all is clear before I try to go up. Next time we may be held by a troop of baboons and it strains the machinery to have it pull against dead weight in that way."

However, it was found no harm had resulted from this experience, and, after reducing the gas pressure, which was taking them too high, Tom set the automatic rudders.

"We'll keep on at slow speed through the night," he explained, "and in the morning we'll be pretty well into the interior. Then we can lay our course for wherever we want to go. Where had we better head for?"

"I don't want to interfere with your plans," said Mr. Anderson, "but I would like to rescue those missionaries. But the trouble is, I don't know just where to look for them. We couldn't get much of a line in Majumba on where the country of the red pygmies is located. What do you think about it, Mr. Durban?"

"As far as elephant hunting goes we can probably do as well in the pygmy land as anywhere else," answered the veteran, "and perhaps it will be well to head for that place. If we run across any elephant herds in the meanwhile, we can stop, get the ivory, and proceed."

They discussed this plan at some length, and agreed that it was the best thing to do. Mr. Durban had a map of the country around the center of Africa, and he marked on it, as nearly as he could, the location of the pygmies' country, while Mr. Anderson also had a chart, showing the location of the mission which had been wiped out of existence. It was in the midst of a wild and desolate region.

"We'll do the best we can," declared Tom, "and I think we'll succeed. We ought to be there in about a week, if we have no bad luck."

All that night the Black Hawk flew on over Africa, covering mile after mile, passing over jungle, forest, plains, rivers and lakes, and, doubtless, over many native villages, though they could not be seen.

Morning found the travelers above a great, grassy plain, dotted here and there with negro settlements which were separated by rivers, lakes or thin patches of forest.

"Well, we'll speed up a bit," decided Tom after breakfast, which was eaten to the weird accompaniment of hundreds of native warning-drums, beaten by the superstitious blacks.

Tom went to the engine room, and turned on more speed. He was about to go back to the pilot house, to set the automatic steering apparatus to coincide with the course mapped out, when there was a crash of metal, an ominous snapping and buzzing sound, followed by a sudden silence.

"What's that?" cried Ned, who was in the motor compartment with his chum.

"Something's gone wrong!" exclaimed the young inventor, as he sprang back toward the engine. The propellers had ceased revolving, and as there was no gas in the bag at that time, it having been decided to save the vapor for future needs, the Black Hawk began falling toward the earth.

"We're going down!" yelled Ned.

"Yes, the main motor has broken!" exclaimed Tom. "We'll have to descend to repair it."

"Say!" yelled Mr. Damon, rushing in, "we're right over a big African village! Are we going to fall among the natives?"

"It looks that way," admitted Tom grimly, as he hastened to the pilot house to shift the wings so that the craft could glide easily to the ground.

"Bless my shoe blacking!" cried the eccentric man as he heard the beating of drums, and the shouts of the savages.

A little later the airship had settled into the midst of a crowd of Africans, who swarmed all about the craft.

CHAPTER XIII

ON AN ELEPHANT TRAIL

"Get ready with your guns, everybody!" cried the old elephant hunter, as he prepared to leave the cabin of the Black Hawk. "Tom Swift, don't forget your electric rifle. There'll be trouble soon!"

"Bless my cartridge belt!" gasped Mr. Damon. "Why? What will happen?"

"The natives," answered Mr. Durban. "They'll attack us sure as fate! See, already they're getting out their bows and arrows, and blowguns! They'll pierce the gas bag in a hundred places!"

"If they do, it will be a bad thing for us," muttered Tom. "We can't have that happen."

He followed the old elephant hunter outside, and Mr. Anderson, Ned Newton and Mr. Damon trailed after, each one with a gun, while Tom had his electric weapon. The airship rested on its wheels on some level ground, just in front of a large hut, surrounded by a number of smaller ones. All about were the natives, tall, gaunt black men, hideous in their savagery, wearing only the loin cloth, and with their kinky hair stuck full of sticks, bones and other odd objects they presented a curious sight.

Some of them were dancing about, brandishing their weapons—clubs spears, bows, and arrows, or the long, slender blowguns, consisting merely of a hollow reed. Women and children there were, too, also dancing and leaping about, howling at the tops of their voices. Above the unearthly din could be heard the noise of the drums and tom-toms, while, as the adventurers drew up in front of their airship, there came a sort of chant, and a line of natives, dressed fantastically in the skins of beasts, came filing out of the large hut.

"The witch-doctors!" exclaimed Tom, who had read of them in African travel books.

"Are they going to attack us?" cried Ned.

"Bless my hymn book! I hope not!" came from Mr. Damon. "We wouldn't have any chance at all in this horde of black men. I wish Eradicate Sampson and his mule Boomerang were here. Maybe he could talk their language, and tell them that we meant no harm."

"If there's any talking to be done, I guess our guns will have to do it," said Tom grimly.

"I can speak a little of their language," remarked Mr. Durban, "but what in the world are the beggars up to, anyhow? I supposed they'd send a volley of arrows at us, first shot, but they don't seem to be going to do that."

"No, they're dancing around us," said Tom.

"That's it!" exclaimed Mr. Anderson. "I have it! Why didn't I think of it before? The natives are welcoming us!"

"Welcoming us?" repeated Ned.

"Yes," went on the missionary seeker. "They are doing a dance in our honor, and they have even called out the witch-doctors to do us homage."

"That's right," agreed Mr. Durban, who was listening to the chanting of the natives dressed in animal skins. "They take us for spirits from another land, and are making us welcome here. Listen, I'll see if I can make out what else they are saying."

The character of the shouts and chants changed abruptly, and the dancing increased in fervor, even the children throwing themselves wildly about. The witch-doctors ran around like so many maniacs, and it looked as much like an American Indian war dance as anything else.

"I've got it!" shouted Mr. Durban, for he had to call loudly to be heard above the din. "They are asking us to make it rain. It seems there has been a dry spell here, and their own rain-makers and witch-doctors haven't been able to get a drop out of the sky. Now, they take it that we have come to help them. They think we are going to bring rain."

"And if we don't, what will happen?" asked Tom.

"Maybe they won't be quite so glad to see us," was the answer.

"Well, if they don't mean war, we might as well put up our weapons," suggested Mr. Anderson. "If they're going to be friendly, so much the better, and if it should happen to rain while we're here, they'd think we brought it, and we could have almost anything we wanted. Perhaps they have a store of ivory hidden away, Mr. Durban. Some of these tribes do."

"It's possible, but the chances for rain are very small. How long will we have to stay here, Tom Swift?" asked the elephant hunter anxiously.

"Well, perhaps I can get the motor mended in two or three days," answered the young inventor.

"Then we'll have to stay here in the meanwhile," decided Mr. Durban. "Well, we'll make the best of it. Ha, here comes the native king to do us honor," and, as he spoke there came toward the airship a veritable giant of a black man, wearing a leopard skin as a royal garment, while on his head was a much battered derby hat, probably purchased at a fabulous price from some trader. The king, if such he could be called, was accompanied by a number of attendants and witch-doctors. In front walked a small man, who, as it developed, was an interpreter. The little cavalcade advanced close to the airship, and came to a halt. The king made a low bow, either to the craft or to the elephant hunters drawn up in front of it. His attendants followed his example, and then the interpreter began to speak.

Mr. Durban listened intently, made a brief answer to the little man, and then the elephant hunter's face lighted up.

"It's all right," he said to Tom and the others. "The king takes us for wonderful spirits from another land. He welcomes us, says we can have whatever we want, and he begs us to make it rain. I have said we will do our best, and I have asked that some food be sent us. That's always the first thing to do. We'll be allowed to stay here in peace until Tom can mend the ship, and then we'll hit the air trail again."

The talk between Mr. Durban and the interpreter continued for some little time longer. Then the king went back to his hut, refusing, as Mr. Durban said, an invitation to come aboard and see how a modern airship was constructed. The natives, too, seemed anxious to give the craft a wide berth.

The excitement had quieted down now, and, in a short tine a crowd of native women came toward the airship, bearing, in baskets on their heads, food of various kinds. There were bananas, some wild fruits, yams, big gourds of goats' milk, some boiled and stewed flesh of young goats, nicely cooked, and other things, the nature of which could only be guessed at.

"Shall we eat this stuff, or stick to Mr. Damon's cooking?" asked Tom.

"Oh, you'll find this very good," explained Mr. Durban. "I've eaten native cookery before. Some of it is excellent and as this appears to be very good, Mr. Damon can have a vacation while we are here."

The old elephant hunter proved the correctness of his statement by beginning to eat, and soon all the travelers were partaking of the food left by the native women. They placed it down on the ground at a discreet distance from the airship, and hurriedly withdrew. But if the women and men were afraid, the children were not, and they were soon swarming about the ship, timidly touching the sides with their little black fingers, but not venturing on board.

Tom, with Ned and Mr. Damon to help him, began work on the motor right after dinner. He found the break to be worse than he had supposed, and knew that it would take at least four days to repair it.

Meanwhile the airship continued to be a source of wonder to the natives. They were always about it, save at night, but their admiration was a respectful one. The king was anxious for the rain-making incantations to begin, but Mr. Durban put him off.

"I don't want to deceive these simple natives," he said, "and for our own safety we can't pretend to make rain, and fail. As soon as we have a chance we'll slip away from here."

But an unexpected happening made a change in their plans. It was on the afternoon of their third day in the native village, and Tom and his assistants were working hard at the motor. Suddenly there seemed to be great excitement in the vicinity of the king's hut. A native had rushed into the village from the jungle, evidently with some news, for presently the whole place was in a turmoil.

Once more the king and his attendants filed out toward the airship. Once more the interpreter talked to Mr. Durban, who listened eagerly.

"By Jove! here's our chance!" he cried to Tom, when the little man had finished.

"What is it?" asked the young inventor.

"A runner has just come in with news that a large herd of wild elephants is headed this way. The king is afraid the big beasts will trample down all their crops, as often occurs, and he begs us to go out and drive the animals away. It's just what we want. Come on, Tom, and all of you. The airship will be safe here, for the natives think that to meddle with it would mean death or enchantment for then. We'll get on our first elephant trail!"

The old hunter went into the cabin for his big game gun, while Tom hastened to get out his electric rifle. Now he would have a chance to try it on the powerful beasts which he had come to Africa to hunt.

Amid the excited and joyous shouts of the natives, the hunters filed out of the village, led by the dusky messenger who had brought the news of the elephants. And, as Tom and the others advanced, they could hear a distant trumpeting, and a crashing in the jungle that told of the near presence of the great animals.

CHAPTER XIV

A STAMPEDE

"Look to your guns, everybody!" cautioned Mr. Durban. "It's no joke to be caught in an elephant herd with an unloaded rifle. Have you plenty of ammunition, Mr. Damon?"

"Ammunition? Bless my powder bag, I think I have enough for all the elephants I'll kill. If I get one of the big beasts I'll be satisfied. Bless my piano keys! I think I see them, Tom!"

He pointed off through the thick jungle. Surely something was moving there amid the trees; great slate-colored bodies, massive forms and waving trunks! The trumpeting increased, and the crashing of the underbrush sounded louder and nearer.

"There they are!" cried Tom Swift joyously.

"Now for my first big game!" yelled Ned Newton.

"Take it easy," advised Mr. Anderson. "Remember to aim for the spot I mentioned to you as being the best, just at the base of the skull. If you can't make a head shot, or through the eye, try for the heart. But with the big bullets we have, almost any kind of a shot, near a vital spot, will answer."

"And Tom can fire at their TOES and put them out of business," declared Ned, who was eagerly advancing. "How about it, Tom?"

"Well, I guess the electric rifle will come up to expectations. Say, Mr. Durban, they seem to be heading this way!" excitedly cried Tom, as the herd of big beasts suddenly turned and changed their course.

"Yes, they are," admitted the old elephant hunter calmly. "But that won't matter. Take it easy. Kill all you can."

"But we don't want to put too many out of business," said Tom, who was not needlessly cruel, even in hunting.

"I know that," answered Mr. Durban. "But this is a case of necessity. I've got to get ivory, and we have to kill quite a few elephants to accomplish this. Besides the brutes will head for the village and the natives' grain fields, and trample them down, if they're not headed back. So all together now, we'll give them a volley. This is a good place! There they are. All line up now. Get ready!"

He halted, and the others followed his example. The natives had come to a stop some time before, and were huddled together in the jungle back of our friends, waiting to see the result of the white men's shots.

Tom, Ned, Mr. Damon, and the two older hunters were on an irregular line in the forest. Before them was the mass of elephants advancing slowly, and feeding on the tender leaves of trees as they came on. They would reach up with their long trunks, strip off the foliage, and stuff it into their mouths. Sometimes, they even pulled up small trees by the roots for the purpose of stripping them more easily.

"Jove! There are some big tuskers in that bunch!" cried Mr. Durban. "Aim for the bulls, every one, don't kill the mothers or little ones." Tom now saw that there were a number of baby Elephants in the herd, and he appreciated the hunter's desire to spare them and their mothers.

"Here we go!" exclaimed Mr. Durban, as he saw that Tom and the others were ready. "Aim! Fire!"

There were thundering reports that awoke the echoes of the jungle, and the sounds of the rifles were followed by shrill trumpets of rage. When the smoke blew away three elephants were seen prostrate, or, rather two, and part of another one. The last was almost blown to pieces by Tom Swift's electric rifle; for the young inventor had used a little too heavy charge, and the big beast had been almost annihilated.

Mr. Durban had dropped his bull with a well-directed shot, and Mr. Anderson had a smaller one to his credit.

"I guess I missed mine," said Ned ruefully.

"Bless my dress-suit case!" exclaimed Mr. Damon. "So did I!"

"One of you hit that fellow!" cried Mr. Durban. "He's wounded."

He pointed to a fair-sized bull who was running wildly about, uttering shrill cries of anger. The other beasts had gathered in a compact mass, with the larger bulls, or tuskers, on the outside, to protect the females and young.

"I'll try a shot at him," said Tom, and raising his electric, gun, he took quick aim. The elephant dropped in his tracks, for this time the young inventor had correctly adjusted the power of the wireless bullet.

"Good!" cried Mr. Durban. "Give them some more! This is some of the best ivory I've seen yet!"

As he spoke he fired, and bowled over another magnificent specimen. Ned Newton, determined to make a record of at least one, fired again, and to his delight, saw a big fellow drop.

"I got him!" he yelled.

Mr. Anderson also got another, and then Mr. Damon, blessing something which his friends could not make out, fired at one of the largest bulls in the herd.

"You only nipped him!" exclaimed Mr. Durban when the smoke had drifted away. "I guess I'll put him out of his misery!"

He raised his weapon and pulled the trigger but no report followed. He uttered an exclamation of dismay.

"The breech-action has jammed!" he exclaimed. "Drop him, Tom. He's scented us, and is headed this way. The whole herd will follow in a minute."

Already the big brute wounded by Mr. Damon had trumpeted out a cry of rage and defiance. It was echoed by his mates. Then, with upraised trunk, he darted forward, followed by a score of big tuskers.

But Tom had heard and understood. The leading beast had not taken three steps before he dropped under the deadly and certain fire of the young inventor.

"Bless my wishbone!" cried Mr. Damon when he saw how effective the electric weapon was.

There was a shout of joy from the natives in the rear. They saw the slain creatures and knew there would be much fresh meat and feasting for them for days to come.

Suddenly Mr. Durban cried out: "Fire again, Tom! Fire everybody! The whole herd is coming this way. If we don't stop them they'll overrun the fields and village, and may smash the airship! Fire again!"

Almost as he spoke, the rush, which had been stopped momentarily, when Tom dropped the wounded elephant, began again. With shrill menacing cries the score of bulls in the lead came on, followed this time by the females and the young.

"It's a stampede!" yelled Mr. Anderson, firing into the midst of the herd. Mr. Durban was working frantically at his clogged rifle. Ned and Mr. Damon both fired, and Tom Swift, adjusting his weapon to give the heaviest charges, shot a fusillade of wireless bullets into the center of the advancing elephants, who were now wild with fear and anger.

"It's a stampede all right!" said Tom, when he saw that the big creatures were not going to stop, in spite of the deadly fire poured into them.

CHAPTER XV

LIONS IN THE NIGHT

Shouting, screaming, imploring their deities in general, and the white men in particular for protection, the band of frightened natives broke and ran through the jungle, caring little where they went so long as they escaped the awful terror of the pursuing herd of maddened elephants. Behind them came Tom Swift and the others, for it were folly to stop in the path of the infuriated brutes.

"Our only chance is to get on their flank and try to turn them!" yelled Mr. Durban. "We may beat them in getting to the clearing, for the trail is narrow. Run, everybody!"

No one needed his excited advice to cause them to hurry. They scudded along, Mr. Damon's cap falling off in his haste. But he did not stop to pick it up.

The hunters had one advantage. They were on a narrow but well-cleared trail through the jungle, which led from the village where they were encamped, to another, several miles away. This trail was too small for the elephants, and, indeed, had to be taken in single file by the travelers.

But it prevented the elephants making the same speed as did our friends, for the jungle, at this point, consisted of heavy trees, which halted the progress of even the strongest of the powerful beasts. True, they could force aside the frail underbrush and the small trees, but the others impeded their progress.

"We'll get there ahead of them!" cried Tom. "Have you got your rifle in working order yet, Mr. Durban?"

"No, something has broken, I fear. We'll have to depend on your electric gun, Tom. Have you many charges left?"

"A dozen or so. But Ned and the others have plenty of ammunition."

"Don't count—on—me!" panted Mr. Damon, who was well-nigh breathless from the run. "I—can't—aim—straight—any—more!"

"I'll give 'em a few more bullets!" declared Mr. Anderson.

The fleeing natives were now almost lost to sight, for they could travel through the jungle, ignoring the trail, at high speed. They were almost like snakes or animals in this respect. Their one thought was to get to their village, and, if possible, protect their huts and fields of grain from annihilation by the elephants.

Behind our friends, trumpeting, bellowing and crashing came the pachyderms. They seemed to be gaining, and Tom, looking back, saw one big brute emerge upon the trail, and follow that.

"I've got to stop him, or some of the others will do the same," thought the young inventor. He halted and fired quickly. The elephant seemed to melt away, and Tom with regret, saw a pair of fine tusks broken to bits. "I used too heavy a charge," he murmured, as he took up the retreat again.

In a few minutes the party of hunters, who were now playing more in the role of the hunted, came out into the open. They could hear the natives beating on their big hollow tree drums, and on tom-toms, while the witch-doctors and medicine men were chanting weird songs to drive the elephants away.

But the beasts came on. One by one they emerged from the jungle, until the herd was gathered together again in a compact mass. Then, under the leadership of some big bulls, they advanced. It seemed as if they knew what they were doing, and were determined to revenge themselves by trampling the natives' huts under their ponderous feet.

But Tom and the others were not idle. Taking a position off to one side, the young inventor began pouring a fusillade of the electric bullets into the mass of slate-colored bodies. Mr. Anderson was also firing, and Ned, who had gotten over some of his excitement, was also doing execution. Mr. Durban, after vainly trying to get his rifle to work, cast it aside.

"Here! Let me take your gun!" he cried to Mr. Damon, who, panting from the run, was sitting beneath a tree.

"Bless my cartridge belt! Take it and welcome!" assented the eccentric man. It still had several shots in the magazine, and these the old hunter used with good effect.

At first it seemed as if the elephants could not be turned back. They kept on rushing toward the village, which was not far away, and Tom and the others followed at one side, as best they could, firing rapidly. The electric rifle did fearful execution.

Emboldened by the fear that all their possessions would be destroyed a body of the natives rushed out, right in front of the elephants, and beat tom-toms and drums, almost under their feet, at the same time singing wild songs.

"I'm afraid we can't stop them!" muttered Mr. Anderson. "We'd better hurry to the airship, and protect that, Tom."

But, almost as he spoke, the tide of battle turned. The elephants suddenly swung about, and began a retreat. They could not stand the hot fire of the four guns, including Tom's fearful weapon. With wild trumpetings they fled back into the jungle, leaving a number of their dead behind.

"A close call," murmured Tom, as he drew a breath of relief. Indeed this was true, for the tide had turned when the foremost elephants were not a hundred feet away from the first rows of native huts.

"I should say it was," agreed Ned Newton, wiping his face with his handkerchief. He, as well as the others, was an odd-looking sight. They were blackened by powder smoke, scratched by briars, and red from exertion.

"But we got more ivory in this hour than I could have secured in a week of ordinary hunting," declared Mr. Durban. "If this keeps up we won't have to get much more, except that I don't think any of the tusks today are large enough for the special purpose of my customer."

"The sooner we get enough ivory the quicker we can go to the rescue of the missionaries," said Mr. Anderson.

"That's so," remarked Tom. "We must not forget the red pygmies."

The natives were now dancing about, wild in delight at the prospect of unlimited eating, and also thankful for what the white men had done for them. Alone, the blacks would never have been able to stop the stampede. They were soon busy cutting up the elephants ready for a big feast, and runners were sent to tell neighboring tribes, in adjoining villages, of the delights awaiting them.

Mr. Durban gave instructions about saving the ivory tusks, and the valuable teeth, each pair worth about $1,000, were soon cut out and put away for our friends. Some had been lost by the excessive power of

Tom's gun, but this could not be helped. It was necessary to stop the rush at any price.

There was soon a busy scene at the native village, and with the arrival of other tribesmen it seemed as if Bedlam had broken loose. The blacks chattered like so many children as they prepared for the feast.

"Do white men ever eat elephant meat?" asked Mr. Damon, as the adventurers were gathered about the airship.

"Indeed they do," declared Mr. Durban. "Baked elephant foot is a delicacy that few appreciate. I'll have the natives cook some for us."

He gave the necessary orders, and the travelers had to admit that it was worth coming far to get.

For the next few days and nights there was great feasting in that African village, and the praises of the white men, and power of Tom Swift's electric rifle, were sung loud and long.

Our friends had resumed work on repairing the airship, and the young inventor declared, one night, that they could proceed the next day.

They were seated around a small campfire, watching the dancing and antics of some natives who were at their usual work of eating meat. All about our friends were numerous blazes for the cooking of the feasts, and some were on the very edge of the jungle.

Suddenly, above the uncouth sounds of the merry-making, there was heard a deep vibration and roar, not unlike the distant rumble of thunder or the hum of a great steamer's whistle heard afar in the fog.

"What's that?" cried Ned.

"Lions," said Mr. Durban briefly. "They have been attracted by the smell of cooking."

At that moment, and instantly following a very loud roar, there was an agonized scream of pain and terror. It sounded directly in back of the airship.

"A lion!" cried Mr. Anderson. "One of the brutes has grabbed a native!"

Tom Swift caught up his rifle, and darted off toward the dark jungle.

CHAPTER XVI

SEEKING THE MISSIONARIES

"Here! Come back!" yelled Mr. Damon and Mr. Anderson, in the same breath, while the old elephant hunter cried out: "Don't you know you're risking your life, Tom to go off in the dark, to trail a lion?"

"I can't stand it to let the native be carried off!" Tom shouted back.

"But you can't see in the dark," objected Mr. Anderson. He had probably forgotten the peculiar property of the electric rifle. Tom kept on, and the others slowly followed.

The natives had at once ceased their merrymaking at the roaring of the lions, and now all were gathered close about the campfires, on which more wood had been piled, to drive away the fearsome brutes.

"There must be a lot of them," observed Mr. Durban, as menacing growls and roars came from the jungle, along the edge of which Tom and the others were walking just then. "There are so many of the brutes that they are bold, and they must be hungry, too. They came close to our fire, because it wasn't so bright as the other blazes, and that native must have wandered off into the forest. Well, I guess it's all up with him."

"He's screaming yet," observed Ned.

Indeed, above the rumbling roars of the lions, and the crackling of the campfires, could be heard the moaning cries of the unfortunate black.

"He's right close here!" suddenly called Tom. "He's skirting the jungle. I think I can get him!"

"Don't take any risks!" called Mr. Durban, who had caught up his own rifle, that was now in working order again.

Tom Swift was not in sight. He had now penetrated into the jungle— into the black forest where stalked the savage lions, intent on getting other prey. Mr. Durban and Mr. Anderson vainly tried to pierce the darkness to see something at which to shoot. Ned Newton had eagerly started to follow his chum, but could not discern where Tom was. A nameless fear clutched at the lad's heart. Mr. Damon was softly blessing everything of which he could think.

Once more came that pitiful cry from the native, who was, as they afterward learned, being dragged along by the lion, who had grabbed him by the shoulder.

Suddenly in the dense jungle there shone a purple-bluish light. It illuminated the scene like some great sky-rocket for an instant, and in that brief time Ned and the others caught sight of a great, tawny form, bounding along. It was a lion, with head held high, dragging along a helpless black man.

A second later, and before the intense glare had died away, the watchers saw the lion gently sink down, as though weary. He stopped short in his tracks, his head rolled back, the jaws relaxed and the native, who was unconscious now, toppled to one side.

"Tom's killed him with the electric rifle!" cried Mr. Durban.

"Bless my incandescent lamp! so he has," agreed Mr. Damon. "Bless my dynamo! but that's a wonderful gun, it's as powerful as a thunderbolt, or as gentle as a summer shower."

Mr. Durban seeing that the lion was dead, in that brief glance he had had of the brute, called to some of the natives to come and get their tribesman. They came, timidly enough at first, carrying many torches, but when they understood that the lion was dead, they advanced more boldly. They carried the wounded black to a hut, where they applied their simple but effective remedies for the cruel bite in his shoulder.

After Tom had shot several other of the illuminated charges into the jungle, to see if he could discover any more lions, but failed to do so, he and his friends returned to the anchored airship, amid the murmured thanks of the Africans.

Bright fires were kept blazing all the rest of the night, but, though lions could be heard roaring in the jungle, and though they approached alarmingly close to the place where our friends were encamped, none of the savage brutes ventured within the clearing.

With the valuable store of ivory aboard the Black Hawk, which was now completely repaired, an early start was made the next morning. The Africans besought Tom and his companions to remain, for it was not often they could have the services of white men in slaying elephants and lions.

"But, we've got to get on the trail," decided Tom, when the natives had brought great stores of food, and such simple presents as they possessed, to induce the travelers to remain.

"Every hour may add to the danger of the missionaries in the hands of the red pygmies."

"Yes," said Mr. Anderson gravely, "it is our duty to save them."

And so the airship mounted into the air, our friends waving farewells to the simple-hearted blacks, who did a sort of farewell war-dance in their honor, shouting their praises aloud, and beating the drums and tom-toms, so that the echoes followed for some time after the Black Hawk had begun to mount upward toward the sky.

The craft was in excellent shape, due to the overhauling Tom had given it while making the repairs. With the propellers beating the air, and the rudder set to hold them about two thousand feet high, the travelers moved rapidly over clearings, forests and jungles.

It was agreed that now, when they had made such a good start in collecting ivory, that they would spend the next few days in trying to get on the trail of the red pygmies. It might seem a simple matter, after knowing the approximate location of the land of these fierce little natives, to have proceeded directly to it. But Africa is an immense continent, and even in an airship comparatively little of the interior can be seen at a time.

Besides, the red pygmies had a habit of moving from place to place, and they were so small, and so wild, capable of living in very tiny huts or caves, and so primitive, not building regular villages as the other Africans do, that as Ned said, they were as hard to locate as the proverbial flea.

Our friends had a general idea of where to look for them, but on nearing that land, and making inquiries of several friendly tribes, they learned that the red pygmies had suddenly disappeared from their usual haunts.

"I guess they heard that we were after them," said Tom, with a grim smile one day, as he sent the airship down toward the earth, for they were over a great plain, and several native villages could be seen dotted on its surface.

"More likely they are in hiding because they have as captives two white persons," said Mr. Anderson. "They are fierce and fearless, but, nevertheless, they have, in times past, felt the vengeance of the white man, and perhaps they dread that now."

They made a descent, and spent several days making inquiries from the friendly blacks about the race of little men. But scarcely anything was learned. Some of the negro tribes admitted having heard of the red pygmies, and others, with superstitious incantations and imprecations, said they had never heard of them.

One tribe of very large negroes had heard a rumor to the effect that the band of the pygmies was several days' journey from their village, across the mountains, and when Tom sent his airship there, the searchers only found an impenetrable jungle, filled with lions and other wild beasts, but not a sign of the pygmies, and with no elephants to reward their search.

"But we're not going to give up," declared Tom, and the others agreed with him. Forward went the Black Hawk in the search for the imprisoned ones, but, as the days passed, and no news was had, it seemed to grow more and more hopeless.

"I'm afraid if we do find them now," remarked Mr. Anderson at length, "that we'll only recover the bodies of the missionaries."

"Then we'll avenge them," said Tom quietly.

They had stopped at another native village to make inquiries, but without result, and were about to start off again that night when a runner came in to announce that a herd of big elephants was feeding not many miles away.

"Well, we'll stay over a day or so, and get some more ivory," decided Mr. Durban and that night they got ready for what was to prove a big hunt.

CHAPTER XVII

SHOTS FROM ABOVE

"There they are!"

"My, what a lot of big ones!"

"Jove! Mr. Anderson, see those tusks!"

"Yes, you ought to get what you want this time, Mr. Durban."

"Bless my hatband! There must be two hundred of them!" exclaimed Mr. Damon.

"I'm glad I recharged my rifle last night!" exclaimed Tom Swift. "It's fully loaded now."

Then followed exulting cries and shouts of the natives, who were following our friends, the elephant hunters, who had given voice to the remarks we have just quoted.

It was early in the morning, and the hunt was about to start, for the news brought in by the runner the night before had been closely followed by the brutes themselves, and at dawn our friends were astir, for scouts brought in word that the elephants, including many big ones, were passing along only a few miles from the African village.

Cautiously approaching, with the wind blowing from the elephants to them, the white hunters made their way along. Mr. Durban was in the lead, and when he saw a favorable opportunity he motioned for the others to advance. Then, when he noticed the big bull sentinels of the herd look about as if to detect the presence of enemies, he gave another signal and the hunters sank out of sight in the tall grass.

As for the natives, they were like snakes, unseen but ever present, wriggling along on their hands and knees. They were awaiting the slaughter, when there would be fresh meat in abundance.

At length the old elephant hunter decided that they were near enough to chance some shots. As a matter of fact, Tom Swift, with his electric rifle, had been within range some time before, but as he did not want to spoil the sport for the others, by firing and killing, and so alarming the herd, he had held back. Now they could all shoot together.

"Let her go!" suddenly cried Mr. Durban, and they took aim.

There was a fusillade of reports and several of the big brutes toppled over.

"Bless my toothbrush!" cried Mr. Damon, "that's the time I got one!"

"Yes, and a fine specimen, too!" added Mr. Durban, who had only succeeded in downing a small bull, with an indifferent pair of tusks. "A fine specimen, Mr. Damon, I congratulate you!"

As for Tom Swift, he had killed two of the largest elephants in the herd.

But now the hunters had their work cut out for them, since the beasts had taken fright and were charging away at what seemed an awkward gait, but which, nevertheless, took them rapidly over the ground.

"Come on!" cried Mr. Durban. "We must get some more. Some of the finest tusks I have ever seen are running away from us!"

He began to race after the retreating herd, but it is doubtful if he would have caught up to them had not a band of natives, who had crept up and surrounded the beasts, turned them by shouts and the beating of tom-toms. Seeing an enemy in front of them, the elephants turned, and our friends were able to get in several more shots. Tom Swift picked out only those with immense tusks, and soon had several to his credit. Ned Newton also bagged some prizes.

But finally the elephants, driven to madness by the firing and the yells of the natives, broke through the line of black men, and charged off into the jungle, where it was not only useless but dangerous to follow them.

"Well, we have enough," said Mr. Durban, and when the tusks had been collected it was found that indeed a magnificent and valuable supply had been gathered.

"But I have yet to get my prize ones," said the old hunter with a sigh. "Maybe we'll find the elephant with them when we locate the red pygmies."

"If we do, we'll have our work cut out for us," declared Tom.

As on the other occasion after the hunt, there was a great feast for the natives, who invited tribes from miles around, and for two days, while the tusks were being cut out and cleaned, there were barbeques on every side.

It was one afternoon, when they were seated in the shade of the airship, cleaning their guns, and discussing the plans they had best follow next, that our travellers suddenly heard a great commotion amongst the Africans, who had for the past hour been very quiet, most of them sleeping after the feasts. They yelled and shouted, and began to beat their drums.

"Something is coming," said Ned.

"Perhaps there's going to be a fight," suggested Tom.

"Maybe it's the red pygmies," said Mr. Damon. "Bless my—"

But what he was going to bless he did not say, for at that instant it seemed as if every native in sight suddenly disappeared, almost like magic. They sank down into the grass, darted into their huts, or hid in the tall grass.

"What can it be?" cried Tom, as he looked to see that his rifle was in working order.

"Some enemy," declared Mr. Anderson.

"There they are!" cried Ned Newton, and as he spoke there burst into view, coming from the tall grass that covered the plain about the village, a herd of savage, wild buffaloes. On rushed the shaggy creatures, their long, sharp horns seeming like waving spears as they advanced.

"Here's more sport!" cried Tom.

"No! Not sport! Danger!" yelled Mr. Durban. "They're headed right for us!"

"Then we'll stop them," declared the young inventor, as he raised his gun.

"No! No!" begged the old hunter. "It's as much as our lives are worth to try to stop a rush of wild buffaloes. You couldn't do it with Gatling guns. We can kill a few, but the rest won't stop until they've finished us and the aeroplane too."

"Then what's to be done?" demanded Mr. Anderson.

"Get into the airship!" cried Mr. Durban. "Send her up. It's the only way to get out of their path. Then we can shoot them from above, and drive them away!"

Quickly the adventurers leaped into the craft. On thundered the buffaloes. Tom feared he could not get the motor started quickly enough. He did not dare risk rising by means of the aeroplane feature, but at once started the gas machine.

The big bag began to fill. Nearer came the wild creatures, thundering over the ground, snorting and bellowing with rage.

"Quick, Tom!" yelled Ned, and at that instant the Black Hawk shot upward, just as the foremost of the buffaloes passed underneath, vainly endeavoring to gore the craft with their sweeping horns. The air-travelers had risen just in time.

"Now it's our turn!" shouted Ned, as he began firing from above into the herd of infuriated animals below him. Tom, after seeing that the motor was working well, sent the airship circling about, while standing in the steering tower, he guided his craft here and there, meanwhile pouring a fusillade of his wireless bullets into the buffaloes. Many of them dropped in their tracks, but the big herd continued to rush here and there, crashing into the frail native huts, tearing them down, and, whenever a black man appeared, chasing after him infuriatedly.

"Keep at it!" cried Mr. Durban, as he poured more lead into the buffaloes. "If we don't kill enough of them, and drive the others away, there won't be anything left of this village."

CHAPTER XVIII

NEWS OF THE RED PYGMIES

Seldom had it been the lot of Tom and his companions to take part in such a novel hunting scene as that in which they were now participating. With the airship moving quickly about, darting here and there under the guidance of the young inventor, the erratic movements hither and thither of the buffaloes could be followed exactly. Wherever the mass of the herd went the airship hovered over them.

"Want any help, Tom?" called Ned, who was firing as fast as his gun could be worked.

"I guess not," answered the steersman of the Black Hawk, who was dividing his attention between managing the craft and firing his electric rifle.

The others, too, were kept busy with their weapons, shooting down on the infuriated animals. It seemed like a needless slaughter, but it was not. Had it not been for the white men, the native village, which consisted of only frail huts, would have been completely wiped out by the animals. As it was they were kept "milling" about in a circle in an open space, just as stampeded cattle on the western ranges are kept from getting away, by being forced round and round.

Not a native was in sight, all being hidden away in the jungle or dense grass. The white hunters in their airship had matters to themselves.

At last the firing proved even too much for the buffaloes which, as we have said, are among the most dreaded of African beasts. With bellows of fear, the leading bulls of the herd unable to find the enemy above their heads, darted off into the forest the way they had come.

"There they go!" yelled Mr. Durban.

"Yes, and I'm glad to see the last of them," added Mr. Anderson, with a breath of relief.

"Score another victory for the electric rifle," exclaimed Ned.

"Oh, you did as much execution as I did," declared the inventor of the weapon.

"Bless my ramrod!" cried Mr. Damon. "I never shot so much in all my life before."

"Yes, there is enough food to last the natives for a week," observed Mr. Durban, as Tom adjusted the deflecting rudder to send the airship down.

"It won't last much longer at the rate they eat," spoke the young inventor with a laugh. "I never saw such fellows for appetites! They seem to eat in their sleep."

There were many dead buffaloes, but there was no fear that the meat, which was much prized by the Africans, would be wasted. Already the natives were coming from their hiding places, knowing that the danger was over. Once more they sang the praises of the mighty white hunters, and the magical air craft in which they moved about.

With the elephants previously killed, the buffaloes provided material for a great feast, preparations for which were at once gotten under way, in spite of the fact that the blacks had hardly stopped eating since the big hunt began. But it was about all they had to do.

Some of the buffaloes were very large, and there were a number of pairs of fine horns. Tom and Ned had some of the blacks cut them off for trophies, and they were stored in the airship together with the ivory.

Becoming rather tired of seeing so much feasting, our friends bade the Africans farewell the next day, and once more resumed their quest. They navigated through the air for another week, stopping at several villages, and scanning the jungles and plains by means of powerful telescopes, for a sight of the red pygmies. They also asked for news of the sacking of the missionary settlement, but, beyond meager facts, could learn nothing.

"Well, we've got to keep on, that's all," decided Mr. Durban. "We may find them most unexpectedly."

"I'm sorry if I have taken you away from your work of gathering ivory," spoke Mr. Anderson. "Perhaps you had better let me go, and I'll see if I can't organize a band of friendly blacks, and search for the red dwarfs myself."

"Not much!" exclaimed Tom warmly. "I said we'd help rescue those missionaries, and we'll do it, too!"

"Of course," declared the old elephant hunter. "We have quite a lot of ivory and, while we need more to make it pay well, we can look for it after we rescue the missionaries as well as before. Perhaps there will be a lot of elephants in the pygmies' land."

"I was only thinking that we can't go on forever in the airship." said Mr. Anderson. "You'll have to go back to civilization soon, won't you, Tom, to get gasolene?"

"No, we have enough for at least a month," answered the young inventor. "I took aboard an unusually large supply when we started."

"What would happen if we ran out of it in the jungle?" asked Ned.

"Bless my pocketbook! What an unpleasant question!" exclaimed Mr. Damon. "You are almost as cheerful, Ned, as was my friend Mr. Parker, the gloomy scientist, who was always predicting dire happenings."

"Well, I was only wondering," said Ned, who was a little abashed by the manner in which his inquiry was received.

"Oh, it would be all right," declared Tom. "We would simply become a balloon, and in time the wind would blow us to some white settlement. There is plenty of material for making the lifting gas."

This was reassuring, and, somewhat easier in mind, Ned took his place in the observation tower which looked down on the jungle over which they were passing.

It was a dense forest. At times there could be seen, in the little clearings, animals darting along. There were numbers of monkeys, an occasional herd of buffaloes were observed, sometimes a solitary stray elephant was noted, and as for birds, there were thousands of them. It was like living over a circus, Ned declared.

They had descended one day just outside a large native village to make inquiries about elephants and the red pygmies. Of the big beasts no signs had been seen in several months, the hunters of the tribe told Mr. Durban. And concerning the red pygmies, the blacks seemed indisposed to talk.

Tom and the others could not understand this, until a witch-doctor, whom the elephant hunter had met some time ago, when he was on a previous expedition, told him that the tribe had a superstitious fear of speaking of the little men.

"They may be around us—in the forest or jungle at any minute," the witch-doctor said. "We never speak of them."

"Say, do you suppose that can be a clue?" asked Tom eagerly. "They may be nearer at hand than we think."

"It's possible." admitted the hunter. "Suppose we stay here for a few days, and I'll see if I can't get some of the natives to go off scouting in the woods, and locate them, or at least put us on the trail of the red dwarfs."

This was considered good advice, and it was decided to adopt it. Accordingly the airship was put in a safe place, and our friends prepared to spend a week, if necessary, in the native village. Their presence with the wonderful craft was a source of wonder, and by means of some trinkets judiciously given to the native king, and also to his head subjects, and to the witch-doctors (who were a power in the land), the good opinion of the tribe was won. Then, by promising rewards to some of the bolder hunters, Mr. Durban finally succeeded in getting them to go off scouting in the jungle for a clue to the red pygmies.

"Now we'll have to wait," said Mr. Anderson, "and I hope we get good news."

Our friends spent their time observing some of the curious customs of the natives, and in witnessing some odd dances gotten up in their honor. They also went hunting, and got plenty of game, for which their hosts were duly grateful. Tom did some night stalking and found his illuminating bullets a great success.

One hot afternoon Tom and Mr. Damon strolled off a little way into the jungle, Tom with his electric weapon, in case he saw any game. But no animals save a few big monkeys where to be seen, and the young inventor scorned to kill them. It seemed too much like firing at a human being he said, though the natives stated that some of the baboons and apes were fierce, and would attack one on the slightest provocation.

"I believe I'll sit down here and rest," said Tom, after a mile's tramp, as he came to a little clearing in the woods.

"Very well, I'll go on," decided Mr. Damon. "Mr. Durban said there were sometimes rare orchids in these jungles, and I am very fond of those odd flowers. I'm going to see if I can get any."

He disappeared behind a fringe of moss-grown trees, and Tom sat down, with his rifle across his knees. He was thinking of many things, but chiefly of what yet lay before them—the discovery of the red dwarfs and the possible rescue of the missionaries.

He might have been thus day-dreaming for perhaps a half hour, when he suddenly heard great commotion in the jungle, in the direction in which Mr. Damon had vanished. It sounded as though some one was running rapidly. Then came the report of the odd man's gun.

"He's seen some game!" exclaimed Tom, jumping up, and preparing to follow his friend. But he did not have the chance. An instant later Mr. Damon burst through the bushes with every appearance of fright, his gun held above his head with one hand, and his pith helmet swaying to and fro in the other.

"They're coming!" he cried to Tom.

"Who, the red pygmies?"

"No, but a couple of rhinoceroses are after me. I wounded one, and he and his mate are right behind. Don't let them catch me, Tom!"

Mr. Damon was very much alarmed, and there was good occasion for it, as Tom saw a moment later, for two fierce rhinoceroses burst out of the jungle almost on the heels of the fleeing man.

Thought was not quicker than Tom Swift. He raised his deadly rifle, and pressed the button. A charge of wireless electricity shot toward the foremost animal, and it was dropped in its tracks. The other came on woofing and snorting with rage. It was the one Mr. Damon had slightly wounded.

"Come on!" yelled the young inventor, for his friend was in front of the beast, and in range with the rifle. "Jump to one side, Mr. Damon."

Mr. Damon tried, but his foot slipped, and there was no need for jumping. He fell and rolled over. The rhinoceros swerved toward him, with the probable intention of goring the prostrate man with the formidable horn, but it had no chance. Once more the young inventor fired, this time with a heavier charge, and the animal instantly toppled over dead.

"Are you hurt?" asked Tom anxiously, as he ran to his friend. Mr. Damon got up slowly. He felt all over himself, and then answered:

"No, Tom, I guess I'm not hurt, except in my dignity. Never again will I fire at a sleeping rhinoceros unless you are with me. I had a narrow escape," and he shook Tom's hand heartily.

"Did you see any orchids?" asked the lad with a smile.

"No, those beasts didn't give me a chance! Bless my tape measure! but they're big fellows!"

Indeed they were fine specimens, and there was the usual rejoicing among the natives when they brought in the great bodies, pulling them to the village with ropes made of vines.

After this Mr. Damon was careful not to go into the jungle alone, nor, in fact, did any of our friends so venture. Mr. Durban said it was not safe.

They remained a full week in the native village, and received no news. In fact, all but one of the hunters came back to report that there was no sign of the red pygmies in that neighborhood.

"Well, I guess we might as well move on, and see what we can do ourselves," said Mr. Durban.

"Let's wait until the last hunter comes back," suggested Tom. "He may bring word."

"Some of his friends think he'll never come back," remarked Mr. Anderson.

"Why not?" asked Ned.

"They think he has been killed by some wild beast."

But this fear was ungrounded. It was on the second day after the killing of the rhinoceroses that, as Tom was tinkering away in the engine-room of the airship, and thinking that perhaps they had better get under way, that a loud shouting was heard among the natives.

"I wonder what's up now?" mused the young inventor as he went outside. He saw Mr. Durban and Mr. Anderson running toward the ship. Behind them was a throng of blacks, led by a weary man whom Tom recognized as the missing hunter. The lad's heart beat high with hope. Did the African bring news?

On came Mr. Durban, waving his hands to Tom.

"We've located 'em!" he shouted.

"Not the red pygmies?" asked Tom eagerly.

"Yes; this hunter has news of them. He has been to the border of their country, and narrowly escaped capture. Then he was attacked by a lion, and slightly wounded. But, Tom, now we can get on the trail!"

"Good!" cried the young inventor. "That's fine news!" and he rejoiced that once more there would be activity, for he was tired of remaining in the African camp, and then, too, he wanted to proceed to the rescue. Already it might be too late to save the unfortunate missionaries.

CHAPTER XIX

AN APPEAL FOR HELP

The African hunter's story was soon told. He had gone on farther than had any of his companions, and, being a bold and brave man, had penetrated into the very fastness of the jungle where few would dare to venture.

But even he had despaired of getting on the trail of the fierce little red men, until one afternoon, just at dusk he had heard voices in the forest. Crouching behind a fallen tree, he waited and saw passing by some of the pygmy hunters, armed with bows and arrows, and blowguns. They had been out after game. Cautiously the hunter followed them, until he located one of their odd villages, which consisted of little mud huts, poorly made.

The black hunter remained in the vicinity of the pygmies all that night, and was almost caught, for some wild dogs which hung around the village smelled him out, and attracted to him the attention of the dwarf savages. The hunter took to a tree, and so escaped. Then, carefully marking the trail, he came away in the morning. When near home, a lion had attacked him, but he speared the beast to death, after a hand-to-hand struggle in which his leg was torn.

"And do you think we can find the place?" asked Ned, when Mr. Durban had finished translating the hunter's story.

"I think so," was the reply.

"But is this the settlement where the missionaries are?" asked Tom anxiously.

"That is what we don't know," said Mr. Anderson. "The native scout could not learn that. But once we get on the trail of the dwarfs, I think we can easily find the particular tribe which has the captives."

"At any rate, we'll get started and do something," declared Tom, and the next day, after the African hunter had described, as well as he could, where the place was, the Black Hawk was sent up into the air, good-bys were called down, and once more the adventurers were under way.

It was decided that they had better proceed cautiously, and lower the airship, and anchor it, sometime before getting above the place where the pygmy village was.

"For they may see us, and, though they don't know what our craft is, they may take the alarm and hide deeper in the jungle with the prisoners, where we can't find them," said Tom.

His plan was adopted, and, while it had taken the native hunter several days to reach the borders of the dwarfs' land, those in the airship made the trip in one day. That is, they came as far toward it as they thought would be safe, and one night, having located a landmark which Mr. Durban said was on the border, the nose of the Black Hawk was pointed downward, and soon they were encamped in a little clearing in the midst of the dense jungle which was all about them.

With his electric rifle, Tom noiselessly killed some birds, very much like chicken, of which an excellent meal was made and then, as it became dark very early, and as nothing could be done, they lighted a campfire, and retired inside their craft to pass the night.

It must have been about midnight that Tom, who was a light sleeper at times, was awakened by some noise outside the window near which his stateroom was. He sat up and listened, putting out his hand to where his rifle stood in the corner near his bunk. The lad heard stealthy footsteps pattering about on the deck of the airship. There was a soft, shuffling sound, such as a lion or a tiger makes, when walking on bare boards. In spite of himself, Tom felt the hair on his head beginning to creep, and a shiver ran down his back.

"There's something out there!" he whispered. "I wonder if I'd better awaken the others? No, if it's a sneaking lion, I can manage to kill him, but—"

He paused as another suggestion came to him.

The red pygmies! They went barefoot! Perhaps they were swarming about the ship which they might have discovered in the darkness.

Tom Swift's heart beat rapidly. He got softly out of his bunk, and, with his rifle in hand made his way to the door opening on deck. On his way he gently awakened Ned and Mr. Durban, and whispered to them his fear.

"If the red pygmies are out there we'll need all our force," said the old elephant hunter. "Call Mr. Damon and Mr. Anderson, Ned, and tell them to bring their guns."

Soon they were all ready, fully armed. They listened intently. The airship was all in darkness, for lights drew a horde of insects. The campfire had died down. The soft footsteps could still be heard moving about the deck.

"That sounds like only one person or animal," whispered Ned.

"It does," agreed Tom. "Wait a minute, I'll fire an illuminating charge, and we can see what it is."

The others posted themselves at windows that gave a view of the deck. Tom poked his electric rifle out of a crack of the door, and shot forth into the darkness one of the blue illuminations. The deck of the craft was instantly lighted up brilliantly, and in the glare, crouched on the deck, could be seen a powerful black man, nearly naked, gazing at the hunters.

"A black!" gasped Tom, as the light died out. "Maybe it is one from the village we just left. What do you want? Who are you?" called the lad, forgetting that the Africans spoke only their own language. To the surprise of all, there came his reply in broken English:

"Me Tomba! Me go fo' help for Missy Illingway—fo' Massy Illingway. Me run away from little red men! Me Christian black man. Oh, if you be English, help Missy Illingway—she most die! Please help. Tomba go but Tomba be lost! Please help!"

CHAPTER XX

THE FIGHT

Surprise, for the moment, held Tom and the others speechless. To be answered in English, poor and broken as it was, by a native African, was strange enough, but when this same African was found aboard the airship, in the midst of the jungle, at midnight, it almost passed the bounds of possibility.

"Tomba!" mused Tom, wondering where he had heard that name before. "Tomba?"

"Of course!" cried Mr. Anderson, suddenly. "Don't you remember? That's the name of the servant of Mr. and Mrs. Illingway, who escaped and brought news of their capture by the pygmies. That's who Tomba is."

"Yes, but Tomba escaped," objected Mr. Durban. "He went to the white settlements with the news. How comes he here?"

"We'll have to find out," said Tom, simply. "Tomba, are you there?" he called, as he fired another illuminating charge. It disclosed the black man standing up on the deck, and looking at them appealingly.

"Yes, Tomba here," was the answer. "Oh, you be English, Tomba know. Please help Missy and Massy Illingway. Red devils goin' kill 'em pretty much quick."

"Come in!" called Tom, as he turned on the electric lights in the airship. "Come in and tell us all about it. But how did you get here?"

"Maybe there are two Tombas," suggested Ned.

"Bless my safety razor!" cried Mr. Damon "perhaps Ned is right!"

But he wasn't, as they learned when they had questioned the African, who came inside the airship, looking wonderingly around at the many strange things he saw. He was the same Tomba who had escaped the massacre, and had taken news of the capture of his master and mistress to the white settlement. In vain after that he had tried to organize a band to go back with him to the rescue, but the whites in the settlement were too few, and the natives too timid. Then Tomba, with grief in his heart, and not wanting to live while the missionaries whom he had come to care for very much, were captives, he went back into the jungle, determined, if he could not help them, that at least he would share their fate, and endeavor to be of some service to them in their captivity.

After almost unbelievable hardships, he had found the red pygmies, and had allowed himself to be captured by them. They rejoiced greatly in the possession of the big black man, and for some strange reason had not killed him. He was allowed to share the captivity of his master and mistress.

Time went on, and the pygmies did not kill their prisoners. They even treated them with some kindness but were going to sacrifice them at their great annual festival, which was soon to take place. Mr. and Mrs. Illingway, Tomba told our friends in his broken English, had urged him to escape at the first opportunity. They knew if he could get away he would travel through the jungle. They could not, even if they had not been so closely guarded that escape was out of the question.

But Tomba refused to go until Mr. Illingway had said that perhaps he might get word to some white hunters, and so send help to the captives. This Tomba consented to do, and, watching his chance, he did escape. That was several nights ago, and he had been traveling through the jungle ever since. It was by mere accident that he came upon the anchored airship, and his curiosity led him to board her. The rest is known.

"Well, of all queer yarns, this is the limit!" exclaimed Tom, when the black had finished. "What had we better do about it?"

"Get ready to attack the red pygmies at once!" decided Mr. Durban. "If we wait any longer it may be too late!"

"My idea, exactly," declared Mr. Anderson.

"Bless my bowie-knife!" cried Mr. Damon. "I'd like to get a chance at the red imps! Come on, Tom! Let's start at once."

"No, we need daylight to fight by," replied Tom, with a smile at his friend's enthusiasm. "We'll go forward in the morning."

"In the airship?" asked Mr. Damon.

"I think so," answered Tom. "There can be no advantage now in trying to conceal ourselves. We can move upon them from where we are so quickly that they won't have much chance to get away. Besides it will take us too long to make our way through the jungle afoot. For, now that the escape of Tomba must be known, they may kill the captives at once to forestall any rescue."

"Then we'll move forward in the morning," declared Mr. Durban.

They took Tomba with them in the airship the next day, though he prayed fervently before he consented to it. But they needed him to point out the exact location of the pygmies' village, since it was not the one the hunter-scout had been near.

The Black Hawk sailed through the air. On board eager eyes looked down for a first sight of the red imps. Tomba, who was at Tom's side in the steering tower, told him, as best he could, from time to time, how to set the rudders.

"Pretty soon by-em-by be there," said the black man at length. "Pass ober dat hill, den red devils live."

"Well, we'll soon be over that hill," announced Tom grimly. "I guess we'd better get our rifles ready for the battle."

"Are you going to attack them at once?" asked Mr. Damon.

"Well," answered the young inventor, "I don't believe we ought to kill any of them if we can avoid it. I don't like to do such a thing but, perhaps we can't help ourselves. My plan is to take the airship down, close to the hut where the missionaries are confined. Tomba can point it out to us. If we can rescue them without bloodshed, so much the better. But we'll fight if we have to."

Grimly they watched as the airship sailed over the hill. Then suddenly there came into view a collection of mud huts on a vast plain, surrounded by dense jungle on every side. As the travelers looked, they could see little creatures running wildly about. Even without a glass it could be noted that their bodies were covered with a curious growth of thick sandy hair.

"The red pygmies!" cried Tom. "Now for the rescue!"

Eagerly Tomba indicated the hut where his master and mistress were held. Telling his friends to have their weapons in readiness, Tom steered the airship toward the rude shelter whence he hoped to take the missionaries. Down to the ground swiftly shot the Black Hawk. Tom checked her with a quick movement of the deflecting rudder, and she landed gently on the wheels.

"Mr. Illingway! Mrs. Illingway! We have come to rescue you!" yelled the young inventor, as he stepped out on the deck, with his electric rifle in his hand. "Where are you? Can you come out?"

The door of the hut was burst open, and a white man and woman, recognizable as such, even in the rude skins that clothed them, rushed out. Wonder spread over their faces as they saw the great airship. They dropped on their knees.

The next instant a swarm of savage little red men surrounded them, and rudely bore them, strugglingly, back into the hut.

"Come on!" cried Tom, about to leap to the ground. "It's now or never! We must save them!"

Mr. Durban pulled him back, and pointed to a horde of the red-haired savages rushing toward the airship. "They'd tear you to pieces in a minute!" cried the old hunter. "We must fight them from the ship."

There was a curious whistling sound in the air. Mr. Durban looked up.

"Duck, everybody!" he yelled. "They're firing arrows at us! Get under shelter, for they may be poisoned!"

Tom and the others darted into the craft. The arrows rattled on deck in a shower, and hundreds of the red imps were rushing up to give battle. Inside the hut where the missionaries were, it was now quiet. Tom Swift wondered if they still lived.

"Give 'em as good as they send!" cried Mr. Durban. "We will have to fire at them now. Open up with your electric rifle, Tom!"

As he spoke the elephant hunter fired into the midst of the screaming savages. The battle had begun.

CHAPTER XXI

DRIVEN BACK

What the travelers had heard regarding the fierceness and courage of the red pygmies had not been one bit exaggerated. Never had such desperate fighting ever taken place. The red dwarfs, scarcely one of whom was more than three feet high, were strongly built, and there were so many of them, and they battled together with such singleness of purpose, that they were more formidable than a tribe of ordinary-sized savages would have been.

And their purpose was to utterly annihilate the enemy that had so unexpectedly come upon them. It did not matter to them that Tom and the others had arrived in an airship. The strange craft had no superstitious terror for them, as it had for the simpler blacks.

"Bless my multiplication tables!" cried Mr. Damon. "What a mob of them!"

"Almost too many!" murmured Tom Swift, who was rapidly firing his electric rifle at them. "We can never hope to drive them back, I'm afraid."

Indeed from every side of the plain, and even from the depths of the jungle the red dwarfs were now pouring. They yelled most horribly, screaming in rage, brandishing their spears and clubs, and keeping up an incessant fire of big arrows from their bows, and smaller ones from the blowguns.

As yet none of our friends had been hit, for they were sheltered in the airship, and as the windows were covered with a mesh of wire, to keep out insects, this also served to prevent the arrows from entering. There were loopholes purposely made to allow the rifles to be thrust out.

Mercifully, Tom and the others fired only to disable, and not to kill the red pygmies. Wounded in the arms or legs, the little savages would be incapable of fighting, and this plan was followed. But so fierce were they that some, who were wounded twice, still kept up the attack.

Tom's electric rifle was well adapted for this work, as he could regulate the charge to merely stun, no matter at what part of the body it was directed. So he could fire indiscriminately, whereas the others had to aim carefully. And Tom's fire was most effective. He disabled scores of the red imps, but scores of others sprang up to take their places.

After their first rush the pygmies had fallen back before the well-directed fire of our friends, but as their chiefs and head men urged them to the attack again, they came back with still fiercer energy. Some, more bold than the others, even leaped to the deck of the airship, and tried to tear the screens from the windows. They partly succeeded, and in one casement from which Ned was firing they made a hole.

Into this they shot a flight of arrows, and one slightly wounded the bank clerk on the arm. The wound was at once treated with antiseptics, after the window had been barricaded, and Ned declared that he was ready to renew the fight. Tom, too, got an arrow scratch on the neck, and one of the barbs entered Mr. Durban's leg, but the sturdy elephant hunter would not give up, and took his place again after the wound had been bandaged.

From time to time as he worked his electric gun, which had been charged to its utmost capacity, Tom glanced at the hut where the missionaries were prisoners. There was no movement noticed about it, and no sound came from it. Tom wondered what had happened inside—he wondered what was happening as the battle progressed.

Fiercely the fight was kept up. Now the red imps would be driven back, and again they would swarm about the airship, until it seemed as if they must overwhelm it. Then the fire of the white adventurers was redoubled. The electric rifle did great work, and Tom did not have to stop and refill the magazine, as did the others.

Suddenly, above the noise of the conflict, Tom Swift heard an ominous sound. It was a hissing in the air, and well he knew what it was.

"The gas bag!" he cried. "They've punctured it! The vapor is escaping. If they put too many holes in the bag it will be all up with us!"

"What's to be done?" asked Mr. Durban.

"If we can't drive them back we must retreat ourselves!" declared Tom desperately. "Our only hope is to keep the airship safe from harm."

Once more came a rush of the savages. They had discovered that the gas bag was vulnerable, and were directing their arrows against that. It was punctured in several more places. The gas was rapidly escaping.

"We've got to retreat!" yelled Tom. He hurried to the engine-room, and turned on the power. The great propellers revolved, and sent the Black Hawk scudding across the level plain. With yells of surprise the red dwarfs scattered and made way for it.

Up into the air it mounted on the broad wings. For the time being our friends has been driven back, and the missionaries whom they had come to rescue were still in the hands of the savages.

CHAPTER XXII

A NIGHT ATTACK

"Well, what's to be done?"

Tom Swift asked that question.

"Bless my percussion cap! They certainly are the very worst imps for fighting that I ever heard of," commented Mr. Damon helplessly.

"Is the gas bag much punctured?" asked Ned Newton.

"Wait a minute," resumed the young inventor, as he pulled the speed lever a trifle farther over, thereby sending the craft forward more swiftly, "I think my question ought to be answered first. What's to be done? Are we going to run away, and leave that man and woman to their fate?"

"Of course not!" declared Mr. Durban stoutly, "but we couldn't stay there, and have them destroy the airship."

"No, that's so," admitted Tom, "if we lost the airship it would be all up with us and our chances of rescuing the missionaries. But what can we do? I hate to retreat!"

"But what else is there left for us?" demanded Ned.

"Nothing, of course. But we've got to plan to get the best of those red pygmies. We can't go back in the airship, and give them open battle. There are too many of them, and, by Jove! I believe more are coming every minute!"

Tom and the others looked down. From all sides of the plain, hastening toward the village of mud huts, from which our friends were retreating, could be seen swarms of the small but fierce savages. They were coming from the jungle, and were armed with war clubs, bows and arrows and the small but formidable blowguns.

"Where are they coming from?" asked Mr. Damon.

"From the surrounding tribes," explained Mr. Durban. "They have been summoned to do battle against us."

"But how did the ones we fought get word to the others so soon?" Ned demanded.

"Oh, they have ways of signaling," explained Mr. Anderson. "They can make the notes of some of their hollow-tree drums carry a long distance, and then they are very swift runners, and can penetrate into the jungle along paths that a white man would hardly see. They also use the smoke column as a signal, as our own American Indians used to do. Oh, they can summon all their tribesmen to the fight, and they probably will. Likely the sound of our guns attracted the imps, though if we all had electric rifles like Tom's they wouldn't make any noise."

"Well, my rifle didn't appear to do so very much good this time," observed the young inventor, as he stopped the forward motion of the ship now, and let it hover over the plain in sight of the village, the gas bag serving to sustain the craft, and there was little wind to cause it to drift. "Those fellows didn't seem to mind being hurt and killed any more than if mosquitoes were biting them."

"The trouble is we need a whole army, armed with electric rifles to make a successful attack," said Mr. Durban. "There are swarms of them there now, and more coming every minute. I do hope Mr. and Mrs. Illingway are alive yet."

"Yes," added Mr. Anderson solemnly, "we must hope for the best. But, like Tom Swift, I ask, what's to be done?"

"Bless my thinking cap!" exclaimed Mr. Damon. "It seems to me if we can't fight them openly in the daytime, there's only one other thing to do."

"What's that?" asked Tom. "Go away? I'll not do it!"

"No, not go away," exclaimed Mr. Damon, "but make a night attack. We ought to be able to do something then, and with your illuminating rifle, Tom, we'd have an advantage! What do you say?"

"I say it's the very thing!" declared Tom, with sudden enthusiasm. "We'll attack them tonight, when they're off their guard, and we'll see if we can't get the missionaries out of that hut. And to better fool the savages, we'll just disappear now, and make 'em believe we've flown away."

"Then the missionaries will think we're deserting them," objected Mr. Anderson.

But there was no help for it, and so Tom once more turned on the power and the craft sailed away.

Tomba, the faithful black, begged to be allowed to go down, and tell his master and mistress that help would soon be at hand again, even though it looked like a retreat on the part of the rescuers, but this could not be permitted.

"They'd tear you in pieces as soon as you got among those red imps," said Tom. "You stay here, Tomba, and you can help us tonight."

"A'right, me glad help lick red fellows," said the black, with as cheerful a grin as he could summon.

The Black Hawk circled around, with Tom and the others looking for a good place to land. They were out of sight of the village now but did not doubt but that they were observed by the keen eyes of the little men.

"We want to pick out a place where they won't come upon us as we descend," declared Tom. "We've got to mend some leaks in the gas bag, for, while they are not serious, if we get any more punctures they may become so. So we've got to pick out a good place to go down."

Finally, by means of powerful glasses, a desolate part of the jungle was selected. No files of the red dwarfs, coming from their scattered villages to join their tribesmen, had been noted in the vicinity picked out, and it was hoped that it would answer. Slowly the airship settled to earth, coming to rest in a thick grove of trees, where there was an opening just large enough to allow the Black Hawk to enter.

Our friends were soon busy repairing the leaks in the bag, while Mr. Damon got a meal ready. As they ate they talked over plans for the night attack.

It was decided to wait until it was about two o'clock in the morning, as at that hour the dwarfs were most generally asleep, Tomba said. They always stayed up quite late, sitting around camp-fires, and eating the meat which the hunters brought in each day. But their carousings generally ended at midnight, the black said, and then they fell into a heavy sleep. They did not post guards, but since they knew of the presence of the white men in the airship, they might do it this time.

"Well, we've got to take our chance," decided Tom. "We'll start off from here about one o'clock, and I'll send the ship slowly along. We'll get right over the hut where the captives are, if possible, and then descend. I'll manage the ship, and one of you can work the electric rifle if they attack us. We'll make a dash, get Mr. and Mrs. Illingway from the hut, and make a quick get-away."

It sounded good, and they were impatient to put it into operation. That afternoon Tom and his friends went carefully over every inch of their craft, to repair it and have it in perfect working order. Guns were cleaned, and plenty of ammunition laid out. Then, shortly after one o'clock in the morning the ship was sent up, and with the searchlight ready to be turned on instantly, and with his electric rifle near at hand, Tom Swift guided his craft on to the attack. Soon they could see the glow of dying fires in the dwarfs' village, but no sound came from the sleeping hordes of red imps.

CHAPTER XXIII

THE RESCUE

"Can you make out the hut, Tom?" asked Ned, as he stood at his chum's side in the steering tower, and gazed downward on the silent village.

"Not very clearly. Suppose you take a look through the night-glasses. Maybe you'll have better luck."

Ned peered long and earnestly.

"No, I can't see a thing." he said. "It all looks to be a confused jumble of huts. I can't tell one from the other. We'll have to go lower."

"I don't want to do that," objected Tom. "If this attack succeeds at all, it will have to be sharp and quick. If we go down where they can spot us, and work our way up to the hut where the captives are, we'll run the chance of an attack that may put us out of business."

"Yes, we ought to get right over the hut, and then make a sudden swoop down," admitted Ned, "but if we can't see it—"

"I have it!" cried Tom suddenly. "Tomba! That African can see in the dark like a cat. Why, just before we started I dropped a wrench, and I didn't have any matches handy to look for it. I was groping around in the dark trying to get my hands on it, and you know it was pretty black in the jungle. Well, along come Tomba. And he spotted it at once and picked it up. We'll call him here and get him to point out the hut. He can tell me how to steer."

"Good!" cried Ned, and the black was soon standing in the pilot house. He comprehended what was wanted of him, and peered down, seeking to penetrate the darkness.

"Shall I go down a little lower?" asked Tom.

For a moment Tomba did not answer. Then he uttered an exclamation of pleasure.

"Me see hut!" he said, clutching Tom's arm. "Down dere!" He pointed, but neither Tom nor Ned could see it. However, as Tomba was now giving directions, telling Tom when to go to the left or the right, as the wind currents deflected they were certain of soon reaching the place where Mr. and Mrs. Illingway were concealed, if they were still alive.

The Black Hawk was moving slowly, and was not under as good control as if she had been making ninety miles an hour. As it was desired to proceed as quietly as possible, the craft was being used as a dirigible balloon, and the propellers were whirled around by means of a small motor, worked by a storage battery. While not much power was obtained this way, there was the advantage of silence, which was very necessary. Slowly the Black Hawk sailed on through the night. In silence the adventurers waited for the moment of action. They had their weapons in readiness. Mr. Durban was to work the electric rifle, as all Tom's attention would be needed at the machinery. As soon as the craft had made a landing he was to leap out, carrying a revolver in either hand, and, followed by Tomba, would endeavor to gain entrance to the hut, break through the flimsy grass-woven curtain over the doorway, and get Mr. and Mrs. Illingway out. Ned, Mr. Damon and the other two men would stand by to fire on the red pygmies as soon as they commenced the attack, which they would undoubtedly do as soon as the guards of the captives raised the alarm.

The airship was in darkness, for it would have been dangerous to show a light. Some wakeful dwarf might see the moving illumination in the sky, and raise a cry.

"Mos' dere," announced Tomba at length. And then, for the first time, Ned and Tom had a glimpse of the hut. It stood away from the others, and was easy to pick out in daylight, but even the darkness offered no handicap to Tomba. "Right over him now," he suddenly called, as he leaned out of the pilot house window, and looked down. "Right over place. Oh, Tomba glad when he see Missy an' Massy!"

"Yes, I hope you do see them," murmured Tom, as he pulled the lever which would pump the gas from the inflated bag, and compress it into tanks, until it was needed again to make the ship rise. Slowly the Black Hawk sank down.

"Get ready!" called Tom in a low voice.

It was a tense moment. Every one of the adventurers felt it, and all but Tom grasped their weapons with tighter grips. They were ready to spring out as soon as a landing was made. Tom managed the machinery in the dark, for he knew every wheel, gear and lever, and could have put his hand on any one with his eyes shut. The two loaded revolvers were on a shelf in front of him. The side door of the pilot house was ajar, to allow him quick egress.

Tomba, armed with a big club he had picked up in the jungle, was ready to follow. The black was eager for the fray to begin, though how he and the others would fare amid the savages was hard to say.

Still not a sound broke the quiet. It was very dark, for nearly all the camp fires, over which the nightly feast had been prepared, were out. The hut could be dimly made out, however.

Suddenly there was a slight tremor through the ship. She seemed to shiver, and bound upward a little.

"We've landed!" whispered Tom. "Now for it! Come on, Tomba!"

The big black glided after the lad like a shadow. With his two weapons held in readiness our hero went out on deck. The others, with cocked rifles, stood ready for the attack to open. It had been decided that as soon as the first alarm was given by the dwarfs, which would probably be when Tom broke into the hut, the firing would begin.

"Open!" called Tom to Tomba, and the big black dashed his club through the grass curtain over the doorway of the hut. He fairly leaped inside, with a cry of battle on his lips.

"Mr. Illingway! Mrs. Illingway!" called Tom, "We've come to save you. Hurry out. The airship is just outside!"

He fired one shot through the roof of the hut, so that the flash would reveal to him whether or not the two missionaries were in the place. He saw two forms rise up in front of him, and knew that they were the white captives he had observed daring the former attack.

"Oh, what is it?" he heard the woman ask.

"A rescue! Thank the dear Lord!" answered her husband fervently. "Oh, whoever you are, God bless you!"

"Come quickly!" cried Tom, "we haven't a moment to lose!"

He was speaking to absolute blackness now, for it was darker immediately following the revolver flash than before. But he felt a man's hand thrust about his arm, and he knew it was Mr. Illingway.

"Take your wife's hand, and follow me," ordered Tom. "Come, Tomba! Are there any of the red pygmies in here?"

He had not seen any at the weapon's flash, but his question was answered a moment later, for there arose from within and without the hut a chorus of wild yells. At the same time Tom felt small arms grasp him about the legs.

"Come on!" he yelled. "They're awake and after us!"

The din outside increased. Tom heard the rifles of his friends crack. He saw, through the torn door curtain, the flashes of fire. Then came a blue glare, and Tom knew that Mr. Durban was using the electric weapon.

By these intermittent gleams Tom managed to see sufficiently to thrust Mr. and Mrs. Illingway ahead of him. Tomba was at their side. The yells inside the hut were almost deafening. All the red dwarfs left to guard the captives had awakened, and they could see well enough to attack Tom. Fortunately they had no weapons, but they fairly threw themselves upon the sturdy lad, trying to pull him down.

"Go on! Go on!" he yelled to the captives, fairly pushing them along. Then, knowing they were out of the way, he turned and fired his two revolvers as fast as he could pull the triggers, into the very faces of the red imps who were seeking to drag him down. Again and again he fired, until he had emptied both cylinders of his weapons.

He felt the grasps of the fiendish little men relax one by one. Tom finally dragged himself loose, and staggered out of the hut. The captives and Tomba were right in front of him. At the airship, which loomed up in the flashes from the guns and electric rifle, Tom's friends were giving battle. About them swarmed the hordes of savages, with more of the imps pouring in every moment.

"Get aboard!" cried Tom to the missionaries. "Get on the airship, and we'll move out of this!"

He felt a stinging pain in his neck, where an arrow struck him. He tore the arrow out, and rushed forward. Fairly pushing Mr. and Mrs. Illingway up on deck before him, Tom followed. Tomba was capering about his master and mistress, and he swung his big club savagely. He had not been idle, and many a red imp had gone down under his blows.

"Rescued! Rescued!" murmured Mr. Illingway, as Tom hastened to the pilot house to start the motor.

CHAPTER XXIV

TWO OTHER CAPTIVES

But the rescue was not yet accomplished. Those on the airship were still in danger, and grave peril, for all about them were the red savages, shouting, howling, yelling and capering about, as they were now thoroughly aroused, and realized that their captives had been taken away from them. They determined to get them back, and were rallying desperately to battle. Nearly all of them were armed by this time, and flight after flight of spears and arrows were thrown or shot toward the airship.

Fortunately it was too dark to enable the pygmies to take good aim. They were guided, to an extent, by the flashes of fire from the rifles, but these were only momentary. Still some of our friends received slight wounds, for they stood on the open deck of the craft.

"Bless my eye-glasses!" suddenly exclaimed Mr. Damon. "I'm stuck!"

"Don't mind that!" advised Ned. "Keep on pouring lead into them. We'll soon be away from here!"

"Don't fire any more!" called Mr. Durban. "The gun-flashes tell them where to shoot. I'll use the electric rifle. It's better."

They followed his advice, and put aside their weapons. By means of the electric flash, which he projected into the midst of the savages, without the glare coming on the airship, Mr. Durban was able to tell where to aim. Once he had a mass of red pygmies located, he could keep on shooting charge after charge into their midst.

"Use it full power!" called Tom, as he opened the gas machine to its widest capacity, so the bag would quickly fill, and the craft be sent forward, for it was so dark, and the ground near the huts so uneven, that the Black Hawk could not rise as an aeroplane.

The elephant hunter turned on full strength in the electric gun and the wireless bullets were sent into the midst of the attackers. The result was surprising. They were so closely packed together that when one was hit the electrical shock was sent through his nearly naked body into the naked bodies of his tribesmen who pressed on every side of him. In consequence whole rows of the savages went down at a time, disabled from fighting any more.

Meanwhile Tom was working frantically to hasten the rising of the airship. His neck pained him very much where the arrow had struck him, but he dared not stop now to dress the wound. He could feel the blood running down his side, but he shut his teeth grimly and said nothing.

The two missionaries, scarcely able to believe that they were to be saved, had been shown into an inner cabin by Tomba, who had become somewhat used to the airship by this time, and who could find his way about well in the dark, for no lights had yet been turned on.

Hundreds of pygmies had been disabled, yet still others came to take their places. The gas bag was again punctured in several places, but the rents were small, and Tom knew that he could make the gas faster than it could escape, unless the bag was ripped open.

"They're climbing up the sides!" suddenly called Ned Newton, for he saw several of the little men clambering up. "What shall we do?"

"Pound their fingers!" called Mr. Anderson. "Get clubs and whack them!" It was good advice. Ned remembered on one occasion when he and Tom were looking at Andy Foger's airship, how this method had been proposed when the bank clerk hung on the back fence. As he grabbed up a stick, and proceeded to pound the hands and bare arms of the savages who were clinging to the railing, Ned found himself wondering what had become of the bully. He was to see Andy sooner than he expected.

Suddenly in the midst of the fighting, which was now a hand-to-hand conflict, there was a tremor throughout the length of the airship.

"She's going up!" yelled Ned.

"Bless my check-book!" cried Mr. Damon, "if we don't look out some of these red imps will go up with us, too!"

As he spoke he whacked vigorously at the hands of several of the pygmies, who dropped off with howls of anguish.

The craft quickly shot upward. There were yells of terror from a few of the red savages who remained clinging to different parts of the Black Hawk and then, fearing they might be taken to the clouds, they, too, dropped off. The rescuers and rescued mounted higher and higher, and, when they were far enough up so that there was no danger from the spears or arrows, Tom switched on the lights, and turned the electric current into the search-lantern, the rays of which beamed down on the mass of yelling and baffled savages below.

"A few shots for them to remember us by!" cried Mr. Durban, as he sent more of the paralyzing electric currents into the red imps. Their yell of rage had now turned to shouts of terror, for the gleaming beam of light frightened them more than did the airship, or the bullets of the white men. The red pygmies fled to their huts.

"I guess we gave them a lesson," remarked Tom, as he started the propellers and sent the ship on through the night.

"Why, Tom! You're hurt!" cried Ned, who came into the pilot house at that moment, and saw blood on his chum.

"Only a scratch," the young inventor declared.

"It's more than that," said Mr. Durban who looked at it a little later. "It must be bound up, Tom."

And, while Ned steered the ship back to the jungle clearing whence they had come to make the night attack, Tom's wound was dressed.

Meanwhile the two missionaries had been well taken care of. They were given other garments, even some dresses being provided for Mrs. Illingway, for when the voyage was begun Tom had considered the possibility of having a woman on board, and had bought some ladies' garments. Then, having cast down to earth the ill-smelling skins which formed their clothes while captives, Mr. and Mrs. Illingway, decently dressed, thanked Tom and the others over and over again.

"We had almost given up hope," said the lady, "when we saw them drive you back after the first attack. Oh, it is wonderful to think how you saved us, and in an airship!" and she and her husband began their thanks over again.

A good meal was prepared by Mr. Damon, for the rescuers and rescued ones were hungry, and since they had been held prisoners the two
missionaries had not been given very good food.

"Oh, it hardly seems possible that we are eating with white men
again," said Mr. Illingway, as he took a second cup of coffee, "hardly
possible!"

"And to see electric lights, instead of a camp-fire," added his wife.
"What a wonderful airship you have, Tom Swift."

"Yes, it's pretty good," he admitted. "It came in useful tonight, all
right."

They were now far enough from the savages, and the pygmies' fires,
which had been set aglow anew when the attack began, could no longer
be observed.

"We'll land at the place where we camped before," said Tom, who
had again assumed charge of the ship, "and in the morning we'll start for
civilization."

"No can get two other white men?" suddenly asked Tomba, who had
been sitting, gazing at his recovered master and mistress. "Fly-ship go
back, an' leave two white mans here?" the black asked.

"What in the world does he mean?" demanded Tom. "Of course we're
not going to leave any of our party behind!"

"Let me question him," suggested Mr. Illingway, and he began to talk
to the African in his own tongue. A rapid conversation followed, and a
look of amazement spread over the faces of the two missionaries, as they
listened.

"What is it?" asked Mr. Durban. "What does Tomba say?"

"Why the pygmies have two other white men in captivity," said Mr.
Illingway. "They were brought in yesterday, after you were driven away.
Two white men, or, rather a white man and a youth, according to Tomba.
They are held in one of the huts near where we were, but tied so they
couldn't escape in the confusion."

"How does Tomba know this?" asked Mr. Damon.

"He says," translated Mr. Illingway, after more questioning of the
black, "that he heard the red pygmies boasting of it after we had escaped.
Tomba says he heard them say that, though we were gone, and could not
be killed, or sacrificed, the other two captives would meet that horrible
fate."

"Two other white captives in the hands of the red imps!" murmured
Tom. "We must rescue them!"

"You're not going to turn back now, are you?" asked Mr. Durban.

"No, but I will as soon as I look the ship over. We'll come back to-morrow. And we'll have to make a day attack or it will be too late to save them. Two other white captives! I wonder who they can be."

There was a big surprise in store for Tom Swift.

CHAPTER XXV

THE ROGUE ELEPHANT—CONCLUSION

Early the next day the airship was again afloat. The night, what little of darkness remained after the rescue, had been spent in the clearing in the dense jungle. Some slight repairs had been made to the craft, and it was once more in readiness to be used in battle against the relentless savages.

"We can't wait for darkness," declared Tom. "In the first place there isn't time, and again, we don't know in what part of the village the other captives are. We'll have to hunt around."

"And that means going right down into the midst of the imps and fighting them hand to hand," said Ned.

"That's what it means," assented Tom grimly, "but I guess the powder bombs will help some."

Before starting they had prepared a number of improvised bombs, filled with powder, which could be set off by percussion. It was the plan to drop these down from the airship, into the midst of the savages. When the bomb struck the ground, or even on the bodies of the red dwarfs, it would explode. It was hoped that these would so dismay the little men that they would desert the village, and leave the way clear for a search to be made for the other captives.

On rushed the Black Hawk. There was to be no concealment this time, and Tom did not care how much noise the motors made. Accordingly he turned on full speed.

It was not long before the big plain was again sighted. Everything was in readiness, and the bombs were at hand to be dropped overboard. Tom counted on the natives gathering together in great masses as soon as they sighted the airship, and this would give him the opportunity wanted.

But something different transpired. No sooner was the craft above the village, than from all the huts came pouring out the little red men. But they did not gather together—at least just then. They ran about excitedly, and it could be seen that they were bringing from the huts the rude household utensils in which they did their primitive cooking. The women had their babies, and some, not so encumbered, carried rolls of grass matting. The men had all their weapons.

"Bless my wagon wheel!" cried Mr. Damon. "What's going on?"

"It looks like moving day," suggested Ned Newton.

"That's just what it is!" declared Mr. Durban. "They are going to migrate. Evidently they have had enough of us, and they're going to get out of the neighborhood before we get a chance to do any more damage. They're moving, but where are the white captives?"

He was answered a moment later, for a crowd of the dwarfs rushing to a certain hut, came out leading two persons by means of bark ropes tied about their necks. It was too far off to enable Tom or the others to recognize them, but they could tell by the clothing that they were white captives.

"We've got to save them!" exclaimed the young inventor.

"How?" asked Mr. Damon. And, indeed, it did seem a puzzle for, even as Tom looked, the whole tribe of red imps took up the march into the jungle, dragging the white persons with them. The captives looked up, saw the airship, and made frantic motions for help. It was too far off, yet, to hear their voices. But the distance was lessening every moment, for Tom had speeded the motor to the highest pitch.

"What are you going to do?" demanded Ned.

"I'll show you," answered his chum. "Take some of those bombs, and be ready to drop them overboard when I give the word."

"But we may kill those white people," objected Ned.

"Not the way I'm going to work it. You drop them when I give the word."

Tom steered the airship toward the head of the throng of blacks. The captives were in the rear, and the van of the strange procession was near the edge of the jungle now. Once the red dwarfs got into the tangle of underbrush they could never be found, and their captives would die a miserable death.

"We've got to stop them," murmured Tom. "Are you ready, Ned?"

"Ready!"

"Then drop the bombs!"

Ned dropped them. A sharp explosion was heard, and the head of the procession was blown apart and thrown into confusion. The throng halted.

"Drop more!" cried Tom, sending the ship about in a circle, and hovering it over the middle of the press of savages.

More of the deadly bombs exploded. The pygmies were running about wildly. Tom, who was closely watching the rear of the cavalcade, suddenly called out:

"Now's our chance! They've let their captives go, and are running into the jungle. We must swoop down, and get the prisoners!"

It was no sooner said than the nose of the Black Hawk was pointed downward. Onward it flew, the two captives wildly waving their hands to the rescuers. There was no more danger from the red savages. They had been thrown into panic and confusion, and wore rapidly disappearing into the forest. The terrible weapons of the whites had been too much for them.

"Quick! Get on board!" called Tom, as he brought the machinery to a stop. The airship now rested on the ground, close to the former captives. "Get in here!" shouted the young inventor. "They may change their minds and come back."

The two white persons ran toward the Black Hawk. Then one of them— the smaller—halted and cried out:

"Why, it's Tom Swift!"

Tom turned and glanced at the speaker. A look of astonishment spread over his face.

"Andy Foger—here!" gasped Tom. "How in the world—?"

"I dink besser as ve git on der board, und dalk aftervard!" exclaimed Andy's companion, who spoke with a strong German accent. "I like not dose red little mans."

In another minute the two rescued ones were safe on Tom Swift's airship, and it had arisen high enough to be out of all danger.

"How in the world did you ever get here?" asked Tom of the lad who had so often been his enemy.

"I'll tell you soon," spoke Andy, "but first, Tom, I want to ask your forgiveness for all I've done to you, and to thank you, from the bottom of my heart, for saving us. I thought we were going to be killed by those dwarfs; didn't you, Herr Landbacher?"

"Sure I did. But ve are all right now. Dis machine is efen besser as mine vot vos lost. Is dere anyt'ing to eats, on board, if you vill excuse me for being so bolt as to ask?"

"Plenty to eat," said Tom, laughing, "and while you eat you can tell us your story. And as for you, Andy, I hope we'll be friends from now on," and Tom held out his hand.

There was not much to tell that the reader has not already guessed. Andy and the German, as has been explained, went abroad to give airship flights. They were in the lower part of Egypt, and a sudden gale drove them into Africa.

For a long time they sailed on, and then their fuel gave out, and they had to descend into the jungle. They managed to fall in with some friendly blacks, who treated them well. The airship was useless without gasolene, and it was abandoned.

Andy and the German inventor were planning to walk to some white settlement, when the tribe they were with was attacked by the red dwarfs and vanquished. Andy and his friend were taken prisoners, and carried to the very village where the missionaries were, just before the latter's rescue.

Then came the fight, and the saving of Andy and the German, almost at the last minute.

"Well, you certainly had nearly as many adventures as we did," said Tom. "But I guess they're over now."

But they were not. For several days the airship sailed on over the jungles without making a descent. Mr. and Mrs. Illingway wished to be landed at a white settlement where they had other missionary friends. Tom would go with them. This was done, and Tom and the others spent some time in this place, receiving so many kinds of thanks that they had to protest.

Andy and Herr Landbacher asked to be taken back to the coast, where they could get a steamer to America. Andy was a very different lad now, and not the bully of old.

"Well, hadn't we better be thinking of getting back home?" asked Tom one day.

"Not until we get some more ivory," declared Mr. Durban. "I think we'll have to have another elephant hunt."

They did, about a week later, and got some magnificent tusks. Tom's electric rifle did great work, to the wonder of Andy and Mr. Landbacher, who had never before seen such a curious weapon. They also did some night hunting.

"But we haven't got that pair of extra large tusks that I want," said the old hunter, as he looked at the store of ivory accumulated after the last hunt. "I want those, and then I'll be satisfied. There is one section of the country that we have not touched as yet, and I'd like to visit that."

"Then let's go," proposed Tom, so, good-bys having been said to the missionaries, who sent greetings to their friends in America, and to the church people who had arranged for their rescue, the airship was once more sent to the deepest part of a certain jungle, where Mr. Durban hoped to get what he wanted.

They had another big hunt, but none of the elephants had any remarkable tusks, and the hunter was about to give up in despair, and call the expedition over, when one afternoon, as they were sailing along high enough to merely clear the tops of the trees, Tom heard a great crashing down below.

"There's something there," he called to Mr. Durban. "Perhaps a small herd of elephants. Shall we go down?"

Before Mr. Durban could answer there came into view, in a small clearing, an elephant of such size, and with such an enormous pair of tusks, that the young inventor and the old hunter could not repress cries of astonishment.

"There's your beast!" said Tom. "I'll go down and you can pot him," and, as he spoke, Tom stopped the propellers, so that the ship hung motionless in the air above where the gigantic brute was.

Suddenly, as though possessed by a fit of rage, the elephant rushed at a good-sized tree and began butting it with his head. Then, winding his trunk around it he pulled it up by the roots, and began trampling on it out of a paroxysm of anger.

"A rogue elephant!" exclaimed Mr. Durban. "Don't go down if you value your life, or the safety of the airship. If we attacked that brute on the ground, we would be the hunted instead of the hunters. That's a rogue elephant of the worst kind, and he's at the height of his rage."

This was indeed so, for the beast was tearing about the clearing like mad, breaking off trees, and uprooting them in sheer wantonness. Tom knew what a "rogue" elephant was. It is a beast that goes away from the herd, and lives solitary and alone, attacking every living thing that comes in his way. It is a species of madness, a disease which attacks elephants and sometimes passes away. More often the afflicted creature gives battle to everything and every animal he meets until he is killed or carried off by his malady. It was such an elephant that Tom now saw, and he realized what the hunter said about attacking one, as he saw the brute's mad rushes.

"Well, if it's dangerous to attack him on the ground, we'll kill him from up above," said the young inventor. "Here is the electric rifle, Mr. Durban. I'll let you have the honor of getting those tusks. My! But they're whoppers! Better use almost a full charge. Don't take any chances on merely wounding him, and having him rush off to the jungle."

"I won't," said the old hunter, and he adjusted the electric rifle which Tom handed him.

As the great beast was tearing around, trumpeting shrilly and breaking off trees Mr. Durban fired. The creature sank down, instantly killed, and was out of his misery, for often it is great pain which makes an otherwise peaceable elephant become a "rogue."

"He's done for," said Ned. "I guess you have the tusks you want now, Mr. Durban."

"I think so," agreed the hunter, and when the airship was sent down, and the ivory cut out, it was found that the tusks were even larger than they had supposed. "It is a prize worth having," said Mr. Durban. "I'm sure my customer will think so, too. Now I'm ready to head for the coast."

Tom Swift went to the engine room, while the last big tusks were being stored away with the other ivory. Several parts of the motor needed oiling, and Ned was assisting in this work.

"Going to start soon?" asked Mr. Durban, appearing in the doorway.

"Yes; why?" inquired Tom, who noted an anxious note in the voice of the hunter.

"Well, I don't like staying longer in this jungle than I can help. It's not healthy in the first place, and then it's a wild and desolate place, where all sorts of wild beasts are lurking, and where wandering hands of natives may appear at any time."

"You don't mean that the red pygmies will come back; do you?" asked Ned.

"There's no telling," replied Mr. Durban with a shrug of his shoulders. "Only, as long as we've got what we're after, I'd start off as soon as possible."

"Yes, don't run any chances with those little red men," begged Andy Foger, who had given himself up for lost when he and his companion fell into their hands.

"Radder vould I be mit cannibals dan dose little imps!" spoke the German fervently.

"We'll start at once," declared Tom. "Are you all aboard, and is everything loaded into the airship?"

"Everything. I guess." answered Mr. Anderson.

Tom looked to the motor, saw that it was in working order, and shoved over the lever of the gas machine to begin the generating of the lifting vapor. To his surprise there was no corresponding hiss that told of the gas rushing into the bag.

"That's odd," he remarked. "Ned, see if anything is wrong with that machine. I'll pull the lever again."

The bank clerk stood beside the apparatus, while Tom worked the handle, but whatever was the matter with it was too intricate or complicated for Ned to solve.

"I can't see what ails it," he called to his chum. "You better have a peep."

"All right, I'll look if you work the handle."

The passengers on the airship, which now rested in a little clearing in the dense jungle, gathered at the engine room door, looking at Tom and Ned as they worked over the machine.

"Bless my pulley wheel!" exclaimed Mr. Damon "I hope nothing has gone wrong."

"Well something has!" declared the young inventor in a muffled voice, for he was down on his hands and knees peering under the gas apparatus. "One of the compression cylinders has cracked," he added dubiously. "It must have snapped when we landed this last time. I came down too heavily."

"What does that mean?" asked Mr. Durban, who did not know much about machinery.

"It means that I've got to put a new cylinder in," went on Tom. "It's quite a job, too, but we can't make gas without it!"

"Well, can't you do it just as well up in the air as down here?" asked Mr. Durban. "Make an ascension, Tom, and do the repairs up above, where we've got good air, and where—"

He paused suddenly, and seemed to be listening.

"What is it?" asked the young inventor quickly. There was no need to answer, for, from the jungle without, came the dull booming of the war drums of some natives.

"That's what I was afraid of!" cried the old elephant hunter, catching up his gun. "Some black scout has seen us and is summoning his tribesmen. Hurry, Tom, send up the ship, and we'll take care of the savages."

"But I CAN'T send her up!" cried Tom.

"You can't? Why not?"

"Because the gas machine won't work until I put in a new cylinder, and that will take at least a half a day."

"Go up as an aeroplane then!" cried Mr. Damon. "Bless my monkey wrench, Tom, you've often done it before."

For answer Tom waved his hand toward the thick jungle all about them.

"We haven't room to get a running start of ten feet." he said, "and without a start the airship can never rise as a mere aeroplane. The only way we can get up from the jungle is like a balloon, and without the gas—"

He paused significantly. The sound of the war drums became louder, and to it was added a weird singing chant.

"The natives!" cried Mr. Anderson. "They're coming right this way! We must fight them off if they attack us!"

"Where's the electric rifle?" asked Ned. "Get that out, Tom!"

"Wait!" suggested Mr. Durban. "This is serious! It looks as if they were going to attack us, and they have us at a disadvantage. Our only safety is in flight, but as Tom says we can't go up until the gas machine is fixed, he will have to attend to that part of it while we keep off the black men. Tom, we can't spare you to fight this time! You repair the ship as soon as you can, and we'll guard her from the natives. And you've got to work lively!"

"I will!" cried the young inventor. "It's luck we have a spare cylinder!"

Suddenly there was a louder shout in the jungle and it was followed by a riot of sound. War drums were beaten, tom-toms clashed and the natives howled.

"Here they are!" cried Mr. Anderson.

"Bless my suspenders!" shouted Mr. Damon. "Where is my gun?"

"Here, you take mine, and I'll use the electric rifle," answered the elephant hunter. As he spoke there was a hissing sound in the air and a flight of spears passed over the airship.

The defenders slipped outside, while Tom, with Ned to help him, worked feverishly to repair the break. They were in a serious strait, for with the airship practically helpless they were at the mercy of the natives. And as Tom glanced momentarily from the window, he saw scores of black, half-naked forms slipping in and out among the trees and trailing vines.

Soon the rifles of his friends began to crack, and the yells of the natives were changed to howls of anguish. The electric weapon, though it made no noise, did great execution.

"I only hope they don't puncture the gas bag," murmured Tom, as he began taking the generating machine apart so as to get out the cracked cylinder.

"If they do, it's all up with us," murmured Ned.

After their first rush, finding that the white men were on the alert, the blacks withdrew some distance, where their spears and arrows were not so effective. Our friends, including Andy Foger, and the German, kept up a hot fire whenever a skulking black form could be seen.

But, though the danger from the spears and arrows was less, a new peril presented itself. This was from the blow guns. The curious weapons shot small arrows, tipped with tufts of a cottony substance in place of feathers, and could be sent for a long distance. The barbs were not strong enough to pierce the tough fabric of the gas bag, as a spear or arrow would have done, but there was more danger from them to our friends who were on deck.

"Those barbs may be poisoned," said Mr. Durban, "and in case any one is wounded, the wound, though it be but a scratch, must be treated with antiseptics. I have some."

This course was followed, the elephant hunter being wounded twice, and Andy Foger and Mr. Damon once each. There was not a native to be seen now, for they were hiding behind the trees of the jungle, but every now and then a blowgun barb would whizz out of the forest.

Finally Mr. Durban suggested that they erect improvised shelters, behind which they could stand with their rifle, and breastworks were made out of packing boxes. Then our friends were comparatively safe. But they had to be on the alert, and it was nervous work, for they could not tell what minute the blacks would rush from the jungle, and, in spite of the fire from the electric rifle and other guns, overwhelm the ship.

It was very trying to Tom and Ned, for they had to work hard and rapidly in the close engine room. The sweat dripped down off them, but they kept at it. It was three hours before the broken cylinder was removed, and it was no light task to put in the other, for the valves had to be made very tight to prevent leakage.

The two lads stopped to get something to eat, while the guards kept sharp watch against a surprise. At intervals came a flight of barbs, and occasionally a black form could be seen, when it was instantly fired at. Several times the barbaric noise of the tom-toms and war drums, with which the shouts of the natives mingled, broke out deafeningly.

"Think you can repair it by night?" asked Mr. Durban anxiously of Tom.

"I hope so," was the response.

"Because if we have to stay here after dark—well, I don't want to do it if I can help it," finished the hunter.

Neither did the young inventor, and he redoubled his efforts to make the repairs. It was getting dark when the last belt was in place, and it was high time, too, for the natives were getting bolder, creeping up through the forest to within shooting distance with their arrows and spears.

"There!" cried Tom at length. "Now we'll see if she works!" Once more he pulled the starting lever, and this time there was the welcome hiss of the gas.

"Hurrah!" cried Ned.

The young inventor turned the machine on at full power. In a few minutes the Black Hawk trembled through her length.

"She's going up! Bless my balloon basket! She's going up!" cried Mr. Damon.

The natives must have suspected that something unusual was going on, for they made a sudden rush, yelling and beating their drums. Mr. Durban and the others hurried out on deck and fired at them, but there was little more need. With a bound the airship left the earth, being rapidly carried up by the gas. The blacks sent a final shower of spears after her, but only one was effective, slightly wounding the German. Then Tom started the motor, the propellers whizzed, and the Black Hawk was once more under way, just as night settled over the jungle, and upon the horde of black and howling savages that rushed around, maddened over the escape of their intended victims.

No further accidents marred the trip to the coast, which was reached in due time, and very glad our friends were to be away from the jungle and the land of the red pygmies.

A division was made of the ivory, and Tom's share was large enough to provide him with a substantial amount. Ned and Mr. Damon were also given a goodly sum from the sale of the tusks. The big ones, from the "rogue," were shipped to the man who had commissioned Mr. Durban to secure them for him.

"Well, now for home," said Tom, when the airship had been taken apart for shipment. "I guess you'll be glad to get back to the United States, won't you, friends?"

"That's what," agreed Andy Foger. "I think I'm done with airships. Ugh! When I think of those red dwarfs I can't sleep nights!"

"Yah, dot iss so!" agreed the German.

"Well, I'm going to settle down for a time," declared Tom. "I've had enough adventures for a while, but those in elephant land—"

"They certainly put it all over the things that happen to some people!" interrupted Ned with a laugh.

"Bless my fish-line, that's so!" agreed Mr. Damon.

But Tom Swift was not done with adventures, and what farther happened to him may be learned by reading the next volume of this series, which will be entitled, "Tom Swift in the City of Gold; or, Marvelous Adventures Underground."

They all made a safe and pleasant voyage home, and as news of the rescue of the missionaries had been cabled to America, Tom and his friends were met, as they left the steamer, by a crowd of newspaper reporters, who got a good story of the battle with the red pygmies, though Tom was inclined to make light of his part in the affair.

"Now for Shopton, home, Dad, Eradicate Sampson and his mule!" exclaimed Tom, as they boarded a train in New York.

"And somebody else, too, I guess; eh?" asked Ned of his chum, with a laugh.

"That's none of your affair!" declared Tom, as he blushed, and then he, too, joined in the merriment.

And now, for a time, we will say good-by to the young inventor and his friends.

TOM SWIFT IN THE CITY OF GOLD

OR, MARVELOUS ADVENTURES UNDERGROUND

CHAPTER I

WONDERFUL NEWS

"Letter for you, Tom Swift."

"Ah, thanks, Mr. Wilson. This is the first mail I've had this week. You've been neglecting me," and the young inventor took the missive which the Shopton postman handed to him over the gate, against which Tom was leaning one fine, warm Spring day.

"Well, I get around as often as I can, Tom. You're not home a great deal, you know. When you're not off in your sky racer seeing how much you can beat the birds, you're either hunting elephants in Africa, or diving down under the ocean, or out in a diamond mine, or some such out-of-the-way place as that. No wonder you don't get many letters. But that one looks as if it had come quite a distance."

"So it does," agreed Tom, looking closely at the stamp and postmark. "What do you make out of it, Mr. Wilson?" and then, just as many other persons do when getting a strange letter, instead of opening it to see from whom it has come, Tom tried to guess by looking at the handwriting, and trying to decipher the faint postmark. "What does that say?" and the young inventor pointed to the black stamp.

"Hum, looks like Jube—no, that first letter's a 'K' I guess," and Mr. Wilson turned it upside down, thinking that would help.

"I made it out a 'G'," said Tom.

"So it is. A 'G'—you're right. Gumbo—Twamba—that's what it is—Gumba Twamba. I can make it out now all right."

"Well, where, for the love of my old geography, is Gumba Twamba?" asked the lad with a laugh.

"You've got me, Tom. Must be in Sweden, or Holland, or some of those foreign countries. I don't often handle letters from there, so I can't say. Why don't you open your letter and find out who its from?"

"That's what I ought to have done at first." Quickly Tom ripped open the much worn and frayed envelope, through the cracks of which some parts of the letter already could be seen, showing that it had traveled many thousand miles before it got to the village of Shopton, in New York State.

"Well, I've got to be traveling on," remarked the postman, as Tom started to read the mysterious letter. "I'm late as it is. You can tell me the news when I pass again, Tom."

But the young inventor did not reply. He was too much engaged in reading the missive, for, no sooner had he perused the first few lines than his eyes began to open wide in wonder, and his manner plainly indicated his surprise. He read the letter once, and then over again, and when he had finished it a second time, he made a dash for the house.

"I say dad!" cried Tom. "This is great! Great news here! Where are you, dad? Say, Mrs. Baggert," he called as he saw the motherly house-keeper, "where's father? I've got great news for him? Where is he?"

"Out in the shop, I think. I believe Mr. Damon is with him."

"And blessing everything as usual, from his hat to his shoe laces, I'll wager," murmured Tom as he made his way to the shop where his father, also an inventor like himself, spent much of his time. "Well, well, I'm glad Mr. Damon is here, for he'll be interested in this."

Tom fairly rushed into the building, much of the space of which, was taken up by machinery, queer tools and odd devices, many of them having to do with the manufacture of aeroplanes, for Tom had as many of them as some people have of automobiles.

"I say, dad!" cried Tom, waving the letter above his head, "what do you think of this? Listen to—"

"Easy there now, Tom! Easy, my boy, or you'll oblige me to do all my work over again," and an aged man, beside whom a younger one was standing, held up a hand of caution, while with the other hand he was adjusting some delicate piece of machinery.

"What are you doing?" demanded the son.

"Bless my scarf pin!" exclaimed the other man—Mr. Wakefield Damon—"Bless my rubbers, Tom Swift! What should your father be doing but inventing something new, as he always is. I guess he's working on his new gyroscope, though it is only a guess, for he hasn't said ten words to me since I came out to talk to him. But that's like all inventors, they—"

"I beg your pardon, Mr. Damon," spoke Mr. Swift with a smile, "I'm sure—"

"Say, can't you listen to me for five minutes?" pleaded Tom. "I've got some great news—simply great, and your gyroscope can wait, dad. Listen to this letter," and he prepared to read it.

"Who's it from?" asked Mr. Damon.

"Mr. Jacob Illingway, the African missionary whom you and I rescued, together with his wife, from the red pigmies!" cried Tom. "Think of that! Of all persons to get a letter from, and such a letter! such news in it. Why, it's simply great! You remember Mr. and Mrs. Illingway; don't you Mr. Damon? How we went to Africa after elephant's tusks, with Mr. Durban the hunter, and how we got the missionaries away from those little savages in my airship—don't you remember?"

"I should say I did!" exclaimed Mr. Damon. "Bless my watch chain— but they were regular imps—the red Pygmies I mean, not the missionaries. But what is Mr. Illingway writing to you about now, Tom? I know he sent you several letters since we came back from Africa. What's the latest news?"

"I'll tell you," replied the young inventor, sitting down on a packing box. "It would take too long to read the letter so I'll sum it up, and you can go over it later."

"To be brief, Mr. Illingway tells of a wonderful golden image that is worshiped by a tribe of Africans in a settlement not far from Gumba Twamba, where he is stationed. It's an image of solid gold—"

"Solid gold!" interrupted Mr. Swift.

"Yes, dad, and about three feet high," went on Tom, referring to the letter to make sure. "It's heavy, too, no hollows in it, and these Africans regard it as a god. But that's not the strangest part of it. Mr. Illingway goes on to say that there is no gold in that part of Africa, and for a time he was at a loss how to account for the golden image. He made some inquiries and learned that it was once the property of a white traveler who made his home with the tribe that now worships the image of gold. This traveler, whose name Mr. Illingway could not find out, was much liked by the Africans. He taught them many things, doctored them when they were sick, and they finally adopted him into the tribe."

"It seems that he tried to make them better, and wanted them to become Christians, but they clung to their own beliefs until he died. Then, probably thinking to do his memory honor, they took the golden image, which was among his possessions, and set it up as a god."

"Bless my hymn book!" exclaimed Mr. Damon. "What did they do that for?"

"This white man thought a great deal of the image," said Tom, again referring to the letter, "and the Africans very likely imagined that, as he was so good to them, some of his virtues had passed into the gold. Then, too, they may have thought it was part of his religion, and as he had so often wanted them to adopt his beliefs, they reasoned out that they could now do so, by worshiping the golden god."

"Anyhow, that's what they did, and the image is there today, in that far-off African village. But I haven't got to the real news yet. The image of solid gold is only a part of it."

"Before this traveler died he told some of the more intelligent natives that the image had come from a far-off underground city—a regular city of gold—nearly everything in it that was capable of being made of metal, being constructed of the precious yellow gold. The golden image was only one of a lot more like it, some smaller and some larger—"

"Not larger, Tom, not larger, surely!" interrupted Mr. Swift. "Why, my boy, think of it! An image of solid gold, bigger even than this one Mr. Illingway writes of, which he says is three feet high. Why, if there are any larger they must be nearly life size, and think of a solid gold statue as large as a man—it would weigh—well, I'm afraid, to say how much, and be worth—why, Tom, it's impossible. It would be worth millions—all the wealth of a world must be in the underground city. It's impossible Tom, my boy!"

"Well, that may be," agreed Tom. "I'm not saying it's true. Mr. Illingway is telling only what he heard."

"Go on! Tell some more," begged Mr. Damon. "Bless my shirt studs, this is getting exciting!"

"He says that the traveler told of this underground city of gold," went on Tom, "though he had never been there himself. He had met a native who had located it, and who had brought out some of the gold, including several of the images, and one he gave to the white man in return for some favor. The white man took it to Africa with him."

"But where is this underground city, Tom?" asked Mr. Swift. "Doesn't Mr. Illingway give you any idea of its location."

"He says it is somewhere in Mexico," explained the lad. "The Africans haven't a very good idea of geography, but some of the tribesmen whom the white traveler taught, could draw rude maps, and Mr. Illingway had a native sketch one for him, showing as nearly as possible where the city of gold is located."

"Tom Swift, have you got that map?" suddenly cried Mr. Damon. "Bless my pocketbook, but—"

"I have it!" said Tom quietly, taking from the envelope a piece of paper covered with rough marks. "It isn't very good, but—"

"Bless my very existence!" cried the excitable man. "But you're not going to let such a chance as this slip past; are you Tom? Are you going to hunt for that buried city of gold?"

"I certainly am," answered the young inventor quietly.

"Tom! You're not going off on another wild expedition?" asked Mr. Swift anxiously.

"I'm afraid I'll have to," answered his son with a smile.

"Go? Of course he'll go!" burst out Mr. Damon. "And I'm going with him; can't I, Tom?"

"Surely. The reason Mr. Illingway sent me the letter was to tell me about the city of gold. He thought, after my travels in Africa, that to find a buried city in Mexico would be no trouble at all, I suppose. Anyhow he suggests that I make the attempt, and—"

"Oh, but, Tom, just when I am perfecting my gyroscope!" exclaimed Mr. Swift. "I need your help."

"I'll help you when I come back, dad. I want to get some of this gold."

"But we are rich enough, Tom."

"It isn't so much the money, dad. Listen. There is another part to the letter. Mr. Illingway says that in that underground city, according to the rumor among the African natives, there is not only gold in plenty, and a number of small gold statues, but one immense big one—of solid gold, as large as three men, and there is some queer mystery about it, so that white traveler said. A mystery he wanted to solve but could not."

"So, dad, I'm going to search for that underground city, not only for the mere gold, but to see if I can solve the mystery of the big gold statue. And if I could bring it away," cried Tom in great excitement as he waved the missionary's letter above his head, "it would be one of the wonders of the world—dad, for, not only is it very valuable, but it is most beautifully carved."

"Well, I might as well give up my gyroscope work until you come back from the city of gold, Tom, I can see that," said Mr. Swift, with a faint smile. "And if you go, I hope you come back. I don't want that mysterious image to be the undoing of you."

"Oh, I'll come back all right!" cried Tom confidently. "Ho! for the city of gold and the images thereof! I'm going to get ready to start!"

"And so am I!" cried Mr. Damon. "Bless my shoe strings, Tom, but I'm with you! I certainly am!" and the little man excitedly shook hands with Tom Swift, while the aged inventor looked on and nodded his head doubtfully. But Tom was full of hope.

CHAPTER II

AN UNSUSPECTED LISTENER

For a few moments after Tom Swift had announced his decision to start for the city of gold, and Mr. Damon had said he would accompany the young inventor, there was a silence in the workshop. Then Mr. Swift laid aside the delicate mechanism of the new model gyroscope on which he had been working, came over to his son, and said:

"Well, Tom, if you're going, that means you're going—I know enough to predict that. I rather wish you weren't, for I'm afraid no good will come of this."

"Now, dad, don't be talking that way!" cried Tom gaily. "Pack up and come along with us." Lovingly he placed his arm around the bent shoulders of his father.

"No, Tom, I'm too old. Home is the place for me."

"Bless my arithmetic tables!" exclaimed Mr. Damon, "you're not so much older than I am, and I'm going with Tom. Come on, Mr. Swift."

"No, I can't put up with dangers, hardship and excitement as I used to. I'd better stay home. Besides, I want to perfect my new gyroscope. I'll work on that while you and Tom are searching for the city of gold. But, Tom, if you're going you'd better have something more definite to look for than an unknown city, located on a map drawn by some African bushman."

"I intend to, dad. I guess when Mr. Illingway wrote his letter he didn't really think I'd take him up, and make the search. I'm going to write and ask him if he can't get me a better map, and also learn more about the location of the city. Mexico isn't such a very large place, but it would be if you had to hunt all over it for a buried city, and this map isn't a lot of help," and Tom who had shown it to his father and Mr. Damon looked at it closely.

"If we're going, we want all the information we can get," declared the odd man. "Bless my gizzard, Tom, but this may mean a lot to us!"

"I think it will," agreed the young inventor. "I'm going to write to Mr. Illingway at once, and ask for all the information he can get."

"And I'll help you with suggestions," spoke Mr. Damon. "Come on in the house, Tom. Bless my ink bottle, but we're going to have some adventures again!"

"It seems to me that is about all Tom does—have adventures—that and invent flying machines," said Mr. Swift with a smile, as his son and their visitor left the shop. Then he once more bent over his gyroscope model, while Tom and Mr. Damon hurried in to write the letter to the African missionary.

And while this is being done I am going to ask your patience for a little while—my old readers, I mean—while I tell my new friends, who have never yet met Tom Swift, something about him.

Mr. Swift spoke truly when he said his son seemed to do nothing but seek adventures and invent flying machines. Of the latter the lad had a goodly number, some of which involved new and startling ideas. For Tom was a lad who "did things."

In the first volume of this series, entitled "Tom Swift and His Motor-Cycle," I told you how he became acquainted with Mr. Damon. That eccentric individual was riding a motor-cycle, when it started to climb a tree. Mr. Damon was thrown off in front of Tom's house, somewhat hurt, and the young inventor took him in. Tom and his father lived in the village of Shopton, New York, and Mr. Swift was an inventor of note. His son followed in his footsteps. Mrs. Swift had been dead some years, and they had a good housekeeper, Mrs. Baggert.

Another "member" of the family was Eradicate Sampson, a colored man of all work, who said he was named "Eradicate" because he "eradicated" the dirt. He used to do odd jobs of whitewashing before he was regularly employed by Mr. Swift as a sort of gardener and watchman.

In the first book I told how Tom bought the motor-cycle from Mr. Damon, fixed it up, and had many adventures on it, not the least of which was saving some valuable patent models of his father's which some thieves had taken.

Then Tom Swift got a motor-boat, as related in the second volume of the series, and he had many exciting trips in that craft. Following that he made his first airship with the help of a veteran balloonist and then, not satisfied with adventures in the air, he and his father perfected a wonderful submarine boat in which they went under the ocean for sunken treasure.

The automobile industry was fast forging to the front when Tom came back from his trip under water, and naturally he turned his attention to that. But he made an electric car instead of one that was operated by gasolene, and it proved to be the speediest car on the road.

The details of Tom Swift and his wireless message will be found in the book of that title. It tells how he saved the castaways of Earthquake Island, and among them was Mr. Nestor, the father of Mary, a girl whom Tom thought—but there, I'm not going to be mean, and tell on a good fellow. You can guess what I'm hinting at, I think.

It was when Tom went to get Mary Nestor a diamond ring that he fell in with Mr. Barcoe Jenks, who eventually took Tom off on a search for the diamond makers, and he and Tom, with some friends, discovered the secret of Phantom Mountain.

One would have thought that these adventures would have been enough for Tom Swift, but, like Alexander, he sighed for new worlds to conquer. How he went to the caves of ice in search of treasure, and how his airship was wrecked is told in the eighth volume of the series, and in the next is related the details of his swift sky-racer, in which he and Mr. Damon made a wonderfully fast trip, and brought a doctor to Mr. Swift in time to save the life of the aged inventor.

It was when Tom invented a wonderful electric rifle, and went to Africa with a Mr. Durban, a great hunter, to get elephants' tusks, that he rescued Mr. and Mrs. Illingway, the missionaries, who were held captive by red pygmies.

That was a startling trip, and full of surprises. Tom took with him to the dark continent a new airship, the Black Hawk, and but for this he and his friends never would have escaped from the savages and the wild beasts.

As it was, they had a hazardous time getting the missionary and his wife away from the jungle. It was this same missionary who, as told in the first chapter of this book, sent Tom the letter about the city of gold. Mr. Illingway and his wife wanted to stay in Africa in an endeavor to christianize the natives, even after their terrible experience. So Tom landed them at a white settlement. It was from there that the letter came.

But the missionaries were not the only ones whom Tom saved from the red pygmies. Andy Foger, a Shopton youth, was Tom's enemy, and he had interfered with our hero's plans in his trips. He even had an airship made, and followed Tom to Africa. There Andy Foger and his companion, a German were captured by the savages. But though Tom saved his life, Andy did not seem to give over annoying the young inventor. Andy was born mean, and, as Eradicate Sampson used to say, "dat meanness neber will done git whitewashed outer him—dat's a fack!"

But if Andy Foger was mean to Tom, there was another Shopton lad who was just the reverse. This was Ned Newton, who was Tom's particular chum, Ned had gone with our hero on many trips, including the one to Africa after elephants. Mr. Damon also accompanied Tom many times, and occasionally Eradicate went along on the shorter voyages. But Eradicate was getting old, like Mr. Swift, who, of late years, had not traveled much with his son.

When I add that Tom still continued to invent things, that he was always looking for new adventures, that he still cared very much for Mary Nestor, and thought his father the best in the world, and liked Mr. Damon and Ned Newton above all his other acquaintances, except perhaps Mrs. Baggert, the housekeeper, I think perhaps I have said enough about him; and now I will get back to the story.

I might add, however, that Andy Foger, who had been away from Shopton for some time, had now returned to the village, and had lately been seen by Tom, riding around in a powerful auto. The sight of Andy did not make the young inventor feel any happier.

"Well, Tom, I think that will do," remarked Mr. Damon when, after about an hour's work, they had jointly written a letter to the African missionary.

"We've asked him enough questions, anyhow," agreed the lad. "If he answers all of them we'll know more about the city of gold, and where it is, than we do now."

"Exactly," spoke the odd man. "Now to mail the letter, and wait for an answer. It will take several weeks, for they don't have good mail service to that part of Africa. I hope Mr. Illingway sends us a better map."

"So do I," assented Tom. "But even with the one we have I'd take a chance and look for the underground city."

"I'll mail the letter," went on Mr. Damon, who was as eager over the prospective adventure as was Tom. "I'm going back home to Waterfield I think. My wife says I stay here too much."

"Don't be in a hurry," urged Tom. "Can't you stay to supper? I'll take you home tonight in the sky racer. I want to talk more about the city of gold, and plan what we ought to take with us to Mexico."

"All right," agreed Mr. Damon. "I'll stay, but I suppose I shouldn't. But let's mail the letter."

It was after supper, when, the letter having been posted, that Tom, his father and Mr. Damon were discussing the city of gold.

"Will you go, even if Mr. Illingway can't send a better map?" asked Mr. Damon.

"Sure," exclaimed Tom. "I want to get one of the golden images if I have to hunt all over the Aztec country for it."

"Who's talking of golden images?" demanded a new voice, and Tom looked up quickly, to see Ned Newton, his chum, entering the room. Ned had come in unannounced, as he frequently did.

"Hello, old stock!" cried Tom affectionately. "Sir, there's great news. It's you and me for the city of gold now!"

"Get out! What are you talking about?"

Then Tom had to go into details, and explain to Ned all about the great quantity of gold that might be found in the underground city.

"You'll come along, won't you, Ned?" finished the young inventor. "We can't get along without you. Mr. Damon is going, and Eradicate too, I guess. We'll have a great time."

"Well, maybe I can fix it so I can go," agreed Ned, slowly, "I'd like it, above all things. Where did you say that golden city was?"

"Somewhere about the central part of Mexico, near the city of—"

"Hark!" suddenly exclaimed Ned, holding up a hand to caution Tom to silence.

"What is it?" asked the young inventor in a whisper.

"Some one is coming along the hall," replied Ned in a low voice.

They all listened intently. There was no doubt but that some one was approaching along the corridor leading to the library where the conference was being held.

"Oh, it's only Mrs. Baggert," remarked Tom a moment later, relief showing in his voice. "I know her step."

There was a tap on the door, and the housekeeper pushed it open, for it had been left ajar. She thrust her head in and remarked:

"I guess you've forgotten, Mr. Swift, that Andy Foger is waiting for you in the next room. He has a letter for you."

"Andy Foger!" gasped Tom. "Here."

"That's so, I forgot all about him!" exclaimed Mr. Swift jumping up. "It slipped my mind. I let him in a while ago, before we came in the library, and he's probably been sitting in the parlor ever since. I thought he wanted to see you, Tom, so I told him to wait. And I forgot all about him. You'd better see what he wants."

"Andy Foger there—in the next room," murmured Tom. "He's been there some time. I wonder how much he heard about the city of gold?"

CHAPTER III

ANDY IS WHITEWASHED

The parlor where Mr. Swift had asked Andy to wait, adjoined the library, and there was a connecting door, over which heavy curtains were draped. Tom quickly pulled them aside and stepped into the parlor. The connecting door had been open slightly, and in a flash the young inventor realized that it was perfectly possible for any one in the next room to have heard most of the talk about the city of gold.

A glance across the room showed Andy seated on the far side, apparently engaged in reading a book.

"Did you want to see me?" asked Tom sharply. His father and the others in the library listened intently. Tom wondered what in the world Andy could want of him, since the two were never in good tame, and Andy cherished a resentment even since our hero had rescued him from the African jungle.

"No, I didn't come to see you," answered Andy quickly, laying aside the book and rising to face Tom.

"Then what—"

"I came to see your father," interrupted the red-haired bully. "I have a letter for him from my father; but I guess Mr. Swift misunderstood me when he let me in."

"Did you tell him you wanted to see me?" asked Tom suspiciously, thinking Andy had made a mistatement in order to have a longer time to wait.

"No, I didn't, but I guess your father must have been thinking about something else, for he told me to come in here and sit down. I've been waiting ever since, and just now Mrs. Baggert passed and saw me. She—"

"Yes, she said you were here," spoke Tom significantly. "Well, then it's my father you want to see. I'll tell him."

Tom hurried back to the library.

"Dad," he said, "it's you that Andy wants to see. He has a letter from Mr. Foger for you."

"For me? What in the world can it be about? He never wrote to me before. I must have misunderstood Andy. But then it's no wonder for my head is so full of my new gyroscope plans. There is a certain spring I can't seem to get right—"

"Perhaps you'd better see what Andy wants," suggested Mr. Damon gently. He looked at Tom. They were both thinking of the same thing.

"I will," replied Mr. Swift quickly, and he passed into the library.

"I wonder how much Andy heard?" asked Ned, in a low voice.

"Oh, I don't believe it could have been very much," answered Tom.

"No, I stopped you just in time," rejoined his chum, "or you might have blurted out the name of the city near where the buried gold is."

"Yes, we must guard our secret well, Tom," put in Mr. Damon.

"Well, Andy couldn't have known anything about the letter I got," declared Tom, "and if he only heard snatches of our talk it won't do him much good."

"The only trouble is he's been there long enough to have heard most of it." suggested Ned. They could talk freely now, for in going into the parlor Mr. Swift had tightly closed the door after him. They could just hear the murmur of his voice speaking to Andy.

"Well, even if he does guess about the city of gold, and its location, I don't believe he'll try to go there," remarked Tom, after a pause.

A moment later they heard Mr. Swift letting Andy out of the front door, and then the inventor rejoined his son and the others. He held an open letter in his hand.

"This is strange—very strange," he murmured.

"What is it?" asked Tom quickly.

"Why. Mr. Foger has written to me asking to be allowed to sell some of our patents and machines on commission."

"Sell them on commission!" exclaimed his son. "Why does a millionaire like Mr. Foger want to be selling goods on commission? It's only a trick!"

"No, it's not a trick," said Mr. Swift slowly. "He is in earnest. Tom, Mr. Foger has lost his millions. His fortune has been swept away by unfortunate investments, he tells me, and he would be glad of any work I could give him. That's why Andy brought the letter tonight. I just sent him back with an answer."

"What did you say, dad?"

"I said I'd think it over."

"Mr. Foger's millions gone," mused Tom.

"And Andy in there listening to what we said about the city of gold," added Ned. "No wonder he was glad the door was open. He'd be there in a minute, Tom, if he could, and so would Mr. Foger, if he thought he could get rich. He wouldn't have to sell goods on commission if he could pick up a few of the golden images."

"That's right," agreed Tom, with an uneasy air. "I wish I knew just how much Andy had heard. But perhaps it wasn't much."

The time was to come, however, when Tom was to learn to his sorrow that Andy Foger had overheard a great deal.

"Bless my bankbook!" exclaimed Mr. Damon. "I never dreamed of such a thing! Andy had every reason in the world for not wanting us to know he was in there! No wonder he kept quiet. I'll wager all the while he was as close to the open door as he could get, hoping to overhear about the location of the place, so he could help his father get back his lost fortune. Bless my hatband! It's a good thing Mrs. Baggert told us he was there."

They all agreed with this, and then, as there was no further danger of being overheard, they resumed their talk about the city of gold. It was decided that they would have to wait the arrival of another letter from Mr. Illingway before starting for Mexico.

"Well, as long as that much is settled, I think I'd better be going home," suggested Mr. Damon. "I know my wife will be anxious about me."

"I'll get out the sky racer and you'll be in Waterford in a jiffy," said Tom, and he kept his word, for the speedy aeroplane carried him and his guest rapidly through the night, bringing Tom safely back home.

It was several days after this, during which time Tom and Ned had had many talks about the proposed trip. They had figured on what sort of a craft to use in the journey. Tom had about decided on a small, but very powerful, dirigible balloon, that could be packed in a small compass and taken along.

"This city may be in some mountain valley, and a balloon will be the only way we can get to it," he told Ned.

"That's right," agreed his chum. "By the way, you haven't heard any more about Andy; have you?"

"Not a thing. Haven't even seen him. None of us have."

"There goes Rad, I wonder if he's seen him."

"No, or he'd have mentioned it to me. Hey, Rad," Tom called to the colored man, "what are you going to do?"

"Whitewash de back fence, Massa Tom. It's in a mos' disrupted state ob disgrace. I'se jest natchally got t' whitewash it."

"All right, Rad, and when you get through come back here. I've got another job for you."

"A'right, Massa Tom, I shorely will," and Rad limped off with his pail of whitewash, and the long-handled brush.

It may have been fate that sent Andy Foger along the rear road a little later, and past the place where Eradicate was making the fence less "disrupted." It may have been fate or Andy may have just been sneaking along to see if he could overhear anything of Tom's plans—a trick of which he was frequently guilty. At any rate, Andy walked, past where Eradicate was whitewashing. The colored man saw the red-haired lad coming and murmured:

"Dere's dat no 'count white trash! I jest wish Massa Tom was hear now. He'd jest natchally wallop Andy," and Eradicate moved his long-handled brush up and down, as though he were coating the Foger lad with the white stuff.

As it happened, Eradicate was putting some of the liquid on a particularly rough spot in the fence, a spot low down, and this naturally made the handle of his brush stick out over the sidewalk, and at this moment Andy Foger got there.

"Here, you black rascal!" the lad angrily exclaimed. "What do you mean by blocking the sidewalk that way? It's against the law, and I could have you arrested for that."

"No, could yo' really now?" asked Eradicate drawlingly for he was not afraid of Andy.

"Yes, I could, and don't you give me any of your back-talk! Get that brush out of the way!" and Andy kicked the long handle.

The natural result followed. The other end of the brush, wet with whitewash, described a curve through the air, coming toward the mean bully. And as the blow of Andy's foot jarred the brush loose, the next moment it fell right on Andy's head, the white liquid trickling down on his clothes, for Eradicate was not a miser when it came to putting on whitewash.

For a moment Andy could not speak. Then he burst out with:

"Hi! You did that on purpose! I'll have you in jail for that! Look at my hat, it's ruined! Look at my clothes! They're ruined! Oh, I'll make you pay for this!"

"Deed, it shore was a accident," said Eradicate, trying not to laugh. "You done did it yo'se'f!"

"I did not! You did it on purpose; Tom Swift put you in on this! I'll—I'll—"

But Andy had to stop and splutter for some of the lime ran down off his hat into his mouth, and he yelled:

"I'll—I'll—Ouch! Phew! Woof! Oof! Oh!"

Then, in his rage, he made a blind rush for Eradicate. Now the colored man had no fear of Andy, but he did not want the pail of whitewash to upset, and the said pail was right in the path of the advancing youth.

"Look out!" cried Eradicate.

"I'll make you look out!" spluttered Andy. "I'll thrash you for this!"

Eradicate caught up his pail. He did not want to have the trouble of mixing more of the liquid. Just as he lifted it Andy aimed a kick for him. But he mis-calculated, and his foot struck the bottom of the pail and sent it flying from the hands of the colored man. Sent it flying right toward Andy himself, for Eradicate jumped back out of the way.

And the next moment a veritable deluge of whitewash was sprayed and splashed and splattered over Andy, covering him with the snowy liquid from head to foot!

CHAPTER IV

A PERILOUS FLIGHT

There was silence for a moment—there had to be—for Eradicate was doubled over with mirth and could not even laugh aloud, and as for Andy the whitewash running down his face and over his mouth effectually prevented speech. But the silence did not last long.

Just as Eradicate caught his breath, and let out a hearty laugh, Andy succeeded in wiping some of the liquid from his face so that it was safe to open his mouth. Then he fairly let out a roar of rage.

"I'll have you put in jail far that, Eradicate Sampson!" he cried. "You've nearly killed me: You'll suffer for this! My father will sue you for damages, too! Look at me! Look at me!"

"Dat's jest what I'se doin', honey! Jest what I'se doin'!" gasped Eradicate, hardly able to speak from laughter. "Yo' suah am a most contrary lookin' specimen! Yo' suah is! Ha! Ha!"

"Stop it!" commanded Andy. "Don't you dare laugh at me, after throwing whitewash on me."

"I didn't throw no whitewash on you!" protested the colored man. "Yo' done poured it over yo'se'f, dat's what yo' done did. An' I jest cain't help laughin', honey. I jest natchally cain't! Yo' look so mortally distressed, dat's what yo' does!"

Andy's rage might have been dangerous, but the very excess of it rendered him incapable of doing anything. He was wild at Eradicate and would willingly have attacked him, but the whitewash was beginning to soak through his clothes, and he was so wet and miserable that soon all the fight oozed out of him.

Then, too, though Eradicate was old, he was strong and he still held the long handle of the whitewash brush, no unformidable weapon. So Andy contented himself with verbal abuse. He called Eradicate all the mean names he could think of, ending up with:

"You won't hear the last of this for a long time, either. I'll have you, and your old rack of bones, your mule Boomerang, run out of town, that's what I will."

"What's dat? Yo' all gwine t'hab Boomerang run out ob town?" demanded Eradicate, a sudden change coming over him. His mule was his most beloved possession. "Lemme tell yo' one thing, Massa Andy. I'se an old colored man, an' I ain't much 'count mebby. But ef yo' dare lay one finger on mah mule Boomerang, only jest one finger, mind you', why I'll—I'll jest natchally drown yo'—all in whitewash, dat's what I'll do!"

Eradicate drew himself up proudly, and boldly faced Andy. The bully shrank back. He knew better than to arouse the colored man further.

"You'll suffer for this," predicted the bully. "I'm not going to forget it. Tom Swift put you up to this, and I'll take it out of him the next time I see him. He's to blame."

"Now looky heah, honey!" said Eradicate quick. "Doan' yo' all git no sich notion laik dat in yo' head. Massa Tom didn't tell me to do noth'in an I ain't. He ain't eben 'round yeh. An' annudder thing. Yo'se t' blame to' this yo' own se'f. Ef yo' hadn't gone fo' is kick de bucket it nebber would 'a happened. It's yo' own fault, honey, an' doan't yo' forgit dat! No, yo' better go home an' git some dry clothes on."

It was good advice, for Andy was soaking wet. He glared angrily at Eradicate, and then swung off down the road, the whitewash dripping from is garments at every step.

"Land a massy! But he suah did use up all mah lime." complained Eradicate, as he picked up the overturned pail. "I's got t' make mo'. But I doan't mind," he added cheerfully, and then, as he saw the woe-begone figure of Andy shuffling along, he laughed heartily, fitted the brush on the handle and went to tell Tom and Ned what had happened, and make more whitewash.

"Hum! Served him right," commented the young inventor.

"I suppose he'll try to play some mean trick on you now," commented Ned. "He'll think you had some hand in what Rad did."

"Let him," answered Tom. "If he tries any of his games I'll be ready for him."

"Maybe we'll soon be able to start for the city of gold," suggested Ned.

"I'm afraid not in some time," was his chum's reply. "It's going to take quite a while to get ready, and then we've got to wait to hear from Mr. Illingway. I wonder if it's true that Mr. Foger has lost his fortune; or was that only a trick?"

"Oh, it's true enough," answered Ned. "I heard some of the bank officials talking about it the other day." Ned was employed in one of the Shopton banks, an institution in which Tom and his father owned considerable stock. "He hasn't hardly any money left, and he may leave town and go out west, I heard."

"He can't go any too soon to suit me," spoke Tom, "and I hope he takes Andy with him."

"Your father isn't going to have any business dealings with Mr. Foger then?"

"I guess not. Dad doesn't trust him. But say, Ned, what do you say to a little trip in my sky racer? I want to go over to Waterford and see Mr. Damon. We can talk about our trip, and he was going to get some big maps of Central Mexico to study. Will you come?"

"I will this afternoon. I've got to go to the bank now."

"All right, I'll wait for you. In the meanwhile I'll be tuning up the motor. It didn't run just right the other night."

The two chums separated, Ned to go downtown to the bank, while Tom hastened to the shed where he kept his speedy little air craft. Meanwhile Eradicate went on whitewashing the fence, pausing every now and then to chuckle at the memory of Andy Foger.

Tom found that some minor adjustments had to be made to the motor, and they took him a couple of hours to complete. It was nearly noon when he finished, and leaving the sky racer in the open space in front of the shed, he went in the house to wash up, for his face and hands were begrimed with dirt and oil.

"But the machine's in good shape," he said to the housekeeper when she objected to his appearance, "and Ned and I will have a speedy spin this afternoon."

"Oh, you reckless boys! Risking your lives in those aeroplanes!" exclaimed Mrs. Baggert.

"Why, they're safer than street cars!" declared Tom with a laugh. "Just think how often street cars collide, and you never heard of an aeroplane doing that."

"No, but think what happens when they fall."

"That's it!" cried Tom gaily, "when they fall you don't have time to think. But is dinner ready? I'm hungry."

"Never saw you when you weren't." commented the housekeeper laughing. "Yes, you can sit right down. We won't wait for your father. He said he'd be late as he wants to find something about his gyroscope. I never did any such people as inventors for spoiling their meals," she added as she put dinner on the table.

Mr. Swift came in before his son had finished.

"Was Andy Foger here to see me again?" he asked.

"No, why do you ask?" inquired Tom quickly.

"I just saw him out by the aeroplane shed, and—"

Tom jumped up without another word, and hurried to where his sky racer rested on its bicycle wheels.

He breathed more easily when he saw that Andy was not in sight, and a hurried inspection of the aeroplane did not disclose that it had been tampered with.

"Anything the matter?" asked Mr. Swift, as he followed his son.

"No, but when you mentioned that Andy was out here I thought he might have been up to some of his tricks. He had a little trouble with Eradicate this morning, and he threatened to get even with me for it." And Tom told of the whitewashing incident.

"I just happened to see him as I was coming to dinner," went on the aged inventor. "He hurried off—when he noticed me, but I thought he might have been here to leave another letter."

"No," said Tom. "I must tell Eradicate to keep his weather eye open for him, though. No telling what Andy'll do. Well, I must finish eating, or Ned will be here before I'm through."

After dinner, Ned arrived, and helped Tom start the motor. With a roar and a bang the swift little machine rapidly got up speed, the propellers whizing so fast that they looked like blurs of light. The sky racer was held back by a rope, as Tom wanted to note the "pull" of the propellers, the force they exerted against the air being registered on a spring balance.

"What does it say, Ned?" cried the young inventor as he adjusted the carburettor.

"A shade over nine hundred pounds."

"Guess that'll do. Hop in, and I'll cast off from the seat."

This Tom frequently did when there was no one available to hold the aeroplane for him while he mounted. He could pull a cord, loosen the retaining rope, and away the craft would go.

The two chums were soon seated side by side and then Tom, grasping the steering wheel, turned on full power and jerked the releasing rope.

Over the ground shot the sky racer, quickly attaining speed until, with a deft motion, the young inventor tilted the deflecting rudder and up into the air they shot.

"Oh, this is glorious!" cried Ned, for, though he had often taken trips with Tom, every time he went up he seemed to enjoy it more.

Higher and higher they rose, and then with the sharp nose of the craft turned in the proper direction they sailed off well above the trees and houses toward Waterford.

"Guess I'll go up a bit higher," Tom yelled into his chums ear when they were near their destination. "Then I can make a spiral glide to earth. I haven't practiced that lately."

Up and up went the sky racer, until it was well over the town of Waterford, where Mr. Damon lived.

"There's his place!" yelled Ned, pointing downward. He had to yell to be heard above the noise of the motor. Tom nodded in reply. He, too, had picked out Mr. Damon's large estate. There were many good landing places on it, one near the house for which Tom headed.

The aeroplane shot downward, like a bird darting from the sky. Tom grasped the rudder lever more firmly. He looked below him, and then, suddenly he uttered a cry of terror.

"What is it?" yelled Ned.

"The rudder! The deflecting rudder! It's jammed, and I can't throw her head up! We're going to smash into the ground, Ned! I can't control her! Something has gone wrong!"

CHAPTER V

NEWS FROM AFRICA

Blankly, and with fear in his eyes, Ned gazed at Tom. The young inventor was frantically working at the levers, trying to loosen the jammed rudder—the rudder that enabled the sky racer to be tilted upward.

"Can't you do it?" cried Ned.

Tom shook his head helplessly, but he did not give up. Madly he worked on, and there was need of haste, for every moment the aeroplane was shooting nearer and nearer to the earth.

Ned glanced down. They were headed for the centre of a large grass plot and the bank employee found himself grimly thinking that at least the turf would be softer to fall on than bare ground.

"I—I can't imagine what's happened!" cried Tom.

He was still yanking on the lever, but it would not move, and unless the head of the aeroplane was thrown up quickly, to catch the air, and check its downward flight, they would both be killed.

"Shut off the engine and vol-plane!" cried Ned.

"No use," answered Tom. "I can't vol-plane when I can't throw her head up to check her."

But he did shut off the banging, throbbing motor, and then in silence they continued to fall. Ned had half a notion to jump, but he knew that would mean instant death, and there was just a bare chance that if he stayed in the machine it would take off some of the shock.

They could see Mr. Damon now. The old man had run out of his house at the sight of the approaching aeroplane. He knew it well, for he had ridden with Tom many times. He looked up and waved his hand to the boys, but he had no idea of their danger, and he could not have helped them had he been aware of it.

He must have soon guessed that something was wrong though, for a moment later, the lads could hear him shout in terror, and could see him motion to them. Later he said he saw that Tom was coming down at too great an inclination, and he feared that the machine could not be thrown up into the wind quickly enough!

"Here goes something—the lever or the rudder!" cried Tom in desperation, as he gave it a mighty yank. Up to now he had not pulled with all his strength as he feared to break some connecting-rod, wire or lever. But now he must take every chance. "If I can get that rudder up even a little we're safe!" he went on.

Once more he gave a terrific pull on the handle. There was a snapping sound and Tom gave a yell of delight.

"That's the stuff!" he cried. "She's moving! We're all right now!"

And the rudder had moved only just in time, for when the aeroplane was within a hundred feet of the earth the head was suddenly elevated and she glided along on a level "keel."

"Look out!" yelled Ned, for a new danger presented. They were so near the earth that Tom had over-run his original stepping place, and now the sky racer was headed directly for Mr. Damon's house, and might crash into it.

"All right! I've got her in hand!" said the young inventor reassuringly.

Tom tilted the rudder at a sharp angle to have the air pressure act as a brake. At the same time he swerved the craft to one side so that there was no longer any danger of crashing into the house.

"Bless my—" began Mr. Damon, but in the excitement he really didn't know what to bless, so he stopped short.

A moment later, feeling that the momentum had been checked enough to make it safe to land, Tom directed the craft downward again and came gracefully to earth, a short distance away from his eccentric friend.

"Whew!" gasped the young inventor, as he leaped from his seat. "That was a scary time while it lasted."

"I should say so!" agreed Ned.

"Bless my straw hat!" cried Mr. Damon. "What happened? Did you lose control of her, Tom?"

"No, the deflecting rudder got jammed, and I couldn't move it. I must look and see what's the matter."

"I thought it was all up with you," commented Mr. Damon, as he followed Tom and Ned to the front end of the craft, where the deflecting mechanism was located.

Tom glanced quickly over it. His quick eye caught something, and he uttered an exclamation.

"Look!" the young inventor cried. "No wonder it jammed!" and from a copper sleeve, through which ran the wire that worked the rudder, he pulled a small iron bolt. "That got between the sleeve and the wire, and I couldn't move it," he explained. "But when I pulled hard I loosened it."

"How did it fall in there?" asked Ned.

"It didn't fall there." spoke Tom quietly. "It was put there."

"Put there! Bless my insurance policy! Who did such a dastardly trick?" cried Mr. Damon.

"I don't know," answered Tom still quietly, "but I suspect it was Andy Foger, and he was never any nearer to putting us out of business than a little while ago, Ned."

"Do you mean to say that he deliberately tried to injure you?" asked Mr. Damon.

"Well, he may not have intended to hurt us, but that's what would have happened if I hadn't been able to throw her up into the wind when I did," replied Tom. Then he told of Mr. Swift having seen the red-haired bully near the aeroplane. "Andy may have only intended to put my machine out of working order," went on the young inventor, "but it might have been worse than that," and he could not repress a shudder.

"Are you going to say anything to him?" asked Ned.

"I certainly am!" replied Torn quickly. "He doesn't realize that he might have crippled us both for life. I sure am going to say something to him when I get back."

But Tom did not get the chance, for when he and Ned returned to Shopton,—the sky racer behaving beautifully on the homeward trip,—it was learned that Mr. Foger had suddenly left town, taking Andy with him.

"Maybe he knew I'd be after him," said Tom grimly, and so that incident was closed for the time being, but it was a long time before Tom and Ned got over their fright.

They had a nice visit with Mr. Damon, and talked of the city of gold to their heart's content, looking at several large maps of Mexico that the eccentric man had procured, and locating, as well as they could from the meager map and description they had, where the underground treasures might be.

"I suppose you are getting ready to go, Mr. Damon?" remarked Ned.

"Hush!" cautioned the odd man, looking quickly around the room. "I haven't said anything to my wife about it yet. You know she doesn't like me to go off on these 'wild goose chases' as she calls them, with you, Tom Swift. But bless my railroad ticket! It's half the fun of my life."

"Then don't you think you can go?" asked the young inventor eagerly, for he had formed a strong like for Mr. Damon, and would very much regret to go without him.

"Oh, bless my necktie! I think I'll be able to manage it," was the answer. "I'm not going to tell her anything about it until the last minute, and then I'll promise to bring her back one of the golden images. She won't object then."

"Good!" exclaimed Tom. "I hope we can all bring back some of the images."

"Yes, I know who you'll bring one for," said Ned with a laugh, and he took care to get beyond the reach of Tom's fist. "Her first name is Mary," he added.

"You get out!" laughed Tom, blushing at the same time.

"Ah! What a thing it is to be young!" exclaimed Mr. Damon with a mock sigh. The boys laughed, for the old man, though well along in years, was a boy at heart.

They talked at some length, speculating when they might hear from Mr. Illingway, and discussing the sort of an outfit that would be best to take with them.

Then, as the afternoon was drawing to a close, Tom and Ned went back in the aeroplane, hearing the news about the Fogers as I have previously mentioned.

"Well, I'll have to wait until I do see Andy to take it out of his hide," remarked Tom grimly. "I'm glad he's out of the way, though. There won't be any more danger of his overhearing our plans, and I can work in peace on the dirigible balloon."

Though Tom had many air crafts, the one he thought best suited to take with them on their search for the city of gold would have to be constructed from parts of several machines, and it would take some time.

Tom began work on it the next day, his father helping him, as did Mr. Damon and Ned occasionally. Several weeks were spent in this way, meanwhile the mails being anxiously watched for news from Africa.

"Here you are, Tom!" called the postman one morning, as he walked out to the shop where the young inventor was busy over the balloon. "Here's another letter from that Buggy-wuggy place."

"Oh, you mean Gumba Twamba, in Africa!" laughed the lad. "Good! That's what I've been waiting for. Now to see what the missionary says."

"I hope you're not going to go as a missionary to Africa, Tom," said the postman.

"No danger. This is just a letter from a friend there. He sent me some facts so I can go off on another expedition."

"Oh, you're always going off on wild adventures," commented Uncle Sam's messenger with a shake of his head as he hurried away, while Tom tore open the letter from Africa and eagerly read it.

CHAPTER VI

"BEWARE THE HEAD-HUNTERS!"

"That's what I want!" exclaimed the young inventor, as he finished the perusal of the missionary's missive.

"What is it?" asked Mr. Swift, entering the shop at that moment.

"News from Africa, dad. Mr. Illingway went to a lot of trouble to get more information for us about the city of gold, and he sends a better map. It seems there was one among the effects of the white man who died near where Mr. Illingway has his mission. With this map, and what additional information I have, we ought to locate the underground city. Look, dad," and the lad showed the map.

"Humph!" exclaimed Mr. Swift with a smile. "I don't call that a very clear map. It shows a part of Central Mexico, that's true, but it's on such a small scale I don't see how you're going to tell anything by it."

"But I have a description," explained Tom. "It seems according to Mr. Illingway's letter, that you have to go to the coast and strike into the interior until you are near the old city of Poltec. That used to be it's name, but Mr. Illingway says it may be abandoned now, or the name changed. But I guess we can find it."

"Then, according to what he could learn from the African natives, who talked with the white man, the best way is to hire ox carts and strike into the jungle. That's the only way to carry our baggage, and the dirigible balloon which I'm going to take along."

"Pretty uncertain way to look for a buried city of gold," commented Mr. Swift. "But I suppose even if you don't find it you'll have the fun of searching for it, Tom."

"But we are going to find it!" the lad declared. "We'll get there, you'll see!"

"But how are you going to know it when you see it?" asked his father. "If it's underground even a balloon won't help you much."

"It's true it is underground," agreed Tom, "but there must be an entrance to it somewhere, and I'm going to hunt for that entrance. Mr. Illingway writes that the city is a very old one, and was built underground by the priests of some people allied to the Aztecs. They wanted a refuge in times of war and they also hid their valuables there. They must have been rich to have so much gold, or else they didn't value it as we do."

"That might be so," assented Mr. Swift. "But I still maintain, Tom, that it's like looking for a needle in a haystack."

"Still, I'm going to have a try for it," asserted the lad. "If I can once locate the plain of the big temple I'll be near the entrance to the underground city."

"What is the 'plain of the big temple,' Tom?"

"Mr. Illingway writes," said the lad, again referring to the letter, "that somewhere near the beginning of the tunnel that leads into the city of gold, there is an immense flat plain, on which the ancient Aztecs once built a great temple. Maybe they worshiped the golden images there. Anyhow the temple is in ruins now, near an overgrown jungle, according to the stories the white man used to tell. He once got as near the city of gold as the big temple, but hostile natives drove him and his party back. Then he went to Africa after getting an image from someone, and died there. So no one since has ever found the city of gold."

"Well, I hope you do, Tom, but I doubt it. However, I suppose you will hurry your preparations for going away, now that you have all the information you can get."

"Right, dad. I must send word to Mr. Damon and Ned at once. A few more days' work, and my balloon will be in shape for a trial flight, and then I can take it apart, pack it up, and ship it. Then ho! for the city of gold!"

Mr. Swift smiled at his son's enthusiasm, but he did not check it. He knew Tom too well for that.

Naturally Mr. Damon and Ned were delighted with the additional information the missionary had sent, and Ned agreed with Tom that it was a mere matter of diligent search to find the underground city.

"Bless my collar button!" cried Mr. Damon. "It may not be as easy as all that, but Tom Swift isn't the kind that gives up! We'll get there!"

Meanwhile Tom worked diligently on his balloon. He sent a letter of thanks to Mr. Illingway, at the same time requesting that if any more information was obtained within the next three weeks to cable it, as there would not be time for a letter to reach Shopton ere Tom planned to leave for Mexico.

The following days were busy ones for all. There was much to be done, and Tom worked night and day. They had to get rifles ready, for they might meet hostile natives. Then, too, they had to arrange for the proper clothing, and other supplies.

To take apart and ship the balloon was no small task, and then there were the passages to engage on a steamer that would land them at the nearest point to strike into the interior, the question of transportation after reaching Mexico, and many other matters to consider.

But gradually things began to shape themselves and it looked as though the expedition could start for the city of gold in about two weeks after the receipt of the second letter from the missionary.

"I think I'll give the balloon a trial tomorrow," said Tom one night, after a hard day's work, "It's all ready, and it ought to work pretty good. It will be just what we need to sail over some dense jungle and land down on the plain by the great temple."

"Bless my slippers!" exclaimed Mr. Damon. "I must think up some way of telling my wife that I'm going."

"Haven't you told her yet?" asked Ned.

The eccentric man shook his head.

"I haven't had a good chance," he said, "but I think I'll tell her tomorrow, and promise her one of the gold images. Then she won't mind."

Tom was just a little bit nervous when he got ready for a trial flight in the new dirigible balloon. To tell the truth he much preferred aeroplanes to balloons, but he realized that in a country where the jungle growth prevailed, and where there might be no level places to get a "take off," or a starting place for an aeroplane, the balloon was more feasible.

But he need have had no fears, for the balloon worked perfectly. In the bag Tom used a new gas, much more powerful even than hydrogen, and which he could make from chemicals that could easily be carried on their trip.

The air craft was small but powerful, and could easily carry Tom, Ned and Mr. Damon, together with a quantity of food and other supplies. They intended to use it by starting from the place where they would leave the most of their baggage, after getting as near to the city of gold as they could by foot trails. Tom hoped to establish a camp in the interior of Mexico, and make trips off in different directions to search for the ruined temple. If unsuccessful they could sail back each night, and if he should discover the entrance to the buried city there was food enough in the car of the balloon to enable them to stay away from camp for a week or more.

In order to give the balloon a good test, Tom took up with him not only Ned and Mr. Damon, but Eradicate and Mr. Swift to equalize the weight of food and supplies that later would be carried. The test showed that the craft more than came up to expectations, though the trial trip was a little marred by the nervousness of the colored man.

"I doan't jest laik dis yeah kind of travelin'," said Eradicate. "I'd radder be on de ground."

Most of the remaining two weeks were spent in packing the balloon for shipment, and then the travelers got their own personal equipment ready. They put up some condensed food, but they depended on getting the major portion in Mexico.

It was two days before they were to start. Their passage had been engaged on a steamer, and the balloon and most of their effects had been shipped. Mr. Damon had broken the news to his wife, and she had consented to allow him to go, though she said it would be for the last time.

"But if I bring her back a nice, big, gold image I know she'll let me go on other trips with you, Tom." said the eccentric man. "Bless my yard stick, if I couldn't go off on an adventure now and then I don't know what I'd do."

They were in the library of the Swift home that evening. Tom, Ned, Mr. Damon and the aged inventor, and of course the only thing talked of was the prospective trip to the city of gold.

"What I can't understand," Mr. Swift was saying, "is why the natives made so many of the same images of gold, and why there is that large one in the underground place. What did they want of it?"

"That's part of the mystery we hope to solve," said Tom. "I'm going to bring that big image home with me if I can. I guess—"

He was interrupted by a ring at the front door.

"I hope that isn't Andy Foger," remarked Ned.

"No danger," replied Tom. "He'll keep away from here after what he did to my aeroplane."

Mrs. Baggert went to the door.

"A message for you, Tom," she announced a little later, handing in an envelope.

"Hello, a cablegram!" exclaimed the young inventor. "It must be from Mr. Illingway, in Africa. It is," he added a moment later as he glanced at the signature.

"What does he say?" asked Mr. Swift.

"Can he give us any more definite information about the city of gold?" inquired Ned.

"I'll read it," said Tom, and there was a curious, strained note in his voice. "This is what it says:"

"'No more information obtainable. But if you go to the city of gold beware of the head-hunters!'"

"Head-hunters!" exclaimed Mr. Damon. "Bless my top-knot, what are they?"

"I don't know," answered Tom simply, "but whatever they are we've got to be on the lookout for them when we get to the gold city, and that's where I'm going, head-hunters or no head-hunters!"

CHAPTER VII

TOM MAKES A PROMISE

It may well be imagined that the cable warning sent by Mr. Illingway caused our friends considerable anxiety. Coming as it did, almost at the last minute, so brief—giving no particulars—it was very ominous. Yet Tom was not afraid, nor did any of the others show signs of fear.

"Bless my shotgun!" exclaimed Mr. Damon, as he looked at the few words on the paper which Tom passed around. "I wish Mr. Illingway had said more about the head-hunters—or less."

"What do you mean?" asked Ned.

"Well, I wish he'd given us more particulars, told us where we might be on the lookout for the head-hunters, what sort of chaps they were, and what they do to a fellow when they catch him."

"Their name seems plainly to indicate what they do," spoke Mr. Swift grimly. "They cut off the head of their enemies, like that interesting Filipino tribe. But perhaps they may not get after you. If they do—"

"If they do," interrupted Tom with a laugh, "we'll hop in our dirigible balloon, and get above their heads, and then I guess we can give a good account of ourselves. But would you rather Mr. Illingway had said less about them, Mr. Damon?"

"Yes, I wish, as long as he couldn't tell us more, that he'd kept quiet about them altogether. It's no fun to be always on the lookout for danger. I'm afraid it will get on my nerves, to be continually looking behind a rock, or a tree, for a head-hunter. Bless my comb and brush!"

"Well, 'forewarned is forearmed,'" quoted Ned. "We won't think anything more about them. It was kind of Mr. Illingway to warn us, and perhaps the head-hunters have all disappeared since that white traveler was after the city of gold. Some story which he told his friends, the natives in Africa, is probably responsible for the missionary's warning. Let's check over our lists of supplies, Tom, and see if we have everything down!"

"Can't you do that alone, Ned?"

"Why?" and Ned glanced quickly at his chum. Mr. Damon and Mr. Swift had left the room.

"Well, I've get an engagement—a call to make, and—"

"Enough said, old man. Go ahead. I know what it is to be in love. I'll check the lists. Go see—"

"Now don't get fresh!" advised Tom with a laugh, as he went to his room to get ready to pay a little visit.

"I say, Tom," called Ned after him. "What about Eradicate? Are you going to take him along? He'd be a big help."

"I know he would, but he doesn't want to go. He balked worse than his mule Boomerang when I spoke about an underground city. He said he didn't want to be buried before his time. I didn't tell him we were going after gold, for sometimes Rad talks a bit too much, and I don't want our plans known."

"But I did tell him that Mexico was a great place for chickens, and that he might see a bull fight."

"Did he rise to that bait?"

"Not a bit of it. He said he had enough chickens of his own, and he never did like bulls anyhow. So I guess we'll have to get along without Rad."

"It looks like it. Well, go and enjoy yourself. I'll wait here until you come back, though I know you'll be pretty late, but I want to make sure of our lists."

"All right, Ned," and Tom busied himself with his personal appearance, for he was very particular when going to call on young ladies.

A little later he was admitted to her house by Miss Mary Nestor, and the two began an animated conversation, for this was in the nature of a farewell call by Tom.

"And you are really about to start off on your wild search?" asked the girl. "My! It seems just like something out of a book!"

"Doesn't it?" agreed Tom. "However, I hope there's more truth in it than there is in some books. I should hate to be disappointed, after all our preparation, and not find the buried city after all."

"Do you really think there is so much gold there?"

"Of course there's a good deal of guesswork about it," admitted the young inventor, "and it may be exaggerated, for such things usually are when a traveler has to depend on the accounts of natives."

"But it is certain that there is a big golden image in the interior of Africa, and that it came from Mexico. Mr. Illingway isn't a person who could easily be deceived. Then, too, the old Aztecs and their allies were wonderful workers in gold and silver, for look at what Cortez and his soldiers took from them."

"My! This is quite like a lecture in history!" exclaimed Mary with a laugh. "But it's interesting. I wonder if there are any small, golden images there, as you say there are so many in the underground city."

"Lots of them!" exclaimed Tom, as confidently as though he had seen them. "I'll tell you what I'll do, Mary. I'll bring you back one of these golden images for an ornament. It would look nice on that shelf I think," and Tom pointed to a vacant space on the mantle. "I'll bring you a large one or a small one, or both, Mary."

"Oh, you reckless boy! Well, I suppose it would be nice to have two, for they must be very valuable. But I'm not going to tax you too much. If you bring me back two small ones, I'll put one down here and the other—"

She paused and blushed slightly.

"Yes, and the other," suggested Tom.

"I'll put the other up in my room to remember you by," she finished with a laugh, "so pick out one that is nicely carved. Some of those foreign ones, such as the Chinese have, are hideous."

"That's right," agreed Tom, "and I'll see that you get a nice one. Those Aztecs used to do some wonderful work in gold and silver carving. I've seen specimens in the museum."

Then the two young people fell to talking of the wonderful trip that lay before Tom, and Mary, several times, urged him to be careful of the dangers he would be likely to encounter.

Tom said nothing to her of the head-hunters. He did not want to alarm Miss Nestor, and then, too, he thought the less he allowed his mind to dwell on that unpleasant feature of the journey, the less likely it would be to get on the nerves of all of them.

Ned was right when he predicted that Tom would make quite a lengthy visit. There was much to talk about and he did not expect to see Mary again for some time. But finally he realized that he must leave, and with a renewed promise to bring back with him the two small gold images, and after saying good-bye to Mr. and Mrs. Nestor, Tom took his leave.

"If you get marooned in the underground city, Tom," said Mr. Nestor, "I hope you can rig up a wireless outfit, and get help, as you did for us on Earthquake Island."

"I hope so," answered our hero with a laugh, and then, a little saddened by his farewell, and pondering rather solemnly on what lay before him—the dangers of travel as well as those of the head-hunters—Tom hastened back to his own home.

The young inventor found Ned busy over the list of supplies, diligently checking it and comparing it with the one originally made out, to see that nothing had been omitted. Mr. Damon had gone to his room, for he was to remain at the Swift house until he left with the gold-hunting expedition.

"Oh, you've got back, have you?" asked Tom's chum, with a teasing air. "I thought you'd given up the trip to the city of gold."

"Oh, cheese it!" invited Tom. "Come on, now I'll help you. Where's Eradicate? I want him to go out and see that the shop is locked up."

"He was in here a while ago and he said he was going to look after things outside. He told me quite a piece of news."

"What was it?"

"It seems that the Foger house has been sold, the furniture was all moved out today, and the family has left, bag and baggage. I asked Rad if he had heard where to, and he said someone down in the village was saying that Andy and his father have engaged passage on some ship that sails day after tomorrow."

"Day after tomorrow!" cried Tom. "Why, that's when ours sails! I hope Andy didn't hear enough of our plans that night to try to follow us."

"It would be just like him," returned Ned, "but I don't think they'll do it. They haven't enough information to go on. More likely Mr. Foger is going to try some new ventures to get back his lost fortune."

"Well, I hope he and Andy keep away from us. They make trouble everywhere they go. Now come on, get busy."

And, though Tom tried to drive from his mind the thoughts of the Fogers, yet it was with an uneasy sense of some portending disaster that he went on with the work of preparing for the trip into the unknown. He said nothing to Ned about it, but perhaps his chum guessed.

"That'll do," said Tom after an hour's labor. "We'll call it a night's work and quit. Can't you stay here—we've got several spare beds."

"No, I'm expected home."

"I'll walk a ways with you," said Tom, and when he had left his chum at his house our hero returned by a street that would take him past the Foger residence. It was shrouded in darkness.

"Everybody's cleared out," said Tom in a low voice as he glance at the gloomy house. "Well, all I hope is that they don't camp on our trail."

CHAPTER VIII

ERADICATE WILL GO

"I guess everything is all ready," remarked Tom,

"I can't think of anything more to do," said Ned.

"Bless my grip-sack!" exclaimed Mr. Damon, "if there is, someone else has got to do it. I'm tired to death! I never thought getting ready to go off on a simple little trip was so much work. We ought to have made the whole journey from start to finish in an airship, Tom, as we've done before."

"It was hardly practical," answered the young inventor. "I'm afraid we'll be searching for this underground city for some time, and we'll only need an airship or a dirigible balloon for short trips here and there. We've got to go a good deal by information the natives can furnish us, and we can't get at them very well when sailing in the air."

"That's right," agreed the eccentric man. "Well, I'm glad we're ready to start."

It was the evening of the day before they were to leave for New York, there to take steamer to a small port on the Mexican coast, and every one was busy putting the finishing details to the packing of his personal baggage.

The balloon, taken apart for easy transportation, had been sent on ahead, as had most of their supplies, weapons and other needed articles.

All they would carry with them were handbags, containing some clothing.

"Then you've fully made up your mind not to go; eh Rad?" asked Tom of the colored man, who was busy helping them pack. "You won't take a chance in the underground city?"

"No, Massa Tom, I's gwine t' stay home an' look after yo' daddy. 'Sides, Boomerang is gettin' old, an' when a mule gits along in yeahs him temper ain't none ob de best."

"Boomerang's temper never was very good, anyhow," said Tom. "Many's the time he's balked on you, Rad."

"I know it, Massa Tom, but dat jest shows what strong character he done hab. Nobody kin manage dat air mule but me, an' if I were to leave him, dere suah would be trouble. No, I cain't go to no underground city, nohow."

"But if you found some of the golden images you could buy another mule—two of 'em if you wanted that many," said Ned, and a moment later he remembered that Tom did not want the colored man to know anything about the trip after gold. He had been led to believe that it was merely a trip to locate an ancient city.

"Did yo' done say golden images?" asked Eradicate, his eyes big with wonder.

Ned glanced apologetically at Tom, and said, with a shrug of his shoulders:

"Well, I—"

"Oh, we might as well tell him," interrupted the young inventor. "Yes, Rad, we expect to bring back some images of solid gold from the underground city. If you go along you might get some for your self. Of course there's nothing certain about it, but—"

"How—how big am dem gold images, Massa Tom?" asked Eradicate eagerly.

"You've got him going now, Tom," whispered Ned.

"How big?" repeated Tom musingly. "Hum, well, there's one that is said to be bigger than three men, and there must be any number of smaller ones—say boy's size, and from that on down to the real little ones, according to Mr. Illingway."

"Real gold—yellow, gold images as big as a man," said Eradicate in a dreamy voice. "An'—an' some big as boys. By golly, Massa Tom, am yo' suah ob dat?"

"Pretty sure. Why, Rad?"

"Cause I's gwine wid yo', dat's why! I didn't know yo' all was goin' after gold. My golly I's gwine along! Look out ob mah way, ef yo' please,—Mr. Damon. I'se gwine t' pack up an' go. Am it too late to git me a ticket, Massa Tom?"

"No, I guess there's room on the ship. But say, Rad, I don't want you to talk about this gold image part of it. You can say we're going to look for an underground city, but no more, mind you!"

"Trust me, Massa Tom; trust me. I—I'll jest say brass images, dat's what I'll say—brass! We's gwine after brass, an' not gold. By golly, I'll fool 'em!"

"No, don't say anything about the images—brass or gold," cautioned Tom. "But, Rad, there's another thing. We may run across the head-hunters down there in Mexico."

"Head-Hunters? What's dem?"

"They crush you, and chop off your head for an ornament."

"Ha! Ha! Den I ain't in no danger, Massa Tom. Nobody would want de head ob an old colored man fo' an ornament. By golly! I's safe from dem head-hunters! Yo' can't scare me dat way. I's gwine after some of dem gold images, I is, an' ef I gits some I'll build de finest stable Boomerang ever saw, an' he kin hab oats fo' times a day. Dat's what I's gwine t' do. Now look out ob mah way, Mr. Damon, ef yo' pleases. I's gwine t' pack up," and Eradicate shuffled off, chuckling to himself and muttering over and over again: "Gold images! Gold images! Images ob solid gold! Think ob dat! By golly!"

"Think he'll give the secret away, Tom?" asked Ned.

"No. And I'm glad he's going. Four makes a nice party, and Rad will make himself useful around camp. I've been sorry ever since he said he wouldn't go, on account of the good cooking I'd miss, for Rad is sure a fine cook."

"Bless my knife and fork, that's so!" agreed Mr. Damon.

So complete were the preparations of our friends that nothing remained to do the next morning. Eradicate had his things all in readiness, and when good-byes had been said to Mr. Swift, and Mrs. Baggert, Tom, Ned and Mr. Damon, followed by the faithful colored man, set off for the depot to take the train for New York. There they were to take a coast steamer for Tampico, Mexico, and once there they could arrange for transportation into the interior.

The journey to New York was uneventful, but on arrival there they met with their first disappointment. The steamer on which they were to take passage had been delayed by a storm, and had only just arrived at her dock.

"It will take three days to get her cargo out, clean the boilers, load another cargo in her and get ready to sail," the agent informed them.

"Then what are we to do?" asked Ned.

"Guess we'll have to wait; that's all," answered Tom. "It doesn't much matter. We're in no great rush, and it will give us three days around New York. We'll see the sights."

"Bless my spectacles! Its an ill wind that blows nobody good," remarked Mr. Damon, "I've been wanting to visit New York for some time, and here's my chance."

"We'll go to a good hotel," said Tom "and enjoy ourselves as long as we have to wait for the steamer."

CHAPTER IX

"THAT LOOKED LIKE ANDY!"

What seemed at first as if it was going to be a tedious time of waiting, proved to be a delightful experience, for our friends found much to occupy their attention in New York.

Tom and Ned went to several theatrical performances, and wanted Mr. Damon to go with them, but the odd man said he wanted to visit several museums and other places of historical interest, so, while he was browsing around that way, the boys went to Bronx Park, and to Central Park, to look at the animals, and otherwise enjoy themselves.

Eradicate put in his time in his own way. Much of it was spent in restaurants where chicken and pork chops figured largely on the bills of fare, for Tom had plentifully supplied the colored man with money, and did not ask an accounting.

"What else do you do besides eat, Rad?" asked Ned with a laugh, the second day of their stay in New York.

"I jest natchally looks in de jewelery store windows," replied Eradicate with a grin on his honest black face. "I looks at all de gold ornaments, an' I tries t' figger out how much better mah golden images am gwine t' be."

"But don't you go in, and ask what a gold image the size of a man would be worth!" cautioned Tom. "The jeweler might think you were crazy, and he might suspect something."

"No, Massa Tom, I won't do nuffin laik dat," promised Eradicate. "But, Massa Tom, how much does yo' 'spect a image laik dat would be worth?"

"Haven't the least idea, Rad. Enough, though, to make you rich for the rest of your life."

"Good land a' massy!" gasped Eradicate, and he spent several hours trying to do sums in arithmetic on scraps of paper.

"Hurrah!" cried Tom, when, on the morning of the third day of their enforced stay in New York, a letter was sent up to his room by the hotel clerk.

"What's up?" asked Ned. "I didn't know that you sent Mary word that you were here."

"I didn't, you old scout!" cried Tom. "This is from the steamship company, saying that the steamer Maderia, on which we have taken passage for Mexico, will sail tonight at high tide. That's the stuff! At last we'll really get on our way."

"Bless my notebook!" cried Mr. Damon. "I hoped we'd stay at least another day here. I haven't seen half enough in the museums."

"You'll see stranger things than in any museum when we get to the underground city," predicted Tom. "Come on, Ned, we'll take in a moving picture show, have our last lunch in the big city, and then go aboard."

So impatient were the travelers to go on board the steamer that they arrived several hours before the time set for sailing. Many others did the same thing, however, as supper was to be served on the Maderia.

Though it was within a few hours of leaving time there seemed so much to be done, such a lot of cargo to stow away, and so much coal to put into the bunkers, that Tom and the others might well be excused for worrying about whether or not they really would sail.

Big trucks drawn by powerful horses thundered down the long dock. Immense automobiles laden with boxes, barrels and bales puffed to the loading gangways. There was the puffing and whistling of the donkey engines as they hoisted into the big holds the goods intended for export.

At the side of the steamer were grimy coal barges, into which was dipped an endless chain of buckets carrying the coal to the bunkers. Stevadores were running here and there, orders and counter-orders were being given, and the confusion must have been maddening to any one not accustomed to it.

"Bless my walking stick!" exclaimed Mr. Damon. "We'll never get off tonight, I'm positive."

"Dat's right," agreed Eradicate. "Look at all dat coal dey's got to load in."

"Oh, they knew how to hustle at the last minute," said Tom, and so it proved. Gradually the loading was finished. The coal barges were emptied and towed away. Truck after truck departed from the dock empty, having left its load in the interior of the steamer. One donkey engine after another ceased to puff, and the littered decks were cleared.

"Let's watch the late-comers get aboard," suggested Ned to Tom, when they had arranged things in their stateroom. The two boys and Mr. Damon had a large one to themselves and Eradicate had been assigned a small one not far from them.

"That'll make the time pass until supper is ready," agreed the young inventor, so they took their station near the main gangway and watched the passengers hurrying up. There were many going to make the trip to Mexico it seemed, and later the boys learned that a tourist agency had engaged passage for a number of its patrons.

"That fat man will never get up the slope unless some one pushes him," remarked Ned, pointing to a very fleshy individual who was struggling up the steep gangplank, carrying a heavy valise. For the tide was almost at flood and the deck of the steamer was much elevated. Indeed it seemed at one moment as if the heavy-weight passenger would slide backward instead of getting aboard.

"Go give him a hand, Rad," suggested Tom, and the colored man obligingly relieved the fat man of his grip, thereby enabling him to give all his attention to getting up the plank.

And it was this simple act on the part of Rad that was the cause of an uneasy suspicion coming to Tom and Ned. For, as Eradicate hastened to help the stout passenger, two others behind him, a man and a boy, started preciptably at the sight of the colored helper. So confused were they that it was noticed by Ned and his chum.

"Look at that!" said Ned in a low voice, their attention drawn from the fat man to the man and youth immediately behind him. "You'd think they were afraid of meeting Rad."

"That's right," agreed Tom, for the man and youth had halted, and seemed about to turn back, Then the man, with a quick gesture, tossed a steamer rug he was carrying over his shoulder up so that it hid his face. At the same time the lad with him, evidently in obedience to some command, pulled his cap well down over his face and turned up the collar of a light overcoat he was wearing. He also seemed to shrink down, almost as if he were deformed.

"Say!" began Ned in wondering tones, "Tom, doesn't that look like—"

"Andy Foger and his father!" burst out the young inventor in a horse whisper. "Ned, do you think it's possible?"

"Hardly, and yet—"

Ned paused in his answer to look more closely at the two who had aroused the suspicions of himself and Tom. But they had now crowded so close up behind the fat man whom Eradicate was assisting up the plank, that he partly hid them from sight, and the action of the two in covering their faces further aided them in disguising themselves, if such was their intention.

"Oh, it can't be!" declared Tom. "If they were going to follow us they wouldn't dare go on the same steamer. It must be some one else. But it sure did look like Andy at first."

"That's what I say," came from Ned. "But we can easily find out."

"How?"

"Ask the purser to show us the passenger list. Even if they are down under some other names he'd know the Fogers if we described them to him."

"That's right, we'll do it."

By this time the fat man, who was being assisted by Eradicate had reached the top of the gang plank. He must have been expected, for several friends rushed to greet him, and for a moment there was a confusing little throng at the place where the passengers came abroad. Tom and Ned hurried up, intent on getting a closer view of the man and youth who seemed so anxious to escape observation.

But several persons got in their way, and the two mysterious ones taking advantage of the confusion, slipped down a companionway to their stateroom, so that when our two lads managed to extricate themselves from the throng around the fat man, who insisted on thanking them for allowing Eradicate to help him, it was too late to effect any identification, at least for the time being.

"But we'll go to the purser," said Tom. "If Andy and his father are on this steamer we want to know it."

"That's right," agreed Ned.

Just then there was the usual cry:

"All ashore that's going ashore! Last warning!"

A bell rang, there was a hoarse whistle, the rattle of the gangplank being drawn in, a quiver through the whole length of the ship, and Tom cried:

"We're off!"

"Yes," added Ned, "if Andy and his father are here it's too late to leave them behind now!"

CHAPTER X

MYSTERIOUS PASSENGERS

Ned and Tom did not escape the usual commotion that always attends the sailing of a large steamer. The people on the dock were waving farewells to those on the boat, and those on the deck of the Maderia shook their handkerchiefs, their steamer rugs, their hands, umbrellas—in short anything to indicate their feelings. It was getting dark, but big electric lights made the dock and the steamer's deck brilliantly aglow.

The big whistle was blowing at intervals to warn other craft that the steamer was coming out of her slip. Fussy little tugs were pushing their blunt noses against the sides of the Maderia to help her and, in brief, there was not a little excitement.

"Bless my steamer chair!" exclaimed Mr. Damon. "We're really off at last! And now for the land of—"

"Hush!" exclaimed Tom, who stood near the odd gentleman. "You're forgetting. Some one might hear you."

"That's so, Tom. Bless my soul! I'll keep quiet after this."

"Mah golly!" gasped Eradicate as he saw the open water between the ship and the deck, "I can't git back now if I wanter—but I doan't wanter. I hope yo' father takes good care ob Boomerang, Massa Tom."

"Oh, I guess he will. But come on, Ned, we'll go to the purser's office now."

"What for? Is something wrong?" asked Mr. Damon.

"No, we just want to see if—er—if some friends of ours are on board," replied the young inventor, with a quick glance at his chum.

"Very well," assented Mr. Damon. "I'll wait for you on deck here. It's quite interesting to watch the sights of the harbor."

As for these same sights they possessed no attractions for the two lads at present. They were too intent on learning whether or not their suspicions regarding the Fogers were correct.

"Now if they are on board," said Tom, as they made their way to the purser's office, "it only means one thing—that they're following us to get at the secret of the city of gold," and Tom whispered this last, even though there seemed to be no one within hearing, for nearly all the passengers were up on deck.

"That's right," agreed Ned. "Of course there's a bare chance, if those two were the Fogers, that Mr. Foger is going off to try and make another fortune. But more than likely they're on our trail, Tom."

"If it's them—yes."

"Hum, Foger—no, I don't think I have any passengers of that name," said the purser slowly, when Tom had put the question. "Let's see, Farday, Fenton, Figaro, Flannigan, Ford, Foraham, Fredericks—those are all the names in the 'Fs'. No Fogers among them. Why, are you looking for some friends of yours, boys?"

"Not exactly friends," replied Tom slowly, "but we know them, and we thought we saw them come aboard, so we wanted to make sure."

"They might be under some other name," suggested Ned.

"Yes, that is sometimes done," admitted the purser with a quick glance at the two lads, "It's done when a criminal wants to throw the police off his track, or, occasionally, when a celebrated person wants to avoid the newspaper reporters. But I hardly think that—"

"Oh, I don't believe they'd do it," said Tom quickly. He saw at once that the suspicions of the purser had been aroused, and the official might set on foot inquiries that would be distasteful to the two lads and Mr. Damon. Then, too, if the Fogers were on board under some other name, they would hear of the questions that had been put regarding them, and if they were on a legitimate errand they could make it unpleasant for Tom.

"I don't believe they'd do anything like that," the young inventor repeated.

"Well, you can look over the passenger list soon," said the purser. "I'm going to post it in the main saloon. But perhaps if you described the persons you are looking for I could help you out. I have met nearly all the passengers already."

"Mr. Foger is a big man, with a florid complexion and he has a heavy brown moustache," said Ned.

"And Andy has red hair, and he squints," added Tom.

"No such persons on board," declared the official positively. "It's true we have several persons who squint, but no one with red hair—I'm sure of it."

"Then they're not here," declared Ned. "No, we must have been mistaken," agreed Tom, and there was relief in his tone. It was bad enough to have to search for a hidden city of gold, and perhaps have to deal with the head-hunters, without having to fight off another enemy from their trail.

"Much obliged," said the young inventor to the purser, and then the two lads went back on deck.

A little later supper was served in the big dining saloon, and the boys and Mr. Damon were glad of it, for they were hungry. Eradicate ate with a party of colored persons whose acquaintance he had quickly made. It was a gay gathering in which Tom and Ned found themselves, for though they had traveled much, generally it had been in one of Tom's airships, or big autos, and this dining on a big ship was rather a novelty to them.

The food was good, the service prompt, and Tom found himself possessed of a very good appetite. He glanced across the table and noted that opposite him and Ned, and a little way down the board, were two vacant chairs.

"Can't be that anyone is seasick already." he remarked to his chum.

"I shouldn't think so, for we haven't any more motion than a ferryboat. But some persons are very soon made ill on the water."

"If they're beginning thus early, what will happen when we get out where it's real rough?" Tom wanted to know.

"They'll sure be in for it," agreed Ned, and a glance around the dining saloon showed that those two vacant chairs were the only ones.

Somehow Tom felt a vague sense of uneasiness—as if something was about to happen. In a way he connected it with the suspicion that the Fogers were aboard, and with his subsequent discovery that their names were not on the passenger list. Then, with another thought in mind, he looked about to see if he could pick out the man and youth who, on coming up the gang plank, had been taken by both Tom and Ned to be their enemies. No one looking like either was to be seen, and Tom's mind at once went back to the vacant seats at the table.

"By Jove, Ned!" he exclaimed. "I believe I have it!"

"Have what—a fit of seasickness?"

"No, but these empty seats—the persons we saw you know—they belong there and they're afraid to come out and be seen."

"Why should they be—if they're not the Fogers. I guess you've got another think coming."

"Well, I'm sure there's something mysterious about those two—the way they hid their faces as they came on board—not appearing at supper—I'm going to keep my eyes open."

"All right, go as far as you like and I'm with you. Just now you may pass me the powdered sugar. I want some on this pie."

Tom laughed at Ned's matter-of-fact indifference, but when the young inventor turned in to his berth that night he could not stop thinking of the empty seats—the two mysterious passengers—and the two Fogers. They got all jumbled in his head and made his sleep restless.

Morning saw the Maderia well out to sea, and, as there was quite a swell on, the vessel rolled and pitched to an uncomfortable degree. This did not bother Tom and Ned, who were used to sudden changes of equilibrium from their voyages in the air. Nor did Mr. Damon suffer. In fact he was feeling fine and went about on deck like an old salt, blessing so many new things that he had many of the passengers amused.

Poor Eradicate did suffer though. He was very seasick, and kept to his berth most of the time, while some of his new friends did what they could for him.

Tom had in mind a plan whereby he might solve the identity of the mysterious passengers. He was going to do it by a process of elimination—that is he would carefully note all on board until he had fixed on the two who had aroused his suspicions. And he had to do this because so many of the passengers looked very different, now that they had on their ship "togs," than when first coming on board.

But the rough weather of the first day prevented the lad from carrying out his plan, as many of the travelers kept to their staterooms, and there were a score of vacant places at the tables.

The next day, however, was fine, and with the sea like the proverbial mill pond, it seemed that everyone was out on deck. Yet when meal time came there were these same two vacant seats.

"What do you think of it, Ned?" asked Tom, with a puzzled air.

"I don't know what to think, Tom. It sure is queer that these two—whoever they are—don't ever come to meals. They can't be seasick on a day like this, and they certainly weren't the first night."

"That's right. I'm going to ask one of the stewards where their stateroom is, and why they don't come out."

"You may get into trouble."

"Oh, I guess not. If I do I can stand it. I want to solve this mystery." Tom did put his question to one of the dining saloon stewards and it created no suspicions.

"Ah, yes, I guess you must mean Mr. Wilson and his son." spoke the steward when he had referred to a list that corresponded with the numbers of the vacant places at the table. "They have their meals served in their stateroom."

"Why?" asked Tom, "are they ill?"

"I really couldn't say, sir. They prefer it that way, and the captain consented to it from the first."

"But I should think they'd want to get out for a breath of air," put in Ned. "I can't stay below decks very long."

"They may come out at night," suggested the steward. "Some of our travelers think they are less likely to be seasick if they come out at night. They don't see the motion of the waves then."

"Guess that's it," agreed Tom with a wink at Ned. "Much obliged. Glad we're not seasick," and he linked his arm in that of his chum's and marched him off.

"Why the wink?" asked Ned, when they were out of earshot of the steward.

"That was to tip you off to say nothing more. I've got a plan I'm going to work."

"What is it?"

"Well, we know who the mysterious ones are, anyhow—at least we know their names—Wilson."

"It may not be the right one."

"That doesn't make any difference. I can find out their stateroom by looking at the passenger list."

"What good will that do."

"Lots. I'm going to keep a watch on that stateroom until I get a good look at the people in it. And if they only come out at night, which it begins to look like, I'm going to do some night watching. This thing has got to be settled, Ned. Our trip to the city of gold is too important to risk having a mysterious couple on our trail—when that same couple may be the Fogers. I'm going to do some detective work, Ned!"

CHAPTER XI

THE MIDNIGHT ALARM

"Whew! What a lot of 'em!"

"Bless my fish line! It's a big school!"

"Look how they turn over and over, and leap from the water."

"By golly, dere is suttinly some fish dere!"

These were the exclamations made by our four friends a few days later, as they leaned over the rail of the Maderia and watched a big school of porpoises gamboling about in the warm waters of the gulf stream. It was the second porpoise school the ship had come up with on the voyage, and this was a much larger one than the first, so that the passengers crowded up to see the somewhat novel sight.

"If they were only good eating now, we might try for a few," observed Ned.

"Some folks eat them, but they're too oily for me," observed a gentleman who had struck up an acquaintance with the boys and Mr. Damon. "Their skin makes excellent shoe laces though, their oil is used for delicate machinery—especially some that comes from around the head, at least so I have heard."

"Wow! Did you see that?" cried Tom, as one large porpoise leaped clear of the water, turned over several times and fell back with a loud splash. "That was the biggest leap yet."

"And there goes another," added Ned.

"Say, this ought to bring those two mysterious passengers out of their room," observed Tom to his chum in a low voice. "Nearly everyone else seems to be on deck."

"You haven't been able to catch a glimpse of them; eh Tom?"

"Not a peak. I stayed up several nights, as you know, and paced the deck, but they didn't stir out. Or, if they did, it must have been toward morning after I turned in. I can't understand it. They must be either criminals, afraid of being seen, or they are the Fogers, and they know we're on to their game."

"It looks as if it might be one or the other, Tom. But if they are criminals we don't have to worry about 'em. They don't concern us."

"No, that's right. Split mackerel! Look at that fellow jump. He's got 'em all beat!" and Tom excitedly, pointed at the porpoises, the whole school of which was swimming but a short distance from the steamer.

"Yes, a lot of them are jumping now. I wonder—"

"Look! Look!" cried the man who had been talking to Mr. Damon. "Something out of the ordinary is going on among those porpoises. I never saw them leap out of the water like that before."

"Sharks! It's sharks!" cried a sailor who came running along the deck. "A school of sharks are after the porpoises!" "I believe he's right," added Mr. Sander, the gentleman with Mr. Damon. "See, there's the ugly snout of one now. He made a bite for that big porpoise but missed."

"Bless my meat axe!" cried the odd man. "So he did. Say, boys, this is worth seeing. There'll be a big fight in a minute."

"Not much of a fight," remarked Mr. Sander. "The porpoise isn't built for fighting. They're trying to get away from the sharks by leaping up."

"Why don't they dive, and so get away?" asked Ned.

"The sharks are too good at diving," went on Mr. Sander. "The porpoises couldn't escape that way. Their only hope is that something will scare the sharks away, otherwise they'll kill until their appetites are satisfied, and that isn't going to be very soon I'm afraid."

"Look! Look!" cried Ned. "A shark leaped half way out of the water then."

"Yes, I saw it," called Tom.

There was now considerable excitement on deck. Nearly all the passengers, many of the crew and several of the officers were watching the strange sight. The porpoises were frantically tumbling, turning and leaping to get away from their voracious enemies.

"Oh, if I only had my electric rifle!" cried Tom. "I'd make some of those ugly sharks feel sick!"

"Bless my cartridge belt!" cried Mr. Damon. "That would be a good idea. The porpoises are such harmless creatures. It's a shame to see them attacked so."

For the activity of the sharks had now redoubled, and they were darting here and there amid the school of porpoises biting with their cruel jaws. The other fish were frantically leaping and tumbling, but the strange part of it was that the schools of sharks and porpoises kept about the same distance ahead of the ship, so that the passengers had an excellent view of the novel and thrilling sight.

"Rifle!" said Mr. Sander, catching at the word. "I fancy the captain may have some. He's quite a friend of mine, I'll speak to him."

"Get me one, too, if you please," called Ned as the gentleman hurried away.

"And I'll also try my luck at potting a shark. Bless my gunpowder if I won't!" said Mr. Damon.

The captain did have several rifles in his stateroom, and he loaned them to Mr. Sander. They were magazine weapons, firing sixteen shots each, but they were not of as high power as those Tom had packed away.

"Now we'll make those sharks sing a different tune, if sharks sing!" cried the young inventor.

"Yes, we're coming to the rescue of the porpoises!" added Ned.

The passengers crowded up to witness the marksmanship, and soon the lads and Mr. Damon were at it.

It was no easy matter to hit a shark, as the big, ugly fish were only seen for a moment in their mad rushes after the porpoises, but both Tom and Ned were good shots and they made the bullets tell.

"There, I hit one big fellow!" cried Mr. Damon. "Bless my bull's eye, but I plugged him right in the mouth, I think."

"I hope you knocked out some of his teeth," cried Ned.

They fired rapidly, and while they probably hit some of the innocent porpoises in their haste, yet they accomplished what they had set out to do—scare off the sharks. In a little while the "tigers of the sea" as some one has aptly called them, disappeared.

"That's the stuff!" cried Mr. Damon. "Now we can watch the porpoises at play."

But they did not have that sight to interest them very long. For, as suddenly as the gamboling fish had appeared, they sank from sight—all but a few dead ones that the sharks had left floating on the calm surface of the ocean. Probably the timid fish had taken some alarm from the depths into which they sank.

"Well, that was some excitement while it lasted," remarked Tom, as he and Ned took the rifles back to the captain.

"But it didn't bring out the mysterious passengers," added Ned. Tom shook his head and on their return to deck he purposely went out of his way to go past Stateroom No. 27, where the "Wilsons" were quartered. The door was closed and a momentary pause to listen brought our hero no clue, for all was silent in the room.

"It's too much for me," he murmured, shaking his head and he rejoined his chum.

Several more days passed, for the Maderia was a slow boat, and could not make good time to Mexico. However, our travelers were in no haste, and they fully enjoyed the voyage.

Try as Tom did to get a glimpse of the mysterious passengers he was unsuccessful. He spent many hours in a night, and early morning vigil, only to have to do his sleeping next day, and it resulted in nothing.

"I guess they want to get on Mexican soil before any one sees their faces," spoke Ned, and Tom was inclined to agree with his chum.

They awoke one morning to find the sea tempestuous. The ship tossed and rolled amid the billows, and the captain said they had run into the tail end of a gulf hurricane.

"Two days more and we'll be in port," he added, "and I'm sorry the voyage had to be marred even by this blow."

For it did blow, and, though it was not a dangerous storm, yet many passengers kept below.

"I'm afraid this settles it," remarked Tom that night, when the ship was still pitching and tossing. "They won't come out now, and this is likely to keep up until we get to port. Well, I can't help it."

But fate was on the verge of aiding Tom in an unexpected way. Nearly every one turned in early that night for it was no pleasure to sit in the saloons, and to lie in one's berth made it easier to stand the rolling of the vessel.

Tom and Ned, together with Mr. Damon, had fallen into slumber in spite of the storm, when, just as eight bells announced midnight there was a sudden jar throughout the whole ship.

The Maderia quivered from stem to stern, seemed to hesitate a moment as though she had been brought to a sudden stop, and then plowed on, only to bring up against some obstruction again, with that same sickening jar throughout her length.

"Bless my soul! What's that?" cried Mr. Damon, springing from his berth.

"Something has happened!" added Tom, as he reached out and switched on the electric lights.

"We hit something!" declared Ned.

The ship was now almost stopped and she was rolling from side to side.

Up on deck could be heard confused shouts and the running to and fro of many feet. The jangling of bells sounded—hoarse orders were shouted—and there arose a subdued hubbub in the interior of the ship.

"Something sure is wrong!" cried Tom. "We'd better get our clothes on and get on deck! Come on, Ned and Mr. Damon! Grab life preservers!"

CHAPTER XII

INTO THE UNKNOWN

"Bless my overshoes! I hope we're not sinking!" cried Mr. Damon, as he struggled into some of his clothes, an example followed by Ned and Tom.

"This boat has water-tight compartments, and if it does sink it won't do it in a hurry," commented Tom.

"I don't care to have it do it at all," declared Ned, who found that he had started to get into his trousers hindside before and he had to change them. "Think of all our baggage and supplies and the balloon on board." For the travelers had shipped their things by the same steamer as that on which they sailed.

"Well, let's get out and learn the worst," cried Tom.

He was the first to leave the stateroom, and as he rushed along the passages which were now brilliant with light he saw other half-clad passengers bent on the same errand as himself, to get on deck and learn what had happened.

"Wait, Tom!" called Ned.

"Come along, I'm just ahead of you," yelled his chum from around a corner. "I'm going to see if Eradicate is up. He's an awful heavy sleeper."

"Bless my feather bed! That shock was enough to awaken anyone!" commented Mr. Damon, as he followed Ned, who was running to catch up to Tom.

Suddenly a thought came to our hero. The mysterious passengers in Stateroom No. 27! Surely this midnight alarm would bring them out, and he might have a chance to see who they were.

Tom thought quickly. He could take a turn, go through a short passage, and run past the room of the mysterious passengers getting on deck as quickly as if he went the usual way.

"I'll go look after Rad!" Tom shouted to Ned. "You go up on deck, and I'll join you."

Eradicate's stateroom was on his way, after he had passed No. 27. Tom at once put his plan into execution. As he ran on, the confusion on deck seemed to increase, but the lad noted that the vessel did not pitch and roll so much, and she seemed to be on an even keel, and in no immediate danger of going down.

As Tom neared Stateroom No. 27 he heard voices coming from it, voices that sent a thrill through him, for he was sure he had heard them before.

"Where are the life preservers? Oh, I know we'll be drowned! I wish I'd never come on this trip! Look out, those are my pants you're putting on! Oh, where is my collar? Hand me my coat! Look out, you're stepping on my fingers!"

These were the confused and alarmed cries that Tom heard. He paused for a moment opposite the door, and then it was suddenly flung open. The lights were glaring brightly inside and a strange sight met the gaze of the young inventor.

There stood Mr. Foger and beside him—half dressed—was his son—Andy! Tom gasped. So did Andy and Mr. Foger, for they had both recognized our hero.

But how Mr. Foger had changed! His moustache was shaved off, though in spite of this Tom knew him. And Andy! No longer was his hair red, for it had been dyed a deep black and glasses over his eyes concealed their squint. No wonder the purser had not recognized them by the descriptions Tom and Ned had given.

"Andy Foger!" gasped Tom.

"Tom—it's Tom Swift, father!" stammered the bully.

"Close the door!" sharply ordered Mr. Foger, though he and his son had been about to rush out.

"I won't do it!" cried Andy. "The ship is sinking and I'm not going to be drowned down here."

"So it was you—after all," went on Tom. "What are you doing here?"

"None of your business!" snapped Andy. "Get out of my way, I'm going on deck."

Tom realized that it was not the proper time to hold a conversation, with a possibly sinking ship under him. He looked at Mr. Foger, and many thoughts shot through his mind. Why were they on board? Had it anything to do with the city of gold? Had Andy overheard the talk? Or was Mr. Foger merely looking for a new venture whereby to retrieve his lost fortune.

Tom could not answer. The bully's father glared at our hero and then, slipping on a coat, he made a dash for the door.

"Get out of my way!" he shouted, and Tom stood aside.

Andy was already racing for the deck, and as the noise and confusion seemed to increase rather than diminish, Tom concluded that his wisest move would be to get out and see what all the excitement was about.

He stopped on his way to arouse Eradicate but found that he and all the colored persons had left their staterooms. A few seconds later Tom was on deck.

"It's all right, now! It's all right!" several officers were calling. "There is no danger. Go back to your staterooms. The danger is all over."

"Is the ship sinking?"

"What happened?"

"Are we on fire?"

"Are you sure there's no danger?"

These were only a few of the questions that were flying about, and the officers answered them as best they could.

"We hit a derelict, or some bit of wreckage," explained the first mate, when he could command silence. "There is a slight hole below the water-line, but the bulkheads have been closed, and there is not the slightest danger."

"Are we going to turn back for New York?" asked one woman.

"No, certainly not. We're going right on as soon as a slight break to one of the engines can be repaired. We are in no danger. Only a little water came in before the automatic bulkheads were shut. We haven't even a list to one side. Now please clear the decks and go back to bed."

It took more urging, but finally the passengers began to disperse. Tom found Ned and Mr. Damon, who were looking for him.

"Bless my life preserver!" cried the odd man. "I thought surely this was my last voyage, Tom!"

"So did I," added Ned. "What's the matter, Tom, you look as though you'd seen a ghost."

"I have—pretty near. The Fogers are on board."

"No! You don't mean it!"

"It's a fact. I just saw them. They are the mysterious passengers." And Tom related his experience.

"Where are they now?" demanded Ned, looking about the deck.

"Gone below again, I suppose. Though I don't see what object they can have in concealing their identity any longer."

"Me either. Well, that surely is a queer go."

"Bless my hot cross buns! I should say so!" commented Mr. Damon when he heard about it. "What are you going to do, Tom?"

"Nothing. I can't. They have a right on board. But if they try to follow us—well, I'll act then," and Tom shut his jaws grimly.

Our three friends went back to their state-room, and Eradicate also retired. The excitement was passing, and soon the ship was under way again, the sudden shock having caused slight damage to one of the big engines. But it was soon repaired and, though the storm still continued, the ship made her way well through the waves.

A stout bow, water-tight compartments, and the fact (learned later) that she had struck the derelict a glancing blow, had combined to save the Maderia.

There were many curious ones who looked over the side next morning to see the gaping hole in the bow. A canvas had been rigged over it, however, to keep out the waves as much as possible, so little could be viewed. Then the thoughts of landing occupied the minds of all, and the accident was nearly forgotten. For it was announced that they would dock early the next morning.

In spite of the fact that their presence on board was known to Tom and his friends, the Fogers still kept to their stateroom, not even appearing at meals. Tom wondered what their object could be, but could not guess.

"Well, here we are at last—in Mexico," exclaimed Ned the next morning, when, the Maderia having docked, allowed the passengers to disembark, a clean bill of health having been her good luck.

"Yes, and now for a lot of work!" added Tom. "We've got to see about getting ox teams, carts and helpers, and no end of food for our trip into the interior."

"Bless my coffee pot! It's like old times to be going off into the jungle or wilderness camping," said Mr. Damon.

"Did you see anything of the Fogers?" asked Ned of his chum.

"Not a thing. Guess they're in their stateroom, and they can stay there for all of me. I'm going to get busy."

Tom and his friends went to a hotel, for they knew it would take several days to get their expedition in shape. They looked about for a sight of their enemies, but saw nothing of them.

It took five days to hire the ox carts, get helpers, a supply of food and other things, and to unload the balloon and baggage from the ship. In all this time there was no sign of the Fogers, and Tom hoped they had gone about their own business.

Our friends had let it be known that they were going into the interior to prospect, look for historic relics and ruins, and generally have a sort of vacation.

"For if it is even hinted that we are after the city of gold," said Tom, "it would be all up with us. The whole population of Mexico would follow us. So keep mum, everyone."

They all promised, and then they lent themselves to the task of getting things in shape for travel. Eradicate was a big help, and his cheerful good nature often lightened their toil.

At last all was in readiness, and with a caravan of six ox carts (for the balloon and its accessories took up much space) they started off, the Mexican drivers cracking their long whips, and singing their strange songs.

"Ho, for the interior!" cried Ned gaily.

"Yes, we're off into the unknown all right," added Tom grimly, "and there's no telling when we'll get back, if we ever will, should the head-hunters get after us."

"Bless my collar and tie! Don't talk that way. It gives me the cold shivers!" protested Mr. Damon.

CHAPTER XIII

FOLLOWED

"Well, this is something like it!" exclaimed Ned as he sat in front of the campfire, flourishing a sandwich in one hand, and in the other a tin cup of coffee.

"It sure is," agreed Tom. "But I say, old man, would you just as soon wave your coffee the other way? You're spilling it all over me."

"Excuse me!" laughed Ned. "I'll be more careful in the future. Mr. Damon will you have a little more of these fried beans—tortillas or fri-joles or whatever these Mexicans call 'em. They're not bad. Pass your plate, Mr. Damon."

"Bless my eyelashes!" exclaimed the odd man. "Water, please, quick!" and he clapped his hand over his mouth.

"What's the matter?" demanded Tom.

"Too much red pepper! I wish these Mexicans wouldn't put so much of it in. Water!"

Mr. Damon hastily swallowed a cup of the liquid which Ned passed to him.

"I spects dat was my fault," put in Eradicate, who did the cooking for the three whites, while the Mexicans had their own. "I were just a little short ob some ob dem funny fried beans, an' I took some from ober dere," and the colored man nodded toward the Mexican campfire. "Den

I puts some red pepper in 'em, an' I done guess somebody'd put some in afo' I done it."

"I should say they had!" exclaimed Mr. Damon, drinking more water. "I don't see how those fellows stand it," and he looked to where the Mexican ox drivers were eagerly devouring the highly-spiced food.

It was the second day of their trip into the interior, and they had halted for dinner near a little stream of good water that flowed over a grassy plain. So far their trip had been quite enjoyable. The ox teams were fresh and made good time, the drivers were capable and jolly, and there was plenty of food. Tom had brought along a supply especially for himself and his friends, for they did not relish the kind the Mexican drivers ate, though occasionally the gold-seekers indulged in some of the native dishes.

"This is lots of fun," Ned remarked again, when Mr. Damon had been sufficiently cooled off. "Don't you think so, Tom?"

"Indeed I do. I don't know how near we are to the place we're looking for, nor even if we're going in the right direction, but I like this sort of life."

"How long Massa Tom, befo' dat gold—" began Eradicate.

"Hush!" interrupted the young inventor quickly, raising a hand of caution, and glancing toward the group of Mexicans. He hoped they had not heard the word the colored man so carelessly used, for it had been the agreed policy to keep the nature of their search a secret. But at the mention of "gold" Miguel Delazes, the head ox driver, locked up quickly, and sauntered over to where Tom and the others were seated on the grass. This Delazes was a Mexican labor contractor, and it was through him that Tom had hired the other men and the ox carts.

"Ah, senors!" exclaimed Delazes as he approached, "I fear you are going in the wrong direction to reach the gold mines. If I had known at the start—"

"We're not looking for gold mines!" interrupted Tom quickly. He did not like the greedy look in the eyes of Delazes, a look that flared out at the mention of gold—a look that was crafty and full of cunning.

"Not looking for gold mines!" the contractor repeated incredulously. "Surely I heard some one say something about gold," and he looked at Eradicate.

"Oh, you mustn't mind what Rad says," cried Tom laughing, and he directed a look of caution at the colored man. "Rad is always talking about gold; aren't you, Rad?"

"I 'spects I is, Massa Tom. I shore would laik t' find a gold mine, dat's what I would."

"I guess that's the case with all of us," put in Ned.

"Rad, get the things packed up," directed Tom quickly. "We've had enough to eat and I want to make a good distance before we camp for the night." He wanted to get the colored man busy so the Mexican would have no chance to further question him.

"Surely the senors are not going to start off again at once—immediately!" protested Delazes. "We have not yet taken the siesta—the noonday sleep, and—"

"We're going to cut out the siestas on this trip," interposed Tom. "We don't want to stay here too long. We want to find some good ruins that we can study, and the sooner we find them the better."

"Ah, then it is but to study—to photograph ruined cities and get relics, that the senors came to Mexico?"

Once more that look of cunning came in the Mexican's eyes.

"That's about it," answered Tom shortly. He did not want to encourage too much familiarity on the part of the contractor. "So, no siestas if you please, Senor Delazes. We can all siesta tonight."

"Ah, you Americanos!" exclaimed the Mexican with a shrug of his shoulders. He stroked his shiny black moustache. "You are ever so on the alert! Always moving. Well, be it so, we will travel on—to the ruined city—if we can find one," and he gave Tom a look that the latter could not quite understand.

It was hot—very hot—but Tom noticed that about a mile farther on, the trail led into a thick jungle of trees, where it would be shady, and make the going more comfortable.

"We'll be all right when we get there," he said to the others.

It was not with very good grace that the Mexicans got their ox teams ready. They had not objected very much when, on the day before Tom had insisted on starting off right after the mid-day meal, but now when it seemed that it was going to be a settled policy to omit the siesta, or noon sleep, there was some grumbling.

"They may make trouble for us, Tom," said in a low voice. "Maybe you'd better give in to them."

"Not much!" exclaimed the young inventor. "If I do they'll want to sleep all the while, and we'll never get any where. We're going to keep on. They won't kick after the first few times, and if they try any funny business—well, we're well armed and they aren't," and he looked at his own rifle, and Ned's. Mr. Damon also carried one, and Eradicate had a large revolver which he said he preferred to a gun. Each of our white friends also carried an automatic pistol and plenty of ammunition.

"I took care not to let the Mexicans have any guns," Tom went on. "It isn't safe."

"I'll wager that they've got knives and revolvers tucked away somewhere in their clothes," spoke Ned.

"Bless my tackhammer!" cried Mr. Damon. "Why do you say such blood-curdling things Ned? You make me shiver!"

In a little while they took up the trail again, the ox carts moving along toward the comparatively cool woods. Our friends had a cart to themselves, one fitted with padded seats, which somewhat made up for the absence of springs, and Eradicate was their driver. Tom had made this arrangement so they might talk among themselves without fear of being overheard by the Mexicans. At first Senor Delazes had suggested that one of his own drivers pilot Tom's cart, saying:

"I know what the senors fear—that their language may be listened to, but I assure you that this man understands no English, do you, Josef?" he asked the man in question, using the Spanish.

The man shook his head, but a quick look passed between him and his employer.

"Oh, I guess we'll let Rad drive," insisted Tom calmly, "it will remind him of his mule Boomerang that he left behind."

"As the senor will," Delazes had replied with a shrug of his shoulders, and he turned away. So it was that Tom, Ned and Mr. Damon, in their own cart, piloted by the colored man, were in the rear of the little cavalcade.

"Have you any idea where you are going, Tom?" asked Ned, after they had reached the shade, when it was not such a task to talk.

"Oh, I have a good general idea," replied the young inventor. "I've studied the map Mr. Illingway sent, and according to that the city of— well, you know the place we're looking for—lies somewhere between Tampico and Zacatecas, and which the plain of the ruined temple which used to be near the ancient city of Poltec, is about a hundred and fifty miles north of the city of Mexico. So I'm heading for there, as near as I can tell. We ought to fetch it in about a week at this rate."

"And what are we to do when we get there?" inquired Mr. Damon. "If we keep on to that place where the images are to be found, with this rascally crew of Mexicans, there won't be much gold for us." He had spoken in low tones, though the nearest Mexican cart was some distance ahead.

"I don't intend to take them all the way with us," said Tom. "When I think we are somewhere near the temple plain I'm going to make the Mexicans go into camp. Then we'll put the balloon together and we four will go off in that. When we find what we're looking for we'll go back, pick up the Mexicans, and make for the coast."

"If the head-hunters let us," put in Ned grimly.

"Bless my nail file! There you go again!" cried Mr. Damon. "Positively, Ned, you get on my nerves."

"Yais, Massa Ned, an' I jest wish yo' wouldn't mention dem head gen'men no mo'," added Eradicate. "I can't drive straight when I hears yo' say dem words, an' goodness knows dese oxes is wusser t' drive dan my mule Boomerang."

"All right I'll keep still," agreed Ned, and then he and Tom, together with Mr. Damon, studied the map, trying to decide whether or not they were on the proper trail.

They made a good distance that day, and went into camp that night near the foot of some low hills.

"It will be cooler traveling tomorrow," said Tom. "We will be up higher, and though we'll have to go slower on account of the up grade, it will be better for all of us."

They found the trail quite difficult the next day, as there were several big hills to climb. It was toward evening, and they were looking for a good place to camp for the night, when Delazes, who was riding in the first cart, was observed to jump down and hasten to the rear.

"I wonder what he wants?" spoke Tom, as he noted the approaching figure.

"Probably he's going to suggest that we take a few days' vacation," ventured Ned. "He doesn't like work."

"Senor," began Delazes addressing Tom, who called to Eradicate to bring his oxen to a halt, "are you aware that we are being followed?"

"Followed? What do you mean?" cried the young inventor, looking quickly around.

"Bless my watch chain!" gasped Mr. Damon. "Followed? By whom?" He, too, looked around, as did Ned, but the path behind them was deserted.

"When last we doubled on our own trail, to make the ascent of the big hill a little easier," on the Mexican, "I saw, on the road below us two ox carts, such as are hired out to prospectors or relic seekers like yourself. At first I thought nothing of it. That was early this morning. When we stopped for dinner, once more having to double, I had another view of the trail, I saw the same two carts. And now, when we are about to camp, the same two carts are there."

He pointed below, for the caravan was on quite an elevation now, and down on the faint trail, which was in plain view, for it wound up the mountain like a corkscrew, were two ox carts, moving slowly along.

"They are the same ones," went on Delazes, "and they have been following us all day—perhaps longer—though this is the first I have noted them."

"Followed!" murmured Tom. "I wonder—" From his valise he took a small but powerful telescope. In the fast-fading light he focused it on the two ox carts. The next moment he uttered an exclamation of anger and dismay.

"Who is it?" asked Ned, though he was almost sure what the answer would be.

"Andy Foger and his father!" cried Tom. "I might have known they'd follow us—to learn—" and then he stopped, for Senor Delazes was regarding him curiously.

CHAPTER XIV

A WEARY SEARCH

"Are you sure it's them?" asked Ned.

"Bless my toothpick!" cried Mr. Damon. "It isn't possible, Tom?"

"Yes, it is," said the young inventor. "It's the Fogers all right. Take a look for yourself, Ned."

The other lad did, and confirmed his chum's news, and then Mr. Damon also made sure, by using the glass.

"No doubt of it," the odd man said. "But what are you going to do, Tom?"

Our hero thought for a moment. Then, once more, he looked steadfastly through the glass at the other carts. The occupants of them did not appear to know that they were under observation, and at that distance they could not have made out our friends without a telescope. Tom ascertained that the Fogers were not using one.

"Has Senor Swift any orders?" asked Delazes. "Who are these Fogers? Enemies of yours I take it. Why should they follow you merely to find a ruined city, that the ruins and relics may be studied?"

"Here are the orders," spoke Tom, a bit sharply, not answering the question. "We'll camp and have supper, and then we'll go on and make all the distance we can after dark."

"What, travel at night?" cried the Mexican, as if in horror at the suggestion.

"Yes; why not?" asked Tom calmly. "They can't see us after dark, and if we can strike off on another trail we may throw them off our track. Surely we'll travel after supper."

"But it will be night—dark—we never work after dark," protested Delazes.

"You're going to this time," declared Tom grimly.

"But the oxen—they are not used to it."

"Nothing like getting used to a thing," went on the young inventor. "They won't mind after a rest and a good feed. Besides, there is a moon tonight, and it will be plenty light enough. Tell the men, Senor Delazes."

"But they will protest. It is unheard of, and—"

"Send them to me," said Tom quickly. "There'll be double pay for night work. Send them to me."

"Ah, that is good. Senor Swift. Double pay! I think the men will not object," and with a greedy look in his black eyes the Mexican contractor hastened to tell his men of the change of plans.

Tom took another look at the approaching Fogers. Their carts were slowly crawling up the trail, and as Tom could plainly see them, he made no doubt but that his caravan was also observed by Andy and his father.

"I guess that's the best plan to throw them off," agreed Ned, when they were once more underway. "But how are you going to explain to Delazes, Tom, the reason the Fogers are following us? He'll get suspicious, I'm afraid."

"Let him. I'm not going to explain. He can think what he likes, I can't stop him. More than likely though, that he'll put it down to some crazy whim of us 'Americanos.' I hope he does. We can talk loudly, when he's around, about how we want to get historical relics, and the Fogers are after the same thing. There have been several expeditions down this way from rival colleges or museums after Aztec relics, and he may think we're one of them. For the golden images are historical relics all right," added Tom in a lower voice.

The Mexicans made no objections to continuing on after supper, once they learned of the double pay, and a little later they went into camp. A turn of the trial hid the Fogers from sight, but Tom and his friends had no doubt but what they were still following.

It was rather novel, traveling along by the light of the brilliant moon, and the boys and Mr. Damon thoroughly enjoyed it. Orders had been given to proceed as quietly as possible, for they did not want the Fogers to learn of the night trip.

"They may see us," Tom had said when they were ready to start, "but we've got to take a chance on that. If the trail divides, however, we can lose them."

"It does separate, a little farther on," Delazes had said.

"Good!" cried Tom, "then we'll fool our rival relic hunters and our museum will get the benefit." He said this quite loudly.

"Ah, then you want the relics for a museum?" asked the Mexican contractor quickly.

"Yes, if they pay enough," replied Tom, and he meant it, for he had no doubt that many museums would be glad to get specimens of the golden images.

Just as they were about to start off Tom had swept the moonlit trail with his night-glass, but there was no sign of the Fogers, though they may have seen their rivals start off.

"Let her go!" ordered Tom, and they were once more underway.

It was about five miles to where the trail divided, and it was midnight when they got there, for the going was not easy.

"Now, which way," asked Delazes, as the caravan came to a halt. "To the left or right?"

"Let me see," mused Tom, trying to remember the map the African missionary had sent him. "Do these roads come together farther on?"

"No, but there is a cross trail about twenty miles ahead by which one can get from either of these trails to the other."

"Good!" cried the young inventor. "Then we'll go to the right, and we can make our way back. But wait a minute. Send a couple of carts on the left trail for about two miles. We'll wait here until they come back."

"The senor is pleased to joke," remarked the Mexican quickly.

"I never was more earnest in all my life," replied Tom.

"What's the answer?" asked Ned.

"I want to fool the Fogers. If they see cart tracks on both roads they won't know which one we took. They may hit on the right one first shot, and again, they may go to the left until they come to the place where our two carts turn back. In that case we'll gain a little time."

"Good!" cried Ned. "I might have known you had a good reason, Tom."

"Send on two carts," ordered the young inventor, and now Delazes understood the reason for the strategy. He chuckled as he ordered two of the drivers to start off, and come back after covering a couple of miles.

It was rather dreary waiting there at the fork of the trail, and to beguile the time Tom ordered fires lighted and chocolate made. The men appreciated this, and were ready to start off again when their companions returned.

"There," announced Tom, when they were on the way once more, "I think we've given them something to think over at any rate. Now for a few more miles, and then we'll rest until morning."

All were glad enough when Tom decided to go into camp, and they slept later than usual the next morning. The trail was now of such a character that no one following them could be detected until quite close, so it was useless to worry over what the Fogers might do.

"We'll just make the best time we can, and trust to luck," Tom said.

They traveled on for two days more, and saw nothing of the Fogers. Sometimes they would pass through Mexican villages where they would stop to eat, and Tom would make inquiries about the ancient city of Poltec and the plain of the ruined temple. In every case the Mexicans shook their heads. They had never heard of it. Long before this Tom had ascertained that neither Delazes nor any of his men knew the location of this plain nor had they ever heard of it.

"If there is such a place it must be far in—very far in," the contractor had said. "You will never find it."

"Oh, yes, I will," declared Tom.

But when a week passed, and he was no nearer it than at first even Tom began to get a little doubtful. They made inquiries at every place they stopped, of villagers, of town authorities, and even in some cases of the priests who obligingly went over their ancient church records for them. But there was no trace of the temple plain, and of course none of the city of gold.

Peasants, journeying along the road, parties of travelers, and often little bodies of soldiers were asked about the ruined temple, but always the answer was the same. They had never heard of it, nor of the head-hunters either.

"Well, I'm glad of the last," said Mr. Damon, looking apprehensively around, while Eradicate felt of his head to see if it was still fast on his shoulders.

It was a weary search, and when two weeks had passed even Tom had to admit that it was not as easy as it had seemed at first. As for the Mexicans, they kept on, spurred by the offer of good wages. Delazes watched Tom narrowly, for a sign or hint of what the party was really after, but the young inventor and his friends guarded their secret well.

"But I'm not going to give up!" cried Tom. "Our map may be wrong, and likely it is, but I'm sure we're near the spot, and I'm going to keep on. If we don't get some hint of it in a few days, though, I'll establish a camp, go up in the air and see what I can pick out from the balloon."

"That's the stuff!" cried Ned. "It will be a relief from these rough ox carts."

So for the next few days they doubled and redoubled on their trail, criss-crossing back and forth, ever hoping to get some trace of the temple, which was near the entrance to the city of gold. In all that time nothing was seen of the Fogers.

"We'll try the balloon tomorrow," decided Tom, as they went into camp one night after a weary day. Every one was tired enough to sleep soundly under the tents which were set up over the carts, in which beds were laid. It must have been about midnight when Tom, who felt a bit chilly (for the nights were cool in spite of the heat of the day), got up to look at the campfire. It was almost out so he went over to throw on some more logs.

As he did so he heard a noise as if something or somebody had leaped down out of a tree to the ground. A moment later, before he could toss on the sticks he had caught up, Tom was aware of two eyes of greenish brightness staring at him in the glow of the dying fire, and not ten feet away.

CHAPTER XV

THE GOLDEN IMAGE

For a moment the young inventor felt a cold chill run down his spine, and, while his hair did not actually "stand up" there was a queer sensation on his scalp as if the hairs wanted to stand on end, but couldn't quite manage it.

Involuntarily Tom started, and one of the sticks he held in his hand dropped to the ground. The green eyes shifted—they came nearer, and the lad heard a menacing growl. Then he knew it was some wild animal that had dropped down from a tree and was now confronting him, ready to spring on the instant.

Tom hardly knew what to do. He realized that if he moved it might precipitate an attack on him, and he found himself dimly wondering, as he stood there, what sort of an animal it was.

He had about come to the conclusion that it was something between a cougar and a mountain lion, and the next thought that came to him was a wonder whether any one else in the camp was awake, and would come to his rescue.

He half turned his head to look, when again there came that menacing growl, and the animal came a step nearer. Evidently every movement Tom made aroused the beast's antagonism, and made him more eager to come to the attack.

"I've got to keep my eyes on him," mused the lad. "I wonder if there's any truth in the old stories that you can subdue a wild beast with your eyes—by glaring at him. But whether that's so or not, I've got to do it—keep looking him in the face, for that's all I can do."

True, Tom held in his hand some light sticks, but if it came to a fight they would be useless. His gun was back in the tent, and as far as he could learn by listening there was not another soul in the camp awake.

Suddenly the fire, which had almost died out, flared up, as a dying blaze sometimes will, and in the bright glare the young inventor was able to see what sort of beast confronted him. He saw the tawny, yellow body, the twitching tail, the glaring eyes and the cruel teeth all too plainly, and he made up his mind that it was some species of the cougar family. Then the embers flared out and it was darker than before. But it was not so dark but what Tom could still see the glaring eyes.

"I've got to get away from him—scare him—or shoot him," the lad decided on the instant. "I'd like to bowl him over with a bullet, but how can I get my gun?"

He thought rapidly. The gun was in the tent back of him, near where he had been sleeping. It was fully loaded.

"I've got to get it," reflected Tom, and then he dropped the other sticks in his hand. Once more the beast growled and came a step nearer—soft, stealthy steps they were, too, making no sound on the ground.

Then Tom started to make a cautious retreat backwards, the while keeping his eyes focused on those of the beast. He made up his mind that he would give that "hypnotism" theory a trial, at any rate.

But at his first backward step the beast let out such a fierce growl, and came on with such a menacing leap that Tom stood still in very terror. The animal was now so close to him that a short jump would hurl the beast upon the lad.

"This won't do," thought Tom. "Every time I go back one step he comes on two, and it won't take him long to catch up to me. And then, too, he'll be in the tent in another minute, clawing Ned or Mr. Damon. What can I do? Oh, for a gun!"

He stood still, and this seemed to suit the animal, for it remained quiet. But it never took its eyes off Tom, and the switching tail, and the low growls now and then, plainly indicated that the beast was but waiting its time to leap and give the death blow.

Then an idea came to Tom. He remembered that he had once read that the human voice had a wonderful effect on wild animals. He would try it.

"And I'm not going to sing him any slumber song, either," mused Tom. "I'll start on a low tone to call for Ned, and gradually raise my voice until I wake him up. Then I'll tell Ned to draw a bead on the beast and plunk him while I hold his attention."

Tom lost no time in putting his plan into operation.

"Ned! Ned! Say, old man, wake up! I'm in trouble! There's a beast as big as a lion out here. Ned! Ned! Ned!"

Tom began in a low voice, but increased his tones with each word. At first the beast seemed uneasy, and then it stopped switching its tail and just glared at Tom.

"Ned! I say Ned! Wake up!"

Tom listened. All was silent within the tent.

"Ned! Oh, Ned!"

Louder this time, but still silence.

"Hey, Ned! Are you ever going to wake up! Get your gun! Your gun! Shoot this beast! Ned! Ned!"

Tom waited. It seemed as if the beast was nearer to him. He called once more.

"Ned! Ned!" He was fairly shouting now. Surely some one must hear him.

"What's that? What's the matter? Tom? Where are you?"

It was Ned's voice—a sleepy voice—and it came from the interior of the tent.

"Here!" called Tom. "Out in front—by the fire—get your gun, and get him with the first shot, or it's all up with yours truly."

"Get who with the first shot. Who are you talking about?"

"This cougar! Hurry Ned, he's creeping nearer!"

Tom heard a movement behind him. He dared not turn his head, but he knew it was his chum. Then he heard a gasp and he knew that Ned had seen the beast. Then all Tom could do was to wait. And it was not easy waiting. At any moment the beast might spring, and, as far as he was concerned it would be all over.

Nearer and nearer crept the brute. Again Tom felt that queer sensation down his spine.

"Hurry, Ned," he whispered.

"All right," came back the reassuring answer.

There was a moment of silence.

Crack! A sliver of flame cut the darkness. There was a report that sounded like a cannon, and it was followed by an unearthly scream. Instinctively Tom leaped back as he saw the greenish eyes change color.

The young inventor felt a shower of dirt thrown over him by the claws of the dying cougar, and then he realized that he was safe. He raced toward the tent, to be met by Ned, and the next instant the camp was in wild commotion.

"Bless my slippers!" cried Mr. Damon. "What has happened. Tell me at once?"

"Fo' de lob of chicken!" yelled Eradicate from a tent he had all to himself—the cook tent.

"Santa Maria! Ten thousand confusions! What is it?" fairly screamed Delazes.

"Are you all right, Tom?" called Ned.

"Sure. It was a good shot."

And then came explanations. Wood was thrown on the fire, and as the Mexicans gathered around the blaze they saw, twitching in the death throes, a big cougar, or some animal allied to it. Neither Tom nor his friends had ever seen one just like it, and the Mexican name for it meant nothing to them. But it was dead, and Tom was saved and the way he grasped Ned's hand showed how grateful he was, even if he did not say much.

Soon the excitement died out, after Tom had related his experience, and though it was some time before he and the others got to sleep again, they did finally, and the camp was once more quiet.

An early start was made the next day, for Tom had reconsidered his determination to assemble the balloon and explore in that air craft, And the reason for his reconsideration was this:

They had not gone far on their journey before they met a solitary Mexican, and of him they asked the usual question about the plain of the temple.

He knew nothing, as might have been expected, but he stated that there was a large village not far distant in which dwelt many old Mexicans.

"They might know something," he said.

"It's worth trying," decided Tom. "I'll wait until tomorrow about the balloon. We can make the village by noon, I guess. Perhaps we can get a clue there."

But it was nearly night when the ox carts drew into the Mexican settlement, for there was an accident in the afternoon, one of the vehicles breaking down.

There were fires blazing in many places in the village, which was one of the most primitive sort, when our friends entered. They were curiously watched as they drove through on their way to a good camping site beyond.

And here, once more, fate stepped in to aid Tom in his search for the city of gold.

As they were out of corn meal, and needed some for supper, Tom told Eradicate to stop at one of the larger houses to buy some. The lad followed the colored man into the building, which seemed to be used by several families.

"We'll be obliged to yo' all fo' some corn meal," began Eradicate, picking out an aged Mexican to whom he addressed his request.

"What is it?" asked the Mexican in Spanish.

Tom put the question in that language, and he was on the point of explaining that they were travelers, when he stopped midway, and stared at something on a rude shelf in the main room of the house.

"Look! Look, Ned!" whispered Tom.

"What is it?" asked his chum.

"On that shelf! That image! The image of gold! One just like the drawing Mr. Illingway sent from Africa! Ned, we're on the trail at last, for there is one of the small images from the city of gold!" and Tom, with a hand that trembled in spite of himself, pointed at the small, yellow figure.

CHAPTER XVI

THE MAP ON THE GOLD

Naturally, when Tom pointed at the golden image, the eyes of all the Mexicans in the room, as well as those of the friends of the young inventor, followed. For a moment there was silence and then the aged Mexican, whom Eradicate had asked for corn meal, rapidly uttered something in Spanish.

"Yes! Yes!" chorused his companions, and they followed this up, by crying aloud when he had said something else: "No! No!" Then there was confused talking, seemingly directed at Tom, who, though he had lowered his hand, continued to stare at the golden image.

"What in the world are they saying?" asked Ned, who only knew a little Spanish.

"I can't get on to all of it," explained Tom above the confusion. "Evidently they think we've come to take the image away from them and they are objecting."

"Offer to buy it then," suggested Ned.

"That's what I'm going to do," answered Tom, and once more addressing the aged Mexican, who seemed to be at the head of the household, Tom offered to purchase the relic which meant so much to him, agreeing to pay a large sum.

This seemed to create further confusion, and one of the women of the household hastily took down the little statute and was carrying it into an inner room, when Miguel Delazes came up. He looked into the open doorway, glanced about the room which was illuminated by several rude oil lamps, saw the looks of wonder and surprise on the faces of Tom and his companions, noted the excitement among the Mexicans, and then he caught sight of the golden image which the woman held.

"Ah!" exclaimed Delazes, and there was a world of meaning in his tone. His small dark eyes glittered. They roved from the image to Tom, and back to the little golden figure again. "Ah!" muttered the contractor. "And so the senor has found that for what he was searching? It is gold after all, but such gold as never I have seen before. So, the senor hopes to get many relics like that for his museum? So, is it not? Ah, ha! But that is worth coming many miles to get!"

Tom realized that if he did not act quickly Delazes might have his secret, and once it was known that Tom was seeking the buried city of gold, the Mexicans could never be shaken off his trail. He decided on a bold step.

"Look here, Senor Delazes," said the young inventor. "I had no more idea that golden image was here than you did. I would like to buy it, in fact I offered to, but they don't seem to want to sell it. If you can purchase it for me I'll pay you a good price for it."

"And doubtless the senor would like many more," suggested Delazes, with an open sneer.

"Doubtless the senor would!" snapped Tom. "Look here, Delazes, I'm here on business, to get all the relics I can—this kind or any other that I may fancy. You can think we're after buried treasure if you want to—I'm not going to take the trouble to contradict you. I hired you and your men for a certain purpose. But if you don't want to stay and let me and my friends run things, the sooner you tell me so the better. But I don't want any more of your underhand remarks. Understand?"

For a moment Delazes stared at Tom with snapping eyes, as though he would like to have attacked him. Then, knowing that Tom and his friends were well armed, and doubtless thinking that strategy was better than open force he bowed, smiled in what he probably meant for a friendly fashion, and said:

"The senor is pleased to joke. Very well, I shall believe what I like. Meanwhile, does Senor Swift commission me to buy the image for him?"

Tom hesitated a moment. He feared he would be no match for the shrewd Mexican, and he wondered how much Delazes already knew. Then he decided on keeping up his end baldly, as that had seemed to have the best effect.

"You can have a try at buying the image after I have failed," he said. "I'll try my hand first."

"Very well," assented the contractor. The talk had been in English, and none of the Mexicans gave any signs of having understood it. Tom realized that he was playing a dangerous game, for naturally Delazes would privately tell the Mexicans to put so high a price on the statute as to prevent Tom from getting it and then the contractor would make his own terms.

But Tom decided that this was the only course, and he followed it.

"We'll stay here in the village for tonight," he went on. "Delazes, you and your men can make yourselves comfortable with any friends you may find here. We'll set up our tent as usual, after we get some corn meal for supper. I'll talk to them about the relic tomorrow. They seem to be afraid now."

"Very well," assented the contractor again, and then he said something in Spanish to the aged Mexican. What it was Tom could not catch, for Delazes spoke rapidly and seemed to use some colloquial, or slang phrases with which our hero was not familiar. The old Mexican assented by a nod, and then he brought out some corn meal which Eradicate took. The woman with the golden image had gone into an inner room.

"Bless my pocketbook!" exclaimed Mr. Damon, when he, Tom, Ned and Eradicate were busy setting up their tent near a campfire just on the edge of the village. "This is most unexpected. What are you going to do, Tom?"

"I hardly know. I want to have a talk with whoever owns that image, to learn where they got it. One thing is sure, it proves that Mr. Illingway's information about the city of gold is correct."

"But it doesn't tell us where it is," said Ned.

"It must be somewhere around here," declared his chum. "Otherwise the image wouldn't be here."

"Bless my gaiters, that's so!" exclaimed the odd man.

"Not necessarily," insisted Ned. "Why one of the images is away over in Africa, and this one may have been brought hundreds of miles from the underground city."

"I don't believe so," declared Tom. "We're somewhere in the neighborhood of the city, according to Mr. Illingway's map, I'm sure. That would be true, image or no image. But when you take the little gold statue into consideration it makes me positive that I'm near the end of the trail. I've just got to have a talk with those people to learn where the statue came from."

"Look out for Delazes," warned Ned.

"I intend to. As soon as I can, I'm going to leave him and his men behind and set off in the balloon. But first I want to get an idea of where to head for. We must locate the plain on which stands the ruined temple."

"It's getting exciting," remarked Ned. "I wish—"

"Supper am serbed in de dinin' cah!" interrupted Eradicate with a laugh, as he imitated a Pullman porter.

"That's the best thing you could wish for," put in Tom gaily. "Come on, we'll have a good meal, a sleep, and then we'll be ready to play detectives again tomorrow."

They all slept soundly that night, though Tom had some idea of staying awake to see if Delazes paid any secret visits to the house where the golden image was kept. But he realized that the Mexican, if he wanted to, could easily find means to outwit him, so the young inventor decided to get all the rest he could and trust to chance to help him out.

His first visit after breakfast was to the house of the aged Mexican. The image was not in sight, though Tom and Ned and Mr. Damon looked eagerly around for it. There was a curious light in the eyes of the old man as Tom asked for the little statue of gold. Delazes was not in evidence. Tom had to conduct the conversation in Spanish, no particularly easy task for him, though he made out all right.

"Will you sell the image?" he asked.

"No sell," replied the Mexican quickly.

"Will you please let me look at it?"

The Mexican hesitated a moment, called a command to some one in the next room, and, a moment later the old woman shuffled in, bearing the wonderful golden image. Tom could not repress a little gasp of delight as he saw it at close range, for it was beautifully carved out of solid, yellow gold.

The woman set it on a rude table, and the young inventor, Ned and Mr. Damon drew near to look at the image more closely. It was the work of a master artist. The statue was about eight inches high, and showed a man, dressed in flowing robes, seated crosslegged on a sort of raised pedestal. On the head was a crown, many pointed and the face beneath it showed calm dignity like that of a superior being. In one extended hand was a round ball, with lines on it to show the shape of the earth, though only the two American continents appeared. In the other hand was what might be tables of stone, a book, or something to represent law-giving authority.

"How much?" asked Tom.

"No sell," was the monotonous answer.

"Five hundred dollars," offered our hero.

"No sell."

"One thousand dollars."

"No sell."

"Why is it so valuable to you?" Tom wanted to know.

"We have him for many years. Bad luck come if he go." Then the Mexican went on to explain that the image had been in his family for many generations, and that once, when it had been taken by an enemy, death and poverty followed until the statue was recovered. He said he would never part with it.

"Where did it come from?" asked Tom, and he cared more about this than he did about buying the image.

"Far, far off," said the Mexican. "No man know. I no know—my father he no know—his father's father no know. Too many years back—many years."

He motioned to the woman to take the statue away, and Tom and his friend realized that little more could be learned. The young inventor stretched out his hand with an involuntary motion, and the Mexican understood. He spoke to the woman and she handed the image to Tom. The Mexican had recognized his desire for a moment's closer inspection and had granted it.

"Jove! It's as heavy as lead!" exclaimed Tom. "And solid gold."

"Isn't it hollow up the middle?" asked Ned. "Look on the underside, Tom."

His chum did so. As he turned the image over to look at the base he had all he could do not to utter a cry of surprise. For there, rudely scratched on the plain surface of the gold, was what was unmistakably a map. And it was a map showing the location of the ruined temple—the temple and the country surrounding it—the ancient city of Poltec, and the map was plain enough so that Tom could recognize part of the route over which they had traveled.

But, better than all, was a tiny arrow, something like the compass mark on modern maps. And this arrow pointed straight at the ruins of the temple, and the direction indicated was due west from the village where our travelers now were. Tom Swift had found out what he wanted to know.

Without a word he handed back the image and then, trying not to let his elation show in his face, he motioned to Ned and Mr. Damon to follow him from the house.

"Bless my necktie!" exclaimed the odd man, when they were out of hearing distance. "What's up, Tom."

"I know the way to the ruined temple. We'll start at once," and he told them of the map on the image.

"Who do you suppose could have made it?" asked Ned.

"Probably whoever took the image from the city of gold. He wanted to find his way back again, or show some one, but evidently none of the recent owners of the image understand about the map, if they know it's there. The lines are quite faint, but it is perfectly plain."

"It's lucky I saw it. I don't have to try to buy the image now, nor seek to learn where it came from. Anyhow, if they told me they'd tell Delazes, and he'd be hot after us. As it is I doubt if he can learn now. Come, we'll get ready to hit the trail again."

And they did, to the no small wonder of the contractor and his men, who could not understand why Tom should start out without the image, or without having learned where it came from, for Delazes had questioned the old Mexican, and learned all that took place. But he did not look on the base of the statue.

Due west went the cavalcade, and then a new complication arose. Tom did not want to take the Mexicans any nearer to the plain of the temple than possible, and he did not know how many miles it was away. So he decided on taking a longer balloon voyage than at first contemplated.

"We'll camp tonight at the best place we can find," he said to Delazes, "and then I'm going on in the balloon. You and your men will stay in camp until we come back."

"Ha! And suppose the senors do not come back with the balloon?"

"Wait a reasonable time for us, and then you can do as you wish. I'll pay you to the end of the month and if you wait for us any longer I have given instructions for the bank in Tampico to pay you and your men what is right."

"Good! And the senors are going into the unknown?"

"Yes, we don't know where we'll wind up. This hunting for relics is uncertain business. Make yourselves comfortable in camp, and wait."

"Waiting is weary business, Senor Swift. If we could come with you—" began Delazes, with an eager look in his eyes.

"Out of the question," spoke Tom shortly. "There isn't room in the balloon."

"Very well, senor," and with a snapping glance from his black eyes the contractor walked away.

CHAPTER XVII

THE RUINED TEMPLE

Though Tom had his portable balloon in shape for comparatively quick assembling it was several days, after they went into permanent camp, before it was in condition for use.

The Mexicans were not of much help for several reasons. Some of them were ignorant men, and were very superstitious, and would have nothing to do with the "Air Fiend" as they called it. In consequence Tom, Ned, Mr. Damon and Eradicate had to do most of the work. But Tom and Ned were a host in themselves, and Mr. Damon was a great help, though he often stopped to bless something, to the no small astonishment of the Mexicans, one of whom innocently asked Tom if this eccentric man was not "a sort of priest in his own country, for he called down so many blessings?"

"Bless my pen wiper!" exclaimed Mr. Damon, when Tom had told him. "I must break myself of that habit. Bless my—" and then he stopped and laughed, and went on with the work of helping to install the motor.

Another reason why some of the Mexicans were of little service was because they were so lazy. They preferred to sit in the shade and smoke innumerable cigarettes, or sleep. Then, too, some of them had to go out after some small game with which that part of the country abounded, for though there was plenty of tinned food, fresh meat was much more appreciated.

But Tom and Ned labored long and hard, and in about a week after making camp they had assembled the dirigible balloon in which they hoped to set out to locate the plain of the ruined temple, and also the entrance to the underground city of gold.

"Well, I'll start making the gas tomorrow," decided Tom, in their tent one night, after a hard day's work. "Then we'll give the balloon a tryout and see how she behaves in this part of the world. The motor is all right, we're sure of that much," for they had given the engine a test several days before.

"Which way are we going to head?" asked Ned.

"North, I think," answered Tom.

"But I thought you said that the temple was west—"

"Don't you see my game?" went on the young inventor quickly, and in a low voice, for several times of late he had surprised some of the Mexicans sneaking about the tent. "As soon as we start off Delazes is going to follow us."

"Follow us?" cried Mr. Damon. "Bless my shoe horn, what do you mean?"

"I mean that he still suspects that we are after gold, and he is going to do his best to get on our trail. Of course he can't follow us through the air, but he'll note in what direction we start and as soon as we are out of sight he and his men will hit the trail in the same direction."

"What, and leave the camp?" asked Ned.

"Yes, though they'll probably skip off with some of our supplies. That's why I'm going to take along an unusually large supply. We may not come back to this camp at all. In fact, it won't be much use after Delazes and his crowd clean it out and leave."

"And you really think they'll do that, Tom?" asked his chum.

"I'm almost sure of it, from the way the Mexicans have been acting lately. Delazes has been hinting around trying to surprise me into saying which direction we're going to take. But I've been careful. The sight of that golden image aroused him and his men. They're hungry for gold, and they'd do away with us in a minute if they thought they could find what we're looking for and get it without us. But our secret is ours yet, I'm glad to say. If only the balloon behaves we ought soon to be in the—"

"Hark!" exclaimed Ned, holding up a warning hand. They heard a rustling outside the tent, and one side bulged in, as if some one was leaning against it.

"Some one's listening," whispered Ned.

Tom nodded. The next moment he drew his heavy automatic revolver and remarked in loud tones:

"My gun needs cleaning. I'm going to empty it through the tent where that bulge is—look out, Ned."

The bulge against the canvas disappeared as if by magic, and the sound of some one crawling or creeping away could be heard outside. Tom laughed.

"You see how it is," he said. "We can't even think aloud."

"Bless my collar button; who was it?" asked Mr. Damon.

"Some of Delazes's men—or himself," replied the young inventor. "But I guess I scared him."

"Maybe it was Andy Foger," suggested Ned with a smile.

"No, I guess we've lost track of him and his father," spoke Tom. "I've kept watch of the back trail as much as I could, and haven't seen them following us. Of course they may pick up our trail later and come here, and they may join forces with the Mexicans. But I don't know that they can bother us, once we're off in the balloon."

To Tom's disappointment, the next day proved stormy, a heavy rain falling, so it was impossible to test the balloon with the gas. The camp was a disconsolate and dreary place, and even Eradicate, usually so jolly, was cross and out of sorts.

For three days the rain kept up, and Tom and Ned thought they would never see the last of it, but on the fourth morning the sun shone, wet garments and shoes were dried out, tents were opened to the warm wind and everyone was in better spirits. Tom and his chum at once set about making gas for the big bag, their operations being closely watched by the Mexicans.

As I have explained before, Tom had the secret of making a very powerful gas from comparatively simple ingredients, and the machinery for this was not complicated. So powerful was it that the bag of the dirigible balloon did not need to be as large as usual, a distinct saving in space.

In a short time the bag began to distend and then the balloon took shape and form. The bag was of the usual cigar shape, divided into many compartments so that the puncture of one would not empty out all the vapor.

Below the bag was a car or cabin made of light wood. It was all enclosed and contained besides the motor, storage tanks for gasolene, oil and other things, sleeping berths, a tiny kitchen, a pilot house, and a room to be used for a living apartment. Everything was very compact, and there was not half the room there was in some of Tom Swift's other airships. But then the party did not expect to make long voyages.

They could take along a good supply of canned and also compressed food, much of which was in tablet or capsule form, and of course they would take their weapons, and ammunition.

"And I hope you'll leave room for plenty of gold," said Ned in a whisper to Tom, as they completed arrangements for the gas test.

"I guess we can manage to store all that we can get out of the underground city," replied his chum. "I'm going to find a place for the big gold statue if we can manage to lift it."

"Say, we'll be millionaires all right!" exulted Ned.

Though much still remained to be done on the balloon, it was soon in shape for an efficient test, and that afternoon Tom, Ned and Mr. Damon went up in it to the no small wonder, fear and delight of the Mexicans. Some, who had never seen an air craft before, fell on their knees and prayed. Others shouted, and when Tom started the motor, and showed how he could control his aircraft, there were yells of amazement.

"She'll do!" cried the young inventor, as he let out some gas and came down.

Thereupon followed busy days, stocking the airship for the trip to discover the ruined temple. Food and supplies were put aboard, spare garments, all their weapons and ammunition, and then Tom paid Delazes and his men, giving them a month's wages in advance, for he told them to wait in camp that long.

"But they won't," the young inventor predicted to Ned.

There was nothing more to be done. All that they could do, to insure success had been completed. From now on they were in the hands of fate.

"All aboard!" cried Tom, as he motioned for Eradicate to take his place in the car. Mr. Damon and Ned followed, and then the young inventor himself. He shook hands with Delazes, though he did not like the man.

"Good bye," said Tom. "We may be back before the month is up. If we are not, go back to Tampico."

"Si, senor," answered the contractor, bowing mockingly.

Tom turned the lever that sent more gas into the bag. The balloon shot up. The young gold-seeker was about to throw on the motor, when Delazes waved his hand to the little party.

"Bon voyage!" he called. "I hope you will find the city of gold!"

"Bless my soul!" cried Mr. Damon. "He knows our secret!"

"He's only guessing at it," replied Tom calmly. "He's welcome to follow us—if he can."

Up shot the aircraft, the propellers whirling around like blades of light. Up and up, higher and higher, and then forward, while down below the Mexicans yelled and swung their hats.

Straight for the north Tom headed his craft, so as to throw the eagerly watching ones off the track. He intended to circle around and go west when out of sight.

And then the very thing Tom had predicted came to pass. The balloon was scarcely half a mile high when, as the young inventor looked down, he uttered a cry.

"See!" he said. "They're breaking camp to follow us."

And it was so. Riding along in one of the lightest ox carts was Delazes, his eyes fixed on the balloon overhead, while behind him came his followers.

"They're following us," said Tom, "but they're going to get sadly left."

In an hour Tom knew his balloon would not be visible to the Mexicans, and at the end of that time he pointed for the west. And then, flying low so as to use the trees as a screen, but going at good speed. Tom and his friends were well on their way to the city of gold.

"We must keep a good lookout down below," said Tom, when everything was in working order. "We don't want to fly over the plain of the ruined temple."

"We may in the night," suggested Ned.

"No night flying this time," said his chum. "We'll only move along daytimes. We'll camp at night."

For three days they sailed along, sometimes over vast level plains on which grazed wild cattle, again over impenetrable jungles which they could never have gotten through in their ox carts. They crossed rivers and many small lakes, stopping each night on the ground, the airship securely anchored to trees. Tom could make the lifting gas on board so what was wasted by each descent was not missed.

One day it rained, and they did not fly, spending rather a lonely and miserable twelve hours in the car. Another time a powerful wind blew them many miles out of their course. But they got back on it, and kept flying to the west.

"We must strike it soon," murmured Tom one day.

"Maybe we're too far to the north or south," suggested Ned.

"Then we'll have to beat back and forth until we get right," was Tom's reply. "For I'm going to locate that ruined temple."

They ate breakfast and dinner high in the air, Eradicate preparing the meals in the tiny kitchen. Ever did they keep looking downward for a sight of a great plain, with a ruined temple in the midst of it.

In this way a week passed, the balloon beating back and forth to the North or South, and they were beginning to weary of the search, and even Tom, optimistic as he was, began to think he would never find what he sought.

It was toward the close of day, and the young inventor was looking for a good place to land. He was flying over a range of low hills, hoping the thick forest would soon come to an end when, as he crossed the last of the range of small mountains, he gave a cry, that drew the attention of Ned and Mr. Damon.

"What is it?" demanded his chum.

"Look!" said Tom. "There is the great plain!"

Ned gazed, and saw, spread out below them a vast level plateau. But this was not all he saw, for there, about in the centre, was a mass of something—something that showed white in the rays of the setting sun.

"Bless my chimney!" cried Mr. Damon. "That's some sort of a building."

"The ruined temple," said Tom softly. "We've found it at last," and he headed the balloon for it and put on full speed.

CHAPTER XVIII

FINDING THE TUNNEL

In silence, broken only by the noise of the motor, did the gold-seekers approach the temple. As they neared it they could see its vast proportions, and they noted that it was made of some white stone, something like marble. Then, too, as they drew closer, they could see the desolate ruin into which it had fallen.

"Looks as if a dynamite explosion had knocked it all apart," observed Ned.

"It certainly does," agreed Mr. Damon.

"Maybe Cortez, or some of those early explorers, blew it up with gunpowder after fighting the Aztecs, or whatever the natives were called in those days," suggested Tom.

"Bless my bookcase! You don't mean to say you think this temple goes back to those early days," spoke Mr. Damon.

"Yes, and probably farther," declared Tom. "It must be very ancient, and the whole country about here is desolate. Why, the way the woods have grown up everywhere but on this plain shows that it must be three or four hundred years ago. There must have been a city around the temple, probably Poltec, and yet there isn't a trace of it that we have seen as we came along. Oh, yes, this is very ancient."

"It will be jolly fun to explore it," decided Ned. "I wish it wasn't so near night."

"We can't do much now," decided Tom. "It will be too dark, and I don't altogether fancy going in those old ruins except by daylight."

"Do you think any of those old Aztec priests, with their knifes of glass, will sacrifice you on a stone altar?" asked Ned, with a laugh.

"No, but there might be wild beasts in there," went on the young inventor, "and I'm sure there are any number of bats. There must be lots of nooks and corners in there where a whole army could hide. It's an immense place."

The ruined temple certainly was large in extent, and in its glory must have been a wonderful place. The balloon came nearer, and then Tom let it sink to rest on the sand not far from the ancient ruin. Out he leaped, followed by his friends, and for a moment they stood in silent contemplation of the vast temple. Then as the last rays of the setting sun turned the white stones to gold, Tom exclaimed:

"A good omen! I'm sure the city of gold must be near here, and in the morning we'll begin our search for the secret tunnel that leads to it."

"That's the stuff!" cried Ned enthusiastically.

An instant later it seemed to get dark very suddenly, as it does in the tropics, and almost with the first shadows of night there came a strange sound from the ruined temple.

It was a low moaning, rumbling sound, like a mighty wind, afar off, and it sent a cold shiver down the spines of all in the little party.

"Good land a' massy! What am dat?" moaned Eradicate, as he darted back toward the balloon.

"Bless my looking glass!" cried Mr. Damon.

A second later the noise suddenly increased, and something black, accompanied by a noise of rapidly beating wings rushed from one of the immense doorways.

"Bats!" cried Tom. "Thousands of bats! I'm glad we didn't go in after dark!" And bats they were, that had made the noise as they rushed out on their nightly flight.

"Ugh!" shuddered Mr. Damon. "I detest the creatures! Let's get under cover."

"Yes," agreed Tom, "we'll have supper, turn in, and be up early to look for the tunnel. We're here at last. I'll dream of gold tonight."

Eradicate soon had a meal in preparation, though he stopped every now and then to peer out at the bats, that still came in unbroken flight from the old temple. Truly there must have been many thousands of them.

Whether Tom dreamed of gold that night he did not say, but he was the first one up in the morning, and Ned saw him hurrying over the sands toward the temple.

"Hold on, Tom!" his chum called as he hastened to dress. "Where you going?"

"To have a hunt for that tunnel before breakfast. I don't want to lose any time. No telling when Delazes and his crowd may be after us. And the Fogers, too, may strike our trail. Come on, we'll get busy."

"Where do you think the tunnel will be?" asked Ned, when he had caught up to Tom.

"Well, according to all that Mr. Illingway could tell us, it was some-where near this temple. We'll make a circle of it, and if we don't come across it then we'll make another, and so on, increasing the size of the circles each time, until we find what we're looking for."

"Let's have a look inside the temple first," suggested Ned. "It must have been a magnificent place when it was new, and with the processions of people and priests in their golden robes."

"You ought to have been an Aztec," suggested Tom, as he headed for one of the big doorways.

They found the interior of the temple almost as badly in ruins as was the outside. In many places the roof had fallen in, the side walls con-tained many gaping holes, and the stone floor was broken away in many places, showing yawning, black caverns below. They saw hundreds of bats clinging to projections, but the ugly creatures were silent in sleep now.

"Bur-r-r-r!" murmured Ned. "I shouldn't like any of 'em to fall on me."

"No, it's not a very nice place to go in," agreed Tom.

They saw that the temple consisted of two parts, or two circular buildings, one within the other. Around the outer part were many rooms, which had evidently formed the living apartments of the priests. There were galleries, chambers, halls and assembly rooms. Then the whole of the interior of the temple, under a great dome that had mostly fallen in, consisted of a vast room, which was probably where the worship went on. For, even without going farther than to the edge of it, the youths could see stone altars, and many strangely-carved figures and statues. Some had fallen over and lay in ruins on the floor. The whole scene was one of desolation.

"Come on," invited Tom, "it's healthier and more pleasant outside. Let's look for that tunnel."

But the lads soon realized that it was not going to be as easy to locate this as they had hoped. They were looking for some sort of slanting opening, going down into the earth—the entrance to the underground city—but though they both made a complete circuit of the temple, each at a varying distance from the outer walls, no tunnel entrance showed.

"Breakfast! Breakfast!" called Eradicate, when Tom was about to start on a second round.

"Let's eat," suggested Ned, "and then we four can circle around together." Tom agreed that this would be a good plan. A little later then, with Tom nearest the temple walls, the four began their march around them.

Four times that morning they made the circuit, and the same number in the afternoon, until they were nearly half a mile away from the ruin, but no tunnel showed.

"Well, we'll have to keep at it tomorrow," suggested Tom. "It's too soon to give up."

But the morrow brought no better success, nor did the following two days. In fact for a week they kept up the search for the tunnel, but did not come upon it, and they had now pretty well covered the big plain. They found a few ruins of the ancient city of Poltec.

"Well, what about it?" asked Ned one night as they sat in the balloon, talking it over. "What next, Tom?"

"We've got to keep at it, that's all. I think we'll go up in the balloon, circle around over the plain at just a little elevation, and maybe we can spot it that way."

"All right, I'm with you."

But they did not try that plan. For in the middle of the night Ned suddenly awakened. Something had come to him in his sleep.

"Tom! Tom!" he cried. "I have it! What chumps we were!"

"What's the matter, old man?" asked Tom anxiously. "Are you sick— talking in your sleep?"

"Sleep nothing! I've just thought of it. That tunnel entrance is inside the temple. That's the most natural place in the world for it. I'll bet it's right in the middle of the big inner chamber, where the priests could control it. Why didn't we look there before?"

"That's right; why didn't we?" agreed Tom. "I believe you're right, Ned! We'll look the first thing in the morning."

They did not wait for breakfast before trying the experiment, and Mr. Damon and Eradicate went with Tom and Ned. It was no easy work to make their way over the ruins to the inner auditorium. Wreckage and ruin was all around, and they had to avoid the yawning holes on every side. But when they got to the main, or sacrificial chamber, as Ned insisted on calling it, they found the floor there solid. In the centre was a great altar, but to their chagrin there was not a sign of a tunnel opening.

"Fooled again!" said Tom bitterly.

"Maybe some of those holes outside is the entrance," suggested Mr. Damon.

"I don't believe so," objected Tom. "They seemed to go only to the cellar, if a temple has such a thing."

Bitterly disappointed, Tom strolled over and stood in front of the big stone altar. It seemed that he must give up the search. Idly he looked at the sacrificial stone. Projecting from it was a sort of a bundle.

Tom took hold of it, and to his surprise he found that it could be moved. Hardly knowing what he was doing, he pulled it toward him.

The next instant he uttered a cry of horror, for the immense stone altar, with a dull rumbling, rolled back as though on wheels, and there, over where it had stood was a hole of yawning blackness, with a flight of stone steps leading down into it. And Tom stood so near the edge that he almost toppled in.

"Look! Look!" he cried when he could get his gasping breath, and step back out of danger.

"The tunnel entrance!" cried Ned. "That's what it is! You've found it, Tom! The entrance to the city of gold at last!"

CHAPTER XIX

THE UNDERGROUND RIVER

They gathered around the opening so unexpectedly disclosed to them, and stared down into the black depths. Beyond the first few steps of the flight that led to they knew not where, nothing could be seen. In his impatience Tom was about to go down.

"Bless my match box!" cried Mr. Damon. "What are you going to do, Tom, my boy?"

"Go down there, of course! What else? I want to get to the underground city."

"Don't!" quickly advised the odd man. "You don't know what's there. It may be a trap, where the old Aztecs used to throw their victims. There may be worse things than bats there. You'll need torches—lights—and you'd better wait until the air clears. It may have been centuries since that place was opened."

"I believe that's right," agreed Ned. "Whew; Smell it! It's as musty as time!"

An unpleasant odor came up the tunnel entrance, and it was stifling to stand too close. Tom lighted a match and threw it down. Almost instantly the flame was snuffed out.

"We couldn't live down there a minute," said the young inventor. "We've got to wait for it to clear. We'll go back to the balloon and get some electric flash lamps. I brought along a lot of 'em, with extra strong batteries. I thought we'd need some if we did find the city of gold, and it looks as if we were almost there now."

Tom's plan was voted good so they hurried out of the temple, their feet echoing and re-echoing over the stone floor. The place, ruined and desolate as it was, had no terrors for them now. In fact they were glad of the very loneliness, and Tom and Ned actually looked about apprehensively as they emerged, fearing they might see a sign of the Mexicans or the Fogers.

"Guess they can't pick up our trail," said Tom, when, he saw of what Ned was thinking.

"No, we've got the place to ourselves. I wonder how long it will take for the air to get fresh?"

"Not so very long, I guess. There was a good draught. There must be some opening in the underground city by which the air is sucked in. They'd never have only one opening to it. But we don't need to look for the other. Come on, we'll get out the torches."

These electrical contrivances are familiar to all boys. A small electric lamp is set in the end of a hollow tube of tin, and about the lamp is a reflector. Dry electrical batteries are put in the tin tube, and by means of a push button the circuit is closed, illuminating the lamp, which gives a brilliant glow. Tom had a special kind of lamp, with tungsten filaments, which gave a very powerful light, and with batteries designed to last a long time. A clip on the spring controlling the push button made it so that the lamp could be made to give a steady glow. Thus they were well prepared for exploring the tunnel.

It took some little time to get the flash lamps ready, and when they were all charged and they had eaten, they went back to the opening to see if the air had cleared. Tom tested it by dropping a match down, and, to his delight it burned with a clear flame.

"It's all right!" he exclaimed. "The air is pure. Now to see where we will bring up. Come on, everybody."

"Jest one minute, Massa Tom," begged Eradicate, as the young inventor was about to descend the steps, which even the brightness of his lamp did not disclose the end. "Is yo' gwine down dar, Massa Tom?"

"Certainly, Rad."

"An' is yo'—'scuse me—but is yo' expectin' me fo' t' follow yo'?"

"Certainly, Rad."

"Den, all I's got t' say is dat yo' is 'spectin' too much. I ain't gwine t' bury mahse'f alive not yit."

"But, Rad, this is where the gold images are. If you don't come down with us you won't get any gold."

"Am dat so? No gold?" The colored man scratched his head. "Well, I shore does want gold," he murmured. "I reckon I'd better trot along. But one thing mo', Massa Tom."

"What is it, Rad?"

"Was yo' all aimin' t' stay down thar any length ob time? 'Case if yo' is yo' all'd better take along a snack ob suffin' t' eat. 'Case when I gits among gold I don't want t' come out very soon, an' we might stay dar all day."

"Good advice, Rad," exclaimed Ned with a laugh. "I think we may get hungry. You go back and put us up a lunch. We'll wait for you."

"Bless my napkin ring! I think you're right!" exclaimed Mr. Damon, and Eradicate hurried back to the balloon to get some of the condensed food.

He was soon back and then, with Tom in the lead, and with everyone carrying an electric torch, with a spare one in reserve, and with their weapons in readiness the party descended the stone steps.

Their footfalls echoed solemnly as they went down—down into the unknown blackness. They kept their bright lights playing here and there, but even these did not dispell the gloom. On every side was stone—stone walls—stone steps. It was like going down into some vast stretch of catacombs.

"Say, will we ever get to the bottom?" asked Ned, when they had counted several hundred steps. "Maybe this goes down to the middle of the earth."

"Well, ef it do I'm gwine right along!" called Eradicate. "I's gwine t' hab one ob dem gold images or bust!"

"And I'm with you!" cried Tom. "We'll have to get to the bottom sooner or later."

Hardly had he spoken than he came to the last step, and saw stretching off before him a long tunnel, straight and level, lined on both sides, and bottom, with smooth stones that gleamed like marble.

"Now we are really in the tunnel," declared Ned. "I wonder what's at the end?"

"The city of gold, of course," answered Tom confidently.

Eagerly they hurried on. There was a slightly musty smell to the air, but it was fresher than might have been expected.

Suddenly Tom, who was in advance, uttered a cry. It sounded like one of alarm, and Ned yelled:

"What's the matter?"

"Look here!" cried Tom. They hurried up to him, to find him standing before a sort of niche in the wall. And the niche was lined with a yellow metal that gleamed like gold, while in it was one of the golden images, the second one they had seen, and the third they heard about.

"We're on the trail! We're on the trail!" cried Tom.

"Heah! Let me hab dat!" cried Eradicate. "I may not git anudder," and he reached up for the statue.

"Let it stay until we come back," suggested Mr. Damon.

"Somebody might take it," said the colored man.

"Who?" laughed Tom. "There's not a soul here but ourselves. But take it, if you want it, Rad," and Eradicate did so, stuffing the image, which was only about four inches high, into his pocket.

Then they went on, and they saw several other images, though not of gold. Several niches were lined with yellow metal, but whether it was gold or not they could not tell. They did not want to stop, as they were anxious to get to the underground city.

"Hark! What's that?" asked Tom, when they had gone about a mile along the tunnel. "Don't you hear something?"

"Sounds like a roaring," agreed Ned. "Maybe it's more of the bats."

"Doesn't sound like bats," declared Tom. "It's more like a waterfall. Come on."

They hurried forward, the strange sound increasing at every step, until it filled the tunnel with its menacing roar.

"That's strange," said Tom in worried tones. "I hope we don't come to a waterfall."

Suddenly the tunnel made a turn, and as they went around the curve in the wall the sound smote on their ears with increased violence. Tom raced forward, focusing his electric lamp down on the stone corridor. The next instant he cried out:

"A river! It's an underground river and we can't go any further! We're blocked!"

The others came to his side, and there, in the glare of their lamps, they saw rushing along, between two walls of stone, a dark stream which caused the roaring sound that had come to them. The tunnel was cut squarely in two by the stream, which was at least thirty feet wide, and how deep they could only guess. Swiftly it flowed on, its roar filling the tunnel.

CHAPTER XX

THE CITY OF GOLD

"Well, I guess this is the end of it," remarked Ned ruefully, as they stood contemplating the roaring stream by the gleam of their electric flash lamps. "We can't go on to the city of gold unless we swim that river, and—"

"And none of us is going to try that!" interrupted Tom sharply. "The strongest swimmer in the world couldn't make a yard against that current. He'd be carried down, no one knows where."

"Bless my bathing suit, yes!" exclaimed Mr. Damon. "But what are we to do? Can't we make a raft, or get a boat, or something like that?"

"Hab t' be a mighty pow'ful boat t' git across dat ribber ob Jordan," spoke Eradicate solemnly.

"That's right," agreed Ned. "But say, Tom, don't you think we could go back, get a lot of trees, wood and stuff and make some sort of a bridge? It isn't so very wide—not more than thirty or forty feet. We ought to be able to bridge it."

"I'm afraid not," and Tom shook his head. "In the first place any trees that would be long enough are away at the far edge of the big plain, and we'd have a hard job getting them to the temple, to say nothing of lugging them down the tunnel. Then, too, we don't know much about building a bridge, and with no one on the other side to help us, we'd have our hands full. One slip and we might be all drowned. No, I guess we've got to go back," and Tom spoke regretfully. "It's hard luck, but we've got to give up and go back."

"Den I's pow'ful glad I got ma golden image when I did, dat's suah!" exclaimed Eradicate. "Ef we doan't git no mo' I'll hab one. But I'll sell it and whack up wid yo' all, Massa Tom."

"You'll do nothing of the sort, Rad!" exclaimed the young inventor. "That image is yours, and I'm sorry we can't get more of them."

He turned aside, and after another glance at the black underground river which flowed along so relentlessly he prepared to retrace his steps along the tunnel.

"Say, look here!" suddenly exclaimed Ned. "I'm not so sure, after all that we've got to turn back. I think we can go on to the city of gold, after all."

"How do you mean?" asked Tom quickly. "Do you think we can bring the balloon down here and float across?"

"Bless my watch chain!" exclaimed Mr. Damon, "but that would be a way. I wonder—"

"No, I don't mean that way at all," went on Ned. "But it seems to me as if this river isn't a natural one—I mean that it flows along banks of smooth stone, just as if they were cut for it, a canal you know."

"That's right," said Tom, as he looked at the edge of the channel of the underground stream. "These stones are cut as cleanly as the rest of the tunnel. Whoever built that must have made a regular channel for this river to flow in. And it's square on the other side, too," he added, flashing his lamp across.

"Then don't you see," continued Ned, "that this river hasn't always been here."

"Bless my gaiters!" gasped Mr. Damon, "what does he mean? The river not always been here?"

"No," proceeded Tom's chum. "For the ancients couldn't have cut the channel out of stone, or made it by cementing separate stones together while the water was here. The channel must have been dry at one time, and when it was finished they turned the water in it."

"But how is that going to help us?" asked Tom. "I grant you that the river may not have been here at one time, but it's here now, which makes it all the worse for us."

"But, Tom!" cried his chum, "if the river was turned aside from this channel once it can be done again. My notion is that the ancients could make the river flow here or not, just as they choose. Probably they turned it into this channel to keep their enemies from crossing to the city of gold, like the ancient moats. Now if we could only find—"

"I see! I see!" cried Tom enthusiastically. "You mean there must be some way of shutting off the water."

"Exactly," replied his chum. "We've got to shut that stream of water off, or turn it into some other channel, then we can cross, and keep on to the city of gold. And I think there must be some valve—some lever, or handle or something similar to the one that moved the altar-near here that does the trick. Let's all look for it."

"Bless my chopping block!" cried Mr. Damon. "That's the strangest thing I ever heard of! But I believe you're right, Ned. We'll look for the handle to the river," and he laughed gaily.

Every one was in better spirits, now that there seemed a way out of the difficulty, and a moment later they were eagerly flashing their lamps on the sides, floor and ceiling of the tunnel, to discover the means of shutting off the water. At first they feared that, after all, Ned's ingenious theory was not to be confirmed. The walls, ceiling and floor were as smooth near the edge of the river as elsewhere.

But Eradicate, who was searching as eagerly as the others, went back a little, flashing his lamp on every square of stone. Suddenly he uttered a cry.

"Look yeah, Massa Tom! Heah's suffin' dat looks laik a big door knob. Maybe yo' kin push it or pull it."

They rushed to where he was standing in front of a niche similar to the one where he had found the golden image. Sunken in the wall was a round black stone. For a moment Tom looked at it, and then he said solemnly:

"Well, here goes. It may shut off the water, or it may make it rise higher and drown us all, or the whole tunnel may cave in, but I'm going to risk it. Hold hard, everybody!"

Slowly Tom put forth his hand and pushed the knob of stone. It did not move. Then he pulled it. The result was the same—nothing.

"Guess it doesn't work any more," he said in a low tone.

"Twist it!" cried Ned. "Twist it like a door knob."

In a flash Tom did so. For a moment no result was apparent, then, from somewhere far off, there sounded a low rumble, above the roar of the black stream.

"Something happened!" cried Mr. Damon.

"Back to the river!" shouted Tom, for they were some distance away from it now. "If it's rising we may have a chance to escape."

They hurried to the edge of the stone channel, and Ned uttered a cry of delight.

"It's going down!" he yelled, capering about. "Now we can go on!"

And, surely enough, the river was falling rapidly. It no longer roared, and it was flowing more slowly.

"The water is shut off," remarked Tom,

"Yes, and see, there are steps which lead across the channel," spoke Ned, pointing to them as the receding water revealed them. "Everything is coming our way now."

In a short time the water was all out of the channel, and they could see that it was about twenty feet deep. Truly it would have been a formidable stream to attempt to swim over, but now it had completely vanished, merely a few little pools of water remaining in depressions on the bottom of the channel. There were steps leading down to the bottom, and other steps ascending on the other side, showing that the river was used as a barrier to further progress along the tunnel.

"Forward!" cried Tom gaily, and they went on.

They went down into the river channel, taking care not to slip on the wet steps, and a few seconds later they had again ascended to the tunnel, pressing eagerly on.

Straight and true the tunnel ran through the darkness, the only illumination being their electric flash lamps. On and on they went, hoping every minute to reach their goal.

"Dish suah am a mighty long tunnel," remarked Eradicate. "Dey ought t' hab a trolley line in yeah."

"Bless my punching bag!" cried Mr. Damon, "so they had! Now if those ancients were building today—"

He stopped suddenly, for Tom, who was in the lead, had uttered a cry. It was a cry of joy, there was no mistaking that, and instinctively they all knew that he had found what he had sought.

All confirmed it a moment later, for, as they rushed forward, they discovered Tom standing at the place where the tunnel broadened out— broadened out into a great cave, a cave miles in extent, for all they could tell, as their lamps, powerful as they were, only illuminated for a comparatively short distance.

"We're here!" cried Tom. "In the city of gold at last!"

"The city of gold!" added Ned. "The underground city of gold!"

"And gold there is!" fairly shouted Mr. Damon. "See it's all over! Look at the golden streets—even the sides of the buildings are plated with it—and see, in that house there are even gold chairs! Boys, there is untold wealth here!"

"An' would yo' all look at dem golden statues!" cried Eradicate, "dey mus' be millions ob 'em! Oh, golly! Ain't I glad I comed along!" and he rushed into one of the many houses extending along the street of the golden city where they stood, and gathered up a fairly large statue of gold—an image exactly similar to the one he already had, except as to size.

"I never would have believed it possible!" gasped Tom. "It's a city of almost solid gold. We'll be millionaires a million times over!"

CHAPTER XXI

THE BIG IMAGE

Could the light of day have penetrated to that mysterious and ancient underground city of gold our friends might have had some idea of its magnificence. As it was they could only view small parts of it at a time by the illumination of their electric torches. But even with them they saw that it was a most wonderful place.

"I don't believe there's another city like it in all the world," spoke Tom in awed accents, "there never was, and never will be again. Those Aztecs must have brought all their treasures of gold here."

"Bless my cake box! that's so," agreed Mr. Damon.

"Let's take a look around," advised Ned, "and then we can decide on what will be best to take away."

"It won't take me long t' make up mah mind," spoke Eradicate. "I's goin' t' take all dem images I kin find."

"I was going to say we'd have plenty of time to look about and pick what we wanted," said Tom, "but I think perhaps we'd better hurry."

"Why?" asked Mr. Damon.

"There's no telling when Delazes and his gang may find this place, and even the Fogers may be nearer than we think. But I believe our best plan would be this: To take some gold now, and several of the statues, go back to our balloon, and make some kind of big lamps, so we can light this place up. Then, too, I think we'd better move the balloon into the old temple. It will be safer there. Then we can come back here, pack up as much gold as we can carry, and be off. I don't like to think of being underground when Delazes and the Fogers are on the surface. It might not be altogether safe for us."

"Bless my insurance policy!" cried the odd man. "Now you're giving me the cold shivers, Tom. But I believe you're right. We must look ahead a bit."

With all their electric flash lamps turned on, the four advanced farther into the underground city of gold. As they went on they saw the precious yellow metal on every side of them. It was used lavishly, showing that to the ancients it was as common as iron or steel is today. But they did not use the gold merely as common material in the construction of buildings or objects of use. Instead, the gold seemed to be brought into play to beautify the city. An artistic scheme was carried out, and while it was true that in many buildings common objects were made of gold, yet each one was beautiful in itself.

"What a wonderful place this must have been when it was lighted up," spoke Tom.

"Do you think it was ever lighted up?" asked his chum.

"It must have been," declared the young inventor. "My idea is that this city was the home of the priests of the temple, and their friends. I don't believe the common people ever came here. Perhaps the officers of the army, the rulers and the royal family were admitted, but not the ordinary people. That's why it's so far underground, and so well guarded by the river."

"Probably the priests and others collected so much gold they didn't know what to do with it, and built this city to use it up, and, at the same time have a safe place to store it. And they must have had some means of lighting the place, for they couldn't go about in darkness—they couldn't have seen the gold if they did. Yes, this must have been wonderfully beautiful then. The priests probably came here to study, or perhaps to carry out some of their rites. Of course it's only guesswork, but it seems true to me."

"I believe you're right, Tom," said Mr. Damon.

As our friends walked about they saw that the city, while smaller than they had at first supposed, was laid out with regular streets. Each one was straight, and at certain places in the stone pavement plates of gold were set, so that literally the streets were paved with gold. There were houses or buildings on each side of the streets, and most of these were open at the doors or windows, for there was no need of heat in that buried city.

All about were the golden images such as they had seen in the Mexican's house, and like the one in far off Africa. Some of the images were almost life size, and others were only an inch or two inches in height. Not a house but had half a dozen or more in various places, and there were also the images on golden pedestals about the streets.

"This must have been their chief god, or else a representation of some great personage to whom they paid the highest honor," said Mr. Damon. "Perhaps he was the reigning king or ruler, and he, himself, might have ordered the images made out of vanity, like some men of today."

The boys agreed that this was a natural theory. As for Eradicate he was busy collecting numbers of the small golden statues, and stuffing them in his pockets.

"Why don't you take bigger ones, and not so many of them?" asked Tom.

"'Case as how I doan't want all mah eggs in one basket," replied the colored man. "I kin carry mo' ob de little fellers," and he persisted in this plan.

They found in some of the houses utensils of solid gold, but there appeared to be no way of cooking food, and that was probably done outside, or in the great temple. In many houses were articles evidently used in the sacrificial rites or in worship of strange gods. They did not stay to half examine the wonderful city of gold, for it would have taken several days. But on Tom's advice, they took up a considerable quantity of the precious metal in the most convenient form to carry, including a number of the statues and art objects and started back along the tunnel.

"We'll rig up some sort of lamps," Tom explained, "and come back to make a thorough examination of this place. I think the scientific men and historians will be glad to know about this city, and I'm going to make some notes about it."

They soon came again to the place of the underground river and found no water there. Ned wanted to turn the stream back into the channel again, but Tom said they might not be able to work the ancient mechanism, so they left the black knob as it was, and hurried on. They decided that the knob must have worked some counter-balance, or great weight that let down a gate and cut off the river from one channel, to turn it into another.

When they emerged at the top of the steps, and came out at the opening which had been revealed by the rolling back of the great altar, they saw there that counter weights, delicately balanced, had moved the big stone.

"We might close that opening," said Tom, "and then if any one should come along and surprise us, they wouldn't know how to get to the underground city." This was done, the altar rolling back over the staircase.

"Now to get the balloon in the temple, make the lamps, and go back," suggested Tom, and, storing the gold they had secured in a safe place in the temple, they went back to move the airship.

This was an easy matter, and soon they had floated the big gas bag and car in through one of the immense doorways and so into the great middle part of the temple where the big stone altar was located.

"Now we're prepared for emergencies," remarked Tom, as he looked up at the yawning hole in the dome-like roof. "If worst comes to worst, and we have to run, we can float right up here, out of the temple, and skip."

"Do you think anything is going to happen?" asked Mr. Damon anxiously.

"You never can tell," replied Tom. "Now to make some lamps. I think I'll use gas, as I've got plenty of the chemicals."

It took two days to construct them, and Tom ingeniously made them out of some empty tins that had contained meat and other foods. The tins were converted into tanks, and from each one rose a short piece of pipe that ended in a gas tip. On board the dirigible were plenty of tools and materials. Into the cans were put certain chemicals that generated a gas which, when lighted, gave a brilliant glow, almost like calcium carbide.

"Now, I guess we can see to make our way about," remarked Tom, on the morning of the third day, when they prepared to go back to the city of gold. "And we'll take plenty of lunch along, for we may stay until nearly night."

It did not take them long to roll back the altar, descend into the tunnel, and reach the underground city. The river channel was now dry, even the small pools of water in the depressions having evaporated.

The gas torches worked to perfection, and revealed the beauties and wonders of the city of gold to the astonished gaze of our friends. It was even richer in the precious metal than they had at first supposed.

"Before we do any exploring, I think we'd better take some more gold back to the balloon," suggested Tom, "and I think I'll just move the balloon itself more out of sight, so that if any persons come along, and look into the temple, they won't see our airship without looking for it."

This was done, and a considerable quantity of the precious metal, including a number of the larger-sized statues, were stored in the balloon car.

"We can't take much more," Tom warned his friends, "or we'll be over-weighted."

"We've got enough now, to make us all rich," said Ned, contentedly.

"I want moah," spoke Eradicate with a grin.

They went back to the underground city and began to explore it with a view of taking back to civilization some word of its wonders and beauties.

"Didn't Mr. Illingway, in his letters, say something about an immense golden statue here?" asked Ned, when they had almost completed a circuit of the underground place.

"So he did!" exclaimed Tom. "I'd almost forgotten. It must be somewhere in the centre of this place I should think. Let's have a hunt for it. We can't take it with us, but maybe we could get part of an arm or a leg to keep as a relic. Come on."

It was easy to reach the centre of the underground city, for it was laid out on a regular plan. In a short time they were in sight of the central plaza and, even before they reached it the glare of their gas lamps showed them something glittering golden yellow. It was on a tall, golden pedestal.

"There it is!" cried Ned.

"Yes, there's the big golden image all right," agreed Tom, hurrying forward, and a moment later they stood before a most wonderful statue.

CHAPTER XXII

TRAPPED

"Well, that sure is a big statue!" exclaimed Ned as he walked around it.

"An' to t'ink dat it's solid gold!" cried Eradicate his eyes big with wonder. "I suah wish I had dat all fo' mahse'f!"

"We never could carry that in the balloon," spoke Tom with a shake of his head. "I guess we'll have to leave it here. But I would like to take say the head. It would be worth a lot as a relic to some museum—worth more than the value of the gold itself. I've a notion to do it."

"How could you get the head off?" asked Mr. Damon.

"Oh, pull the statue down or overturn it, as the American patriots did to the Bowling Green, New York, lead statue of King George III during the Revolutionary days," answered Tom. "I think that's what I'll do."

"I say, look here!" called Ned, who had made a circuit of the statue. "There's some sort of an inscription here. See if you can read it, Tom."

They went around to the front of the big, golden image where Ned stood. On a sort of a plate, with raised letters, was an inscription in a strange language. Part of it seemed to be the name of the person or god whom the statue represented, and what followed none could make out.

"It's something like the ancient Greek or Persian language," declared Mr. Damon, who was quite a scholar. "I can make out a word here and there, and it seems to be a warning against disturbing the statue, or damaging it. Probably it was put there to warn small boys thousands of years ago, if they ever allowed small boys in this place."

"Does it say what will be done to whoever harms the statue?" asked Tom with a laugh.

"Probably it does, but I can't make out what it is," answered Mr. Damon.

"Then here goes to see if we can't overturn it and hack off the head," went on Tom. "I've got a sharp little hatchet, and gold is very soft to cut. Over she goes."

"You never can upset that statue," declared Ned.

"Yes, I can," cried the young inventor. "I brought a long, thin, but very strong rope with me, and I think if we all pull together we can do it."

Tom made a noose and skillfully threw it over the head of the statue. It settled about the neck, and then, all taking hold, and walking away a short distance, they gave a "long pull, a strong pull, and a pull altogether."

At first the statue would not move, but when they strained on the rope, the image suddenly tilted, and, a moment later it tumbled to the stone pavement. But the fall was not as heavy as should have resulted from a statue of solid metal. There was a tinkling sound.

"That's queer!" cried Tom. "It didn't make half the fuss I expected," and he hurried up to look at the fallen statue. "Why!" he cried in astonishment, "it's hollow—the big golden statue is hollow—it's a fake!"

And so it was. The big image was only a shell of gold.

"Not so valuable as it looked," commented Ned. "We could take that with us in the balloon, if it wasn't so big."

"Well, here goes for the head, anyhow!" exclaimed Tom, and with a few blows of his keen little axe he severed the neck. As he held it up for all to see—rather a grewsome sight it was, too, in the flickering light of the gas torches—there sounded throughout the underground city, a dull, booming noise, like distant thunder.

"What's that?" cried Ned.

"Bless my bath sponge!" exclaimed Mr. Damon, "I hope the water isn't rising in the river."

"Oh land a massy!" gasped Eradicate.

Without a word Tom dropped the golden head and made for the street that led to the tunnel. The others followed, and soon caught up to the young inventor. On and on they ran, with only the light of their electric flash torches to guide them. Suddenly Tom stopped.

"Go on!" cried Ned. "See what's happened! Go on!"

"I can't," answered Tom, and they all wondered at his voice. "There's a big block of stone across the tunnel, and I can't go another step. The stone gate has fallen. We're trapped here in the underground city of gold!"

"Bless my soul! The tunnel closed?" cried Mr. Damon.

"Look," said Tom simply and in hopeless tones, as he flashed his light. And there, completely filling the tunnel, was a great block of stone, fitting from ceiling to floor and from side wall to side wall, completely cutting off all escape.

"Trapped!" gasped Ned. "The Mexicans or Andy Foger did this."

"No, I don't think so," spoke Tom solemnly. "I think the pulling down of the statue released this stone gate. We trapped ourselves. Oh, why didn't I leave the statue alone!"

"That can't have done it!" declared Ned.

"We can soon tell," spoke Mr. Damon. "Let's go back and look. Later maybe we can raise the block," and they returned to the fallen gold statue. Tom casting back a hopeless look at the barrier that had buried them alive in the city of gold.

CHAPTER XXIII

"IS IT A RESCUE?"

"Can you see anything, Tom? Any lever or anything by which we can raise the stone gate?"

It was Ned who spoke, and he addressed his chum, who was closely examining the pedestal of the fallen golden statue.

"Bless my soul!" exclaimed Mr. Damon, "we've get to find some way out of here soon—or—"

He did not finish the sentence, but they all knew what he meant.

"Oh good landy!" cried Eradicate. "What's gwine t' become ob us?"

"Don't you see anything, Tom?" repeated Ned.

"Not a thing. Not a sign of a lever or handle by which the stone might be raised. But wait, I'm going to get on top of the pedestal."

He managed to scramble up by stepping on and clinging to various ornamental projections, and soon gained the flat place where the big golden statue had rested. But he saw at a glance that it was as smooth as a billiard table.

"Nothing here!" he called down to Ned.

"Then how do you suppose the gate closed down when the statue was pulled off?" asked Ned.

"It must have been because of the disturbance of the equilibrium, or due to a change of weight. Probably this pedestal rests on a platform, like the platform of a large scale. Its weight, with that of the statue, rested on certain concealed levers, and held the stone up out of sight in the roof of the tunnel. When I yanked down the statue I made the weight uneven, and the stone fell, and there doesn't seem to be any way of putting the weight back again."

"No, we never could get the statue back on the pedestal," said Ned. "But maybe there's some mechanism at the stone gate, or near it, like the black knob which turned off the water. We may be able to work that and raise the big stone slab."

"It's the only thing to try, as long as we haven't dynamite to blast it," agreed Tom. "Come on, we'll take a look."

They went back to where the rock closed the tunnel, but a long and frantic search failed to show the least projection, lever, handle or any other thing, that could be moved.

"What in the world do you suppose those ancients made such a terrible contrivance for?" Ned wanted to know.

"Well, if we could read the warning on the statue we might know," replied Mr. Damon. "That probably says that whoever disturbs the status will close up the golden city forever."

"Maybe there's another way out—or in," suggested Tom hopefully. "We didn't look for that. It must be our next move. We must not let a single chance go by. We'll look for some way of getting out, at the far end of this underground city."

Filled with gloomy and foreboding thoughts, they walked away from the stone barrier. To search for another means of egress would take some time, and the same fear came to all of them—could they live that long?

"It was a queer thing, to make that statue hollow," mused Ned as he walked between Mr. Damon and Tom. "I wonder why it was done, when all the others are solid gold?"

"Maybe they found they couldn't melt up, and cast in a mould, enough gold to make a solid statue that size," suggested Mr. Damon. "Then, too, there may have been no means of getting it on the pedestal if they made it too heavy."

They discussed these and other matters as they hurried on to seek for some way of escape. In fact to talk seemed to make them less gloomy and sad, and they tried to keep up their spirits.

For several hours they searched eagerly for some means of getting out of the underground city. They went to the farthest limits of it, and found it to be several miles in diameter, but eventually they came to solid walls of stone which reached from roof to ceiling, and there was no way out.

They found that the underground city was exactly like an overturned bowl, or an Esquimo ice hut, hollow within, and with a tunnel leading to it—but all below the surface of the earth. The city had been hollowed out of solid rock, and there was but one way in or out, and that was closed by the seamless stone.

"There's no use hunting any longer," declared Tom, when, weary and footsore, they had completed a circuit of the outer circumference of the city, "the rock passage is our only hope."

"And that's no hope at all!" declared Ned.

"Yes, we must try to raise that stone slab, or—break it!" cried Tom desperately. "Come on."

"Wait a bit," advised Mr. Damon. "Bless my dinner plate! but I'm hungry. We brought some food along, and my advice to you is to eat and keep up our strength. We'll need it."

"By golly gracious, that's so!" declared Eradicate. "I'll git de eatin's."

Fortunately there was a goodly supply, and, going in one the houses they ate off a table of solid gold, and off dishes of the precious, yellow metal. Yet they would have given it all—yes, even the gold in their dirigible balloon—for a chance for freedom.

"I wonder what became of the chaps who used to live here?" mused Ned as he finished the rather frugal meal.

"Oh, they probably died—from a plague maybe, or there may have been a war, or the people may have risen in revolt and killed them off," suggested Tom grimly.

"But then there ought to be some remains—some mummies or skeletons or something."

"I guess every one left this underground city—every soul." suggested Mr. Damon, "and then they turned on the river and left it. I shouldn't be surprised but what we are the first persons to set foot here in thousands of years."

"And we may stay here for a thousand years," predicted Tom.

"Oh, good land a' massy; doan't say dat!" cried Eradicate. "Why we'll all be dead ob starvation in dat time."

"Before then, I guess," muttered Tom. "I wonder if there's any water in this hole?"

"We'll need it—soon," remarked Ned, looking at the scanty supply they had brought in with them. "Let's have a hunt for it."

"Let Rad do that, while we work on the stone gate," proposed the young inventor. "Rad, chase off and see if you can find some water."

While the colored man was gone, Tom, Ned and Mr. Damon went back to the stone gate. To attack it without tools, or some powerful blasting powder seemed useless, but their case was desperate and they knew they must do something.

"We'll try chipping away the stone at the base," suggested Tom. "It isn't a very hard rock, in fact it's a sort of soft marble, or white sand stone, and we may be able to cut out a way under the slab door with our knifes."

Fortunately they had knives with big, strong blades, and as Tom had said, the stone was comparatively soft. But, after several hours' work they only had a small depression under the stone door.

"At this rate it will take a month," sighed Ned.

"Say!" cried Tom, "we're foolish. We should try to cut through the stone slab itself. It can't be so very thick. And another thing. I'm going to play the flames from the gas torches on the stone. The fires will make it brittle and it will chip off easier."

This was so, but even with that advantage they had only made a slight impression on the solid stone door after more than four hours of work, and Eradicate came back, with a hopeless look on his face, to report that he had been unable to find water.

"Then we've got to save every drop of what we've got," declared Tom. "Short rations for everybody."

"And our lights, too," added Mr. Damon. "We must save them."

"All out but one!" cried Tom quickly. "If we're careful we can make them gas torches last a week, and the electric flashes are good for several days yet."

Then they laid out a plan of procedure, and divided the food into as small rations as would support life. It was grim work, but it had to be done. They found, with care, that they might live for four days on the food and water and then—

Well—no one liked to think about it.

"We must take turns chipping away at the stone door," decided Tom. "Some of us will work and some will sleep—two and two, I guess."

This plan was also carried out, and Tom and Eradicate took the first trick of hacking away at the door.

How they managed to live in the days that followed they could never tell clearly afterward. It was like some horrible nightmare, composed of hours of hacking away at the stone, and then of eating sparingly, drinking more sparingly, and resting, to get up, and do it all over again.

Their water was the first to give out, for it made them thirsty to cut at the stone, and parched mouths and swollen tongues demanded moisture. They did manage to find a place where a few drops of water trickled through the rocky roof, and without this they would have died before five days had passed.

They even searched, at times for another way out of the city of gold, for Tom had insisted there must be a way, as the air in the underground cave remained so fresh. But there must have been a secret way of ventilating the place, as no opening was found, and they went back to hacking at the stone.

Just how many days they spent in their horrible golden prison they never really knew. Tom said it was over a week, Ned insisted it was a month, Mr. Damon two months, and Eradicate pitifully said "it seem mos' laik a yeah, suah!"

It must have been about eight days, and at the end of that time there was not a scrap of food left, and only a little water. They were barely alive, and could hardly wield the knives against the stone slab. They had dug a hole about a foot deep in it, but it would have to be made much larger before any one could crawl through, even when it penetrated to the other side. And how soon this would be they did not know.

It was about the end of the eighth day, and Tom and Ned were hacking away at the rocky slab, for Mr. Damon and Eradicate were too weary.

Tom paused for a moment to look helplessly at his chum. As he did so he heard, amid the silence, a noise on the other side of the stone door.

"What—what's that?" Tom gasped faintly.

"It sounds—sounds like some one—coming," whispered Ned. "Oh, if it is only a rescue party!"

"A rescue party?" whispered Tom. "Where would a rescue party—"

He stopped suddenly. Unmistakably there were voices on the other side of the barrier—human voices.

"It is a rescue party!" cried Ned.

"I—I hope so," spoke Tom slowly.

"Mr. Damon—Eradicate!" yelled Ned with the sudden strength of hope, "they're coming to save us! Hurry over here!"

And then, as he and Tom stood, they saw, with staring eyes, the great stone slab slowly beginning to rise!

CHAPTER XXIV

THE FIGHT

The talk sounded more plainly now—a confused murmur of voices—many of them—the sound coming under the slowly raising stone doorway.

"Who can it be—there's a lot of them," murmured Ned.

Tom did not answer. Instead he silently sped back to where they had slept and got his automatic revolver.

"Better get yours," he said to his companions. "It may be a rescue party, though I don't see how any one could know we were in here, or it may be—"

He did not finish. They all knew what he meant, and a moment later four strained and anxious figures stood on the inner side of the stone door, revolvers in hand, awaiting what might be revealed to them. Would it be friend or foe?

At Tom's feet lay the golden head—the hollow head of the statue. The scene was illumined by a flickering gas torch—the last one, as the others had burned out.

Slowly the stone went up, very slowly, for it was exceedingly heavy and the mechanism that worked it was primitive. Up and up it went until now a man could have crawled under. Ned made a motion as if he was going to do so, but Tom held him back.

Slowly and slowly it went up. On the other side was a very babble of voices now—voices speaking a strange tongue. Tom and his companions were silent.

Then, above the other voices, there sounded the tones of some one speaking English. Hearing it Tom started, and still more as he noted the tones, for he heard this said:

"We'll be inside in a minute, dad, and I guess we'll show Tom Swift that he and his crowd can't fool us. We've got to the city of gold first!"

"Andy Foger!" hoarsely whispered Tom to Ned.

The next moment the stone gate went up with a rush, and there, in the light of the gas torch, and in the glare of many burning ones of wood, held by a throng of people on the other side, stood Andy Foger, his father, Delazes, and a horde of men who looked as wild as savages.

For a moment both parties stood staring at one another, too startled to utter a sound. Then as Tom noticed that some of the natives, who somewhat resembled the ancient Aztecs, had imitation human heads stuck on the ends of poles or spears, he uttered two words:

"Head-hunters!"

Like a flash there came to him the warning of the African missionary: "Beware of the head-hunters!" Now they were here—being led on by the Mexican and the Fogers—the enemies of our friends.

For another moment there was a silence, and then Andy Foger cried out:

"They're here! Tom Swift and his party! They got here first and they may have all the gold!"

"If they have they will share it with us!" cried Delazes fiercely.

"Quick!" Tom called hoarsely to Ned, Mr. Damon and Eradicate. "We've got to fight. It's the only way to save our lives. We must fight, and when we can, escape, get to the airship and sail away. It's a fight to the finish now."

He raised his automatic revolver, and, as he did so one of the savages saw the golden head of the statue lying at Tom's feet. The man uttered a wild cry and called out something in his unknown tongue. Then he raised his spear and hurled it straight at our hero.

Had not Mr. Damon pulled Tom to one side, there might have been a different ending to this story. As it was the weapon hissed through the air over the head of the young inventor. The next minute his revolver spat lead and fire, but whether he hit any one or not he could not see, as the place was so filled with smoke, from the powder and from the torches. But some one yelled in pain.

"Crouch down and fire!" ordered Tom. "Low down and they'll throw over our heads." It was done on the instant, and the four revolvers rang out together.

There were howls of pain and terror and above them could be heard the gutteral tones of Delazes, while Andy Foger yelled:

"Look out dad! Here, help me to get behind something or I may be hit. Mr. Delazes, can't you tell those savages to throw spears at Tom Swift and his gang?"

"They are doing it, Senor Foger," replied the Mexican. "Oh, why did I not think to bring my gun! We haven't one among us." Then he called some command to the head-hunters who had apparently been enlisted on the side of himself and the two Fogers.

The automatic revolvers were soon emptied, and the place was now so full of smoke that neither party could see the other. The torches burned with a red glare.

"Reload!" ordered Tom, "and we'll make a rush for it! We can't keep this up long!"

It took but an instant to slip in another lot of cartridges and then, on Tom's advice, they slipped the catches to make the automatic weapons simple ones, to be fired at will.

They sent several more shots through the door-way but no cries of pain followed, and it was evident that their enemies had stepped back out of the line of fire.

"Now's our chance!" cried Tom. "The way is clear. Come on!"

He and the others dashed forward, Tom carrying the golden head, though it was hard work. It was not very heavy but it was awkward.

As they rushed through the now open gateway they crouched low to avoid the spears, but, as it was one grazed Tom's shoulder, and Eradicate was pierced in the fleshy part of his arm.

"Forward! Forward!" cried Tom. "Come on!"

And on they went, through the smoke and darkness, Ned flashing his electric torch which gave only a feeble glow as the battery was almost exhausted. On and on! Now they were through the stone gateway, now out in the long tunnel.

Behind them they could hear feet running, and several spears clattered to the stone floor. Lights flickered behind them.

"If only the river bed is dry!" gasped Tom. "We may yet escape. But if they've filled the channel—"

He did not dare think of what that would mean as he ran on, turning occasionally to fire, for he and the others had again reloaded their revolvers.

CHAPTER XXV

THE ESCAPE—CONCLUSION

The noise behind our friends increased. There were shouts of rage, yells of anger at the escape of the prey. High above the other voices were the shrill war-cries of the head-hunters—the savages with their grewsome desires.

"Can—can we make it, Tom?" panted Ned.

They were almost at the river channel now, and in another instant they had reached it.

By the feeble rays of Ned's electric torch they saw with relief that it was empty, though they would have given much to see just a trickle of water in it, for they were almost dead from thirst.

Together they climbed up the other side, and as yet their pursuers had not reached the brink. For one moment Tom had a thought of working the black knob, and flooding the channel, but he could not doom even the head-hunters, much less the Fogers and Delazes, to such a death as that would mean.

On ran Tom and his companions, but now they could glance back and see the foremost of the other crowd dipping down into the dry channel.

"The steps! The steps!" suddenly cried Ned, when they had run a long distance, as a faint gleam of daylight beyond shewed the opening beneath the stone altar. "We're safe now."

"Hardly, but a few minutes will tell," said Tom. "The balloon is in shape for a quick rise, and then we'll leave this horrible place behind."

"And all the gold, too," murmured Ned regretfully. "We've got some," said Mr. Damon, "and I wouldn't take a chance with those head-hunters for all the gold in the underground city."

"Same here!" panted Tom. Then they were at the steps and ran up them.

Out into the big auditorium they emerged, weak and faint, and toward the hidden dirigible balloon they rushed.

"Quick!" cried Tom, as he climbed into the car, followed by Mr. Damon and Eradicate. "Shove it right under the broken dome, Ned, and I'll turn on the gas machine. It's partly inflated."

A moment later the balloon was right below the big opening. The blue sky showed through it—a welcome sight to our friends. The hiss of the gas was heard, and the bag distended still more.

"Hop in!" cried Tom. "She'll go up I guess."

"There they come!" shouted Ned, as he spoke the foremost of the head-hunters emerged from the hole beneath the stone altar. He was followed by Delazes.

"Stop them! Get them! Spear them!" cried the contractor. They evidently thought our friends had all the gold from the underground city.

Fortunately the temple was so large that the balloon was a good distance from the hole leading to the tunnel, and before the foremost of the head-hunters could reach it the dirigible began to rise.

"If they throw their spears, and puncture the bag in many places we're done for," murmured Tom. But evidently the savages did not think of this, though Delazes screamed it at them.

Up went the balloon, and not a moment too soon, for one of the head-hunters actually grabbed the edge of the car, and only let go when he found himself being lifted off the temple floor.

Up and up it went and, as it was about to emerge from the broken dome, Tom looked down and saw a curious sight.

Mr. Foger and Andy, who brought up in the rear of the pursuing and attacking party, had just emerged from the hole by the great stone altar when there suddenly spouted from the same opening a solid column of water. A cry of wonder came from all as they saw the strange sight. A veritable geyser was now spurting in the very middle of the temple floor, and the head-hunters, the Mexicans and the Fogers ran screaming to get out of the way.

"Look!" cried Ned. "What happened?"

"The underground river must be running the wrong way!" answered Tom, as he prepared to set in motion the motor. "Either they accidentally turned some hidden lever, or when they raised the stone door they did it. The tunnel is flooded and—"

"Bless my match box! So is the underground city!" cried Mr. Damon. "I guess we've seen the last of it and its gold. We were lucky to escape with our lives, and these fellows might have been drowned like rats in a trap, if they hadn't followed us. The underground city will never be discovered again."

"And now for home!" cried Tom, when they had eaten and drunk sparingly until they should get back their strength, and had seen to their slight wounds.

"And our trip wasn't altogether a failure," said Mr. Damon. "We'd have had more gold if the stone door hadn't trapped us. But I guess we have enough as it is. I wonder how the Fogers ever found us?"

"They must have followed our trail, though how we'll never know and they came up to where Delazes and his men were, joined forces with them, and hunted about until they found the temple," remarked Tom, "Then they saw the opening, went down, and found the stone door."

"But how did they get it open? and what were they doing with the head-hunters, and why didn't the head-hunters attack them?" Ned wanted to know.

"Well, I guess perhaps Delazes knew how to handle those head-hunters," replied Tom. "They may be a sort of lost tribe of Mexicans, and perhaps their ancestors centuries ago owned the city of gold. At any rate I think some of them knew the secret of raising the door." And later Tom learned in a roundabout way from the Fogers that this was so. The father and son had after much hardship joined forces with Delazes and he, by a promise of the heads of the party of our friends, and much tobacco, had gained the head-hunters as allies.

On and on sailed the balloon and our friends regained their strength after partaking of the nourishing food. They looked at their store of gold and found it larger than they had thought. Soon they left far behind them the great plain of the ruined temple, which, had they but known it was a lake now, for the underground river, perhaps by some break in the underground mechanism that controlled it, or a break in the channel, overflowed and covered temple, plain and underground city with water many fathoms deep.

"Are we going all the way home in the balloon?" asked Ned on the second day of their voyage in the air, when they had stopped to make slight repairs.

"No, indeed," replied Tom. "As soon as we get to some city where we can pack it up, and ship our gold without fear of being robbed, I'm coming to earth, and go home in a steamer."

This plan was carried out; and a week later, with the gold safely insured by an express company, and the balloon packed for transportation, our friends went to a railroad station, and took a train for Tampico, there to get a steamer for New York.

"Bless my top knot!" exclaimed Mr. Damon a few days after this, as they were on the vessel. "I think for queer adventures this one of ours in the city of gold, Tom, puts it all over the others we had."

"Oh, I don't know," answered the young inventor, "we certainly had some strenuous times in the past, and I hope we'll have some more in the future."

"The same here," agreed Ned.

And whether they did or not I will leave my readers to judge if they peruse the next book in this series, which will be called, "Tom Swift and His Air Glider; Or, Seeking the Platinum Treasure."

They arrived safely in Shopton in due course of time, and found Mr. Swift well. They did not become millionaires, for they found, to their regret that their gold was rather freely alloyed with baser metals, so they did not have more than half the amount in pure solid gold. But there was a small fortune in it for all of them.

In recognition of Mr. Illingway, the African missionary having put Tom on the track of the gold, a large sum was sent to him, to help him carry on his work of humanity.

Tom had many offers for the big golden head, but he would not sell it, though he loaned it to a New York museum, where it attracted much attention. There were many articles written about the underground city of gold from the facts the young inventor furnished.

Eventually the Fogers got home, but they did not say much about their experiences, and Tom and his friends did not think it worth while to prosecute them for the attack. As for Delazes, Tom never saw nor heard from him again, not in all his reading could he find any account of the head-hunters, who must have been a small, little known tribe.

"And you really kept your promise, and brought me a golden image?" asked Mary Nestor of Tom, when he called on her soon after reaching home.

"Indeed I did, the two that I promised and a particularly fine one that I picked up almost at the last minute," and Tom gave her the valuable relics.

"And now tell me about it," she begged, when she had admired them, and then sat down beside Tom: and there we will leave our hero for the present, as he is in very good company, and I know he wouldn't like to be disturbed.

TOM SWIFT AND HIS AIR GLIDER

OR, SEEKING THE PLATINUM TREASURE

CHAPTER I

A BREAKDOWN

"Well, Ned, are you ready?"

"Oh, I suppose so, Tom. As ready as I ever shall be."

"Why, Ned Newton, you're not getting afraid; are you? And after you've been on so many trips with me?"

"No, it isn't exactly that, Tom. I'd go in a minute if you didn't have this new fangled thing on your airship. But how do you know how it's going to work—or whether it will work at all? We may come a cropper."

"Bless my insurance policy!" exclaimed a man who was standing near the two lads who were conversing. "You'd better keep near the ground, Tom."

"Oh, that's all right, Mr. Damon," answered Tom Swift. "There isn't any more danger than there ever was, but I guess Ned is nervous since our trip to the underground city of gold."

"I am not!" indignantly exclaimed the other lad, with a look at the young inventor. "But you know yourself, Tom, that putting this new pro-peller on your airship, changing the wing tips, and re-gearing the motor has made an altogether different sort of a craft of it. You, yourself, said it wasn't as reliable as before, even though it does go faster."

"Now look here, Ned!" burst out Tom. "That was last week that I said it wasn't reliable. It is now, for I've tried it out several times, and yet, when I ask you to take a trip with me, to act as ballast—"

"Is that all you want me for, Tom, to act as ballast? Then you'd better take a bag of sand—or Mr. Damon here!"

"Me? I guess not! Bless my diamond ring! My wife hasn't forgiven me for going off on that last trip with you, Tom, and I'm not going to take any more right away. But I don't blame Ned—"

"Say, look here!" cried Tom, a little out of patience, "you know me better than that, Ned. Of course you're more than ballast—I want you to help me manage the craft since I made the changes on her. Now if you don't want to come, why say so, and I'll get Eradicate. I don't believe he'll be afraid, even if he—"

"Hold on dar now, Massa Tom!" exclaimed an aged colored man, who was an all around helper at the Swift homestead, "was yo' referencin' t' me when yo' spoke?"

"Yes, Rad, I was saying that if Ned wouldn't go up in the airship with me you would."

"Well, now, Masa Tom, I shorely would laik t' 'blige yo', I shore would. But de fack ob de mattah am dat I has a mos' particular job ob white washin' t' do dish mornin', an' I 'spects I'd better be gittin' at it. It's a mos' particular job, an', only fo' dat, I'd be mos' pleased t' go up in de airship. But as it am, I mus' ax yo' t' 'scuse me, I really mus'," and the colored man shuffled off at a faster gait than he was in the habit of using.

"Well, of all things!" gasped Tom. "I believe you're all afraid of the old airship, just because I made some changes in her. I'll go up alone, that's what I will."

"No, I'll go with you," interposed Ned Newton who was Tom's most particular chum. "I only wanted to be sure it was all right, that was all."

"Well, if you've fully made up your mind," went on the young inventor, a little mollified, "lend me a hand to get her in shape for a run. I expect to make faster time than I ever did before, and I'm going to head out Waterford way. You'd better come along, Mr. Damon, and I'll drop you off at your house."

"Bless my feather bed!" gasped the man. "Drop me off! I like that, Tom Swift!"

"Oh, I didn't mean it exactly that way," laughed Tom. "But will you come."

"No, thanks, I'm going home by trolley," and then as the odd man went in the house to speak to Tom's father, the two lads busied themselves about the airship.

This was a large aeroplane, one of the largest Tom Swift had ever constructed, and he was a lad who had invented many kinds of machinery besides crafts for navigating the upper regions. It was not as large as his combined aeroplane and dirigible balloon of which I have told you in other books, but it was of sufficient size to carry three persons besides other weight.

Tom had built it some years before, and it had seemed good enough then. Later he constructed some of different models, besides the big combination affair, and he had gone on several trips in that.

He and his chum Ned, together with Eradicate Sampson, the colored man, and Mr. Damon, had been to a wonderful underground city of gold in Mexico, and it was soon after their return from this perilous trip that

Tom had begun the work of changing his old aeroplane into a speedier craft.

This had occupied him most of the Winter, and now that Spring had come he had a chance to try what a re-built motor, changed propellers, and different wing tips would do for the machine.

The time had come for the test and, as we have seen, Tom had some difficulty in persuading anyone to go along with him? But Ned finally got over his feeling of nervousness.

"Understand, Tom," spoke Ned, "it isn't because I don't think you know how to work an aeroplane that I hesitated. I've been up in the air with you enough times to know that you're there with the goods, but I don't believe even you know what this machine is going to do."

"I can pretty nearly tell. I'm sure my theory is right."

"I don't doubt that. But will it work out in practice?"

"She may not make all the speed I hope she will, and I may not be able to push her high into the air quicker than I used to before I made the changes," admitted Tom, "but I'm sure of one thing. She'll fly, and she won't come down until I'm ready to let her. So you needn't worry about getting hurt."

"All right—if you say so. Now what do you want me to do, Tom?"

"Go over the wire guys and stays for the first thing. There's going to be lots of vibration, with the re-built motor, and I want everything tight."

"Aye, aye, sir!" answered Ned with a laugh.

Then he set at his task, tightening the small nuts, and screwing up the turn-buckles, while Tom busied himself over the motor. There was some small trouble with the carburetor that needed eliminating before it would feed properly.

"How about the tires?" asked Ned, when he had finished the wires.

"You might pump them up. There, the motor is all right. I'm going to try it now, while you attend to the tires."

Ned had pumped up one of the rubber circlets of the small bicycle wheels on which the aeroplane rested, and was beginning on the second, when a noise like a battery of machine guns going off next to his ear startled him so that he jumped, tripped over a stone and went down, the air pump thumping him in the back.

"What in the world happened, Tom?" he yelled, for he had to use all his lung power to be heard above that racket. "Did it explode?"

"Explode nothing!" shouted Tom. "That's the re-built motor in action."

"In action! I should say it was in action. Is it always going to roar like that?"

Indeed the motor was roaring away, spitting fire and burnt gases from the exhaust pipe, and enveloping the aeroplane in a whitish haze of choking smoke.

No, I have the muffler cut out, and that's why she barks so. But she runs easier that way, and I want to get her smoothed out a bit.

"Whew! That smoke!" gasped his chum. "Why don't you—whew— this is more than I can stand," and holding his hands to his smarting eyes, Ned, gasping and choking, staggered away to where the air was better.

"It is sort of thick," admitted Tom. "But that's only because she's getting too much oil. She'll clear in a few minutes. Stick around and we'll go up."

Despite the choking vapor, the young inventor stuck to his task of regulating the motor, and in a short while the smoke became less, while the big propeller blades whirled about more evenly. Then Tom adjusted the muffler, and most of the noise stopped.

"Come on back, and finish pumping up the tires," he shouted to Ned. "I'm going to stop her now, and then I'll give her the pressure test, and we'll take a trip."

Having cleared his eyes of smoke, Ned came back to his task, and this having been finished, Tom attached a heavy spring balance, or scales, to the rope that held the airship back from moving when her propellers were whirling about.

"How much pressure do you want?" asked Ned.

"I ought to get above twelve hundred with the way the motor is geared, but I'll go up with ten. Watch the needle for me."

It may be explained that when aeroplanes are tested on the earth the propellers are set in motion. This of course would send a craft whizzing over the ground, eventually to rise in the air, but for the fact that a rope, attached to the craft, and to some stationary object, holds it back.

Now if this rope is hooked to a spring balance, which in turn is made fast to the stationary object, the "thrust" of the propellers will be registered in pounds on the scale of the balance. Anywhere from five hundred to nine hundred pounds of thrust will take a monoplane or biplane up. But Tom wanted more than this.

Once more the motor coughed and spluttered, and the big blades whirled about so fast that they seemed like solid pieces of wood. Tom stood on the ground near the levers which controlled the speed, and Ned watched the scale.

"How much?" yelled the young inventor.

"Eight hundred."

Tom turned on a little more gasolene.

"How much?" he cried again.

"Ten hundred. That'll do!"

"No, I'm going to try for more."

Again he advanced the spark and gasolene levers, and the comparatively frail craft vibrated so that it seemed as if she would fly apart.

"Now?" yelled Tom.

"Eleven hundred and fifty!" cried Ned.

"Good! That'll do it. She'll give more after she's been running a while. We'll go up."

Ned scrambled to his seat, and Tom followed. He had an arrangement so that he could slip loose the retaining rope from his perch whenever he was ready.

Waiting until the motor had run another minute, the young inventor pulled the rope that released them. Over the smooth starting ground that formed a part of the Swift homestead darted the aeroplane. Faster and faster she moved, Ned gripping the sides of his seat.

"Here we go!" cried Tom, and the next instant they shot up into the air.

Ned Newton had ridden many times with his chum Tom, and the sensation of gliding through the upper regions was not new to him. But this time there was something different. The propellers seemed to take hold of the air with a firmer grip. There was more power, and certainly the speed was terrific.

"We're going fast!" yelled Ned into Tom's ear.

"That's right," agreed the young inventor. "She'll beat anything but my Sky Racer, and she'd do that if she was the same size." Tom referred to a very small aeroplane he had made some time before. It was like some big bird, and very swift.

Up and onward went the remodeled airship, faster and faster, until, when several miles had been covered, Ned realized that the young inventor had achieved another triumph.

"It's great, Tom! Great!" he yelled.

"Yes, I guess it will do, Ned. I'm satisfied. If there was an international meet now I'd capture some of the prizes. As it is—"

Tom stopped suddenly. His voice which had been raised to overcome the noise of even the muffled motor, sounded unnaturally loud, and no wonder, for the engine had ceased working!

"What's the matter?" gasped Ned.

"I don't know—a breakdown of some kind."

"Can you get it going again?"

"I'm going to try."

Tom was manipulating various levers, but with no effect. The aeroplane was shooting downward with frightful rapidity.

"No use!" exclaimed the young inventor. "Something has broken."

"But we're falling, Tom!"

"I know it. We've done it before. I'm going to volplane to earth."

This, it may be explained, is gliding downward from a height with the engine shut off. Aeroplanists often do it, and Tom was no novice at the art.

They shot downward with less speed now, for the young inventor had thrown up his headplanes to act as a sort of brake. Then, a little later they made a good landing in a field near a small house, in a rather lonely stretch of country, about ten miles from Shopton, where Tom lived.

"Now to see what the trouble is," remarked our hero, as he climbed out of his seat and began looking over the engine. He poked in among the numerous cogs, wheels and levers, and finally uttered an exclamation.

"Find it?" asked Ned.

"Yes, it's in the magneto. All the platinum bearings and contact surfaces have fused and crystallized. I never saw such poor platinum as I've been getting lately, and I pay the highest prices for it, too. The trouble is that the supply of platinum is giving out, and they'll have to find a substitute I guess."

"Can't we go home in her?" asked Ned.

"I'm afraid not. I've got to put in new platinum bearings and contacts before she'll spark. I only wish I could get hold of some of the better kind of metal."

The magneto of an aeroplane performs a service similar to one in an automobile. It provides the spark that explodes the charge of gas in the cylinders, and platinum is a metal, more valuable now than gold, much used in the delicate parts of the magneto.

"Well, I guess it's walk for ours," said Ned ruefully.

"I'm afraid so," went on Tom. "If I only had some platinum, I could—"

"Perhaps I could be of service to you," suddenly spoke a voice behind them, and turning, the youths saw a tall, bearded man, who had evidently come from the lonely house. "Did I hear you say you needed some platinum?" he asked. He spoke with a foreign accent, and Tom at once put him down for a Russian.

"Yes, I need some for my magneto," began the young inventor.

"If you will kindly step up to my house, perhaps I can give you what you want," went on the man. "My name is Ivan Petrofsky, and I have only lately come to live here."

"I'm Tom Swift, of Shopton, and this is my chum, Ned Newton," replied the young inventor, completing the introductions. He was wondering why the man, who seemed a cultured gentleman, should live in such a lonely place, and he was wondering too how he happened to have some platinum.

"Will that answer?" asked Mr. Petrofsky, when they had reached his house, and he had handed Tom several strips of the precious silverlike metal.

"Do? I should say it would! My, but that is the best platinum I've seen in a long while!" exclaimed Tom, who was an expert judge of this metal. "Where did you get it, if I may ask?"

"It came from a lost mine in Siberia," was the unexpected answer.

"A lost mine?" gasped Tom.

"In Siberia?" added Ned.

Mr. Petrofsky slowly nodded his head, and smiled, but rather sadly.

"A lost mine," he said slowly, "and if it could be found I would be the happiest man on earth for I would then be able to locate and save my brother, who is one of the Czar's exiles," and he seemed shaken by emotion.

Tom and Ned stood looking at the bearded man, and then the young inventor glanced at the platinum strips in his hand while a strange and daring thought came to him.

CHAPTER II

A DARING PROJECT

While Tom and his chum are in the house of the Russian, who so strangely produced the platinum just when it was most needed, I am going to take just a little time to tell you something about the hero of this story. Those who have read the previous books of this series need no introduction to him, but in justice to my new readers I must make a little explanation.

Tom Swift was an inventor, as was his father before him. But Mr. Swift was getting too old, now, to do much, though he had a pet invention—that of a gyroscope—on which he worked from time to time. Tom lived with his father in the village of Shopton, in New York state. His mother was dead, but a housekeeper, named Mrs. Baggert, looked after the wants of the inventors, young and old.

The first book of the series was called "Tom Swift and His Motor-Cycle," and in that I related how Tom bought the machine from a Mr. Wakefield Damon, of Waterford, after the odd gentleman had unintentionally started to climb a tree with it. That disgusted Mr. Damon with motorcycling, and Tom had lots of fun on the machine, and not a few daring adventures.

He and Mr. Damon became firm friends, and the oddity of the gentleman—mainly that of blessing everything he could think of—was no objection in Tom's mind. The young inventor and Ned Newton went on many trips together, Mr. Damon being one of the party.

In Shopton lived Andy Foger, a bullying sort of a chap, who acted very meanly toward Tom at times. Another resident of the town was a Mr. Nestor, but Tom was more interested in his daughter Mary than in the head of the household. Add Eradicate Sampson, an eccentric colored man who said he got his name because he "eradicated" dirt, and his mule, Boomerang, and I think you have met the principal characters of these stories.

After Tom had much enjoyment out of his motor-cycle, he got a motor boat, and one of his rivals on Lake Carlopa was this same Andy Foger, but our hero vanquished him. Then Tom built an airship, which had been the height of his ambition for some years. He had a stirring cruise in the Red Cloud, and then, deserting the air for the water, Tom and his father built a submarine, in which they went after sunken treasure. In the book, "Tom Swift and His Electric Runabout," I told how, in the speediest car on the road, Tom saved his father's bank from ruin, and in the book dealing with Tom's wireless message I related how he saved the Castaways of Earthquake Island.

When Tom went among the diamond makers, at the request of Mr. Barco Jenks, and discovered the secret of phantom mountain the lad fancied that might be the end of his adventures, but there were more to follow. Going to the caves of ice, his airship was wrecked, but he and his friends managed to get back home, and then it was that the young inventor perfected his sky racer, in which he made the quickest flight on record.

Most startling were his adventures in elephant land whither he went with his electric rifle, and he was the means of saving a missionary, Mr. Illingway and his wife, from the red pygmies.

Tom had not been home from Africa long before he got a letter from this missionary, telling about an underground city in Mexico that was said to be filled with gold. Tom went there, and in the book, entitled, "Tom Swift in the City of Gold," I related his adventures.

How he and his friends were followed by the Fogers, how they eluded them, made their way to the ruined temple in a small dirigible balloon, descended to the secret tunnel, managed to turn aside the underground river, and reach the city of gold with its wonderful gold statues—all this is told in the volume.

Then, after pulling down, in the centre of the underground city, the big golden statue, the door of rock descended, and made our friends prisoners. They almost died, but Andy Foger and his father, in league with some rascally Mexicans and a tribe of head-hunters, finally made their way to the tunnel, and most unexpectedly, released Tom and his friends.

There was a fight, but our hero's party escaped with considerable gold and safely reached Shopton. Now, after a winter spent in work, fixing over an old aeroplane, we again meet Tom.

"Would you mind telling me something about where this platinum comes from, and if you can get any more of it?" asked Tom, after a pause, following the strange statement made by the Russian.

"I will gladly tell you the story," spoke Mr. Petrofsky, "for I am much interested in inventions, and I formerly did something in that line myself, and I have even made a small aeroplane, so you see I know the need of platinum in a high power magneto."

"But where did you get such pure metal?" asked Tom. "I have never seen it's equal."

"There is none like it in all the world," went on the Russian, "and perhaps there never can be any more. I have only a small supply. But in Siberia—in the lost mine—there is a large quantity of it, as pure as this, needing only a little refining."

"Can't we get some from there?" asked the young inventor eagerly. "I should think the Russian government would mine it, and export it."

"They would—if they could find it," said Ivan Petrofsky dryly, "but they can't—no one can find it—and I have tried very hard—so hard, in fact, that it is the reason for my coming to this country—that and the desire to find and aid my brother, who is a Siberian exile."

"This is getting interesting," remarked Ned to Tom in a low voice, and the young inventor nodded.

"My brother Peter, who is younger than I by a few years, and I, are the last of our family," began Mr. Petrofsky, motioning Tom and Ned to take chairs. "We lived in St. Petersburg, and early in life, though we were of the nobility, we took up the cause of the common people."

"Nihilists?" asked Ned eagerly, for he had read something of these desperate men.

"No, and not anarchists," said Mr. Petrofsky with a sad smile. "Our party was opposed to violence, and we depended on education to aid our cause. Then, too, we did all we could in a quiet way to help the poor. My brother and I invented several life-saving and labor-saving machines and in this way we incurred the enmity of the rich contractors and government officials, who made more money the more people they could have working for them, for they made the people buy their food and supplies from them.

"But my brother, and I persisted, with the result that we were both arrested, and, with a number of others were sent to Siberia.

"Of the horrors we endured there I will say nothing. However, you have probably read much. In the country near which we were quartered there were many mines, some of salt and some of sulphur. Oh, the horrors of those mines! Many a poor exile has been lost in the windings of a salt mine, there to die miserably. And in the sulphur mines many die also, not from being lost so much as being overcome by stifling gases. It is terrible! And sometimes they are purposely abandoned by their guides, for the government wants to get rid of certain exiles.

"But you are interested in platinum. One day my brother and I who had been sent to work in the salt mines, mistook a turning and wandered on and on for several miles, finally losing our way. We had food and water with us, or we would have perished, and, as it was, we nearly died before we finally found our way out of an abandoned opening.

"We came out in the midst of a terrible snowstorm, and wandered about almost frozen. At last we were found by a serf who, in his sled, took us to his poor cottage. There we were warmed and fed back to life.

"We knew we would be searched for, as naturally, our absence would lead to the suspicion that we had tried to escape. So as soon as we were able, we started back to the town where we were quartered. The serf wanted to take us in his sled, but we knew he might be suspected of having tried to aid us to get away, and he might be arrested. So we went alone.

"As might have been expected, we became lost again, and wandered about for several days. But we had enough food to keep us alive. And it was during this wandering that I came upon the platinum mine. It was down in a valley, in the midst of a country densely wooded and very desolate. There was an outcropping of the ore, and rather idly I put some of it in my pockets. Then we wandered on, and finally after awful suffering in terrific storms, were found by a searching party and brought back to the barracks."

"Did they think you had escaped?" asked Tom.

"They did," replied the Russian, "and they punished us severely for it, in spite of our denials. In time I managed secretly to smelt the platinum ore, and I found I had some of the purest metal I had ever seen. I was wishing I could find the mine, or tell some of my friends about it, when one of the officers discovered the metal in my bed.

"He demanded to know where I had gotten it, and knowing that refusal would only make it the worse for me I told him. There was considerable excitement, for the value of the discovery was recognized, and a search was at once made for the mine.

"But, even with the aid we were able to give, it could not be located. Many expeditions went out to hunt for it but came back baffled. They could not penetrate that wild country."

"They should have used an aeroplane," suggested Tom.

"They did," replied the Russian quickly, "but it was of no use."

"Why not?" the young inventor wanted to know.

"Because of the terrific winds that almost continually sweep over that part of Siberia. They never seem to cease, and there are treacherous air currents and 'pockets' that engulfed more than one luckless aviator. Oh, you may be sure the Russian government spared no means of finding the lost platinum mine, but they could not locate it, or even get near the place where they supposed it to be.

"Then, perhaps thinking that my brother and I were concealing something, they separated us. Where they sent him I do not know, but I was doomed to the sulphur mines. I was heartbroken, and I scarcely cared whether I lived or died. But an opportunity of escape came, and I took it. I wanted to save my brother, but I did not know where he was, and I thought if I could make my way to some civilized country, or to free America, I might later be able to save my brother.

"I went to England, taking some of my precious platinum with me, and stayed there for two years. I learned your language, but my efforts to organize an expedition to search for the lost mine, and for my brother, failed. Then I came here, and—well, I am still trying."

"My! That is certainly interesting!" exclaimed Ned, who had been all attention during the telling of the story.

"And you certainly had a hard time," declared Tom. "I am much obliged for this platinum. Have you set a price on it? It is worth much more than the ordinary kind."

"The price is nothing to you," replied the Russian, with a smile. "I am only too glad to help you fix your aeroplane. Will it take long? I should like to watch you."

"Come along," invited Tom. "I can soon have it going again, and I'll give you a ride, if you like."

"No, thank you, I'm hardly up to that yet, though I may be some day. The machine I made never flew well and I had several bad falls."

Tom and Ned worked rapidly on the magneto, and soon had replaced the defective bits of platinum.

"If the Russians had such a machine as this maybe they could have gotten to that mine," suggested Ned, who was very proud of Tom's craft.

"It would be useless in the terrific winds, I fear," answered Ivan Petrofsky. "But now I care little for the mine. It is my brother whom I want to save. He must be in some of the Siberian mines, and if I had such a craft as this I might be able to rescue him."

Tom Swift dropped the file he was using. A bright light sparkled in his eyes. He seemed strangely excited.

"Mr. Petrofsky!" he cried, "would you let me have a try at finding your brother, and would you come with me?"

"Would I?" asked the Russian eagerly. "I would be your debtor for life, and I would always pray for you, if you could help me to save my brother Peter."

"Then we'll have a try at it!" cried Tom. "I've got a different airship than this—one in which I can travel three thousand miles without coming down. I haven't had any excitement since I got back from the city of gold. I'm going to Russia to help you rescue your brother from exile, and I'm also going to have a try for that lost platinum treasure!"

"Thank heaven, there is some hope for poor Peter at last," murmured Mr. Petrofsky earnestly.

"You never can get to the platinum mine," said Ned. "The winds will tear your airship to pieces."

"Not the kind I'm going to make," declared Tom. "It's going to be an air glider, that will fairly live on high winds. Ho! for Siberia and the platinum mines. Will you come?"

"I don't know what you mean by an air glider, Tom Swift, but I'll go to help rescue my brother," was the quick answer, and then, with the light of a daring resolve shining in his eyes, the young inventor proceeded to get his aeroplane in shape for the trip back to Shopton.

CHAPTER III

THE HAND OF THE CZAR

"Then you won't take a ride with me today?" asked the young inventor, of the Russian, as he completed the repairs to the magneto. "I'd like to have you meet my father, and a friend of his, Mr. Damon. Most likely he'll go to Siberia with us, if his wife will let him. I'd like to talk some plans over with you."

"I shall certainly call on you," answered Ivan Petrofsky, "but," he added with a smile, "I think I should prefer to take my first ride in your larger airship—the one that doesn't come down so often."

"Well, perhaps it is a little easier on an amateur," admitted Tom. "If you'll come over to our house at any time I'll take you out in it, or I'll call for you."

"I'll come over in a few days," answered the escaped exile. "Then I'll tell you all I know of the locality where the platinum mine is located, and we can make our plans. In the meanwhile don't say anything about what I have told you."

"Why?" asked Ned quickly.

Mr. Petrofsky approached closer to the lads, and in a low voice said:

"I am not sure about it, but of late I think I have been shadowed. I have seen strange men in the village near here and they have eyed me rather suspiciously. Then, too, I have surprised several men around my house. I live here all alone, you know, and do most of my own work, a woman coming in occasionally to clean. But I don't like these suspicious characters hanging about.

"Who do you think they are?" asked Tom

"I'm almost afraid to think, but from my past experience I think— nay, I fear—they may be spies, or agents of the Russian government."

"Spies!" cried Ned.

"Hush. Not so loud," cautioned Mr. Petrofsky. "They may even now be in hiding, especially since your aeroplane landed so near my house. They may see something suspicious even in that."

"But why should the Russian government set spies on you?" asked Tom in a low voice.

"For two reasons. I am an escaped exile, and I am not a citizen of the United States. Therefore I may be sent back to the sulphur mines. And another reason is that they may think I know the secret of the platinum treasure—the lost mine."

"Say this is getting interesting!" exclaimed Tom. "If we are going to have a brush with some of the spies of the Russian government so much the better. I'm ready for 'em!"

"So am I!" added Ned.

"You don't know them," said Mr. Petrofsky, and he could not repress a shudder. "I hope they are not on my trail, but if they are—" he paused a moment, straightened himself up, and looked like what he was, a strong man—"if they are let them look out. I'd give my life to save my brother from the awful, living death to which he is consigned!"

"And we're with you!" cried Tom, offering the Russian his hand. "We'll turn the trick yet. Now don't forget to come and see us. Come along, Ned. If I'm going to build an air glider I've got to get busy." And waving farewells to their new friend, the lads took their places in the aeroplane and were soon on their way to Shopton.

"Well, what do you think of it?" asked Ned of his chum, as they sped along at a good elevation, the engine going at half speed to be less noisy and make talking easier.

"Lots. I think we're in for a good time, an exciting one, anyhow, if what he says is true. But what in the world is an air glider, Tom?"

"It's the last word in aeroplanes. You don't need a motor to make it go."

"Don't need a motor?"

"No, the wind does it all. It's a sort of aeroplane, but the motion comes from the wind, acting on different planes, and this is accomplished by shifting weights. In it you can stand still in a fierce gale, if you like."

"How, by tying her fast on the ground?"

"No, hovering in the air. It's all done by getting the proper balance. The harder the wind blows the better the air glider works, and that's why I think it will be just the thing for Siberia. I'm going to get right at work on it, and you'll help me; won't you?"

"I sure will. Say, is platinum worth much?"

"Worth much? I should say it was! It's got gold beat now, and the available supply is very small, and it's getting more scarce. Russia has several mines, and the metal is of good quality. I've used some Russian platinum, but the kind Mr. Petrofsky gave me today was better than the best I ever had. If we can only find that lost mine we'll be millionaires all right."

"That's what we thought when we found the city of gold, but the gold wasn't of as fine a grade as we hoped."

"Well, nothing like that can happen in this platinum deal. It sure is rich ore that Mr. Petrofsky and his brother found. Poor fellow! To think of being an exile in that awful country, not knowing where you may be sent next. No wonder Mr. Petrofsky wants to rescue him."

"That's right. Well, here we are. I wonder what your father will say when he hears you're thinking of another expedition, Tom?"

"Oh, he'll want me to go when he hears about the exile."

"And I'm sure my folks will let me go. How about Mr. Damon?"

"I don't believe we can hold him back. It will make a nice party, just you and I, and Mr. Damon and Mr. Petrofsky. That will leave room for the other Russian—if we can rescue him," and with that Tom shut off the engine and glided to earth.

It may well be imagined that Mr. Swift was surprised when his son told him the latest news, but he did not offer any serious objection to the young inventor going to Siberia.

"Only you must be careful," he said. "Those Russian officers are ugly when it comes to trying to take away any of their prisoners. And this air glider—I don't exactly know about that. It's a new machine, and you want to be sure it works before you trust yourself to it."

"I will," promised Tom. "Say, I've got plenty of work ahead of me,— to get my big airship in shape, and build the glider. You'll have to help me, dad."

"I will, son. Now tell me more about this Mr. Petrofsky." Which Tom did.

The days that followed were indeed busy ones for Tom. The young inventor made a model air glider that sailed fairly well, but he knew it would have to work better to be successful, and he bent all his energies in that direction. Meanwhile Mr. Damon had been told of the prospective trip.

"Bless my bank book! Of course I'll go," he said. "But don't say anything about it to my wife—that is, just yet. I'll bring her around to it gradually. She has always wanted a diamond ring set in platinum, and now I can get it for her. I know she'll let me go if I break it to her gently."

It may be mentioned here that many valuable diamonds are now set in platinum instead of gold.

"I want to keep busy," said Mr. Damon, so Tom set him, Ned and Eradicate at the task of getting the big airship in shape for the trip. This air craft has not figured in any of my previous stories, but as it is so nearly like the one that was crushed in the caves of ice, I will not give a description of it here. Those who care to may refer to the book telling of Tom's trip to the caves of ice for a detailed account of the craft.

Sufficient to say that this latest airship, named the Falcon, was the largest Tom had ever built. It contained much room, many comforts, and could sail for several thousand miles without descending, except in case of accident. It was a combined dirigible balloon and aeroplane, and could be used as either, the necessary gas being made on board. It was large enough to enable the air glider to be taken on it in sections.

It was about a week after their first meeting with him, that Ivan Petrofsky paid a visit to the Swift home. He was warmly welcomed by the aged inventor and Mr. Damon, and, closeted in the library of the house, he proceeded to go more into details of his own and his brother's exile to Siberia, and to tell about the supposed location of the lost platinum mine.

"I don't believe we can start for several weeks yet," said Tom, after some discussion. "It will take me that long to make the glider."

"And I, too, need a little time," said the Russian. "I will write to some friends in St. Petersburg and perhaps they can get some information for us, as to where my brother is.

"That will be good," declared Mr. Damon. "Bless my icicle! But the more I think of this trip the better I like it!"

It was arranged that the Russian should call again soon, when the plans would be nearer in shape, and in the meanwhile he must learn all he could from revolutionary friends in Siberia.

It was a week after this, during which Tom, Ned and the others had been very busy, that Tom decided to take a trip to see their Russian friend. They had not heard from him since his visit, and Tom wanted to learn something about the strength of the Siberian winds.

He and Ned went in one of the small airships and soon they were hovering over the grounds surrounding the lonely house where Ivan Petrofsky lived.

"He doesn't seem to be at home," remarked Ned, as they descended and approached the dwelling.

"No, and it looks quite deserted," agreed the young inventor. "Say, all the doors are open, too! He shouldn't go away and leave his house open like that—with the valuable platinum there."

"Maybe he's asleep," suggested Ned.

They knocked on the opened door, but there was no answer. Then they went inside. To their surprise the house was in confusion. Furniture was overturned, tables and chairs were broken, and papers were scattered about the room.

"There's been a fight here!" cried Tom.

"That's right," agreed Ned. "Maybe he's been hurt—maybe burglars came for the platinum!"

"Come on!" cried Tom, making a dash for the stairs. "We'll see if he's here."

The house was small, and it took but a moment to show that Mr. Petrofsky was not there. Upstairs, as below, was the same confusion—the overturned furniture and the papers scattered about.

Tom stooped and picked up a scrap that looked like a piece torn from a letter. On top was a seal—the black seal of Russia—the imperial arms of the Czar!

"Look!" cried Tom, holding out the paper.

"What is it?" asked Ned.

"The hand of the Czar!" answered his chum. "It has reached out from Russia, and taken Mr. Petrofsky away!"

CHAPTER IV

THE SEARCH

For a moment Ned could scarcely understand what Tom meant. It scarcely seemed possible that such a thing could happen. That some one in far-off Russia—be it the Czar or one of the secret police—could operate from such a distance, seeking out a man in an obscure house in a little American village, and snatching him away.

"It isn't possible!" declared Ned breathlessly.

"What difference does that make?" asked Tom. "The thing has happened, and you can't get out of it. Look at all the evidence—there's been a fight, that's sure, and Mr. Petrofsky is gone."

"But maybe he went away of his own accord," insisted Ned, who was sometimes hard to convince.

"Nonsense! If a man went away of his own accord would he smash up his furniture, leave his papers scattered all about and go off leaving the doors and windows open for any one to walk in? I guess not."

"Well, maybe you're right. But think of it! This isn't Russia!"

"No, but he's a Russian subject, and, by his own confession an escaped exile. If he was arrested in the usual way he could be taken back, and our government couldn't interfere. He's been taken back all right. Poor man! Think of being doomed to those sulphur mines again, and as he escaped they'll probably make it all the harder for him!"

"But I thought our government wouldn't help other nations to get back prisoners convicted of political crimes," suggested Ned. "That's all Mr. Petrofsky was guilty of—politics, trying to help the poor in his own country. It's a shame if our government stands for anything like that!"

"That's just the point!" exclaimed Tom. "Probably the spies, secret police, or whoever the Russian agents were, didn't ask any help from our government. If they did there might be a chance for him. But likely they worked in secret. They came here, sneaked in on him, and took him away before he could get help. Jove! If he could only have gotten word to me I'd have come in the airship, and then there'd be a different ending to this."

"I guess you're right, Tom. Well, that ends it I suppose."

"Ends what?"

"Our trip to the platinum mine."

"Not a bit of it. I'm going to have a hunt for it."

"But how can you when Mr. Petrofsky can't go along to show us the way? Besides, we wanted to help rescue his brother, and now we can't."

"Well, I'm going to make a big try," declared the young inventor firmly. "And the first thing I'm going to do is to get our friend out of the clutches of the Russian police."

"You are? How?"

"I'm going to make a search for him. Look here, Ned, he must have been taken away some time today—perhaps only a few hours ago—and they can't have gone far with him."

"How do you make that out?" Ned wanted to know.

"Well, I guess I'm detective enough for that," and Tom smiled. "Look here, the doors and windows are open. Now it rained last night, and there was quite a wind. If the windows had been open in the storm there'd be some traces of moisture in the rooms. But there isn't a drop. Consequently the windows have been opened since last night."

"Say, that's so!" cried Ned admiringly.

"But that's not all," went on Tom. "Here's a bottle of milk on the table, and it's fresh," which he proved by tasting it. "Now that was left by the milkman either late last night or early this morning. I don't believe it's over twelve hours old."

"Well, what does this mean?" asked Ned, who couldn't quite follow Tom's line of reasoning.

"To my mind it means that the spies were here no later than this morning. Look at the table upset, the dishes on the floor. Here's one with oatmeal in it, and you know how hard and firm cooked oatmeal gets after it stands a bit. This is quite fresh, and soft, and—"

"And that means—" interrupted Ned, who was in turn interrupted by Tom, who exclaimed:

"It means that Mr. Petrofsky was at breakfast when they burst in on him, and took him away. They had hard work overpowering him, I'll wager, for he could put up a pretty good fight. And the broken furniture is evidence of that. Then the spies, after tying him up, or putting him in a carriage, searched the house for incriminating papers. That's as plain as the nose on your face. Then the police agents, or whoever they were, skipped out in a hurry, not taking the trouble to close the windows and doors."

"I believe it did happen that way," agreed Ned, who clearly saw what Tom meant. "But what can we do? How can we find him?"

"By getting on the trail," answered his chum quickly. "There may be more clues in the house, and I'm sure there'll be some out of doors, for they must have left footprints or the marks of carriage wheels. We'll take a look, and then we'll get right on the search. I'm not going to let them take Mr. Petrofsky to Russia if I can help it. I want to get after that platinum, and he's the only one who can pilot us anywhere near the place; and besides, there's his brother we've got to rescue. We'll make a search for the exile."

"I'm with you!" cried Ned. "Jove! Wouldn't it be great if we could rescue him? They can't have gotten very far with him."

"I'm afraid they have quite a start on us," admitted Tom with a dubious shake of his head, "but as long as they're in the United States we have a chance. If ever they get him on Russian soil it's all up with him."

"Come on then!" cried Ned. "Let's get busy. What's the first thing to do?"

"Look for clues," replied Tom. "We'll begin at the top of the house and work down. It's lucky we came when we did, for every minute counts."

Then the two plucky lads began their search for the kidnapped Russian exile. Had those who took him away seen the mere youths who thus devoted themselves to the task, they might have laughed in contempt, but those who know Tom Swift and his sturdy chum, know that two more resourceful and brave lads would be hard to find.

CHAPTER V

A CLUE FROM RUSSIA

"Nothing much up here," remarked Tom, when he and Ned had gone all over the second floor twice. "That scrap of paper, which put me on to the fact that some one from the Russian government had been here, is about all. They must have taken all the documents Mr. Petrofsky had."

"Maybe he didn't have any," suggested Ned.

"If he was wise he'd get rid of them when he knew he was being shadowed, as he told us. Perhaps that was why they broke up the furniture, searching for hidden papers, or they may have done it out of spite because they didn't find anything. But we might as well go downstairs and look there."

But the first floor was equally unproductive of clues, save those already noted, which showed, at least so Tom believed, that Mr. Petrofsky had been surprised and overpowered while at breakfast.

"Now for outside!" cried the young inventor. "We'll see if we can figure out how they got him away."

There were plenty of marks in the soft ground and turf, which was still damp from the night's rain, though it was now afternoon. Unfortunately, however, in approaching the house after leaving the aeroplane, Ned and Tom had not thought to exercise caution, and, not suspecting anything wrong, they had stepped on a number of footprints left by the kidnappers.

But for all that, they saw enough to convince them that several men had been at the lonely house, for there were many marks of shoes. It was out of the question, however, to tell which were those of Mr. Petrofsky and which those of his captors.

"They might have carried him out to a carriage they had in waiting," suggested Ned. "Let's go out to the front gate and look in the road. They hardly would bring the carriage up to the door."

"Good idea," commented Tom, and they hurried to the main thoroughfare that passed the Russian's house.

"Here they are!" cried Ned, Who was in the lead. "There's been a carriage here as sure as you're a foot high and it's a rubber-tired one too."

"GOOD!" cried Tom admiringly. "You're coming right along in your detective training. How do you make that out?"

"See here, where a piece of rubber has been broken or cut out of the tire. It makes a peculiar mark in the dirt every time the wheel goes around."

"That's right, and it will be a good thing to trace the carriage by. Come on, we'll keep right after it."

"Hold on a bit," suggested Ned, who, though not so quick as Tom Swift, frequently produced good results by his very slowness. "Are you going off and leave the airship here for some one to walk off with?"

"Guess they wouldn't take it far," replied the young inventor, "but I'd better make it safe. I'll disconnect it so they can't start it, though if Andy Foger happens to come along he might slash the planes just out of spite. But I guess he won't show up."

Tom took a connecting pin out of the electrical apparatus, making it impossible to start the aeroplane, and then, wheeling it out of sight behind a small barn, he and Ned went back to the carriage marks in the road.

"Hurry!" urged Tom, as he started off in the direction of the village of Hurdtown, near where the cottage stood. "We will ask people living along the highway if they've seen a carriage pass."

"But what makes you think they went off that way?" asked Ned. "I should think they'd head away from the village, so as not to be seen."

"No, I don't agree with you. But wait, we'll look at the marks. Maybe that will help us."

Peering carefully at the marks of horses' hoofs and the wheel impressions, Tom uttered a cry of discovery.

"I have it!" he declared. "The carriage came from the village, and kept right on the other way. You're right, Ned. They didn't go back to town.

"Are you sure?"

"Of course. You can see for yourself; if the carriage had turned around the track would show, but it doesn't and, even if they turned on the grass, there'd be two lines of marks—one coming out here and one returning. As it is there is only a single set—just as if the carriage drove up here, took on its load, and continued on. This way, Ned."

They hurried down the road, and soon came to a cluster of farm houses. Inquiries there, however, failed to bring anything to light, for either the occupants of the house had failed to notice passing vehicles, or there had been so many that any particular carriage was not recalled. And there were now so many impressions in the soft dirt of the highway—so many wheel tracks and hoof imprints—that it was impossible to pick out those of the carriage with the cut rubber tire. "Well, I guess it isn't of much use to go on any farther," spoke Ned, when they had traveled several miles and had learned nothing.

"We'll try one more house, and then go back," agreed Tom. "We'll tell dad about what's happened, and see what he says."

"Carriage?" repeated an old farmer to whom they next put the question. "Wa'al, now, come t' think of it, I did see one drivin' along here early this morning. It had rubber tires on too, for I recollect remarkin' t' myself that it didn't make much noise. Had t' talk t' myself," he added in explanation, "'cause nobody else in the family was up, 'ceptin' th' dog."

"Did the carriage have some Russians in it?" asked Tom eagerly, "and was one a big bearded man?"

"Wa'al, now you've got me," admitted the farmer frankly. "It was quite early you see, and I didn't take no particular notice. I got up early t' do my milkin' 'cause I have t' take it t' th' cheese factory. That's th' reason nobody was up but me. But I see this carriage comin' down th' road, and thinks I t' myself it was pretty middlin' early fer anybody t' be takin' a pleasure ride. I 'lowed it were a pleasure ride, 'cause it were one of them hacks that folks don't usually use 'ceptin' fer a weddin', or a funeral, an' it wa'n't no funeral."

"Then you can't tell us anything more except that it passed?" asked Ned.

"No, I couldn't see inside, 'cause it was rather dark at that hour, and then, too, I noticed that they had th' window shades down."

"That's suspicious!" exclaimed Tom. "I believe they are the fellows we re after," and, without giving any particulars he said that they were looking for a friend who might have been taken away against his will.

"Could you tell where they were going?" asked Tom, scarcely hoping to get an affirmative answer.

"Wa'al, th' man on th' seat pulled up when he see me," spoke the farmer with exasperating slowness, "an' asked me how far it was t' th' Waterville station, an' I told him."

"Why didn't you say so at first?" asked Tom quickly. "Why didn't you tell us they were heading for the railroad?"

"You didn't ask me," replied the farmer. "What difference does it make."

"Every minute counts!" exclaimed the young inventor. "We want to keep right after those fellows. Maybe the agent can tell us where they bought tickets to, and we can trace them that way.

"Shouldn't wonder," commented the farmer. "There ain't many trains out from Waterville at that time of day, an' mighty few passengers. Shouldn't wonder but Jake Applesauer could put ye on th' trail."

"Much obliged," called Tom. "Come on, Ned," and he started back in the direction of the house where the kidnapping had taken place.

"That ain't th' way t' 'vaterville!" the farmer shouted after them.

"I know it, we're going to get our airship," answered Tom, and then he heard the farmer mutter.

"Plumb crazy! That's what they be! Plumb crazy! Going after their airship! Shouldn't wonder but they was escaped lunatics, and the other fellers was keepers after 'em. Hu! Wa'al, I've got my work to do. 'Tain't none of my affair."

"Let him think what he likes," commented Ned as he and his chum hurried on. "We're on the trail all right."

If Jake Applesauer, the agent at the Waterville station, was surprised at seeing two youths drop down out of an aeroplane, and begin questioning him about some suspicious strangers that had taken the morning train, he did not show it. Jake prided himself on not being surprised at anything, except once when he took a counterfeit dollar in return for a ticket, and had to make it good to the company.

But, to the despair of Tom and Ned, he could not help them much. He had seen the party, of course. They had driven up in the hack, and one of the men seemed to be sick, or hurt, for his head was done up in bandages, and the others had to half carry him on the train.

"That was Mr. Petrofsky all right," declared Ned.

"Sure," assented Tom. "They must have hurt and drugged him. But you can't tell us for what station they bought tickets, Mr. Applesauer?"

"No, for they didn't buy any. They must have had 'em, or else they paid on the train. One man drove off in the coach, and that's all I know."

As Tom and Ned started back to Shopton in the aeroplane they discussed what could be done next. A hard task lay before them, and they realized that.

"They could have gotten off at any station between here and New York, or even changed to another railroad at the junction," spoke Tom. "It's going to be a hard job."

"Guess we'll have to get some regular detectives on it," suggested Ned.

"And that's what I'll do," declared the young inventor. "They may be able to locate Mr. Petrofsky before those spies take him out of this country. If they don't—it will be too late. I'm going to talk to dad about it, and if he agrees I'll hire the best private detectives."

Mr. Swift gave his consent when Tom had told the story, and, a day later, one of the best detectives of a well known agency called on Tom in Shopton and assumed charge of the case.

The early reports from the detective were quite reassuring. He got on the trail of the men who had taken Mr. Petrofsky away, and confirmed the suspicion that they were agents of the Russian police. He trailed them as far as New York, and there the clues came to an end.

"Whether they are in the big city, which might easily be, or in some of the nearby towns, will take some time to learn," the detective wrote, and Tom wired back telling him to keep on searching.

But, as several weeks went by, and no word came, even Tom began to give up hope, though he did not stop work on the air glider, which was nearing completion. And then, most unexpectedly a clue came—a clue from far-off Russia.

Tom got a letter one day—a letter in a strange hand, the stamp and postmark showing that it had come from the land of the Czar.

"What do you suppose it contains?" asked Ned, who was with his chum when the communication was received.

"Haven't the least idea; but I'll soon find out."

"Maybe it's from the Russian police, telling you to keep away from Siberia."

"Maybe," answered Tom absently, for he was reading the missive. "I say!" he suddenly cried. "This is great! A clue at last, and from St. Petersburg! Listen to this, Ned!

"This letter is from the head of one of the secret societies over there, a society that works against the government. It says that Mr. Petrofsky is being detained a prisoner in a lonely hut on the Atlantic sea coast, not far from New York—Sandy Hook the letter says—and here are the very directions how to get there!"

"No!" cried Ned, in disbelief. "How in the world could anybody in Russia know that."

"It tells here," said Tom. "It's all explained. As soon as the secret police got Mr. Petrofsky they communicated with the head officials in St. Petersburg. You know nearly everyone is a spy over there, and the letter says that Mr. Petrofsky's friends there soon heard the news, and even about the exact place where he is being held."

"What are they holding him for?" asked Ned.

"That's explained, too. It seems they can't legally take him back until certain papers are received from his former prison in Siberia, and those are now on the way. His friends write to me to hasten and rescue him."

"But how did they ever get your address?"

"That's easy, though you wouldn't think so. It seems, so the letter explains, that as soon as Mr. Petrofsky got acquainted with us he wrote to friends in St. Petersburg, giving my address, and telling them, in case anything ever happened to him, to notify us. You see he suspected that something might, after he found he was being shadowed that way.

"And it all worked out. As soon as his friends heard that he was caught, and learned where he was being held, they wrote to me. Hurrah, Ned! A clue at last! Now to wire the detective—no, hold on, we'll go there and rescue him ourselves! We'll go in the airship, and pick up Detective Trivett in New York."

"That's the stuff! I'm with you!"

"Bless my suspender buttons! So am I, whatever it is!" cried Mr. Damon, entering the room at that moment.

CHAPTER VI

RESCUING MR. PETROFSKY

"We ought to be somewhere near the place now, Tom."

"I think we are, Ned. But you know I'm not going too close in this airship."

"Bless my silk hat!" exclaimed Mr. Damon. "I hope we don't have to walk very far in such a deserted country as this, Tom Swift."

"We'll have to walk a little way, Mr. Damon," replied the young inventor. "If I go too close to the hut they'll see the airship, and as those spies probably know that Mr. Petrofsky has been dealing with me, They'd smell a rat at once, and run away, taking him with them, and we'd have all our work to do over again."

"That's right," agreed Detective Trivett, who was one of the four in the airship that was now hovering over the Atlantic coast, about ten miles below the summer resorts of which Asbury Park was one.

It was only a few hours after Tom had received the letter from Russia informing him of the whereabouts of the kidnapped Russian, and he had acted at once.

His father sanctioned the plan of going to the rescue in one of Tom's several airships and, Mr. Damon, having been on hand, at once agreed to go. Of course Ned went along, and they had picked up the private detective in New York, where he was vainly seeking a clue to the whereabouts of Mr. Petrofsky.

Now the young inventor and his friends were hovering over the sandy stretch of coast that extends from Sandy Hook down the Atlantic seaboard. They were looking for a small fishing hamlet on the outskirts of which, so the Russian letter stated, was situated the lonely hut in which Mr. Petrofsky was held a prisoner.

"Do you think you can pick it out from a distance, Tom?" asked Mr. Damon, as the airship floated slowly along. It was not the big one they intended taking on their trip to Siberia, but it was sufficiently large to accommodate the four and leave room for Mr. Petrofsky, should they succeed in rescuing him.

"I think so," answered the young inventor.

In the letter from Russia a comparatively accurate description of the prisoner's hut had been given, and also some details about his guards. For there is little goes on in political circles in the realm of the Czar that is not known either to the spies of the government or those of the opposition, and the latter had furnished Tom with reliable information.

"That looks like the place," said Tom at length, when, after peering steadily through a powerful telescope, during which time Ned steered the ship, the young inventor "picked up" a fishing settlement. "There is the big fish house, spoken of in the letter," he went on, "and the Russians know a lot about fish. That house makes a good landmark. We'll go down now, before they have a chance to see us."

The others thought this a good idea, and a little later the airship sank to the ground amid a lonely stretch of sand dunes, about two miles from the hamlet on the outskirts of which the prison hut was said to be located.

"Now," said Tom, "we've got to decide on a plan of campaign. It won't do for all of us to go to the hut and make the rescue. Some one has got to stay with the airship, to be ready to start it off as soon as we come back with Mr. Petrofsky—if we do come.

"Then there's no use in me staying here," spoke Detective Trivett. "I don't know enough even to turn on the gasolene."

"No, it's got to be Ned or me," said the young inventor.

"I'll stay," volunteered Ned quickly, for though he would very much have liked to be in at the rescue, he realized that his place was in the airship, as Mr. Damon was not sufficiently familiar with the machinery to operate it.

Accordingly, after looking to everything to see that it was in working order, Tom led the advance. It was just getting dusk, and they figured on getting to the hut after dark.

"Have everything ready for a quick start," Tom said to Ned, "for we may come back running."

"I will," was the prompt answer, and then, getting their bearings, the little party set off.

They had to travel over a stretch of sandy waste that ran along the beach. Back in shore were a few scattered cottages, and not yet opened for the summer, and on the ocean side was the pounding surf. The hut, as Tom recalled the directions, lay just beyond a group of stunted hemlock trees that set a little way back from the ocean, on a bluff overlooking the sea. It was not near any other building.

Slowly, and avoiding going any nearer the other houses than they could help, the little party made its way. They had to depend on their own judgement now, for the minor details of the location of the hut could not be given in the letter from Russia. In fact the spies themselves, in writing to their head officers about the matter, had not described the location in detail.

"That looks like it over there," said Tom at last, when they had gone about a mile and a half, and saw a lonely hut with a light burning in it.

Cautiously they approached and, as they drew nearer, they saw that the light came through the window of a small hut.

"Looks like the place," commented the detective.

"We'll have a look," remarked Tom.

He crept up so he could glance in the window, and no sooner had he peered in, than he motioned for the others to approach.

Looking under a partly-drawn curtain, Mr. Damon and Mr. Trivett saw the Russian whom they sought. He was seated at a table, his head bowed on his hands, and in the room were three men. A rifle stood in one corner, near one of the guards.

"They're taking no chances," whispered Mr. Damon. "What shall we do, Tom?"

"It's three to three," replied the young inventor. "But if we can get him away without a fight, so much the better. I think I have it. I'll go up to the door, knock and make quite a racket, and demand admittance in the name of the Czar. That will startle them, and they may all three rush to answer. Mr. Damon, you and the detective will stay by the window. As soon as you see the men rush for the door, smash in the window with a piece of driftwood and call to Mr. Petrofsky to jump out that way. Then you can run with him toward the airship, and I'll follow. It may work."

"I don't see why it wouldn't," declared the detective. "Go ahead, Tom. We're ready."

Looking in once more, to make sure that the guards were not aware of the presence of the rescuing party, Tom went to the front door of the hut. It was a small building, evidently one used by fishermen.

Tom knocked loudly on the portal, at the same time crying out in a voice that he strove to make as deep and menacing as possible:

"Open! Open in the name of the Czar!"

Looking through the window, ready to act on the instant, Mr. Damon and the detective saw the three guards spring to their feet. One remained near Mr. Petrofsky, who also leaped up.

"Now!" called the detective to his companion. "Smash the window!"

The next instant a big piece of driftwood crashed through the casement, just as the two men were hurrying to the front door to answer Tom's summons.

"Mr. Petrofsky! This way!" yelled Mr. Damon, sticking his head in through the broken sash. "Come out! We've come to save you! Bless my putty blower, but this is great! Come on!"

For a moment the exile stared at the head thrust through the broken window, and he listened to Tom's emphatic knocks and demands. Then with a cry of delight the Russian sprang for the open casement, while the guard that had remained near him made a leap to catch him, crying out:

"Betrayed! Betrayed! It's the Nihilists! Look out, comrades!"

CHAPTER VII

THE AIR GLIDER

Mr. Damon continued to hammer away at the window sash with the piece of driftwood. There were splinters of the frame and jagged pieces of glass sticking out, making it dangerous for the exile to slip through.

"Come on! Come on!" the eccentric man continued to call. "Bless my safety valve! We'll save you! Come on!"

Mr. Petrofsky was leaping across the room, just ahead of the one guard. The other two were at the open door now, through which Tom could be seen. Then the spies, realizing in an instant that they had been deceived, made a dash after their comrade, who had his hand on the tails of the exile's coat.

"Break away! Break loose!" cried Mr. Damon, who, by this time had cleared the window so a person could get through. "Don't let them hold you!"

"I don't intend to!" retorted Mr. Petrofsky, and he swerved suddenly, tearing his coat, from the grasp of the guard.

In another instant the exile was at the casement, and was being helped through by Mr. Damon, and there was need of it, for the three guards were there now, doing their best to keep their prisoner.

"Pull away! Pull away!" cried Mr. Damon.

"We'll help you!" shouted Tom, who, now that his trick had worked, had sped around to the other side of the hut.

"Don't be afraid, we're with you!" exclaimed the detective, who was with the young inventor.

"Grab him! Keep him! Hold him!" fairly screamed the rearmost of the three guards. "It is a plot of the Nihilists to rescue him. Shoot him, comrades. He must not get away!"

"Don't you try any of your shooting games, or I'll take a hand in it!" shouted the detective, and, at the same moment he drew his revolver and fired harmlessly in the air.

"A bomb! A bomb!", yelled the guards in terror.

"Not yet, but there may be!" murmured Tom. The firing of the shot produced a good effect, for the three men who were trying to detain Ivan Petrofsky at once fell back from the window and gave him just the chance needed. He scrambled through, with the aid of Mr. Damon, and before the guards could again spring at him, which they did when the echoes of the shot had died away. They had realized, too late, that it was not a bomb, and that there was no immediate danger for them.

"Come on!" cried Tom. "Make for the airship! We've got to get the start of them!"

Leading the way, he sprinted toward the road that led to the place where the airship awaited them. He was followed by Mr. Damon and the detective, who had Mr. Petrofsky between them.

"Are you all right?" Tom called back to the exile. "Are you hurt? Can you run?"

"I'm all right," was the reassuring answer. "Go ahead; But they'll be right after us."

"Maybe they'll stop when they see this," remarked the detective significantly, and he held his revolver so that the rays of the newly-risen moon glinted on it.

"Here they come!" cried Tom a moment later, as three figures, one after the other, came around the corner of the house. They had not taken the shorter route through the window, as had Mr. Petrofsky, and this gained a little time for our friends.

"Stop! Hold on!" cried one of the guards in fairly good English. "That is our prisoner."

"Not any more!" the young inventor yelled back. "He's ours now."

"Look out! They're going to shoot!" cried Mr. Damon. "Bless my gunpowder! can't you stop them some way or other, Mr. Detective?"

"The only way is by firing first," answered Mr. Trivett, "and I don't want to hurt them. Guess I'll fire in the air again."

He did, and the guards halted. They seemed to be holding a consultation, as Tom learned by glancing hastily back, and he caught the glisten of some weapon. But if the three men had any notion of firing they gave it up, and once more came on running. Doubtless they had orders to get their prisoner back to Russia alive, and did not want to take any chances of hitting him.

"Leg it!" cried Tom. "Leg it!"

He was well ahead, and wanted the others to catch up to him, but none of the men was a good runner, and Mr. Petrofsky, by reason of being rather heavily built, was worse than the other two, so they had to accommodate their pace to his.

"I wonder if we can make it," mused Tom, as he realized that the airship was a good distance off yet the guards, though quite a way in the rear now were coming on fast. "It's going to be a close race," thought the young inventor. "I wish we'd brought the airship a little nearer."

It was indeed a race now, for the guards, seeming to know that they would not be shot at, were coming on more confidently, and were rapidly lessening the distance that separated them from their recent prisoner.

"We've got to go faster!" cried Tom.

"Bless my shoe leather!" yelled Mr. Damon. "I can't go any faster."

Still he did make the attempt, and so did the exile and the detective. Little was said now, for each of the parties was running a dogged race, and in silence. They had gone possibly half a mile, and the first advantage of Tom and his friends was rapidly being lost, when suddenly there sounded in the air above a curious throbbing noise.

"Bless my gasolene! What's that?" cried Mr. Damon.

"The airship! It's the airship!" yelled Tom, as he saw a great dark shape slowly approaching. "Ned is bringing her to met us."

"Good!" cried the detective. "We need it I'm about winded!"

"This way, Ned! This way!" cried Tom, and, an instant later, they were in the midst of a brilliant glow, for Ned had turned the current into the great searchlight on the bow of the air craft, and the beams were focused on our friends. Ned could now see the refugees, and in a moment he sent the graceful craft down, bringing it to a halt on the ground near Tom.

"In with you!" cried the lad. "She's all ready to start up again!"

"Come on!" yelled Tom to the others. "We're all right now, if you hustle!"

"Bless my pin cushion!" gasped Mr. Damon, making a final spurt.

The three guards had halted in confusion on seeing the big, black bulk of the airship, and when they noted the gleaming of the searchlight they must have realized that their chances were gone. They made a rush, however, but it was too late. Over the side of the craft scrambled Tom, Mr. Damon, the detective and Ivan Petrofsky, and an instant later Ned had sent it aloft. The race was over, and the young inventor and his friends had won.

"You're the stuff!" cried Tom to Ned, as he went with his chum to the pilot house to direct the progress of the airship. "It's lucky you came for us. We never could have made the distance. We left the ship too far off."

"That's what I thought after you'd gone," replied his chum. "So I decided to come and meet you. I had to go slowly so as not to pass you in the darkness."

They were speeding off now, and Ned, turning the beams of the great searchlight below them, picked up the three guards who were gazing helplessly aloft after their fast disappearing prisoner.

"You're having your first ride in an airship, Mr. Petrofsky," remarked Tom, when they had gone on for some little distance. "How do you like it?"

"I'm so excited I hardly know, but it's quite a sensation. But how in the world did you ever find me to rescue me?"

Then they told the story of their search, and the unexpected clue from Russia. In turn the exile told how he had been attacked at the breakfast table one morning by the three spies—the very men who had been shadowing him—and taken away secretly, being drugged to prevent his calling for help. He had been kept a close prisoner in the lonely hut, and each day he had expected to be taken back to serve out his sentence in Siberia.

"Another day would have been too late," he told Tom, when he had thanked the young inventor over and over again, "for the papers would have arrived, and the last obstacle to taking me back to Russia would have been removed. They dared not take me out of the United States without official documents, and they would have been forged ones, for they intended trumping up a criminal charge against me, the political one not being strong enough to allow them to extradite me."

"Well I'm glad we got you," said Tom heartily. "We will soon be ready to start for Siberia."

"In this kind of a craft?"

"Yes, only much larger. You'll like it. I only hope my air glider works."

By putting on speed, Tom was able to reach Shopton before midnight, and there was quite an informal celebration in the Swift homestead over the rescue of the exile. The detective, for whom there was no further need, was paid off, and Mr. Petrofsky was made a member of the household.

"You'd better stay here until we are ready to start," Tom said, "and then we can keep an eye on you. We need you to show us as nearly as possible where the platinum field is."

"All right," agreed the Russian with a laugh. "I'm sure I'll do all I can for you, and you are certainly treating me very nicely after what I suffered from my captors."

Tom resumed work on his air glider the next day, and he had an additional helper, for Mr. Petrofsky proved to be a good mechanic.

In brief, the air glider was like an aeroplane save that it had no motor. It was raised by a strong wind blowing against transverse planes, and once aloft was held there by the force of the air currents, just like a box kite is kept up. To make it progress either with or against the wind, there were horizontal and vertical rudders, and sliding weights, by which the equilibrium could be shifted so as to raise or lower it. While it could not exactly move directly against the wind it could progress in a direction contrary to which the gale was blowing, somewhat as a sailing ship "tacks."

And, as has been explained, the harder the wind blew the better the air glider worked. In fact unless there was a strong gale it would not go up.

"But it will be just what is needed out there in that part of Siberia," declared the exile, "for there the wind is never quiet. Often it blows a regular hurricane."

"That's what we want!" cried Tom. He had made several models of the air glider, changing them as he found out his errors, and at last he had hit on the right shape and size.

Midway of the big glider, on which work was now well started, there was to be an enclosed car for the carrying of passengers, their food and supplies. Tom figured on carrying five or six.

For several weeks the work on the air glider progressed rapidly, and it was nearing completion. Meanwhile nothing more had been heard or seen of the Russian spies.

"Well," announced Tom one night, after a day's hard work, "we'll be ready for a trial now, just as soon as there comes a good wind."

"Is it all finished?" asked Ned.

"No, but enough for a trial spin. What I want is a big wind now."

CHAPTER VIII

IN A GREAT GALE

There was a humming in the air. The telegraph wires that ran along on high poles past the house of Tom Swift sung a song like that of an Aeolian harp. The very house seemed to tremble.

"Jove! This is a wind!" cried Tom as he awakened on a morning a few days after his air glider was nearly completed. "I never saw it so strong. This ought to be just what I want I must telephone to Mr. Damon and to Ned."

He hustled into his clothes, pausing now and then to look out of his window and note the effects of the gale. It was a tremendous wind, as was evidenced by the limbs of several trees being broken off, while in some cases frail trees themselves had been snapped in twain.

"Coffee ready, Mrs. Baggert?" asked our hero as he went downstairs. "I haven't got time to eat much though."

In spite of his haste Tom ate a good breakfast and then, having telephoned to his two friends, and receiving their promises to come right over, our hero went out to make a few adjustments to his air glider, to get it in shape for the trial.

He was a little worried lest the wind die out, but when he got outside he noted with satisfaction that the gale was stronger than at first. In fact it did considerable damage in Shopton, as Tom learned later.

It certainly was a strong wind. An ordinary aeroplane never could have sailed in it, and Tom was doubtful of the ability of even his big airship to navigate in it. But he was not going to try that.

"And maybe my air glider won't work," he remarked to himself as he was on his way to the shed where it had been constructed. "The models went up all right, but maybe the big one isn't proportioned right. However, I'll soon see."

He was busy adjusting the balancing weights when Ned Newton came in.

"Great Scott!" exclaimed the lad, as he labored to close the shed door, "this is a blow all right, Tom! Do you think it's safe to go up?"

"I can't go up without a gale, Ned."

"Well, I'd think twice about it myself."

"Why, I counted on you going up with me."

"Burr-r-r-r!" and Ned pretended to shiver. "I haven't an accident insurance policy you know."

"You won't need it, Ned. If we get up at all we'll be all right. Catch hold there, and shift that rear weight a little forward on the rod. I expect Mr. Damon soon."

The eccentric man came in a little later, just as Tom and Ned had finished adjusting the mechanism.

"Bless my socks!" cried Mr. Damon. "Do you really mean to go up today, Tom?"

"I sure do! Why, aren't you going with me?" and Tom winked at Ned.

"Bless my—" began Mr. Damon, and then, evidently realizing that he was being tested he exclaimed: "Well, I will go, Tom! If the air glider is any good it ought to hold me. I will go up."

"Now, Ned, how about you?" asked the young inventor.

"Well, I guess it's up to me to come along, but I sure do wish it was over with," and Ned glanced out of the window to see if the gale was dying out. But the wind was as high as ever.

It was hard work getting the air glider out of the shed, and in position on top of a hill, about a quarter of a mile away, for Tom intended "taking off" from the mound, as he could not get a running start without a motor. The wind, however, he hoped, would raise him and the strange craft.

In order to get it over the ground without having it capsize, or elevate before they were ready for it, drag ropes, attached to bags of sand were used, and once these were attached the four found that they could not wheel the air glider along on its bicycle wheels.

"We'll have to get Eradicate and his mule, I guess," said Tom, after a vain endeavor to make progress against the wind. "When it's up in the air it will be all right, but until then I'll need help to move it. Ned, call Rad, will you?"

The colored man, with Boomerang, his faithful mule, was soon on hand. The animal was hitched to the glider, and pulled it toward the hill.

"Now to see what happens," remarked Tom as he wheeled his latest invention around where the wind would take it as soon as the restraining ropes were cast off, for it was now held in place by several heavy cables fastened to stakes driven in the ground.

Tom gave a last careful look to the weights, planes and rudders. He glanced at a small anemometer or wind gage, on the craft, and noted that it registered sixty miles an hour.

"That ought to do," he remarked. "Now who's going up with me? Will you take a chance, Mr. Petrofsky?"

"I'd rather not—at first."

"Come on then, Ned and Mr. Damon. Mr. Petrofsky and Rad can cast off the ropes."

The wind, if anything, was stronger than ever. It was a terrific gale, and just what was needed. But how would the air glider act? That was what Tom wanted very much to know.

"Cast off!" he cried to the Russian and Eradicate, and they slipped the ropes.

The next moment, with a rush and whizzing roar, the air glider shot aloft on the wings of the wind.

CHAPTER IX

THE SPIES

"We're certainly going up!" yelled Ned, as he sat beside Tom in the cabin of the air glider.

"That's right!" agreed the young inventor rather proudly, as he grasped two levers, one of which steered the craft, the other being used to shift the weights. "We're going up. I was pretty sure of that. The next thing is to see if it will remain stationary in the air, and answer the rudder."

"Bless my top knot!" cried Mr. Damon. "You don't mean to tell me you can stand still in a gale of wind, Tom Swift."

"That's exactly what I do mean. You can't do it in an aeroplane, for that depends on motion to keep itself up in the air. But the glider is different. That's one of its specialties, remaining still, and that's why it will be valuable if we ever get to Siberia. We can hover over a certain spot in a gale of wind, and search about below with telescopes for a sign of the lost platinum mine.

"How high are you going up?" demanded Ned, for the air glider was still mounting upward on a slant. If you' ever scaled a flat piece of tin, or a stone, you'll remember how it seems to slide up a hill of air, when it was thrown at the right angle. It was just this way with the air glider—it was mounting upward on a slant.

"I'm going up a couple of hundred feet at least," answered Tom, "and higher if the gale-strata is there. I want to give it a good test while I'm at it."

Ned looked down through a heavy plate of glass in the floor of the cabin, and could see Mr. Petrofsky and Eradicate looking up at them.

"Bless my handkerchief!" cried Mr. Damon, when his attention had been called to this. "It's just like an airship."

"Except that we haven't a bit of machinery on board," said Tom. "These weights do everything," and he shifted them forward on the sliding rods, with the effect that the air glider dipped down with a startling lurch.

"We're falling!" cried Ned.

"Not a bit of it," answered Tom. "I only showed you how it worked. By sliding the weights back we go up."

He demonstrated this at once, sending his craft sliding up another hill of air, until it reached an elevation of four hundred feet, as evidenced by the barograph.

"I guess this is high enough," remarked Tom after a bit. "Now to see if she'll stand still."

Slowly he moved the weights along, by means of the compound levers, until the air glider was on an "even keel" so to speak. It was still moving forward, with the wind now, for Tom had warped his wing tips.

"The thing to do," said the young inventor, "is to get it exactly parallel with the wind-strata, so that the gale will blow through the two sets of planes, just as the wind blows through a box kite. Only we have no string to hold us from moving. We have to depend on the equalization of friction on the surfaces of the wings. I wonder if I can do it."

It was a delicate operation, and Tom had not had much experience in that sort of thing, for his other airships and aeroplanes worked on an entirely different principle. But he moved the weights along, inch by inch, and flexed the tips, planes and rudders until finally Ned, who was looking down through the floor window, cried out:

"We're stationary!"

"Good!" exclaimed Tom. "Then it's a success."

"And we can go to Siberia?" added Mr. Damon.

"Sure," assented the young inventor. "And if we have luck we'll rescue Mr. Petrofsky's brother, and get a lot of platinum that will be more valuable than gold."

It would not be true to say that the air glider was absolutely stationary. There was a slight forward motion, due to the fact that it was not yet perfected, and also because Tom was not expert enough in handling it.

The friction on the plane surfaces was not equalized, and the gale forced the craft along slightly. But, compared to the terrific power of the wind, the air glider was practically at a standstill, and this was remarkable when one considers the force of the hurricane that was blowing above below and through it.

For actually that was what the hurricane was doing. It was as if an immense box kite was suspended in the air, without a string to hold it from moving, and as though a cabin was placed amidships to hold human beings.

"This sure is great!" cried Ned. "Have you got her in control, Tom?"

"I think so. I'll try and see how she works."

By shifting the weights, changing the balance, and warping the wings, the young inventor sent the craft higher up, made it dip down almost to the earth, and then swoop upward like some great bird. Then he turned it completely about and though he developed no great speed in this test made it progress quarteringly against the wind.

"It's almost perfect," declared Tom. "A few touches and she'll be all right."

"Is it all right?" asked Ivan Petrofsky anxiously, as the three left the cabin, and Eradicate hitched his mule to the glider to take it back to the shed.

"I see where it can be improved," he said, as they made ready to descend. "I'll soon have it in shape."

"Then we can go to Siberia?"

"In less than a month. The big airship needs some repairs, and then we'll be off."

The Russian said nothing, but he looked his thanks to Tom, and the manner in which he grasped the hand of our hero showed his deep feelings.

The glider was given several more trials, and each time it worked better. Tom decided to change some of the weights, and he devoted all his time to this alteration, while Ned, Mr. Damon, and the others labored to get the big airship in shape for the long trip to the land of the exiles.

So anxious was Tom to get started, that he put in several nights working on the glider. Ned occasionally came over to help him, while Mr. Damon was on hand as often as his wife would allow. Mr. Petrofsky spent his nights writing to friends in Russia, hoping to get some clue as to the whereabouts of his brother.

It was on one of these nights, when Tom and Ned were laboring hard, with Eradicate to help them that an incident occurred which worried them all not a little. Tom was adjusting some of the new weights on the sliding rods, and called to Ned:

"I say, old man, hand me that big monkey wrench, will you. I can't loosen this nut with the small one. You'll find it on the bench by that back window."

As Ned went to get the tool he looked from the casement. He started, stood staring through the glass for a moment into the outer darkness, and then cried out:

"Tom, we're being watched! There are some spies outside!"

"What?" exclaimed the young inventor "Where are they? Who are they?"

"I don't know. Those Russian police, maybe out front, and maybe we can catch them!"

Grabbing up the big monkey wrench, Ned made a dash for the large sliding doors, followed by Tom who had an iron bar, and Eradicate with a small pair of pliers.

"By golly!" cried the colored man, "ef I gits 'em I'll pinch dere noses off!"

CHAPTER X

OFF IN THE AIRSHIP

Going from the brightly lighted shop into the darkness of the night, illuminated as it was only by the stars, neither Tom, Ned, nor Eradicate, could see anything at first. They had to stand still for a moment to accustom their eyes to the gloom.

"Can you see them?" cried Tom to his chum.

"No, but I can hear them! Over this way!" yelled Ned, and then, being able to dimly make out objects, so he would not run into them, he started off, followed by the young inventor.

Tom could hear several persons running away now, but he could see no one, and from the sound he judged that the spies, if such they were, were hurrying across the fields that surrounded the shop.

It was almost a hopeless task to pursue them, but the two lads were not the kind that give up. They rushed forward, hoping to be able to grapple with those who had looked in the shop window, but it was not to be.

The sound of the retreating footsteps became more and more faint, until finally they gave no clue to follow.

"Better stop," advised Tom. "No telling where we'll end up if we keep on running. Besides it might be dangerous."

"Dangerous; how?" panted Ned.

"They might dodge around, and wait for us behind some tree or bush."

"An' ef dat Foger feller am around he jest as soon as not fetch one ob us a whack in de head," commented Eradicate grimly.

"Guess you're about right," admitted Ned. "There isn't much use keeping on. We'll go back."

"What sort of fellows were they?" asked Tom, when, after a little further search, the hunt was given up. "Could you see them well, Ned?"

"Not very good. Just as I went to get you that wrench I noticed two faces looking in the window. I must have taken them by surprise, for they dodged down in an instant. Then I yelled, and they ran off."

"Did you see Andy Foger?"

"No, I didn't notice him."

"Was either of them one of the spies who had Mr. Petrofsky in the hut?"

"I didn't see those fellows very well, you remember, so I couldn't say."

"That's so, but I'll bet that's who they were."

"What do you think they're after, Tom?"

"One of two things. They either want to get our Russian friend into their clutches again, or they're after me—to try to stop me from going to Siberia."

"Do you think they'd go to such length as that?"

"I'm almost sure they would. Those Russian police are wrong, of course, but they think Mr. Petrofsky is an Anarchist or something like that, and they think they're justified in doing anything to get him back to the Siberian mines. And once the Russian government sets out to do a thing it generally does it—I'll give 'em credit for that."

"But how do you suppose they know you're going to Russia?"

"Say, those fellows have ways of getting information you and I would never dream of. Why, didn't you read the other day how some fellow who was supposed to be one of the worst Anarchists ever, high up in making bombs, plotting, and all that sort of thing—turned out to be a police spy? They get their information that way. I shouldn't be surprised but what some of the very people whom Mr. Petrofsky thinks are his friends are spies, and they send word to headquarters of every move he makes."

"Why don't you warn him?"

"He knows it as well as I do. The trouble is you can't tell who the spies are until it's too late. I'm glad I'm not mixed up in that sort of thing. If I can get to Siberia, help Mr. Petrofsky rescue his brother, and get hold of some of that platinum I'll be satisfied. Then I won't go back to the land of the Czar, once I get away from there."

"That's right. Well, let's go back and work on the glider."

"And we'll have Eradicate patrolling about the shop to make sure we're not spied on again."

"By golly! Ef I sees any oh 'em, I suah will pinch 'em!" cried the colored man, as he clicked the pliers.

But there was no further disturbance that night, and, when Tom and Ned ceased work, they had made good progress toward finishing the air glider.

The big airship was almost ready to be given a trial flight, with her motors tuned up to give more power, and as soon as the Russian exile had a little more definite information as to the possible whereabouts of his brother, they could start.

In the days that followed Tom and his friends worked hard. The air glider was made as nearly perfect as any machine is, and in a fairly stiff gale, that blew up about a week later, Tom did some things in it that made his friends open their eyes. The young inventor had it under nearly as good control as he had his dirigible balloons or aeroplanes.

The big airship, too, was made ready for the long voyage, extra large storage tanks for gasolene being built in, as it was doubtful if they could get a supply in Siberia without arranging for it in advance, and this they did not want to do. Besides there was the long ocean flight to provide for.

"But if worst comes to worst I can burn kerosene in my motor," Tom explained, for he had perfected an attachment to this end. "You can get kerosene almost anywhere in Russia."

At last word was received from Russia, from some Revolutionist friends of the exile, stating that his brother was supposed to be working in a certain sulphur mine north of the Iablonnoi mountains, and half way between that range and the city of Iakutsk.

"But it might be a salt mine, just as well," said Mr. Petrofsky, when he told the boys the news. "Information about the poor exiles is hard to get."

"Well, we'll take a chance!" cried Tom determinedly.

The preparations went on, and by strict watchfulness none of the spies secured admission to the shop where the air glider was being finished. The big airship was gotten in shape for the voyage, and then, after a final trial of the glider, it was taken apart and put aboard the Falcon, ready for use on the gale-swept plains of Siberia.

The last of the stores, provisions and supplies were put in the big car of the airship, a route had been carefully mapped out, and Tom, after saying good-bye to Mary Nestor, his father, the housekeeper, and Eradicate, took his place in the pilot house of the airship one pleasant morning at the beginning of Summer.

"Don't you wish you were going, Rad?" the young inventor asked, for the colored man had decided to stay at home.

"No indeedy, Massa Tom," was the answer. "Dat's a mighty cold country in Shebeara, an' I laik warm wedder."

"Well, take care of yourself and Boomerang," answered Tom with a laugh. Then he pulled the lever that sent a supply of gas into the big bag, and the ship began to rise.

"I guess we've given those spies the slip," remarked Ned, as they rose from the ground calling good-byes to the friends they left behind.

"I hope so," agreed Tom, but could he have seen two men, of sinister looks, peering at the slowly-moving airship from the shelter of a glove of trees, not far off, he might have changed his opinion, and so would Ned.

Then, as the airship gathered momentum, it fairly sprang into the air, and a moment later, the big propellers began revolving. They were off on their long voyage to find the lost platinum mine, and rescue the exile of Siberia.

CHAPTER XI

A STORM AT SEA

Tom had the choice of two routes in making his voyage to far-off Siberia. He could have crossed the United States, sailed over the Pacific ocean, and approached the land of the Czar from the western coast above Manchuria. But he preferred to take the Atlantic route, crossing Europe, and so sailing over Russia proper to get to his destination. There were several reasons for this.

The water voyage was somewhat shorter, and this was an important consideration when there was no telling when he might have an accident that would compel him to descend. On the Atlantic he knew there would be more ships to render assistance if it was needed, although he hoped he would not have to ask for it.

"Then, too," he said to Ned, when they were discussing the matter, "we will have a chance to see some civilized countries if we cross Europe, and we may land near Paris."

"Paris!" cried Ned. "What for?"

"To renew our supply of gasolene, for one thing," replied the young inventor. "Not that we will be out when we arrive, but if we take on more there we may not have to get any in Russia. Besides, they have a very good quality in France, so all told, I think the route over Europe to be the best."

Ned agreed with him, and so did Mr. Petrofsky. As for Mr. Damon, he was so busy getting his sleeping room in order, and blessing everything he could think of, that he did not have time to talk much. So the eastern route was decided on, and as the big airship, carrying our friends, their supplies, and the wonderful air glider rose higher and higher, Tom gradually brought her around so that the pointed nose of the gas bag aimed straight across the Atlantic.

They were over the ocean on the second day out, for Tom did not push the craft to her limit of speed, now they had time to consider matters at their leisure, for they had been rather hurried on leaving.

The machinery was working as nearly to perfection as it could be brought, and Tom, after finding out that his craft would answer equally well as a dirigible balloon or an aeroplane, let it sail along as the latter.

"For," he said, "we have a long trip ahead of us and we need to save all the elevating gas we can save. If worst comes to worst, and we can't navigate as an aeroplane any more, we can even drift along as a dirigible. But while we have the gasolene we might as well make speed and be an aeroplane."

The others agreed with him, and so it was arranged. Tom, when he had seen to it that his craft was working well, let Ned take charge and devoted himself to seeing that all the stores and supplies were in order for quick use.

Of course, until they were nearer the land of the Czar, and that part of Siberia where Mr. Petrofsky's brother was held as an exile, they could do little save make themselves as comfortable as possible in the airship. And this was not hard to do.

Naturally, in a craft that had to carry a heavy load, and lift itself into the air, as well as propel itself along, not many things could be taken. Every ounce counted. Still our friends were not without their comforts. There was a well stocked kitchen, and Mr. Damon insisted on installing himself as cook. This had been Eradicate's work but the eccentric man knew how to do almost everything from making soup to roasting a chicken, and he liked it. So he was allowed free run of the galley.

Tom and Ned spent much time in the steering tower or engine room, for, though all of the machinery was automatic, there was need of almost constant attention, though there was an arrangement whereby in case of emergency, the airship would steer herself in any set direction for a certain number of hours.

There were ample sleeping quarters for six persons, a living room and a dining saloon. In short the Falcon was much like Tom's Red Cloud, only bigger and better. There was even a phonograph on board so that music, songs, and recitations could be enjoyed.

"Bless my napkin! but this is great!" exclaimed Mr. Damon, about noon of the second day, when they had just finished dinner and looked down through the glass windows in the bottom of the cabin at the rolling ocean below them. "I don't believe many persons have such opportunities as we have."

"I'm sure they do not," added Mr. Petrofsky. "I can hardly think it true, that I am on my way back to Siberia to rescue my dear brother."

"And such good weather as we're having," spoke Ned. "I'm glad we didn't start off in a storm, for I don't exactly like them when we're over the water."

"We may get one yet," said Tom. "I don't just like the way the barometer is acting. It's falling pretty fast."

"Bless my mercury tube!" cried Mr. Damon. "I hope we have no bad luck on this trip."

"Oh, we can't help a storm or two," answered Tom. "I guess it won't do any harm to prepare for it."

So everything was made snug, and movable articles on the small exposed deck of the airship were lashed fast. Then, as night settled down, our friends gathered about in the cheerful cabin, in the light of the electric lamps, and talked of what lay before them.

As Mr. Damon could steer as well as Tom or Ned, he shared in the night watch. But Mr. Petrofsky was not expert enough to accept this responsibility.

It was when Mr. Damon finished his watch at midnight, and called Tom, that he remarked.

"Bless my umbrella, Tom. But I don't like the looks of the weather."

"Why, what's it doing?"

"It isn't doing anything, but it's clouding up and the barometer is going down."

"I was afraid we were in for it," answered the young inventor. "Well, we'll have to take what comes."

The airship plunged on her way, while her young pilot looked at the various gages, noting that to hold her way against the wind that had risen he would have to increase the speed of the motor.

"I don't like it," murmured Tom, "I don't like it," and he shook his head dubiously.

With a suddenness that was almost terrifying, the storm broke over the ocean about three o'clock that morning. There was a terrific clap of thunder, a flash of lighting, and a deluge of rain that fairly made the staunch Falcon stagger, high in the air as she was.

"Come on, Ned!" cried Tom, as he pressed the electric alarm bell connected with his chum's berth. "I need you, and Mr. Damon, too."

"What's the matter?" cried Ned, awakened suddenly from a sound sleep.

"We're in a bad storm," answered Tom, "and I'll have to have help. We need more gas, to try and rise above it."

"Bless my hanging lamp!" cried Mr. Damon, "I hope nothing happens!"

And he jumped from his berth as the Falcon plunged and staggered through the storm that was lashing the ocean below her into white billow of foam.

CHAPTER XII

AN ACCIDENT

For a few moments it seemed as if the Falcon would surely turn turtle and plunge into the seething ocean. The storm had burst with such suddenness that Tom, who was piloting his air craft, was taken unawares.

He had not been using much power or the airship would have been better able to weather the blast that burst with such fury over her. But as it was, merely drifting along, she was almost like a great sheet of paper. Down she was forced, until the high-flying spray from the waves actually wet the lower part of the car, and Ned, looking through one of the glass windows, saw, in the darkness, the phosphorescent gleam of the water so near to them.

"Tom!" he cried in alarm. "We're sinking!"

"Bless my bath sponge! Don't say that!" gasped Mr. Damon.

"That's why I called you," yelled the young inventor. "We've got to rise above the storm if possible. Go to the gas machine, Ned, and turn it on full strength. I'll speed up the motor, and we may be able to cut up that way. But get the gas on as soon as you can. The bag is only about half full. Force in all you can!

"Mr. Damon, can you take the wheel? It doesn't make any difference which way we go as long as you keep her before the wind, and yank back the elevating rudder as far as she'll go! We must head up."

"All right, Tom," answered the eccentric man, as he fairly jumped to take the place of the young inventor at the helm.

"Can I do anything?" asked the Russian, as Tom raced for the engine room, to speed the motor up to the last notch.

"I guess not. Everything is covered, unless you want to help Mr. Damon. In this blow it will be hard to work the rudder levers."

"All right," replied Ivan Petrofsky, and then there came another sickening roll of the airship, that threatened to turn her completely over.

"Lively!" yelled Tom, clinging to various supports as he made his way to the engine room. "Lively, all hands, or we'll be awash in another minute!"

And indeed it seemed that this might be so, for with the wind forcing her down, and the hungry waves leaping up, as if to clutch her to themselves, the Falcon was having anything but an easy time of it.

It was the work of but an instant however, when Tom reached the engine room, to jerk the accelerator lever toward him, and the motor responded at once. With a low, humming whine the wheels and gears redoubled their speed, and the great propellers beat the air with fiercer strokes.

At the same time Tom heard the hiss of the gas as it rushed into the envelope from the generating machine, as Ned opened the release valve.

"Now we ought to go up," the young inventor murmured, as he anxiously watched the barograph, and noted the position of the swinging pendulum which told of the roll and dip of the air craft.

For a moment she hung in the balance, neither the increased speed of the propellers, nor the force of the gas having any seeming effect. Mr. Damon and the Russian, clinging to the rudder levers, to avoid being dashed against the sides of the pilot house, held them as far back as they could, to gain the full power of the elevation planes. But even this seemed to do no good.

The power of the gale was such, that, even with the motor and gas machine working to their limit, the Falcon only held her own. She swept along, barely missing the crests of the giant waves.

"She's got to go up! She's got to go up!" cried Tom desperately, as if by very will power he could send her aloft. And then, when there came a lull in the fierce blowing of the wind, the elevation rudder took hold, and like a bird that sees the danger below, and flies toward the clouds, the airship shot up suddenly.

"That's it!" cried Tom in relief, as he noted the needle of the barograph swinging over, indicating an ever-increasing height. "Now we're safe."

They were not quite yet, but at last the power of machinery had prevailed over that of the elements. Through the pelting rain, and amid the glare of the lightning, and the thunder of heaven's artillery, the airship forced her way, up and up and up.

Setting the motor controller to give the maximum power until he released it, Tom hastened to the gas-generating apparatus. He found Ned attending to it, so that it was now working satisfactorily.

"How about it, Tom?" cried his chum anxiously.

"All right now, Ned, but it was a close shave! I thought we were done for, platinum mine, rescue of exiles, and all."

"So did I. Shall I keep on with the gas?"

"Yes, until the indicator shows that the bag is full. I'm going to the pilot house."

Running there, Tom found that Mr. Damon and the Russian had about all they could manage. The young inventor helped them and then, when the Falcon was well started on her upward course, Tom set the automatic steering machine, and they had a breathing spell.

To get above the sweep of the blast was no easy task, for the wind strata seemed to be several miles high, and Tom did not want to risk an accident by going to such an elevation. So, when having gone up about a mile, he found a comparatively calm area he held to that, and the Falcon sped along with the occupants feeling fairly comfortable, for there was no longer that rolling and tumbling motion.

The storm kept up all night, but the danger was practically over, unless something should happen to the machinery, and Tom and Ned kept careful watch to prevent this. In the morning they could look down on the storm-swept ocean below them, and there was a feeling of thankfulness in their hearts that they were not engulfed in it.

"This is a pretty hard initiation for an amateur," remarked Mr. Petrofsky. "I never imagined I should be as brave as this in an airship in a storm."

"Oh, you can get used to almost anything," commented Mr. Damon.

It was three days before the storm blew itself out and then came pleasant weather, during which the Falcon flew rapidly along. Our friends busied themselves about many things, talked of what lay before them, and made such plans as they could.

It was the evening of the fifth day, and they expected to sight the coast of France in the morning. Tom was in the pilot house, setting the course for the night run, and Ned had gone to the engine room to look after the oiling of the motor.

Hardly had he reached the compartment than there was a loud report, a brilliant flash of fire, and the machinery stopped dead.

"What is it?" cried Tom, as he came in on the run, for the indicators in the pilot house had told him something was wrong.

"An accident!" cried Ned. "A breakdown, Tom! What shall we do?"

CHAPTER XIII

SEEKING A QUARREL

There was an ominous silence in the engine room, following the flash and the report. The young inventor took in every bit of machinery in a quick glance, and he saw at once that the main dynamo and magneto had short-circuited, and gone out of commission. Almost instantly the airship began to sink, for the propellers had ceased revolving.

"Bless my barograph!" cried Mr. Damon, appearing on the scene. "We're sinking, Tom!"

"It's all right," answered our hero calmly. "It's a bad accident, and may delay us, but there's no danger. Ned, start up the gas machine," for they were progressing as an aeroplane then. "Start that up, and we'll drift along as a dirigible."

"Of course! Why didn't I think of that!" exclaimed Ned, somewhat provoked at his own want of thought. The airship was going down rapidly, but it was the work of but a moment to start the generator, and then the earthward motion was checked.

"We'll have to take our chance of being blown to France," remarked Tom, as he went over to look at the broken electrical machinery. "But we ought to fetch the coast by morning with this wind. Lucky it's blowing our way."

"Then you can't use the propellers?" asked Mr. Petrofsky.

"No," replied Tom, "but if we get to France I can easily repair this break. It's the platinum bearings again. I do hope we'll locate that lost mine, for I need a supply of good reliable metal.

"Then we'll have to land in France?" asked the Russian, and he seemed a trifle uneasy.

"Yes," answered Tom. "Don't you want to?"

"Well, I was thinking of our safety."

"Bless my silk hat!" cried Mr. Damon. "Where is the danger of landing there? I rather hoped we could spend some time in Paris."

"There is no particular danger, unless it be comes known that I am an escaped exile, and that we are on our way to Siberia to rescue another one, and try to find the platinum mine. Then we would be in danger."

"But how are they to know it?" asked Ned, who had come back from the gas machine.

"France, especially in Paris and the larger cities, is a hot-bed of political spies," answered Mr. Petrofsky. "Russia has many there on the secret police, and while the objectors to the Czar's government are also there, they could do little to help us."

"I guess they won't find out about us unless we give it away," was Tom's opinion.

"I'm afraid they will," was the reply of the Russian. "Undoubtedly word has been cabled by the spies who annoyed us in Shopton, that we are on our way over here. Of course they can't tell where we might land, but as soon as we do land the news will be flashed all over, and the word will come back that we are enemies of Russia. You can guess the rest."

"Then let's go somewhere else," suggested Mr. Damon.

"It would be the same anywhere in Europe," replied Ivan Petrofsky. "There are spies in all the large centres."

"Well, I've got to go to Paris, or some large city to get the parts I need," said Tom. "Unfortunately I didn't bring any along for the dynamo and magneto, as I should have done, and I can't get the necessary pieces in a small town. I'll have to depend on some big machine shop. But we might land in some little-frequented place, and I could go in to town alone."

"That might answer," spoke the Russian, and it was decided to try that.

Meanwhile it was somewhat doubtful whether they would reach France, for they were dependent on the wind. But it seemed to be blowing steadily in the desired direction, and Tom noted with satisfaction that their progress was comparatively fast. He tried to repair the broken machinery but found that he could not, though he spent much of the night over it.

"Hurrah!" cried Ned when morning came, and he had taken an observation. "There's some kind of land over there."

The wind freshened while they were at breakfast and using more gas so as to raise them higher Tom directed the course of his airship as best he could. He wanted to get high enough so that if they passed over a city they would not be observed.

At noon it could be seen through the glass that they were over the outskirts of some large place, and after the Russian had taken an observation he exclaimed:

"The environs of Paris! We must not land there!"

"We won't, if the wind holds out," remarked Tom and this good fortune came to them. They succeeded in landing in a field not far from a small village, and though several farmers wondered much as the sight of the big airship, it was thought by the platinum-seekers that they would be comparatively safe.

"Now to get the first train for Paris and get the things I need," exclaimed Tom. He set to work taking off the broken pieces that they might be duplicated, and then, having inquired at an inn for the nearest railroad station, and having hired a rig, the young inventor set off.

"Can you speak French?" asked Mr. Petrofsky. "If not I might be of service, but if I go to Paris I might be—"

"Never mind," interrupted Tom. "I guess I can parley enough to get along with."

He had a small knowledge of the tongue, and with that, and knowing that English was spoken in many places, he felt that he could make out. And indeed he had no trouble. He easily found his way about the gay capital, and located a machine shop where a specialty was made of parts for automobile and airship motors. The proprietor, knowing the broken pieces belonged to an aeroplane, questioned Tom about his craft but the young inventor knew better than to give any clue that might make trouble, so he returned evasive answers.

It was nearly night when he got back to the place where he had left the Falcon, and he found a curious crowd of rustics grouped about it.

"Has anything happened?" he asked of his friends.

"No, everything is quiet, I'm glad to say," replied Mr. Petrofsky. "I don't think our presence will create stir enough so that the news of it will reach the spies in Paris. Still I will feel easier when we're in the air again."

"It will take a day to make the repairs," said Tom, "and put in the new pieces of platinum. But I'll work as fast as I can."

He and Ned labored far into the night, and were at it again the next morning. Mr. Damon and the Russian were of no service for they did not understand the machinery well enough. It was while Tom was outside the craft, filing a piece of platinum in an improvised vise, that a poorly-clothed man sauntered up and watched him curiously. Tom glanced at him, and was at once struck by a difference between the man's attire and his person.

For, though he was tattered and torn, the man's face showed a certain refinement, and his hands were not those of a farmer or laborer in which character he obviously posed.

"Monsieur has a fine airship there," he remarked to Tom.

"Oh, yes, it'll do." Tom did not want to encourage conversation.

"Doubtless from America it comes?"

The man spoke English but with an accent, and certain peculiarities.

"Maybe so," replied the young inventor.

"Is it permit to inspect the interior?"

"No, it isn't," came from Tom shortly. He had hurt his finger with the file, and he was not in the best of humor.

"Ah, there are secrets then?" persisted the stranger.

"Yes!" said Tom shortly. "I wish you wouldn't bother me. I'm busy, can't you see."

"Ah, does monsieur mean that I have poor eyesight?"

The question was snapped out so suddenly, and with such a menacing tone that Tom glanced up quickly. He was surprised at the look in the man's eyes.

"Just as you choose to take it," was the cool answer. "I don't know anything about your eyes, but I know I've got work to do."

"Monsieur is insulting!" rasped out the seeming farmer. "He is not polite. He is not a Frenchman."

"Now that'll do!" cried Tom, thoroughly aroused. "I don't want to be too short with you, but I've really got to get this done. One side, if you please," and having finished what he was doing, he started toward the airship.

Whether in his haste Tom did not notice where he was going, or whether the man deliberately got in his way I cannot say, but at any rate they collided and the seeming farmer went spinning to one side, falling down.

"Monsieur has struck me! I am insulted! You shall pay for this!" he cried, jumping to his feet, and making a rush for our hero.

"All right. It was your own fault for bothering me but if you want anything I'll give it to you!" cried Tom, striking a position of defense.

The man was about to rush at him, and there would have been a fight in another minute, had not Mr. Petrofsky, stepping to the open window of the pilot house, called out:

"Tom! Tom! Come here, quick. Never mind him!"

Swinging away from the man, the young inventor rushed toward the airship. As he entered the pilot house he noticed that his late questioner was racing off in the direction of the village.

"What is it? What's the matter?" he asked of the Russian. "Is something more wrong with the airship?"

"No, I just wanted to get you away from that man.

"Oh, I could take care of myself."

"I know that, but don't you see what his game was? I listened to him. He was seeking a quarrel with you."

"A quarrel?"

"Yes. He is a police spy. He wanted to get you into a fight and then he and you would be arrested by the local authorities. They'd clap you into jail, and hold us all here. It's a game! They suspect us, Tom! The Russian spies have had some word of our presence! We must get away as quickly as we can!"

CHAPTER XIV

HURRIED FLIGHT

The announcement of Ivan Petrofsky came to Tom with startling suddenness. He could say nothing for a moment, and then, as he realized what it meant, and as he recalled the strange appearance and actions of the man, he understood the danger.

"Was he a spy?" he asked.

"I'm almost sure he was," came the answer. "He isn't one of the villagers, that's sure, and he isn't a tourist. No one else would be in this little out-of-the-way place but a police official. He is in disguise, that is certain."

"I believe so," agreed Tom. "But what was his game?"

"We are suspected," replied the Russian. "I was afraid a big airship couldn't land anywhere, in France without it becoming known. Word must have been sent to Paris in the night, and this spy came out directly."

"But what will happen now?"

"Didn't you see where he headed for? The village. He has gone to send word that his trick failed. There will be more spies soon, and we may be detained or thrown into jail on some pretext or other. They may claim that we have no license, or some such flimsy thing as that. Anything to detain us. They are after me, of course, and I'm sorry that I made you run such danger. Perhaps I'd better leave you, and—"

"No, you don't!" cried Tom heartily. "We'll all hang together or we'll hang separately', as Benjamin Franklin or some of those old chaps once remarked. I'm not the kind to desert a friend in the face of danger."

"Bless my revolver! I should say not!" cried Mr. Damon. "What's it all about? Where's the danger?"

They told him as briefly as possible, and Ned, who had been working in the motor room, was also informed.

"Well, what's to be done?" asked Tom. "Had we better get out our ammunition, or shall I take out a French license."

"Neither would do any good," answered the Russian. "I appreciate your sticking by me, and if you are resolved on that the only thing to do is to complete the repairs as soon as possible and get away from here."

"That's it!" cried Ned. "A quick flight. We can get more gasolene here, for lots of autos pass along the road through the village. I found that out. Then we needn't stop until we hit the trail for the mine in Siberia!"

"Hush!" cautioned the Russian. "You can't tell who may be sneaking around to listen. But we ought to leave as soon as we can."

"And we will," said Tom. "I've got the magneto almost fixed!"

"Let's get a hustle on then!" urged Ned. "That fellow meant business from his looks. The nerve of him to try to pick a quarrel that way."

"I might have told by his manner that something was wrong," commented Tom, "but I thought he was a fresh tramp and I didn't take any pains in answering him. But come on, Ned, get busy."

They did, with such good effect that by noon the machinery was in running shape again, and so far there had been no evidence of the return of the spy. Doubtless he was waiting for instructions, and something might happen any minute.

"Now, Ned, if you'll see to having some gasolene brought out here, and the tanks filled, I'll tinker with the dynamo and get that in running shape," said Tom. "It only needs a little adjustment of the brushes. Then we'll be off."

Ned started for the village where there was a gasolene depot. He fancied the villagers regarded him rather curiously, but he did not stop to ask what it meant. Another odd fact was that the usual crowd of curious rustics about the airship was missing. It was as though they suspected trouble might come, and they did not want to be mixed up in it.

Never, Ned thought, had he seen a man so slow at getting ready the supply of gasolene. He was to take it out in a wagon, but first he mislaid the funnel, then the straining cloth, and finally he discovered a break in the harness that needed mending.

"I believe he's doing it on purpose to delay us," thought the youth, "but it won't do to say anything. Something is in the wind." He helped the man all he could, and urged him in every way he knew, but the fellow seemed to have grown suddenly stupid, and answered only in French, though previously he had spoken some English.

But at last Ned, by dint of hard work, got him started, and rode on the gasolene wagon with him. Once at the anchored airship, Tom and the others filled the reserve tanks themselves, though the man tried to help. However he did more harm than good, spilling several gallons of the fluid.

"Oh, get away, and let us do it!" cried Tom at last. "I know what you—"

"Easy!" cautioned Mr. Petrofsky, with a warning look, and Tom subsided.

Finally the tanks were full, the man was paid, and he started to drive away.

"Now to make a quick flight!" cried Tom, as he took his place in the pilot house, while Ned went to the engine room. "Full speed, Ned!"

"Yes, and we'll need it, too," said the Russian.

"Why?" asked Tom.

"Look!" was the answer, and Ivan Petrofsky pointed across the field over which, headed toward the airship, came the man who had sought a quarrel with Tom. And with the spy were several policemen in uniform, their short swords dangling at their sides.

"They're after us!" cried Mr. Damon. "Bless my chronometer they're after us!"

"Start the motor, Ned! Start the motor!" cried Tom, and a moment later the hum of machinery was heard, while the police and the spy broke into a run, shouting and waving their hands.

CHAPTER XV

PURSUED

Slowly the airship arose, almost too slowly to suit those on board who anxiously watched the oncoming officers. The latter had drawn their short swords, and at the sight of them Mr. Damon cried out:

"Bless my football! If they jab them into the gas bag, Tom, we're done for!"

"They won't get the chance," answered the young inventor, and he spoke truly, for a moment later, as the big propellers took hold of the air, the Falcon went up with a rush, and was far beyond the reach of the men. In a rage the spy shook his fist at the fast receding craft, and one of the policemen drew his revolver.

"They're going to fire!" cried Ned.

"They can't do much damage," answered Tom coolly. "A bullet hole in the bag is easily repaired, and anywhere else it won't amount to anything."

The officer was aiming his revolver at the airship, now high above his head, but with a quick motion the spy pulled down his companion's arm, and they seemed to be disputing among themselves.

"I wonder what that means?" mused Mr. Damon.

"Probably they didn't want to risk getting into trouble," replied the Russian. "There are strict laws in France about using firearms, and as yet we are accused of no crime. We are only suspected, and I suppose the spy didn't want to get into trouble. He is on foreign ground, and there might be international complications."

"Then you really think he was a spy?" asked Tom.

"No doubt of it, and I'm afraid this is only the beginning of our trouble."

"In what way?"

"Well, of course word will be sent on ahead about us, and every where we go they'll be on the watch for us. They have our movements pretty well covered."

"We won't make a descent until we get to Siberia," said Tom, "and I guess there it will be so lonesome that we won't be troubled much."

"Perhaps," admitted the Russian, "but we will have to be on our guard. Of course keeping up in the air will be an advantage but they may—"

He stopped suddenly and shrugged his shoulders.

"What were you going to say?" inquired Ned.

"Oh, it's just something that might happen, but it's too remote a possibility to work about. We're leaving those fellows nicely behind," he added quickly, as though anxious to change the subject.

"Yes, at this rate we'll soon be out of France," observed Tom, as he speeded the ship along still more. The young inventor wondered what Mr. Petrofsky had been going to say, but soon after this, some of the repaired machinery in the motor room needed adjusting, and the young inventor was kept so busy that the matter passed from his mind.

The dynamo and magneto were doing much more efficient work since Tom had put the new platinum in, and the Falcon was making better time than ever before. They were flying at a moderate height, and could see wondering men, women and children rush out from their houses, to gaze aloft at the strange sight. Paris was now far behind, and that night they were approaching the borders of Prussia, as Mr. Petrofsky informed them, for he knew every part of Europe.

The route, as laid down by Tom and the Russian, would send the airship skirting the southern coast of the Baltic sea, then north-west, to pass to one side of St. Petersburg, and then, after getting far enough to the north, so as to avoid the big cities, they would head due east for Siberia.

"In that way I think we'll avoid any danger from the Russian police," remarked the exile.

For the next few days they flew steadily on at no remarkable speed, as the extra effort used more gasolene than Tom cared to expend in the motor. He realized that he would need all he had, and he did not want to have to buy any more until he was homeward bound, for the purchase of it would lead to questions, and might cause their detention.

Mr. Damon gave his friends good meals and they enjoyed their trip very much, though naturally there was some anxiety about whether it would have a successful conclusion.

"Well, if we don't find the platinum mine we'll rescue your brother, if there's a possible chance!" exclaimed Tom one day, as he sat in the pilot house with the exile. "Jove! it will be great to drop down, pick him up, and fly away with him before those Cossacks, or whoever has him, know what's up."

"I'm afraid we can't make such a sensational rescue as that," replied Mr. Petrofsky. "We'll have to go at it diplomatically. That's the only way to get an exile out of Siberia. We must get word to him somehow, after we locate him, that we are waiting to help him, and then we can plan for his escape. Poor Peter! I do hope we can find him, for if he is in the salt or sulphur mines it is a living death!" and he shuddered at the memory of his own exile.

"How do you expect to get definite information as to where he might be?" asked Tom.

"I think the only thing to do is to get in touch with some of the revolutionists," answered the Russian. "They have ways and means of finding out even state secrets. I think our best plan will be to land near some small town, when we get to the edge of Siberia. If we can conceal the airship, so much the better. Then I can disguise myself and go to the village."

"Will it be safe?" inquired the young inventor.

"I'll have to take that chance. It's the only way, as I am the only one in our party who can speak Russian."

"That's right," admitted Tom with a laugh. "I'm afraid I could never master that tongue. It's as hard as Chinese."

"Not quite," replied his friend, "but it is not an easy language for an American."

They talked at some length, and then Tom noticing, by one of the automatic gages on the wall of the pilot house, that some of the machinery needed attention, went to attend to it.

He was rather surprised, on emerging from the motor compartment, to see Mr. Damon standing on the open after deck of the Falcon gazing earnestly toward the rear.

"Star-gazing in the day time?" asked Tom with a laugh.

"Bless my individuality!" exclaimed the odd man. "How you startled me, Tom! No, I'm not looking at stars, but I've been noticing a black speck in the sky for some time, and I was wondering whether it was my eyesight, or whether it really is something."

"Where is it?"

"Straight to the rear," answered Mr. Damon, "and it seems to be about a mile up. It's been hanging in the same place this ten minutes."

"Oh, I see," spoke Tom, when the speck had been pointed out to him. "It's there all right, but I guess it's a bird, an eagle perhaps. Wait, I'll get a glass and we'll take a look."

As he was taking the telescope down from its rack in the pilot house, Mr. Petrofsky saw him.

"What's up?" asked the Russian, and the youth told him.

"Must be a pretty big bird to be seen at such a distance as it is," remarked Tom.

"Maybe it isn't a bird," suggested Ivan Petrofsky. "I'll take a look myself," and, showing something of alarm in his manner, he followed Tom to where Mr. Damon awaited them. Ned also came out on deck.

Quickly adjusting the glass, Tom focused it on the black speck. It seemed to have grown larger. He peered at it steadily for several seconds.

"Is it a bird?" asked Mr. Damon.

"Jove! It's another airship—a big biplane!" cried Tom, "and there seems to be three men in her."

"An aeroplane!" gasped Ned.

"Bless my deflecting rudder!" cried Mr. Damon. "An airship in this out-of-the-way place?" for they were flying over a desolate country.

"And they're coming right after us," added Tom, as he continued to gaze.

"I thought so," was the quiet comment of Mr. Petrofsky. "That is what I started to say a few days ago," he went on, "when I stopped, as I hardly believed it possible. I thought they might possibly send an aeroplane after us, as both the French and Russian armies have a number of fast ones. So they are pursuing us. I'm afraid my presence will bring you no end of trouble."

"Let it come!" cried Tom. "If they can catch up to us they've got a good machine. Come on, Ned, let's speed her up, and make them take more of our star dust."

"Wait a minute," advised the Russian, as he took the telescope from Tom, and viewed the ever-increasing speck behind them. "Are you sure of the speed of this craft?" he asked a moment later.

"I never saw the one yet I couldn't pull away from, even after giving them a start," answered the young inventor proudly. "That is all but my little sky racer. I could let them get within speaking distance, and then pull out like the Congressional Limited passing a slow freight."

"Then wait a few minutes," suggested Mr. Petrofsky. "That is an aeroplane all right, but I can't make out from what country. I'd like a better view, and if it's safe we can come closer."

"Oh, it's safe enough," declared Tom. "I'll get things in shape for a quick move," and he hurried back to the machine room, while the others took turns looking at the oncoming aeroplane. And it was coming on rapidly, showing that it had tremendous power, for it was a very large one, carrying three men.

"How do you suppose they got on our track?" asked Ned.

"Oh, we must have been reported from time to time, as we flew over cities or towns," replied Mr. Petrofsky. "You know we're rather large, and can be seen from a good distance. Then too, the whole Russian secret police force is at the service of our enemies."

"But we're not over Russia yet," said Mr. Damon.

Ivan Petrofsky took the telescope and peered down toward the earth. They were not a great way above it, and at that moment they were passing a small village.

"Can you tell where we are?" asked the odd man.

"We are just over the border of the land of the Czar," was the quiet answer. "The imperial flag is flying from a staff in front of one of the buildings down there. We are over Russia."

"And here comes that airship," called Ned suddenly.

They gazed back with alarm, and saw that it was indeed so. The big aeroplane had come on wonderfully fast in the last few minutes.

"Tom! Tom!" cried his chum. "Better get ready to make a sprint."

"I'm all ready," calmly answered our hero. "Shall I go now?"

"If you can give us a few seconds longer I may be able to tell who is after us," remarked Mr. Petrofsky, turning his telescope on the craft behind them.

"I can let them get almost up to us, and get away," replied Tom.

The Russian did not answer. He was gazing earnestly at the approaching aeroplane. A moment later he took the glass down from his eye.

"It's our spy again," he said. "There are two others with him. That is one of the aeroplanes owned by the secret police. They are stationed all over Europe, ready for instant service, and they're on our trail."

The pursuing craft was so near that the occupants could easily be made out with the naked eye, but it needed the glass to distinguish their features, and Mr. Petrofsky had done this.

"Shall I speed up?" cried Tom.

"Yes, get away as fast as you can!" shouted the Russian. "No telling what they may do," and then, with a hum and a roar the motor of the Falcon increased its speed, and the big airship shot ahead.

CHAPTER XVI

THE NIHILISTS

From the pursuing aircraft came a series of sharp explosions that fairly rattled through the clear air.

"Look out for bombs!" yelled Ned.

"Bless my safety match!" cried Mr. Damon. "Are they anarchists?"

"It's only their motor back-firing," cried Tom. "It's all right, They're done for now, we'll leave them behind."

He was a true prophet, for with a continued rush and a roar the airship of our friends opened up a big gap between her rear rudders and the forward planes of the craft that was chasing her. The three men were working frantically to get their motor in shape, but it was a useless task.

A little later, finding that they were losing speed, the three police agents, or spies, whatever they might be, had to volplane to earth and there was no need for the Falcon to maintain the terrific pace, to which Tom had pushed her. The pursuit was over.

"Well, we got out of that luckily," remarked Ned, as he looked down to where the spies were making a landing. "I guess they won't try that trick again."

"I'm afraid they will," predicted Mr. Petrofsky. "You don't know these government agents as I do. They never give up. They'll fix their engine, and get on our trail again."

"Then we'll make them work for what they get," put in Tom, who, having set the automatic speed accelerator, had rejoined his companions. "We'll try a high flight and if they can pick up a trail in the air, and come up to us, they're good ones!"

He ran to the pilot house, and set the elevation rudder at its limit. Meanwhile the spies were working frantically over their motor, trying to get it in shape for the pursuit. But soon they realized that this was out of the question, for the Falcon was far away, every moment going higher and higher, until she was lost to sight beyond the clouds.

"I guess they'll have their own troubles now," remarked Ned. "We've seen the last of them."

"Don't be too sure," spoke the Russian. "We may have them after us again. We're over the land of the Czar now, and they'll have everything their own way. They'll want to stop me at any cost."

"Do you think they suspect that we're after the platinum?" asked Tom.

"They may, for they know my brother and I were the only ones who ever located it, though unless I get in the exact neighborhood I'd have trouble myself picking it out. I remember some of the landmarks, but my brother is better at that sort of work than I am. But I think what they are mostly afraid of is that I have some designs on the life of, say one of the Grand Dukes, or some high official. But I am totally opposed to violent measures," went on Mr. Petrofsky. "I believe in a campaign of education, to gain for the down-trodden people what are their rights."

"Do you think they know you are coming to rescue your brother?" asked Tom.

"I don't believe so. And I hope not, for once they suspected that, they would remove him to some place where I never could locate him."

Calmer feelings succeeded the excitement caused by the pursuit, and our friends, speculating on the matter, came to the conclusion that the aeroplane must have started from some Prussian town, as Mr. Petrofsky said there were a number of Russian secret police in that country. The Falcon was now speeding along at a considerable height, and after running for a number of miles, sufficient to preclude the possibility that they could be picked up by the pursuing aeroplane, Tom sent his craft down, as the rarefied atmosphere made breathing difficult.

It was about three days after the chase when, having carefully studied the map and made several observations through the telescope of the Country over which they were traveling, that Ivan Petrofsky said:

"If it can be managed, Tom, I think we ought to go down about here. There is a Russian town not far away, and I know a few friends there, There is a large stretch of woodland, and the airship can be easily concealed there.

"All right," agreed the young inventor, "down we go, and I hope you get the information you want."

Flying high so as to keep out of the observation of the inhabitants of the Russian town, the young inventor sent his craft in a circle about it, and, having seen a clearing in the forest, he made a landing there, the Falcon having come to rest a second time since leaving Shopton, now several thousand miles away.

"We'll hide here for a few days," observed Tom, "and you can spend as much time in town as you like, Mr. Petrofsky."

The Russian, disguising himself by trimming his beard, and putting on a pair of dark spectacles, went to the village that afternoon.

While he was gone Tom, Ned and Mr. Damon busied themselves about the airship, making a few repairs that could not very well be done while it was in motion. As night came on, and the exile did not return, Tom began to get a little worried, and he had some notion of going to seek him, but he knew it would not be safe.

"He'll come all right," declared Ned, as they sat down to supper. All about them was an almost impenetrable forest, cut here and there by paths along which, as Mr. Petrofsky had told them, the wood cutters drove their wagons.

It was quite a surprise therefor, when, as they were leaving the table, a knock was heard on the cabin door.

"Bless my electric bell!" cried Mr. Damon. "Who can that be?"

"Mr. Petrofsky of course," answered Ned.

"He wouldn't knock—he'd walk right in," spoke Tom, as he went to the door. As he opened it he saw several dark-bearded men standing there, and in their midst Mr. Petrofsky.

For one moment our hero feared that his friend had been arrested and that the police had come to take the rest of them into custody. But a word from the exile reassured him.

"These are some of my friends," said Mr. Petrofsky simply. "They are Nihilists which I am not, but—"

"Nihilists yes! Always!" exclaimed one who spoke English. "Death to the Czar and the Grand Dukes! Annihilation to the government!"

"Gently my friend, gently," spoke Mr. Petrofsky. "I am opposed to violence you know." And then, while his new friends gazed wonderingly at the strange craft, he led them inside. Tom and the others were hardly able to comprehend what was about to take place.

CHAPTER XVII

ON TO SIBERIA

"Has anything happened?" asked Tom. "Are we suspected? Have they come to warn us?"

"No, everything is all right, so far," answered Ivan Petrofsky. "I didn't have the success I hoped for, and we may have to wait here for a few days to get news of my brother. But these men have been very kind to me," he went on, "and they have ways of getting information that I have not. So they are going to aid me."

"That's right!" exclaimed the one who had first spoken. "We will yet win you to our cause, Brother Petrofsky. Death to the Czar and the Grand Dukes!"

"Never!" exclaimed the exile firmly. "Peaceful measures will succeed. But I am grateful for what you can do for me. They heard me describe your wonderful airship," he explained to Tom, "and wanted to see for themselves."

The Nihilists were made welcome after Mr. Petrofsky had introduced them. They had strange and almost unpronounceable names for the ears of our friends, and I will not trouble you with them, save to say that the one who spoke English fairly well, and who was the leader, was called Nicolas Androwsky. There was much jabbering in the Russian tongue, when Mr. Petrofsky and Mr. Androwsky took the others about the craft, explaining how it worked.

"I can't show you the air glider," said Tom, who naturally acted as guide, "as it would take too long to put together, and besides there is not enough wind here to make it operate."

"Then you need much wind?" asked Nicolas Androwsky.

"The harder the gale the better she flies," answered Tom proudly.

"Bless my sand bag, but that's right!" exclaimed Mr. Damon, who, up to now had not taken much part in the conversation. He followed the party about the airship, keeping in the rear, and he eyed the Nihilists as if he thought that each one had one or more dynamite bombs concealed on his person.

"Ha!" exclaimed Mr. Androwsky, turning suddenly to the odd man. "Are you not one of us? Do you not believe that this terrible kingdom should be destroyed—made as nothing, and a new one built from its ashes? Are you not one of us?" and with a quick gesture he reached into his pocket.

"No! No!" exclaimed Mr. Damon, starting back. "Bless my election ticket! No! Never could I throw a bomb. Please don't give me one." Mr. Damon started to run away.

"A bomb!" exclaimed the Nihilist, and then he drew from his pocket some pamphlets printed in Russian. "I have no bombs. Here are some of the tracts we distribute to convert unbelievers to our cause," he went on. "Read them and you will understand what we are striving for. They will convert you, I am sure."

He went on, following the rest of the party, while Mr. Damon dropped back with Ned.

"Bless my gas meter!" gasped the odd man, as he stared at the queerly-printed documents in his hand. "I thought he was going to give me a bomb to throw!"

"I don't blame you," said Ned in a low voice. "They look like desperate men, but probably they have suffered many hardships, and they think their way of righting a wrong is the only way. I suppose you'll read those tracts," he added with a smile.

"Hum! I'm afraid not," answered Mr. Damon. "I might just as well try to translate a Chinese laundry check. But I'll save 'em for souvenirs," and he carefully put them in his pocket, as if he feared they might unexpectedly turn into a bomb and blow up the airship.

The tour of the craft was completed and the Nihilists returned to the comfortable cabin where, much to their surprise, they were served with a little lunch, Mr. Damon bustling proudly about from the table to the galley, and serving tea as nearly like the Russians drink it as possible.

"Well, you certainly have a wonderful craft here—wonderful," spoke Mr. Androwsky. "If we had some of these in our group now, we could start from here, hover over the palace of the Czar, or one of the Grand Dukes, drop a bomb, utterly destroy it, and come back before any of the hated police would be any the wiser."

"I'm afraid I can't lend it to you," said Tom, and he could scarcely repress a shudder at the terrible ideas of the Nihilists.

"It would never do," agreed Ivan Petrofsky. "The campaign of education is the only way."

There were gutteral objections on the part of the other Russians, and they turned to more cheerful subjects of talk.

"What are your plans?" asked Tom of the exile. "You say you can get no trace here of your brother?"

"No, he seems to have totally disappeared from sight. Usually we enemies of the government can get some news of a prisoner, but poor Peter is either dead, or in some obscure mine, which is hidden away in the forests or mountains."

"Maybe he is in the lost platinum mine," suggested Ned.

"No, that has not been discovered," declared the exile, "or my friends here would have heard of it. That is still to be found."

"And we'll do it, in the air glider," declared Tom. "By the way, Mr. Petrofsky, would it not be a good plan to ask your friends the location of the place where the winds constantly blow with such force. It occurs to me that in some such way we might locate the mine."

"It would be of use if there was only one place of the gales," replied the exile. "But Siberia has many such spots in the mountain fastnesses— places which, by the peculiar formation of the land, have constant eddys of air over them. No, the only way is for us to go as nearly as possible to the place where my brother and I were imprisoned, and search there."

"But what is that you said about us having to stay here, to get some news of your brother?" asked Tom.

"I had hoped to get some information here," resumed Mr. Petrofsky, "but my friends here are without news. However, they are going to make inquiries, and we will have to stay here until they have an answer. It will be safe, they think, as there are not many police in town, and the local authorities are not very efficient. So the airship will remain here, and, from time to time I will go to the village, disguised, and see if any word has come."

"And we will bring you news as soon as we get it," promised Mr. Androwsky. "You are not exactly one of us, but you are against the government, and, therefor, a brother. But you will be one of us in time."

"Never," replied the exile with a smile. "My only hope now is to get my brother safely away, and then we will go and live in free America. But, Tom, I hope I won't put you out by delaying here."

"Not a bit of it. More than half the object of our trip is to rescue your brother. We must do that first. Now as to details," and they fell to discussing plans. It was late that night when the Nihilists left the airship, first having made a careful inspection to see that they were not spied upon. They promised at once to set to work their secret methods of getting information.

For several days the airship remained in the vicinity of the Russian town. Our friends were undisturbed by visitors, as they were in a forest where the villagers seldom came and the nearest wood-road was nearly half a mile off.

Every day either Mr. Petrofsky went in to town to see the Nihilists or some of them came out to the Falcon, usually at night.

"Well, have you any word yet?" asked Tom, after about a week had passed.

"Nothing yet," answered the exile, and his tone was a bit hopeless. "But we have not given up. All the most likely places have been tried, but he is not there. We have had traces of him, but they are not fresh ones. He seems to have been moved from one mine to another. Probably they feared I would make an attempt to rescue him. But I have not given up. He is somewhere in Siberia."

"And we'll find him!" cried Tom with enthusiasm.

For three days more they lingered, and then, one night, when they were just getting ready to retire, there was a knock on the cabin door. Mr. Petrofsky had been to the village that day, and had received no news. He had only returned about an hour before.

"Some one's knocking," announced Ned, as if there could be any doubt of it.

"Bless my burglar alarm!" gasped Mr. Damon.

"I'll see who it is," volunteered Mr. Petrofsky, and Tom looked toward the rack of loaded rifles, for that day a man, seemingly a wood cutter had passed close to the airship, and had hurried off as if he had seen a ghost.

The knock was repeated. It might be their friends, and it might be—

But Mr. Petrofsky solved the riddle by throwing back the portal, and there stood the Nihilist, Nicolas Androwsky.

"Is there anything the matter?" asked the exile quickly.

"We have news," was the cautious answer, as the Nihilist slipped in, and closed the door behind him.

"News of my brother?"

"Of your brother! He is in a sulphur mine in the Altai Mountains, near the city of Abakansk."

"Where's that?" asked Tom for he had forgotten most of his Russian geography.

"The Altai Mountains are a range about the middle of Siberia," explained Mr. Petrofsky. "They begin at the Kirghiz Steppes, and run west. It is a wild and desolate place. I hope we can find poor Peter alive."

"And this city of Abakansk?" went on the young inventor.

"It is many miles from here, but I can give you a good map," said the Nihilist. "Some of our friends are there," he added with a half-growl. "I wish we could rescue all of them."

"We'd like to," spoke Tom. "But I fear it is impossible. But now that we have a clue, come on! Let's start at once! It may be dangerous to stay here. On to Siberia!"

CHAPTER XVIII

IN A RUSSIAN PRISON

The news they had waited for had come at last. It might be a false clue, but it was something to work on, and Tom was tired of inaction. Then, too, even after they had started, the prisoner might be moved and they would have to trace him again.

"But that is the latest information we could get," said Mr. Androwsky. "It came through some of our Anarchist friends, and I believe is reliable. Can you soon make a thousand miles in your airship?"

"Yes," answered Tom, "if I push her to the limit."

"Then do so," advised the Nihilist, "for there is need of haste. In making inquiries our friends might incur suspicions and Peter Petrofsky may be exiled to some other place."

"Oh, we'll get there," cried Tom. "Ned, see to the gas machine. Mr. Damon, you can help me in the pilot house."

"Here is a map of the best route," said the Nihilist, as he handed one to Mr. Petrofsky. "It will take you there the shortest way. But how can you steer when high in the air?"

"By compass," explained Tom. "We'll get there, never fear, and we're grateful for your clue."

"I never can thank you enough!" exclaimed the exile, as he shook hands with Mr. Androwsky.

The Nihilist left, after announcing that, in the event of the success of Tom and his friends, and the rescue of the exile from the sulphur mine, it would probably become known to them, as such news came through the Revolutionary channels, slowly but surely.

"Here we go!" cried the young inventor gaily, as he turned the starting lever in the pilot house, and silently, in the darkness of the night, the Falcon shot upward. There was not a light on board, for, though small signal lamps had been kept burning when the craft was in the forest, to guide the Nihilists to her, now that she was up in the air, and in motion, it was feared that her presence would become known to the authorities of the town, so even these had been extinguished.

"After we get well away we can turn on the electrics," remarked Tom, "and if they see us at a distance they may take us for a meteor. But, so close as this, they'd get wise in a minute."

Mr. Damon, who had done all that Tom needed in the starting of the craft, went to the forward port rail, and idly looked down on the black forest they were leaving. He could just make out the clearing where they had rested for over a week, and he was startled to see lights bobbing in it.

"I say, Mr. Petrofsky!" he called. "Did we leave any of our lanterns behind us?"

"I don't believe so," answered the exile. "I'll ask Tom."

"Lanterns? No," answered the young inventor. "Before we started I took down the only one we had out. I'll take a look."

Setting the automatic steering apparatus, he joined Mr. Damon and the Russian. The lights were now dimly visible, moving about in the forest clearing.

"It's just as if they were looking for something," said Tom. "Can it be that any of your Nihilist friends, Mr. Petrofsky are—"

"Friends—no friends—enemies!" cried the Russian. "I understand now! We got away just in time. Those are police agents who are looking for us! They must have received word about our being there. Androwsky and the others never carry lights when they go about. They know the country too well, and then, too, it leads to detection. No, those are police spies. A few minutes later, and we would have been discovered."

"As it is we're right over their heads, and they don't know it," chuckled Tom. The airship was moving silently along before a good breeze, the propellers not having been started, and Tom let her drift for several miles, as he did not want to give the police spies a clue by the noise of the motor.

The twinkling lights in the forest clearing disappeared from sight, and the seekers went on in the darkness.

"Well, we've got the hardest part of our work yet ahead of us," remarked Tom several hours later when, the lights having been set aglow, they were gathered in the main cabin. There was no danger of being seen now, for they were quite high.

"We've done pretty well, so far," commented Ned. "I think we will have easier work rescuing Mr. Petrofsky's brother than in locating the mine.

"I don't know about that," answered the Russian. "It is almost impossible to rescue a person from Siberia. Of course it is not going to be easy to locate the lost mine, but as for that we can keep on searching, that is if the air glider works, but there are so many forces to fight against in rescuing a prisoner."

They had a long journey ahead of them, and not an easy route to follow, but as the days passed, and they came nearer and nearer to their goal, they became more and more eager.

They were passing over a desolate country, for they avoided the vicinity of large towns and cities.

"I wonder when we'll strike Siberia?" mused Tom one afternoon, as they sat on the outer deck, enjoying the air.

"At this rate of progress, very soon," answered the exile, after glancing at the map. "We should be at the foot of the Ural mountains in a few hours, and across them in the night. Then we will be in Siberia."

And he was right, for just as supper was being served, Ned, who had been making observations with a telescope, exclaimed:

"These must be the Urals!"

Mr. Petrofsky seized the glass.

"They are," he announced. "We will cross between Orsk and Iroitsk. A safe place. In the morning we will be in Siberia—the land of the exiles."

And they were, morning seeing them flying over a most desolate stretch of landscape. Onward they flew, covering verst after verst of loneliness.

"I'm going to put on a little more speed," announced Tom, after a visit to the storeroom, where were kept the reserve tanks of gasolene. "I've got more fluid than I thought I had, and as we're on the ground now I want to hurry things. I'm going to make better time," and he yanked over the lever of the accelerator, sending the Falcon ahead at a rapid rate.

All day this was kept up, and they were just making an observation to determine their position, along toward supper time, when there came the sound of another explosion from the motor room.

"Bless my safety valve!" cried Mr. Damon. "Something has gone wrong again."

Tom ran to the motor, and, at the same time the Falcon which was being used as an aeroplane and not as a dirigible, began to sink.

"We're going down!" cried Ned.

"Well, you know what to do!" shouted his chum. "The gas bag! Turn on the generator!"

Ned ran to it, but, in spite of his quick action, the craft continued to slide downward.

"She won't work!" he cried.

"Then the intake pipe must be stopped!" answered the young inventor. "Never mind, I'll volplane to earth and we can make repairs. That magneto has gone out of business again."

"Don't land here!" cried Ivan Petrofsky.

"Why not?"

"Because we are approaching a large town—Owbinsk I think it is-the police there will be there to get us. Keep on to the forest again!"

"I can't!" cried Tom. "We've got to go down, police or no police."

Running to the pilot house, he guided the craft so that it would safely volplane to earth. They could all see that now they were approaching a fairly large town, and would probably land on its outskirts. Through the glass Ned could make out people staring up at the strange sight.

"They'll be ready to receive us," he announced grimly.

"I hope they have no dynamite bombs for us," murmured Mr. Damon. "Bless my watch chain! I must get rid of that Nihilist literature I have about me, or they'll take me for one," and he tore up the tracts, and scattered them in the air.

Meanwhile the Falcon continued to descend.

"Maybe I can make quick repairs, and get away before they realize who we are," said Tom, as he got ready for the landing.

They came down in a big field, and, almost before the bicycle wheels had ceased revolving, under the application of the brakes, several men came running toward them.

"Here they come!" cried Mr. Damon.

"They are only farmers," said the exile. He had donned his dark glasses again, and looked like anything but a Russian.

"Lively, Ned!" cried Tom. "Let's see if we can't make repairs and get off again."

The two lads frantically began work, and they soon had the magneto in running order. They could have gone up as an aeroplane, leaving the repairs to the gas bag to be made later but, just as they were ready to start, there came galloping out a troop of Cossack soldiers. Their commander called something to them.

"What is he saying?" cried Tom to Mr. Petrofsky.

"He is telling them to surround us so that we can not get a running start, such as we need to go up. Evidently he understands aeroplanes."

"Well, I'm going to have a try," declared the young inventor.

He jumped to the pilot house, yelling to Ned to start the motor, but it was too late. They were hemmed in by a cordon of cavalry, and it would have been madness to have rushed the Falcon into them, for she would have been wrecked, even if Tom could have succeeded in sending her through the lines.

"I guess it's all up with us," groaned Ned.

And it seemed to; for, a moment later, an officer and several aides galloped forward, calling out something in Russian.

"What is it?" asked Tom.

"He says we are under arrest," translated the exile.

"What for?" demanded the young inventor.

Ivan Petrofsky shrugged his shoulders.

"It is of little use to ask—now," he answered. "It may be we have violated some local law, and can pay a fine and go, or we may be taken for just what we are, or foreign spies, which we are not. It is best to keep quiet, and go with them."

"Go where?" cried Tom.

"To prison, I suppose," answered the exile. "Keep quiet, and leave it to me. I will do all I can. I don't believe they will recognize me.

"Bless my search warrant!" cried Mr. Damon. "In a Russian prison! That is terrible!"

A few minutes later, expostulations having been useless, our friends were led away between guards who carried ugly looking rifles, and who looked more ugly and menacing themselves. Then the doors of the Russian prison of Owbinsk closed on Tom and his friends, while their airship was left at the mercy of their enemies.

CHAPTER XIX

LOST IN A SALT MINE

The blow had descended so suddenly that it was paralyzing. Tom and his friends did not know what to do, but they saw the wisdom of the course of leaving everything to Ivan Petrofsky. He was a Russian, and he knew the Russian police ways—to his sorrow.

"I'm not afraid," said Tom, when they had been locked in a large prison room, evidently set apart for the use of political, rather than criminal, offenders. "We're United States citizens, and once our counsel hears of this—as he will—there'll be some merry doings in Oskwaski, or whatever they call this place. But I am worried about what they may do to the Falcon."

"Have no fears on that score," said the Russian exile. "They know the value of a good airship, and they won't destroy her."

"What will they do then?" asked Tom.

"Keep her for their own use, perhaps."

"Never!" cried Tom. "I'll destroy her first!"

"If you get the chance!" interposed the exile.

"But we're American citizens!" cried Tom, "and—"

"You forget that I am not," interrupted Mr. Petrofsky. "I can't claim the protection of your flag, and that is why I wish to remain unknown. We must act quietly. The more trouble we make, the more important they will know us to be. If we hope to accomplish anything we must act cautiously."

"But my airship!" cried Tom.

"They won't do anything to that right away," declared the Russian in a whisper for he knew sometimes the police listened to the talk of prisoners. "I think, from what I overheard when they arrested us, that we either trespassed on the grounds of some one in authority, who had us taken in out of spite, or they fear we may be English or French spies, seeking to find out Russian secrets."

They were served with food in their prison, but to all inquiries made by Ivan Petrofsky, evasive answers were returned. He spoke in poor, broken Russian, so that he would not be taken for a native of that country. Had he been, he would have at once been in great danger of being accused as an escaped exile.

Finally a man who, the exile whispered to his Companions, was the local governor, came to their prison. He eagerly asked questions as to their mission, and Mr. Petrofsky answered them diplomatically.

"I don't think he'll make much out of what I told him," said the exile when the governor had gone. "I let him think we were scientists, or pleasure seekers, airshipping for our amusement. He tried to tangle me up politically, but I knew enough to keep out of such traps."

"What's going to become of us?" asked Ned.

"We will be detained a few days—until they find out more about us. Their spies are busy, I have no doubt, and they are telegraphing all over Europe about us."

"What about my airship?" asked Tom.

"I spoke of that," answered the exile. "I said you were a well-known inventor of the United States, and that if any harm came to the craft the Russian Government would not only be held responsible, but that the governor himself would be liable, and I said that it cost much money. That touched him, for, in spite of their power, these Russians are miserably paid. He didn't want to have to make good, and if it developed that he had made a mistake in arresting us, his superiors would disclaim all responsibility, and let him shoulder the blame. Oh, all is not lost yet, though I don't like the looks of things."

Indeed it began to seem rather black for our friends, for, that night they were taken from the fairly comfortable, large, prison room, and confined in small stone cells down in a basement. They were separated, but as the cells adjoined on a corridor they could talk to each other. With some coarse food, and a little water, Tom and his friends were left alone.

"Say I don't like this!" cried our hero, after a pause.

"Me either," chimed in Ned.

"Bless my burglar alarm!" exclaimed Mr. Damon. "It's an awful disgrace! If my wife ever heard of me being in jail—"

"She may never hear of it!" interposed Tom.

"Bless my heart!" cried the odd man. "Don't say such things."

They discussed their plight at length, but nothing could be done, and they settled themselves to uneasy slumber. For two days they were thus imprisoned, and all of Mr. Petrofsky's demands that they be given a fair trial, and allowed to know the nature of the charge against them, went for naught. No one came to see them but a villainous looking guard, who brought them their poor meals. The governor ignored them, and Mr. Petrofsky did not know what to think.

"Well, I'm getting sick of this!" exclaimed Tom—"I wish I knew where my airship was."

"I fancy it's in the same place," replied the exile. "From the way the governor acted I think he'd be afraid to have it moved. It might be damaged. If I could only get word to some of my Revolutionary friends it might do some good, but I guess I can't. We'll just have to wait."

Another day passed, and nothing happened. But that night, when the guard came to bring their suppers, something did occur.

"Hello! we've got a new one!" exclaimed Tom, as he noted the man. "Not so bad looking, either."

The man peered into his cell, and said something in Russian.

"Nothing doing," remarked the young inventor with a short laugh. "Nixy on that jabbering."

But, no sooner had the man's words penetrated to the cell of Ivan Petrofsky, that the exile called out something. The guard started, hastened to that cell door, and for a few seconds there was an excited dialogue in Russian.

"Boys! Mr. Damon! We're saved!" suddenly cried out Mr. Petrofsky.

"Bless my door knob! You don't say so!" gasped the odd man. "How? Has the Czar sent orders to release us."

"No, but somehow my Revolutionary friends have heard about my arrest, and they have arranged for our release—secretly of course. This guard is affiliated with the Nihilist group that got on the trail of my brother. He bribed the other guard to let him take his place for tonight, and now—"

"Yes! What is it?" cried Tom.

"He's going to open the cell doors and let us out!"

"But how can we get past the other guards, upstairs?" asked Ned.

"We're not going that way," explained Mr. Petrofsky. "There is a secret exit from this corridor, through a tunnel that connects with a large salt mine. Once we are in there we can make our way out. We'll soon be free."

"Ask him if he's heard anything of my airship?" asked Tom. Mr. Petrofsky put the question rapidly in Russian and then translated the answer.

"It's in the same place."

"Hurray!" cried Tom.

Working rapidly, the Nihilist guard soon had the cell doors open, for he had the keys, and our friends stepped out into the corridor.

"This way," called Ivan Petrofsky, as he followed their liberator, who spoke in whispers. "He says he will lead us to the salt mine, tell us how to get out and then he must make his own escape."

"Then he isn't coming with us?" asked Ned.

"No, it would not be safe. But he will tell us how to get out. It seems that years ago some prisoners escaped this way, and the authorities closed up the tunnel. But a cave-in of the salt mine opened a way into it again."

They followed their queer guide, who led them down the corridor. He paused at the end, and then, diving in behind a pile of rubbish, he pulled away some boards. A black opening, barely large enough for a man to walk in upright, was disclosed.

"In there?" cried Tom.

"In there," answered Mr. Petrofsky. He and the guard murmured their good-byes, and then, with a lighted candle the faithful Nihilist had provided, and with several others in reserve, our friends stepped into the blackness. They could hear the board being pulled back into place behind them.

"Forward!" cried the exile, and forward they went.

It was not a pleasant journey, being through an uneven tunnel in the darkness. Half a mile later they emerged into a large salt mine, that seemed to be directly beneath the town. Work in this part had been abandoned long ago, all the salt there was left being in the shape of large pillars, that supported the roof. It sparkled dully in the candle light.

"Now let me see if I remember the turnings," murmured Mr. Petrofsky. "He said to keep on for half an hour, and we would come out in a little woods not far from where our airship was anchored."

Twisting and turning, here and there in the semi-darkness, stumbling, and sometimes falling over the uneven floor, the little party went on.

"Did you say half an hour?" asked Tom, after a while.

"Yes," replied the Russian.

"We've been longer than that," announced the young inventor, after a look at his watch. "It's over an hour."

"Bless my timetable!" cried Mr. Damon.

"Are you sure?" asked Mr. Petrofsky.

"Yes," answered Tom in a low voice.

The Russian looked about him, flashing the candle on several turnings and tunnels. Suddenly Ned uttered a cry.

"Why, we passed this place a little while before!" he said. "I remember this pillar that looks like two men wrestling!"

It was true. They all remembered it when they saw it again.

"Back in the same place!" mused the Russian. "Then we have doubled on our tracks. I'm afraid we're lost!"

"Lost in a Russian salt mine!" gasped Tom, and his words sounded ominous in that gloomy place.

CHAPTER XX

THE ESCAPE

For a space of several seconds no one moved or spoke. In the flickering light of the candle they looked at one another, and then at the fantastic pillars of salt all about them. Then Mr. Damon started forward.

"Bless my trolley car!" he exclaimed. "It isn't possible! There must be some mistake. If we'll keep on we'll come out all right. You know your way about, don't you, Mr. Petrofsky?"

"I thought I did, from what the guard told us, but it seems I must have taken a wrong turning."

"Then it's easily remedied," suggested Tom "All we'll have to do will be to go to the place where we started, and begin over again."

"Of course," agreed Ned, and they all seemed more cheerful.

"And if we start out once more, and get lost again, then what?" asked Mr. Damon.

"Well, if worst comes to worst, we can go, back in the tunnel, go to our cells and ask the guard to come with us and show us the way went on Tom.

"Never!" cried the exile. "It would be the most dangerous thing in the world to go back to the prison. Our escape has probably been discovered by this time, and to return would only be to put our heads in the noose. We must keep on at any cost!"

"But if we can't get out," suggested Tom, "and if we haven't anything to eat or drink, we—"

He did not finish, but they all knew what he meant.

"Oh, we'll get out!" declared Ned, who was something of an optimist. "You've been in salt mines before, haven't you, Mr. Petrofsky?"

"Yes, I was condemned to one once, but it was not in this part of the country, and it was not an abandoned one. I imagine this was only an isolated mine, and that there are no others near it, so when they abandoned it, after all the salt was taken out, most people forgot about it. I remember once a party of prisoners were lost in a large salt mine, and were missed for several days."

"What happened to them?" asked Tom.

"I don't like to talk about it," replied the Russian with a shudder.

"Bless my soul! Was it as bad as that?" asked Mr. Damon.

"It was," replied the exile. "But now let's see if we can find our way back, and start afresh. I'll be more careful next time, and watch the turns more closely."

But he did not get the chance. They could not find the tunnel whence they had started. Turn after turn they took, down passage after passage sometimes in such small ones that they almost had to crawl.

But it was of no use. They could not find their way back to the starting place, and they could not find the opening of the mine. They had used two of the slow burning candles and they had only half a dozen or so left. When these were gone—

But they did not like to think of that, and stumbled on and on. They did not talk much, for they were too worried. Finally Ned gasped:

"I'd give a good deal for a drink of water."

"So would I," added his chum. "But what's the use of wishing? If there was a spring down here it would be salt water. But I know what I would do—if I could."

"What?" asked Mr. Damon.

"Go back to the prison. At least we wouldn't starve there, and we'd have something to drink. If they kept us we know we could get free—sometime."

"Perhaps never!" exclaimed Ivan Petrofsky. "It is better to keep on here, and, as for me, I would rather die here than go back to a Russian prison. We must—we shall get out!"

But it was idle talk. Gradually they lost track of time as they staggered on, and they hardly knew whether a day had passed or whether it was but a few hours since they had been lost.

Of their sufferings in that salt mine I shall not go into details. There are enough unpleasant things in this world without telling about that. They must have wandered around for at least a day and a half, and in all that while they had not a drop of water, and not a thing to eat. Wait, though, at last in their desperation they did gnaw the tallow candles, and that served to keep them alive, and, in a measure, alleviate their awful sufferings from thirst.

Back and forth they wandered, up and down in the galleries of the old salt mine. They were merely hoping against hope.

"It's worse than the underground city of gold," said Ned in hollow tones, as he staggered on. "Worse—much worse." His head was feeling light. No one answered him.

It was, as they learned later, just about two days after the time when they entered the mine that they managed to get out. Forty-eight hours, most of them of intense suffering. They were burning their last candle, and when that was out they knew they would have the horrors of darkness to fight against, as well as those of hunger and thirst.

But fate was kind to them. How they managed to hit on the right gallery they did not know, but, as they made a turn around an immense pillar of salt Tom, who was walking weakly in advance, suddenly stopped.

"Look! Look!" he whispered. "Another candle! Someone—someone is searching for us! We are saved!"

"It may be the police!" said Ned.

"That is not a candle," spoke the Russian in hollow tones as he looked to where Tom pointed, to a little glimmer of light. "It is a star. Friends, we are saved, and by Providence! That is a star, shining through the opening of the mine. We are saved!"

Eagerly they pressed forward, and they had not gone far before they knew that the exile was right. They felt the cool night wind on their hot cheeks.

"Thank heaven!" gasped Tom, as he pushed on.

A moment later, climbing over the rusted rails on which the mine cars had run with their loads of salt, they staggered into the open. They were free—under the silent stars!

"And now, if we can only find the airship," said Tom faintly, "we can—"

"Look there!" whispered Ned, pointing to a patch of deeper blackness that the surrounding night. "What's that."

"The Falcon!" gasped Tom. He started toward her, for she was but a short distance from a little clump of trees into which they had emerged from the opening of the salt mine. There, on the same little plane where they had landed in her was the airship. She had not been moved.

"Wait!" cautioned Ivan Petrofsky. "She may be guarded."

Hardly had he spoken than there walked into the faint starlight on the side of the ship nearest them, a Cossack soldier with his rifle over his shoulder.

"We can't get her!" gasped Ned.

"We've got to get her!" declared Tom. "We'll die if we don't!"

"But the guards! They'll arrest us!" said the exile.

An instant later a second soldier joined the first, and they could be seen conversing. They then resumed their pacing around the anchored craft. Evidently they were waiting for the escaped prisoners to come up when they would give the alarm and apprehend them.

"What can we do?" asked Mr. Damon.

"I have a plan," said Tom weakly. "It's the only chance, for we're not strong enough to tackle them. Every time they go around on the far side of the airship we must creep forward. When they come on this side we'll lie down. I doubt if they can see us. Once we are on hoard we can cut the ropes, and start off. Everything is all ready for a start if they haven't monkeyed with her, and I don't think they have. We've got room enough to run along as an aeroplane and mount upward. It's our only hope."

The others agreed, and they put the plan into operation. When the Cossack guards were out of sight the escaped prisoners crawled forward, and when the soldiers came into view our friends waited in silence.

It took several minutes of alternate creeping and waiting to do this, but it was accomplished at last and unseen they managed to slip aboard. Then it was the work of but a moment to cut the restraining ropes.

Silently Tom crept to the motor room. He had to work in absolute darkness, for the gleam of a light would have drawn the fire of the guards. But the youth knew every inch of his invention. The only worriment was whether or not the motor would start up after the breakdown, not having been run since it was so hastily repaired. Still he could only try.

He looked out, and saw the guards pacing back and forth. They did not know that the much-sought prisoners were within a few feet of them.

Ned was in the pilot house. He could see a clear field in front of him.

Suddenly Tom pulled the starting lever. There was a little clicking, followed by silence. Was the motor going to revolve? It answered the next moment with a whizz and a roar.

"Here we go!" cried the young inventor, as the big machine shot forward on her flight. "Now let them stop us!"

Forward she went until Ned, knowing by the speed that she had momentum enough, tilted the elevation rudder, and up she shot, while behind, on the ground, wildly running to and fro, and firing their rifles, were the two amazed guards.

CHAPTER XXI

THE RESCUE

"Have we—have we time to get a drink?" gasped Ned, when the aeroplane, now on a level keel, had been shooting forward about three minutes. Already it was beyond the reach of the rifles.

"Yes, but take only a little," cautioned Tom. "Oh! it doesn't seem possible that we are free!"

He switched on a few interior lights, and by their glow the faint and starving platinum-seekers found water and food. Their craft had, apparently, not been touched in their absence, and the machinery ran well.

Cautiously they ate and drank, feeling their strength come back to them, and then they removed the traces of their terrible imprisonment, and set about in ease and comfort, talking of what they had suffered.

Onward sped the aeroplane, onward through the night, and then Tom, having set the automatic steering gear, all fell into heavy slumbers that lasted until far into the next day.

When the young inventor awoke he looked below and could see nothing—nothing but a sea of mist.

"What's this?" he cried. "Are we above the clouds, or in a fog over some inland sea?"

He was quite worried, until Ivan Petrofsky informed him that they were in the midst of a dense fog, which was common over that part of Siberia.

"But where are we?" asked Ned.

"About over the province of Irtutsk," was the answer. "We are heading north," he went on, as he looked at the compass, "and I think about right to land somewhere near where my brother is confined in the sulphur mine."

"That's so; we've got to drop," said Tom. "I must get the gas pipe repaired. I wish we could see over what soft of a place we were so as to know whether it would be safe to land. I wish the mist would clear away."

It did, about noon, and they noted that they were over a desolate stretch of country, in which it would be safe to make a landing.

Bringing the aeroplane down on as smooth a spot as he could pick out, Tom and Ned were soon at work clearing out the clogged pipe of the gas generator. They had to take it out in the open air, as the fumes were unpleasant, and it was while working over it that they saw a shadow thrown on the ground in front of them. Startled they looked up, to see a burly Russian staring at them.

The sudden appearance of a man in that lonely spot, his calm regard of the lads, his stealthy approach, which had made it possible for him to be almost upon them before they were aware of his presence, all this made them suspicious of danger. Tom gave a quick glance about, however, and saw no others—no Cossack soldiers, and as he looked a second time at the man he noted that he was poorly dressed, that his shoes were ragged, his whole appearance denoting that he had traveled far, and was weary and ill.

"What do you make of this, Ned?" asked Tom, in a low voice.

"I don't know what to make of it. He can't be an officer, in that rig, and he has no one with him. I guess we haven't anything to be afraid of. I'm going to ask him what he wants."

Which Tom did in his plainest English. At once the man broke into a stream of confused Russian, and he kept it up until Tom held up his hand for silence.

"I'm sorry, but I can't understand you," said the young inventor. "I'll call some one who can, though," and, raising his voice, he summoned Ivan Petrofsky who, with Mr. Damon, was inside the airship doing some small repairs.

"There's a Russian out here, Mr. Petrofsky," said Tom, "and what he wants I can't make out."

The exile was quickly on the scene and, after a first glance at the man, hurried up to him, grasped him by the hand and at once the two were talking such a torrent of hard-sounding words that Tom and Ned looked at each other helplessly, while Mr. Damon, who had come out, exclaimed:

"Bless my dictionary! they must know each other."

For several minutes the two Russians kept up their rapid-fire talk and then Mr. Petrofsky, evidently realizing that his friends must wonder at it, turned to them and said:

"This is a very strange thing. This man is an escaped convict, as I once was. I recognized him by certain signs as soon as I saw him, though I had never met him before. There are certain marks by which a Siberian exile can never be forgotten," he added significantly. "He made his escape from the mines some time ago, and has suffered great hardships since. The revolutionists help him when they can, but he has to keep in concealment and travels from town to town as best he may. He has heard of our airship, I suppose from inquiries the revolutionists have been making in our behalf, and when he unexpectedly came upon us just now he was not frightened, as an ordinary peasant would have been. But he did not know I was aboard."

"And does he know you?" asked Tom. "Does he know you are trying to rescue your brother?"

"No, but I will tell him."

There was another exchange of the Russian language, and it seemed to have a surprising result. For, no sooner had Ivan Petrofsky mentioned his brother, than the other, whose name was Alexis Borious seemed greatly excited. Mr. Petrofsky was equally so at the reply his new acquaintance made, and fairly shouted to Tom, Ned and Mr. Damon.

"Friends, I have unexpected good news! It is well that we met this man or we would have gone many miles out of our way. My brother has been moved to another mine since the revolutionists located him for me. He is in a lonely district many miles from here. This man was in the same mine with him, until my brother was transferred, and then Mr. Borious escaped. We will have to change our plans."

"And where are we to head for now?" asked Tom.

"Near to the town of Haskaski, where my poor brother is working in a sulphur mine!"

"Then let's get a move on!" cried Tom with enthusiasm. "Do you think this man will come with us, Mr. Petrofsky, to help in the rescue, and show us the place?"

"He says he will," translated the exile, "though he is much afraid of our strange craft. Still he knows that to trust himself to it is better than being captured, and sent back to the mines to starve to death!"

"Good!" cried Tom. "And if he wants to, and all goes well, we'll take him out of Russia with us. Now get busy, Ned, and we'll have this machine in shape again soon."

While Ivan Petrofsky took his new friend inside, and explained to him about the workings of the Falcon, Tom and Ned labored over the gas machine with such good effect that by night it was capable of being used. Then they went aloft, and making a change in their route, as suggested by Mr. Borious, they headed for the desolate sulphur region.

For several days they sailed on, and gradually a plan of rescue was worked out. According to the information of the newcomer, the best way to save Mr. Petrofsky's brother was to make the attempt when the prisoners were marched back from the mines to the barracks where they were confined.

"It will be dark then," said Mr. Borious, "and if you can hover in your airship near at hand, and if Mr. Petrofsky can call out to his brother to run to him, we can take him up with us and get away before the guards know what we are doing."

"But aren't the prisoners chained?" asked Tom.

"No, they depend on guards to prevent escapes."

"Then we'll try that way," decided the young inventor.

On and on they sailed, the Falcon working admirably. Verst after verst was covered, and finally, one morning, Mr. Borious, who knew the country well, from having once been a prisoner there, said:

"We are now near the place. If we go any closer we may be observed. We had better remain hidden in some grove of trees so that at nightfall we can go forth to the rescue."

"But how can we find it after dark?" asked Ned.

"You can easily tell by the lights in the barracks," was the answer. "I can stand in the pilot house to direct you, for nearly all these exile prisons are alike. The prisoners will march in a long line from the mine. Then for the rescue."

It was tedious waiting that day, but it had to be done, and to Tom, who was anxious to effect the rescue, and proceed to the place of the winds to try his air glider, it seemed as if dusk would never come as they remained in concealment.

But night finally approached and then the great airship went silently aloft, ready to hover over the prison ground. Fortunately there was little wind; and she could be used as a balloon, thus avoiding the noise of the motor.

"The next thing I do, when I get home," remarked Tom, as they drifted along. "Will be to make a silent airship. I think they would be very useful."

With Mr. Borious in the pilot house, to point out the way, Tom steered through the fast-gathering darkness. The Russian had soon become used to the airship, and was not at all afraid.

"Can you go just where you want to, as a balloon?" asked the new guide.

"No, but almost," replied Tom. "At the last moment I've got to take a chance and start the motor to send us just where we want to go. That's why I think a silent airship would be a great thing. You could get up on the enemy before he knew it."

"There are the prison barracks," said the guide a little later, his talk being translated by Mr. Petrofsky. Below and a little ahead of them could been seen a cluster of lights.

"Yes, that looks like a line of prisoners," remarked Ned, who was peering through a pair of night glasses.

"Where?" asked Tom eagerly, and they were pointed out to him. He took an observation, and exclaimed:

"There they are, sure enough. Now if your brother is only among them, Mr. Petrofsky, we'll soon have him on board."

"Heaven grant that he may be there!" said the exile in a low voice.

A moment later, the Falcon, meanwhile having been allowed to drift as close as possible to the dimly-seen line of prisoners, Tom set in motion the great motor, the propeller blades heating the air fiercely.

At the sound there was a shout on the ground below, but before the excitement had time to spread, or before any of the guards could form a notion of what was about to take place, Tom had sent his craft to earth on a sharp slant, closer to the line of prisoners than he had dared to hope.

Mr. Petrofsky sprang out on deck, and in a loud voice called in Russian:

"Peter! Peter! If you are there, come here! Come quickly! It is I, your brother Ivan who speaks. I have come to save you—save you in the wonderful airship of Tom Swift! Come quickly and we will take you away! Peter Petrofsky!"

For a moment there was silence, and then the sound of some one running rapidly was borne to the ears of the waiting ones. It was followed, a moment later, by angry shouts from the guards.

"Quick! Quick, Peter!" cried the brother, "over this way!"

For an instant only the exile showed a single electric flash light, that his brother might see in which direction to run. The echo of the approaching footsteps came nearer, the shouts of the guards redoubled, and then came the sound of many men running in pursuit.

"Hurry, Peter, hurry!" cried Mr. Petrofsky, and, as he spoke in Russian the guards, of course, understood.

Suddenly a rifle shot rang out, but the weapon seemed to have been fired in the air. A moment later a dark figure clambered aboard the airship.

"Peter, is it you?" cried Ivan Petrofsky, hoarsely.

"Yes, brother! But get away quickly or the whole guard will be swarming about here!"

"Praise the dear Lord you are saved!"

"Is it all right?" cried Tom, who wanted to make sure they were saving the right man.

"Yes! Yes, Tom! Go quickly!" called Ivan Petrofsky, as he folded his brother in his arms. A moment later, with a roar, the Falcon shot away from the earth, while below sounded angry cries, confused shouts and many orders, for the guards and their officers had never known of such a daring rescue as this.

CHAPTER XXII

IN THE HURRICANE

There was a volley of shots from the prison guards, and the flashes of the rifles cut bright slivers of flame in the darkness, but, so rapidly did the airship go up, veering off on a wide slant, under the skillful guidance of Tom that the shots did no harm.

"Bless my bullet pouch!" cried Mr. Damon. "They must be quite excited."

"Shouldn't wonder," calmly observed Ned, as he went to help his chum in managing the airship. "But it won't do them any good. We've got our man."

"And right from under their noses, too," added Ivan Petrofsky exultingly. "This rescue of an exile will go down in the history of Russia."

The two exile brothers were gazing fondly at each other, for now that the Falcon was so high, Tom ventured to turn on the lights.

A moment later the three Russians were excitedly conversing, while Tom and Ned managed the craft, and Mr. Damon, after listening a moment to the rapid flow of the strange language, which quite fascinated him, hurried to the galley to prepare a meal for the rescued one, who had been taken away before he had had a chance to get his supper.

His wonder at his startling and unexpected rescue may well be imagined, but the joy at being reunited to his brother overshadowed everything for the time being. But when he had a chance to look about, and see what a strange craft he was in, his amazement knew no bounds, and he was like a child. He asked countless questions, and Ivan Petrofsky and

Mr. Borious took turns in answering them. And from now on, I shall give the conversation of the two new Russians just as if they spoke English, though of course it had to be translated by Ivan Petrofsky, Peter's brother.

If Peter was amazed at being rescued in an airship, his wonder grew when he was served with a well-cooked meal, while high in the air, and while flying along at the rate of fifty miles an hour. He could not talk enough about it.

By degrees the story of how Tom and his friends had started for Russia was told, and there was added the detail of how Mr. Borious came to be picked up.

"But brother Ivan, you did not come all that distance to rescue me; did you?" asked Peter.

"Yes, partly, and partly to find the platinum mine."

"What? The lost mine that you and I stumbled upon in that terrible storm?"

"That is the one, Peter."

"Then, Tom Swift may as well return. I doubt if we can even locate the district where it was, and if we did find it, the winds blow so that even this magnificent ship could not weather the gales."

"I guess he doesn't understand about my air glider," said Tom with a smile, when this was translated to him. "I wish I had a chance to put it together, and show him how it works."

"Oh, it will work all right," replied Ned, who was very proud of his friend's inventive ability.

"Now, what is the next thing to be done?" asked Tom, a little later that evening, when, supper having been served, they were sitting in the main cabin, talking over the events of the past few days. "I'd like to get on the track of that platinum treasure."

"And we will do all in our power to aid you," said Ivan Petrofsky. "My brother and I owe much to you—in fact Peter owes you his life; do you not?" and he turned to him.

"I do," was the firm answer.

"Oh, nonsense!" exclaimed Tom, who did not like to be praised. "I didn't do much."

"Much! You do not call taking me away from that place—that sulphur mine—that horrible prison barrack with the cruel guards—you do not call that much? My friend," spoke the Russian solemnly, "no one on earth has done so much for me as you have, and if it is the power of man to show you where that lost mine is, my brother and I will do so!"

"Agreed," spoke Ivan quietly.

"Then what plans shall we make?" asked Tom, after a little more talk. "Are we to go about indiscriminately, or is there any possible way of getting on the trail?"

"My brother and I will try and decide on a definite route," spoke Ivan Petrofsky. "It is some time since I have seen him, and longer since we accidently found the mine together, but we will consult each other, and, if possible make some sort of a map."

This was done the next day, the present maps aboard the Falcon being consulted, and the brothers comparing notes. They began to lay out a stretch of country in which it was most likely the lost mine lay. It took several days to do this, for sometimes one brother would forget some point, and again the other would. But at last they agreed on certain facts.

"This is the nearest we can come to it," said Ivan Petrofsky to Tom. "The lost platinum mine lies somewhere between the city of Iakutsk and the first range of the Iablonnoi mountains. Those are the northern and southern boundaries. As for the western one, it is most likely the Lena river, and the eastern one the Amaga river. So you see you have quite a large stretch of country to search, Tom Swift."

"Yes, I should say I had," agreed the young inventor. "But I have had harder tasks. Now that I know where to head for I'll get there as soon as possible."

"And what will you do when you arrive?" asked Ned.

"Fly about in the Falcon, in ever-widening circles, starting as near the centre of that area as possible," replied Tom. "And as soon as I run into a steady hurricane I'll know that I'm at the place of the big winds, and I'll get out my glider, for I'll be pretty sure to be near the place."

"Bless my gas meter!" cried Mr. Damon. "That's the talk!"

Tom put his plan into operation at once, by heading the nose of his craft for the desolate region mapped out by the Russian brothers.

The days that followed were filled with weary searching. It was like the time when they had sought for the plain of the great ruined Temple in Mexico, that they might locate the underground city of gold. Only in this case they had no such landmark as a great Aztec ruin to guide them.

What they were seeking for was something unseen, but which could be felt—a mysterious wind—a wind that might be encountered any time, and which might send the Falcon to the earth a wreck.

The Russian brothers, staggering about in the storm, had seen the mine under different conditions from what it would be viewed now. Then it was winter in Siberia. Now it was summer, though it was not very warm.

On and on sailed the Falcon. The weather could not have been better, but for once Tom wanted bad weather. He wanted a blow—the harder the better—and all eyes anxiously watched the anemometer, or wind gage. But ever it revolved lazily about in the gentle breeze.

"Oh, for a hurricane!" cried Tom.

He got his wish sooner than he anticipated. It was about two days after this, when they were going about in a great circle, about two hundred miles from the imaginary centre of the district in which the mine lay, that, as Mr. Damon was getting dinner a dish he was carrying to the table was suddenly whisked out of his hand.

"I say, what's the matter?" he cried. "Bless my—"

But he had no time to say more. The airship fairly stood on end, and then, turning completely about, was rapidly driven in the opposite direction, though her propellers were working rapidly.

"What's up?" yelled Ned.

"We are capsizing!" shouted Ivan Petrofsky, and indeed it seemed so, for the airship was being forced over.

"I guess we've struck what we want!" cried Tom. "We're in a hurricane all right! This is the place of the big wind! Now for my air glider, if I can get the airship to earth without being wrecked! Ned, lend a hand! We've got our work cut out for us now!"

CHAPTER XXIII

THE LOST MINE

For several moments it seemed as if disaster would overtake the little band of platinum-hunters. In spite of all that Tom and Ned could do, the Falcon was whipped about like a feather in the wind. Sometimes she was pointing her nose to the clouds, and again earthward. Again she would be whirling about in the grip of the hurricane, like some fantastic dancer, and again she would roll dangerously. Had she turned turtle it probably would have been the last of her and of all on board.

"Yank that deflecting lever as far down as it will go!" yelled Tom to his chum.

"I am. She won't go any farther."

"All right, hold her so. Mr. Damon, let all the gas out of the bag. I want to be as heavy as possible, and get to earth as soon as we can."

"Bless my comb and brush!" cried the odd man. "I don't know what's going to become of us."

"You will know, pretty soon, if the gas isn't let out!" retorted Tom grimly, and then Mr. Damon hastened to the generator compartment, and opened the emergency outlet.

Finally, by crowding on all the possible power, so that the propellers and deflecting rudders forced the craft down, Tom was able to get out of the grip of the hurricane, and landed just beyond the zone of it on the ground.

"Whew! That was a narrow squeak!" cried Ned, as he got out. "How'd you do it, Tom?"

"I hardly know myself. But it's evident that we're on the right spot now."

"But the wind has stopped blowing," said Mr. Damon. "It was only a gust."

"It was the worst kind of a gust I ever want to see," declared the young inventor. "My air glider ought to work to perfection in that. If you think the wind has died out, Mr. Damon, just walk in that direction," and Tom pointed off to the left.

"Bless my umbrella, I will," was the reply and the odd man started off. He had not gone far, before he was seen to put his hand to his cap. Still he kept on.

"He's getting into the blow-zone," said Tom in a low voice.

The next moment Mr. Damon was seen to stagger and fall, while his cap was whisked from his head, and sent high into the air, almost instantly disappearing from sight.

"Some wind that," murmured Ned, in rather awe-struck tones.

"That's so," agreed his chum. "But we'd better help Mr. Damon," for that gentleman was slowly crawling back, not caring to trust himself on his feet, for the wind had actually carried him down by its force.

"Bless my anemometer!" he gasped, when Tom and Ned had given him a hand up. "What happened?"

"It was the great wind," explained Tom. "It blows only in a certain zone, like a draft down a chimney. It is like a cyclone, only that goes in a circle. This is a straight wind, but the path of it seems to be as sharply marked as a trail through the forest. I guess we're here all right. Does this location look familiar to you?" he asked of the Russian brothers.

"I can't say that it does," answered Ivan. "But then it was winter when we were here."

"And, another thing," put in Peter. "That wind zone is quite wide. The mine may be in the middle, or near the other edge."

"That's so," agreed Tom. "We'll soon see what we can do. Come on, Ned, let's get the air glider out and put her together. She'll have a test as is a test, now."

I shall not describe the tedious work of re-assembling Tom Swift's latest invention in the air craft line—his glider. Sufficient to say that it was taken out from where it had been stored in separate pieces on board the Falcon, and put together on the plain that marked the beginning of the wind zone.

It was a curious fact that twenty feet away from the path of the wind scarcely a breeze could be felt, while to advance a little way into it meant that one would at once be almost carried off his feet.

Tom tested the speed of it one day with a special anemometer, and found that only a few hundred feet inside the zone the wind blew nearly one hundred miles an hour.

"What is it like inside, I wonder?" asked Ned.

"It must be terrific," was his chum's opinion.

"Dare you risk it, Tom?"

"Of course. The harder it blows the better the glider works. In fact I can't make much speed in a hundred-mile wind for with us all on board the craft will be heavy, and you must remember that I depend on the wind alone to give me motion."

"What do you think causes the wind to blow so peculiarly here Tom?" went on Ned.

"Oh, it must be caused by high mountain ranges on either side, or the effects of heat and cold, the air being evaporated over a certain area because of great heat, say a volcano, or something like that; though I don't know that they have volcanoes here. That creates a vacuum, and other air rushes in to fill the vacant space. That's all wind is, anyhow, air rushing in to fill a vacuum, or low pressure zone, for you remember that nature abhors a vacuum."

It took nearly a week to assemble the Vulture, as Tom had named his latest craft, from the fact that it could hover in the air motionless, like that great bird. At last it was completed and then, weights being taken aboard to steady it, all was ready for the test. Tom would have liked to have taken all his passengers in the glider, for it would work better then, but the three Russians were timid, though they promised to get aboard after the trial.

The test came off early one morning, Tom, Ned and Mr. Damon being the only ones aboard. Bags of sand represented the others. The glider was wheeled to the edge of the wind zone and they took their places in the car. It was hard work for the gale, that had never ceased blowing for an instant since they found its zone, was very strong. But the glider remained motionless in it, for the wing planes, the rudders, and equalizing weights had been adjusted to make the strain of the wind neutral.

"All ready?" asked Tom, when his chum and his friend were in the enclosed car of the glider.

"As ready as I ever shall be," answered Ned.

"Bless my suspenders! Let her go, Tom, and have it over with!" cried the odd man.

The young inventor pulled a lever, and almost instantly the glider darted forward. A moment later it soared aloft, and the three Russians cheered. But their voices were lost in the roar of the hurricane, as Tom sent his craft higher and higher.

It worked perfectly, and he could direct it almost anywhere. The wind acted as the motive power, the bending and warping wings, and the rudders and weights controlling its force.

"I'm going higher, and see if I can remain stationary!" yelled Tom in Ned's ear. His chum only nodded. Mr. Damon was seated on a bench, clinging to the sides of it as if he feared he would fall off.

Higher and higher went the Vulture, ever higher, until, all at once, Tom pulled on another lever and she was still. There she hung in the air, the wind rushing through her planes, but the glider herself as still and quiet as though she rested on the ground in a calm. She hardly moved a foot in either direction, and yet the wind, as evidenced by the anemometer was howling along at a hundred and twenty miles an hour!

"Success!" cried Tom. "Success! Now we can lie stationary in any spot, and spy out the land through our telescope. Now we will find the lost platinum mine!"

"Well, I'm not deaf," responded Ned with a smile, for Tom had fairly yelled as he had at the start, and there was no need of this now, for though the wind blew harder than ever it was not opposed to any of the weights or planes, and there was only a gentle humming sound as it rushed through the open spaces of the queer craft.

Tom gave his glider other and more severe tests, and she answered every one. Then he came to earth.

"Now we'll begin the search," he said, and preparations were made to that end. The Russians, now that they had seen how well the craft worked, were not afraid to trust themselves in her.

As I have explained, there was an enclosed car, capable of holding six. In this were stores, supplies and food sufficient for several days. Tom's plan was to leave the airship anchored on the edge of the wind zone, as a sort of base of supplies or headquarters. From there he intended to go off from time to time in the wind-swept area to look for the lost mine.

There were weary days that followed. Hour after hour was spent in the air in the glider, the whole party being aboard. Observation after observation was taken, sometimes a certain strata of wind enabling them to get close enough to the earth to use their eyes, while again they had to use the telescopes. They covered a wide section but as day after day passed, and they were no nearer their goal, even Tom optimistic as he usually was, began to have a tired and discouraged look.

"Don't you see anything like the place where you found the mine?" he asked of the exile brothers.

They could only shake their heads. Indeed their task was not easy, for to recognize the place again was difficult.

More than a week passed. They had been back and forth to their base of supplies at the airship, often staying away over night, once remaining aloft all through the dark hours in the glider, in a fierce gale which prevented a landing. They ate and slept on board, and seldom descended unless at or near the place where they had left the Falcon. Once they completely crossed the zone of wind, and came to a calm place on the other side. It was as wild and desolate as the other edge.

Nearly two weeks had passed, and Tom was almost ready to give up and go back home. He had at least accomplished part of his desire, to rescue the exile, and he had even done better than originally intended, for there was Mr. Borious who had also been saved, and it was the intention of the young inventor to take him to the United States.

"But the platinum treasure has me beat, I guess," said Tom grimly. "We can't seem to get a trace of it."

Night was coming on, and he had half determined to head back for the airship. Ivan Petrofsky was peering anxiously down at the desolate land, over which they were gliding. He and his brother took turns at this.

They were not far above the earth, but landmarks, such as had to be depended on to locate the mine, could not readily be observed without the glass. Mr. Damon, with a pair of ordinary field glasses, was doing all he could to pick out likely spots, though it was doubtful if he would know the place if he saw it.

However, as chance willed it, he was instrumental in bringing the quest to a close, and most unexpectedly. Peter Petrofsky was relieving his brother at the telescope, when the odd man, who had not taken his eyes from the field glasses, suddenly uttered an exclamation.

"Bless my tooth-brush!" he cried. "That's a most desolate place down there. A lot of trees blown down around a lake that looks as black as ink."

"What's that!" cried Ivan Petrofsky. "A lake as black as ink? Where?"

"We just passed it!" replied Mr. Damon.

"Then put back there, as soon as you can, Tom!" called the Russian. "I want to look at that place."

With a long, graceful sweep the young inventor sent the glider back over the course. Ivan Petrofsky glued his eyes to the telescope. He picked out the spot Mr. Damon had referred to, and a moment later cried:

"That's it! That's near the lost platinum mine! We've found it again, Tom—everybody! Don't you remember, Peter," he said turning to his brother, "when we were lost in the snow we crawled in among a tangle of trees to get out of the blast. There was a sheet of white snow near them, and you broke through into water. I pulled you out. That must have been a lake, though it was lightly frozen over then. I believe this is the lost mine. Go down, Tom! Go down!"

"I certainly will!" cried the youth, and pulling on the descending lever he shunted the glider to earth.

CHAPTER XXIV

THE LEAKING TANKS

Like a bird descending from some dizzy height, the Vulture landed close to the pool of black water. It was a small lake and the darkness must have been caused by its depth, for later when they took some out in a glass it was as clear as a crystal. Then, too, there might have been black rocks on the bottom.

"Can it be possible that we are here at last?" cried Tom, above the noise of the gale, for the wind was blowing at a terrific rate. But our friends knew better now how to adjust themselves to it, and the lake was down in a valley, the sides of which cut off the power of the gale. As for the glider it was only necessary to equalize the balance and it would remain stationary in any wind.

"This is the place! This is the place!" cried Ivan Petrofsky. "Don't you remember, Peter?"

"Indeed I do! I have good cause to! This is where we found the platinum!"

"Bless my soul!" cried Mr. Damon. "Where is it, in the lake?"

"The mine itself is just beyond that barrier of broken and twisted trees," replied the elder Russian brother. "It is an irregular opening in the ground, as though once, centuries ago, an ancient people tried to get out the precious metal. We will go to it at once."

"But it is getting late," objected Ned.

"No matter," said Tom. "If we find any platinum we'll stay here all night, and longer if necessary to get a good supply. This is better than the city of gold, for we're in the open."

"I should say we were," observed Mr. Damon, as he bent to the blast, which was strong, sheltered even as they were.

"Will it be safe to remain all night?" asked Mr. Borious, with a glance about the desolate country.

"We have plenty of food," replied Tom, "and a good place to stay, in the car of the glider. I don't believe we'll be attacked."

"No, not here," said the elder Petrofsky. "But we still have to go back across Siberia to escape."

"We'll do it!" cried Tom. "Now for the platinum treasure!"

They went forward, and it was no easy work. For the wind still blew with tremendous force though nothing like what it did higher up. And the ground was uneven. They had to cling to each other and it was very evident that no airship, not even the powerful Falcon, could have reached the place. Only an air glider would answer.

It took them half an hour to get to the opening of the ancient mine, and by that time it was nearly dark. But Tom had thought to bring electric torches, such as he had used in the underground city of gold, and they dispelled the gloom of the small cavern.

"Will you go in?" asked Ivan Petrofsky, when they had come to the place. He looked at Tom.

"Go in? Of course I'll go in!" cried our hero, stepping forward. The others followed. For some time they went on, and saw no traces of the precious metal. Then Ned uttered a cry, as he saw some dull, grayish particles imbedded in the earth walls of the shaft.

"Look!" he cried.

Tom was at his chum's side in a moment

"That's platinum!" cried the young inventor. "And of the very highest grade! But the lumps are very small."

"There are larger ones beyond," said the younger Russian brother.

Forward they pressed, and a moment later coming around a turn in the cavern where some earth had fallen away, evidently recently, Tom could not repress a cry of joy. For there, in plain sight, were many large lumps of the valuable metal, in as pure a state as it is ever found. For it is always mixed with other metals or chemicals.

"Look at that!" cried Tom. "Look at that! Lumps as large as an egg!" and he dug some out with a small pick he had brought along, and stuffed them into his pocket.

"Bless my check book!" cried Mr. Damon, "and that stuff is as valuable as gold!"

"More so!" cried Tom enthusiastically.

"Oh, here's a whopping big one!" cried Ned. "I'll bet it weighs ten pounds."

"More than that!" cried Tom, as he ran over and began digging it out, and they found later that it did. Platinum is usually found in small granules, but there are records of chunks being found weighing twenty pounds while others, the size of pigeons' eggs, are not uncommon.

"Say, this is great!" yelled Ned, discovering another large piece, and digging it out.

"I am glad we could lead you to it," said the elder Russian brother. "It is a small return for what you did for us!"

"Nonsense!" cried Tom. "These must be a king's ransom here. Everybody dig it out! Get all you can."

They were all busy, but the light of the two torches Tom had brought was not sufficient for good and efficient work, so after getting several thousand dollars worth of the precious metal, they decided to postpone operations until morning, and come with more lights.

They were at the work soon after breakfast, the night in the air glider having passed without incident. The treasure of platinum proved even richer than the Russians had thought, and it was no wonder the Imperial government had tried so hard to locate it, or get on the trail of those who sought it.

"And it's all good stuff!" cried Tom eagerly. "Not like that low-grade gold of the underground city. I can make my own terms when I sell this."

For three days our friends dug and dug in that platinum mine, so many years lost to man, and when they got ready to leave they had indeed a king's ransom with them. But it was to be equally divided. Tom insisted on this, as his Russian friends had been instrumental in finding it. Toward the end of the excavation large pieces were scarce, and it was evident that the mine was what is called a "lode."

"Well, shall we go back now?" asked Tom one day, after the finish of their mining operations. The work was comparatively simple, as the platinum lumps had merely to be dug out of the sides of the cave. But the loneliness and dreariness of the place was telling on them all.

"Can't we carry any more?" asked Ned.

"We could, but it might not be safe. I don't want to take on too much weight, as my glider isn't as stable as the airship. But we have plenty of the metal."

"Indeed we have," agreed Ivan Petrofsky. "Much of mine and my brother's will go toward helping relieve the sufferings of the Siberian exiles," he added.

"And mine, too," said Alexis Borious.

They started back early the next morning in a more terrific gale than in any the glider had yet flown. But she proved herself a stanch craft, and soon they were at the place where they had left the airship. It was undisturbed.

Four days were spent in taking apart the glider and packing it on board the Falcon. Then, with the platinum safely stored away Tom, with a last look at the desolate land that had been so kind to them, sent his craft on her homeward way.

It was when they were near the city of Pirtchina, on the Obi river, that what might have proved a disastrous accident occurred. They were flying along high, and at great speed, for Tom wanted to make all the distance he could, to get out of Siberia the more quickly. They had had a fair passage so far, and were congratulating themselves that they would soon be in civilization again.

Suddenly, Mr. Damon, who had been on the after deck, taking observations through a telescope, came running forward, crying out:

"Tom! Tom! What is that water dripping from the back part of the airship?"

"Water?" exclaimed Tom. "No water is dripping from there."

"Come and look," advised Mr. Damon.

The young inventor raced back with him. He saw a thin, white stream trickling down from the lower part of the craft. Tom sniffed the air suspiciously.

"Gasolene! It's gasolene!" he cried. "We must have a leak in the supply tanks!"

He dashed toward the reserve storeroom, and at that moment, with a suddenness that was startling, the motor stopped and the Falcon lurched toward the earth.

CHAPTER XXV

HOMEWARD BOUND—CONCLUSION

"All right!" yelled Ned, as soon as he heard Tom's cry. "I've got her under control. We'll volplane down."

"Is it dangerous? Are we in danger?" asked Peter Petrofsky of his brother, in Russian.

"I guess there's no danger, where Tom Swift's concerned," was the answer. "I have not volplaned much, but it will be all right I think."

And it was, for with Ned Newton to guide the craft, while Tom did his best to stop the leak, the craft came gently to earth on the outskirts of a fairly large Siberian city. Almost instantly the Falcon was surrounded by a curious throng.

"You had better keep inside," said Ivan Petrofsky to his brother and Mr. Borious. "Descriptions of you are probably out broadcast by now, but I am still sufficiently disguised, I think."

"But what is to be done?" demanded the younger Russian brother. "If the gasolene is gone, how can we leave here?"

"Trust Tom Swift for that," was the reply. "Keep out of sight now, there is a large crowd outside."

Tom came from the tank room. There was a despondent look on his face.

"It's all gone—every drop," he said. "That's what made the motor stop."

"What's gone?" asked Mr. Damon.

"The gasolene. We sprung a leak in the main tank, somehow, and it all flowed out while we were flying along."

"Haven't you any more?"

"Not a bit. I was drawing on the reserve tank, hoping to get to civilization before I needed more. But its too late now. We will have to—"

"Bless my snow shoes!" cried Mr. Damon. "Don't say we'll have to stay here—in Siberia! Don't say that. My wife—"

"No, we won't have to stay here if we can get a supply of kerosene," interrupted Tom. "The motor will burn that. The only trouble is that we may be detained. The authorities probably know us by this time, and are on the watch."

"Then get it before they know we are here," advised Ned.

"I'll try," said Tom, and he at once conferred with the elder Petrofsky. The latter said he was sure kerosene could be had in town, and, rather than risk going in themselves, they hired a wagoner who agreed, for liberal pay, to go and return with a quantity. Until then there was nothing to do but wait.

Meanwhile the crowd of curiosity seekers grew. They thronged around the airship, some of them meddling with various devices, until Tom had to order them away with gestures.

One particularly inquisitive man insisted on pulling or twisting everything, until he happened to touch a couple of live wires, giving himself quite a shock, and then he ran away howling. But still the crowd increased, and at last Mr. Petrofsky said:

"I don't like this, Tom?"

"Why not?" They were all inside the craft, looking out and waiting for the return of the man with the kerosene. The leak in the tank had proved to be a small one, and had quickly been soldered. It had been open a long time, which accounted for the large amount of gasolene escaping. "What don't you like, Mr. Petrofsky?"

"So many men surrounding us. I believe some of them are officers dressed in civilians' clothes, and a Russian officer never does that unless he has some object."

"And you think the object is—?"

"To capture us."

"If it was that, wouldn't they have done it long ago—when we first came down?"

"No, they are evidently waiting for something perhaps for some high official, without whose orders they dare do nothing. Russia is overrun with officialdom."

And a little later Ivan Petrofsky's suspicion proved true. There arrived a man in uniform, who spoke fairly good English, and who politely asked Tom if he would not delay the start of the airship, again, until the governor could arrive from his country place to see it.

"We know you are going to leave us," said the Russian with a smile, "for you have sent for kerosene. But please wait."

"If your governor comes soon we'll wait," replied Tom. "But we are in a hurry. I wish that kerosene fellow would get a move on," he murmured.

"Oh, he will doubtless be here soon," said the officer. "Might I be permitted to come aboard and wait for my chief?"

"Sorry, but it's not allowed," replied our hero, straining his eyes down the road for a sight of the wagoner. At last he came, and Tom breathed easier.

But the crowd was bigger, and some of the men, though poorly dressed, seemed to be persons in authority. Tom had no doubt but what there was a plot afoot to detain him, and arrest the exiles, and that there were disguised soldiers in the throng. But they could not act without the governor's orders, and he was probably on his way with all haste.

"Lively now, get that kerosene in the tanks!" cried Tom to the man, motioning in lieu of using Russian. The youth was not going to meet the governor if he could help it.

Now it was a curious thing, but the more that wagoner and his helpers seemed to try to hurry, and pour the oil from the cans into the tank-opening of the airship, the slower they worked. They got in each others' way, dropped some cans, spilled others, and in general made such poor work at it that Tom saw there was something in the wind.

"Ned!" he exclaimed, "they're doing all they can to detain us. We've got to put that oil in ourselves. Just as we did the gasolene in France. It's the same sort of a delay game."

"Right, Tom! I'm with you."

"And I'll warn the crowd back, by telling them we are likely to blow up any minute!" added Ivan Petrofsky, which warning he shouted in Russian a moment later.

Backward leaped the throng, as though a bomb bad been thrown into their midst, even the supposed officers joining in the retreat. The oil wagon was now easy of access, and Tom and Ned, with Mr. Damon to aid them, hastened toward it. Then the work of filling the tanks went on in something like good old, United States fashion.

The last gallon of kerosene had been put aboard, and Tom and Ned with Mr. Damon, had climbed on deck, when the gaily uniformed officer, who had requested the delay, came riding up furiously.

"Hold! Hold! If you please!" he cried. "The governor has come. He wants to see you."

"Too late!" answered Tom. "Give him our best regards and ask him to come to the United States if he wants to see us. Sorry we haven't cards handy. Ned, take the pilot house, and shoot her up sharp when you get the signal. I'm going to run the motor. I don't know just how she'll behave on the kerosene."

"You must remain!" angrily cried the officer.

"The United States doesn't take 'must' from anybody, from the Czar down!" cried Tom as he disappeared into the motor room. The window was open, and the youth turned on the power the official cried again to him:

"Halt! Here comes the governor! I declared you arrested by his orders, and in the name of the Czar!"

"Nothing doing!" yelled Tom, and then, looking from the window, he saw approaching a troop of Cossacks, in the midst of whom rode a man in a brilliant uniform—evidently the governor.

"Stop! Stop!" cried the official.

"Here we go, Ned!" yelled Tom, and turning on more power the Falcon arose swiftly, before the very eyes of the angry governor, and his staff of Cossack soldiers.

Up and up she went, faster and faster, the motors working well on the kerosene. Higher and higher. The governor and his soldiers were directly below her now.

"Stop! Stop! You must stop. The Imperial governor orders it!" yelled the officer, evidently his Excellency's aide-de-camp.

"We can't hear you!" shouted Tom, waving his hand from the motor room window, and then, turning on still more power he flew over the city, taking his friends and the valuable supply of platinum with him. So surprised were the soldiers that they did not fire a shot, but had they done so it is doubtful if much damage could have been done.

"And now for home!" cried Tom, and homeward hound the Falcon was after a perilous trip through two storms. But she weathered them well.

In due season they reached Paris again, and now, having no reason for concealment, they flew boldly down, to change what remained of the kerosene for gasolene, as the motor worked better on that. The secret police learned that the exiles were aboard, but they could do nothing, as the offenses were political ones, and so Tom kept his friends safe.

Then they started on the long voyage across the Atlantic, and though they had one bad experience in a storm over that mighty ocean, they got safely home to Shopton in due season.

There is little more to tell. The platinum proved to be even more valuable than Tom had expected. He could have sold it all for a large sum, but he preferred to keep most of what he had for his inventive work, and he used considerable of it in his machinery. Ned disposed of his, selling Tom some at a lower price than market quotations, and the Russians got a good price for theirs, turning the money into the fund to help their fellow exiles. Mr. Damon also made a good donation to the cause, as did Tom and Ned.

Mr. Petrofsky and his brother, with the other exile, joined friends in New York, and promised to come and see Tom when they could.

"Well, I suppose you'll take a long vacation now," said Mary Nestor, to Tom, when he called on her one evening to present her a unique ring, with the stones set in some of the platinum he had dug in the Siberian mine.

"Vacation? I have no time for vacations!" said the young inventor. "I'm soon going to work on my silent airship, and on some other things I have in mind. I want more adventures."

"Oh, you greedy boy!" exclaimed Mary with a laugh.

And what adventures Tom had next will be found in the next book of this series, which will be entitled, "Tom Swift in Captivity; Or, a Daring Escape by Airship."

Tom had several offers to give exhibitions in his air glider, from aviation committees at various meets, but he declined.

"I haven't time," he declared. "I'm too busy."

"You ought to rest," his chum Ned advised him.

"'Bless my alarm clock!' as Mr. Damon would say," exclaimed Tom. "The best rest is new work," and then he began sketching his ideas for a silent motor craft, during which we will take leave of him for a while.

Made in the USA
Columbia, SC
30 October 2020